DANA LeCHEMINANT

First Printing: January 2023

ISBN: 978-1-951753-16-0

ONE

IF THERE WAS ONE THING Kit Morgan was good at, it was getting beaten at chess by eight-year-olds. He wasn't proud of that fact, but after he held a tournament at the end of his first teaching year, he had to do it the next year. And the next. And while his students seemed to get better every year, Kit somehow managed to get worse.

"It's all about the strategy," Oliver told him as Kit waffled over his next move. His oldest friend (and now brother-in-law) had been teaching beginner coding classes all school year, and he'd finished up his last class just in time to witness Kit's final stand. "You have to think at least three steps ahead."

Kit resisted the urge to grumble. He still had his whole third grade class watching him, though the bell was set to ring any minute. Maybe he could delay the game long enough and call it a draw.

"Mr. H, you're not supposed to help him," Riley said with a snigger. He looked way too smug for a kid who still sometimes wrote his Gs backwards. Unfortunately, what he lacked in writing skills he made up for with mathematics and strategy.

Kit was pretty sure he'd lost this game the moment he played his first pawn. He was usually good at strategy, and it drove him crazy that chess had always eluded him. He blamed it on the game requiring him to sacrifice certain pieces to save others; that wasn't how he operated.

Oliver laughed, folding his arms and looking way too cool as he leaned against the white board. He and Kit had grown up together and spent their childhoods doing basically everything the same. How had he managed to grow up into the cool teacher while Kit had struggled to keep the attention of his class? Oliver had literally zero teaching training, and yet some of his coding kids—Riley included—were building whole computer programs. Okay, yes, Oliver had always tested close to genius level intelligence, but that didn't give him an automatic ability to teach others.

No, that was just Oliver being Oliver. The man had never met a challenge he couldn't face head-on.

"The bell's about to ring," one of the girls said, her voice quivering with worry. Apparently, the stakes of this game were high.

Kit stifled a groan and took Riley's bishop with his knight. He might as well just admit defeat instead of dragging things out.

Riley didn't hesitate, slapping his own knight into place and shouting, "Check mate!" right as the bell rang.

All of the kids cheered, but whether because it was the last day of school or because Riley completely swept the floor with him, Kit didn't know. He was too busy ignoring the itching sensation that washed over him as yet another school year came to an end.

Oliver waited until the last kid skipped out the door, and then he took Riley's abandoned seat.

"I need to go help with the pickup line," Kit muttered before Oliver could say anything.

Oliver nodded. "I know. You doing okay?"

"It's not like I haven't been through this transition before. This was my seventh year of teaching." The seventh year of the same thing over and over again, leaving Kit feeling unfulfilled and restless. The last day of school was always bittersweet. As he stood and headed outside, Oliver right behind him, Kit reminded himself why he did this.

He loved the kids. He really did. He loved watching them learn and grow and get wiser with every passing day. But for every kid who passed a state test with flying colors and moved onto fourth grade, another kid took their place.

It never ended.

Kit shook off the dissatisfaction that always wormed its way into his tense shoulders at the end of the year. He'd be fine. He had two months of summer vacation to pack in as much creativity as he could before he was back for another round.

"Mr. Morgan, do you have a minute?"

Kit and Oliver both paused right before the doors leading outside, turning to face the middle-aged principal of Mount Pleasant Elementary, Ms. Bundt.

Yes, like the cake. Kit had never been able to fully take her seriously after learning she was named after a cake, particularly when she wore her dark hair in a large round bun atop her head like today.

"Mr. Hamilton," she said with a nod toward Oliver.

He took the hint, clearing his throat before slipping out into the late May sunshine.

"What can I do for you, ma'am?" Kit asked. He made a point not to use her name if he could help it for fear of laughing. It didn't help that her first name was Cherry, so he had to resort to sounding ridiculously formal whenever he spoke to her to maintain professionalism.

Ms. Bundt clasped her hands together. "Well, I was hoping to avoid this, or at the very least speak with you tomorrow, but I'm afraid I have to catch an early flight in the morning. My mother fell yesterday."

"Oh no, is she—"

"Oh, she'll be fine." Bundt waved his concern away, though she seemed to be growing more nervous, fidgeting with her hands and turning rather red.

"Do you need to sit down?" Kit asked, putting a hand on her arm before remembering he generally didn't touch people anymore. Despite knowing he should remember things like that when it had been several years, sometimes moments snuck up on him, pushing through the careful exterior he'd crafted. Now was probably not the best time to suddenly get uncharacteristically affectionate.

Bundt, thankfully, didn't seem to notice his microsecond touch, too busy wringing her hands. "It's not easy to…"

Kit didn't like where this was going. "Ms. Bundt?" He didn't even snicker.

"I'm afraid we're going to have to let you go, Mr. Morgan."

Something shattered in Kit's brain the moment he processed those words, leaving him with a sharp pain somewhere behind his right eye. He adjusted his glasses, as if making them straight would make this moment make more sense. "I'm sorry?"

"Well, you see, there have been budget cuts across the district, and every school is having to cut down on staff."

Was it possible to forget to breathe? Kit had to shift his concentration to his lungs to keep from passing out. "But… But I've been here for seven years."

In the same classroom. Teaching the same subjects. Eating the same school lunch every day.

Did he even like school lunch?

"Unfortunately, the other third grade teachers have more tenure."

"Mrs. Halpert is retiring in a year."

"So you see why we can't let her go."

No, he didn't see. "How many—"

"One teacher from each grade. I know it sounds drastic, but so many parents are homeschooling lately that our class sizes are already smaller, and…"

Kit stopped listening. He was losing his job? The one job he was trained to do? And if there were budget cuts throughout the district, that meant a whole lot of teachers suddenly looking for work that didn't exist.

And with the way Bundt was watching him warily, something told him she knew that.

"How many more teachers do you still need to tell?" he asked, instinctively knowing the answer.

Bundt sighed. "You're the last."

Kit scrubbed his jaw as his head started pounding. "When did you start telling people?"

"Um. Last week. I was trying to keep you, I really was. You were going to be one of the ones that lasted forever. I'm so sorry."

He wanted to tell her she didn't have to worry about him. That he would be fine. But his entire body felt like it was covered in insects, and it was taking everything in him not to fall apart in the middle of the K-through-Third hallway. So he did the only thing he could do and headed outside to make sure his kids made it home safely.

One more time.

Was he supposed to feel relieved? Because he did. Just a little, in the center of his palm. The only place that wasn't itchy. The rest of him? The rest of him was on fire. If he couldn't teach, what could he do?

Anything, a little voice in the back of his head said.

He hadn't heard that voice in a long time.

"Kit!" Oliver suddenly slammed into him, nearly knocking him off his feet.

"Ow! Watch where you're—"

"Kit, it's happening." Oliver grabbed his shoulders, eyes wide and wild.

Kit furrowed his brow. "What's—"

"*Madi.*"

Madi? But what would... Kit froze. "The baby?" he gasped.

Oliver nodded, stuffing his hands into his hair and dropping his phone into the grass under his feet. "I have to get to the... I don't..."

Swallowing, Kit forced a deep breath and shoved down every bit of panic that was threatening to take him out for the rest of the day. If his sister really was having her baby, he couldn't just stand here and wallow in his own existential crisis. Oliver was practically hyperventilating, and there was no way he would be able to get himself to the hospital like this. His wife needed him.

"Give me your keys," Kit said, scooping up the phone. Thankfully, Oliver complied. "Maggie!" He waved to the nearest teacher overseeing pickup, one of the third grade teachers who *hadn't* lost her job. "I've got an emergency. Can you—"

"Sure thing, Kit. We've got it covered."

With that taken care of, Kit grabbed Oliver's arm and pushed him toward the teacher lot. "Who's with her?" he asked Oliver.

"Mom," Oliver said breathlessly, meaning Kit and Madi's mom. "She said Madi's dilated to a—"

"I do *not* need to know that. Get in."

Once sure that Oliver had his seatbelt on, Kit pushed the ignition and tried not to dwell on the fact that Oliver had never let him drive his fancy sports car before now. Kit had never even asked.

Why had he never asked?

Now was not the time for second-guessing his entire life. Shaking away the familiar, dizzy feeling of being completely lost, Kit threw the car into gear and peeled out of the parking lot to the cheers of easily impressed children.

Kit spent six hours on a cramped couch in the waiting room, squished between his friends Cam and Ben. For most of that time, the two of them talked about a TV show Kit hadn't seen, and he did his best to not think about anything at all until his mom finally came to get him so he could meet his new little nephew.

Though Madi looked exhausted, she was happy and healthy, and the minute Kit took hold of the blanket-wrapped bundle Oliver handed him, he didn't want to let go. Madi's baby was perfect.

He was supposed to feel nervous. This baby was a big change in his life, the product of his sister and his oldest friend falling in love, but he only felt utter happiness. He hadn't remembered babies being this tiny, being only two years older than Madi, but it was the greatest thing he'd ever seen. As he gazed down at his new favorite person, he made a silent promise to keep this baby safe and happy for the rest of his life.

"You feel it too?" Oliver asked quietly. They were sitting next to each other on a little loveseat while Madi talked to a nurse.

Kit looked up at him.

Oliver sighed. "This kid is gonna be spoiled rotten. Just look at him." He tucked his pinky beneath the impossibly small fingers.

"We're calling him Orion," Madi said.

"Ri," Oliver added with a smile Kit had never seen before. "I can't believe I have a kid."

The itchiness was back, but Kit couldn't scratch it because little Ri was sound asleep in his arms.

Maybe someday he would get the chance to hold his own kid in his arms, even if that meant risking his heart and opening up to someone again. As terrifying as that prospect was,

Kit had never wanted to go through life alone. Maybe he was ready to try again.

He hoped so.

Kit didn't get home until after midnight, desperate for a shower and a good night's sleep. He'd been putting off thoughts about what Ms. Bundt had told him before he rushed off to the hospital, but as his eyes locked on a stack of books he'd been meaning to bring back to his classroom, his gut twisted.

For the first time since graduating college seven years ago, Kit was jobless.

And he had no idea what to do about that. The itchiness on his skin had settled somewhat, leaving him only mildly uncomfortable. He'd lived with worse discomfort most of his life, so this felt oddly manageable. Or maybe that was the growing excitement he wasn't ready to acknowledge.

For now, he would focus on a shower and his bed and deal with the uncertainty of things tomorrow. Setting his keys on the counter, he trudged up the stairs of his little townhome and ignored the million and a half things he wanted to change about it, like rebuilding the banister and putting in a closet at the top of the stairs to replace the random alcove.

All things he couldn't do if he didn't have a job to pay for them.

He had been piecing his life back together with each remodel, trying to gain control over things again. Four years was a long time to relive all the memories of the disaster of a relationship that had broken all his plans for the future, and now he would have to keep suffering through the reminders of what might have been. Honestly, he was glad things hadn't worked out with Angela, but everything about this house had been for her.

His ex-fiancée, now happily married to her best friend, had probably forgotten all about this house. Why had he even bothered to keep it when the only reason he'd bought it was for her? He would have picked something completely different if he'd been buying a place for himself.

Maybe losing his job was a sign—the universe telling him he had been stuck in a rut for too long. He already knew that part, but he'd been living this boxed-in life for so many years that he wasn't sure how to climb out of it.

Ignoring the siren call of his bed, Kit walked through the dark to the shower and flipped the water on.

The pipes creaked. Groaned. One tiny drop of water came out of the shower head.

"Tomorrow," he breathed, flopping onto his bed without bothering to change. The day had been long enough.

TWO

KIT CAME TO A HORRIFYING realization the next day: it's not a great idea to push laundry day to the limit every single time, particularly during the last week of school when every day involves something especially messy. This discovery came as a result of another realization: you never know when a water main might burst and leave an entire townhouse complex without any water.

The men working on it said they would hopefully have things fixed in three days. Apparently, the breakage had brought to light several other issues that compounded into a major problem.

When Kit stepped into Maravilla Restaurant for his weekly burrito after clearing out his classroom and losing a battle with the laundromat machines down the street from his house, the whole place felt off. Like everything had been shifted two inches to the left and the lightbulbs had been changed from warm to cool light. Not enough to look all that different but enough for Kit to get the itching sensation that always accompanied something new. He might have been able to ignore the feeling if things really had changed, but in reality, everything was exactly how it had been last week. And the week before. And the week before that.

Kit was pretty sick of burritos.

"Hey, Kit." Gloria at the hostess desk waved at him, but instead of her usual million-dollar smile, she wore a deep frown. "I was worried you weren't going to make it in today."

Thanks to the laundromat debacle, he was almost an hour later than usual. He grimaced. "Sorry I'm late."

Gloria grinned at him, and the expression was genuine despite the tension in her shoulders. That helped him relax a bit. "Actually, your food's not ready yet. We had a huge family come in for a birthday party or something, and a few people called in sick, so—" She paused when something shattered around the corner. "I'll go see how long it'll be, okay?"

Kit mumbled something unintelligible and sank onto a vinyl waiting bench. He probably should have gone back home instead of coming to Maravilla, but Gloria had learned to expect him. That was what happened when a man came at the same time every week for three years straight. Dropping his head against the wall, he closed his eyes and pretended he was just tired from the last week of school. Not because his carefully crafted life had split at the seams and left him completely exhausted from trying to hold everything together.

He wasn't quite ready to face what that unraveling meant for the future.

As much as he hated the monotony of his life, at least he knew what to do with it. Losing his job, a new nephew, a useless house…it was like junior high all over again, when he was suddenly surrounded by the unfamiliar and feeling like anything could happen.

The problem with that was the equal chance of the happenings being bad or good. Junior high? That had been bad in the end. Oliver and Madi getting married and having a kid? Good. Falling for Angela? Definitely bad. This chance to find something new? It was too soon to tell. For now, he just needed some time to process and gain a more solid footing before anything else changed or knocked him even further off balance.

"Christopher?"

He jumped up so fast that he hit his head on a light fixture screwed into the wall. Cursing, he rubbed out the pain as he tried to figure out why he responded to his full name so quickly. Usually, he had to think about it, as if he often forgot his own name.

The twenty-something woman who had spoken cringed, her green eyes bouncing to the light fixture before returning to him. "Sorry," she said. "I didn't mean to scare you. But you're Christopher Morgan, right?"

Kit squinted. She looked moderately familiar, her skin fair and freckled beneath strawberry-blonde hair that hung in waves around her shoulders. Was she a parent of one of his students? He usually remembered them pretty well, and nothing was ringing a bell.

Besides, the only time he had gone by Christopher had been in the sixth grade…

Whoever this woman was, she was painfully pretty. Kit wasn't even sure what *painfully pretty* meant, but looking at her was making his chest hurt.

"Yes," he said suddenly, his brain finally recognizing she had asked him a question. "Yeah, that's me."

She took a step closer.

Kit took a step back.

She lifted an eyebrow, like she found all of this amusing. Then she started examining him, her eyes running from his hair to his shoes as if this was an entirely normal interaction.

He didn't know what to do. He wasn't usually this awkward, but he also didn't usually have to wait for his boring food after going through several awful days in a row. That had thrown everything off. Was he supposed to stand there and let her inspect him like a horse up for auction? That didn't sound particularly enjoyable.

He cleared his throat.

Her eyes snapped up to meet his. "You look good," she said.

"I look awful," he replied without thinking. He was standing there in a rumpled shirt and tie, pizza sauce on his slacks and two days' worth of scruff making his face prickle like crazy. He probably smelled, and his hair was a mess, and he was just now noticing a fingerprint smeared on his glasses that was likely part of the reason he had a massive headache right now because everything was blurry in one eye.

For some reason, the woman smiled as she made her way up to the hostess desk just as Gloria returned. "I said what I said," she told Kit before turning to Gloria and announcing, "I have a reservation under Skyler Montague."

Kit's knees gave out, dropping him back onto the bench with a thump.

"Of course," Gloria said breathlessly. "Just so you know, it's probably an hour wait for food, so—"

"That's fine. I'm here for a business meeting anyway."

"Kit? Is an hour okay?"

Kit waved a hand without looking away from the worn carpet under his feet. Skyler Montague. Skyler Montague was in Maravilla. Now he was more convinced than ever that all of this was just some nightmare because there was no way *Skyler Montague* was in Diamond Springs and telling him he looked good.

Outside of a painful pinch to test if he was dreaming—he wasn't—he didn't move until Gloria had taken Skyler around to the main dining area. Then he got to his feet to start pacing— only to realize Gloria had taken Skyler to a booth right on the other side of the half-wall that separated the waiting area from the dining. Kit dropped back down before either woman noticed him.

"This is perfect," he heard Skyler tell Gloria. "I have a few different people meeting me, but only one at a time. They should know to ask for my name."

The more she spoke, the more Kit wanted to hit himself for not recognizing her voice earlier. She had such a unique voice, so velvety that it made him shiver. It had gotten deeper over the years. Sexier.

This time Kit *did* hit himself, slapping his face just in time for Gloria to come back around to her podium.

"Fly," he croaked when she gave him an odd look.

"Do you want a table or something? You can have some chips and salsa while you wait."

Kit might have agreed, despite the tension that filled him at the idea of doing even more out of the norm, if a man who looked like The Rock hadn't come through the front door just then. Kit was used to strong people—his friend Cam and his fiancée Kailani both were made of pure muscle—but this guy was freakishly huge. Kit felt tiny as he passed, which didn't happen often. Kit was well over six feet, and he liked to think he packed a decent amount of muscle.

This guy made Kit feel like a preteen who spent all his time on the computer instead of being active.

Gloria greeted him with wide eyes. "Welcome to Maravilla. How many in your party?"

He looked around the restaurant with narrowed eyes. "I'm meeting a Ms. Montague," he grunted.

Kit stiffened, meeting Gloria's gaze and sharing a worried look with the hostess. What kind of meeting had Skyler set up? Was she looking for a hitman? No, that would be ridiculous. But after the week Kit had had, ridiculous wasn't all that out of the question. Part of him was convinced he had spent the last couple of days in the Twilight Zone.

"Right this way," Gloria squeaked.

As soon as they were around the corner, Kit hopped over to the bench on the other side so his back was to the wall that separated him from Skyler's table. Whatever she was doing, it wasn't any of his business, but he couldn't ignore his curiosity.

"You must be Pete," Skyler said. "Have a seat."

The table creaked, probably Pete squishing himself beneath it. "Let's make this quick," Pete said.

"Of course. Here is all the information you need to know, as well as the amount you'll be paid if I decide you're the right candidate. Twenty-five percent up front, the rest when the job is done."

Kit's stomach twisted itself into knots. The hitman idea had been a joke! But maybe it was more accurate than he wanted. He hadn't seen Skyler in nearly two decades, so it wasn't like he knew anything about her. For all he knew, she was some government official here to put out a hit on someone who was causing problems.

Problems in Diamond Springs? Kit shook his head. Nothing happened in this city. Nothing but budget cuts and water main explosions.

Pete was quiet for a second except for some shuffling papers. Maybe he was looking at the target. "How many people?" he asked.

"As many as it takes."

As many as... Was Kit supposed to call 911 in this scenario? Was he about to become an unwitting accomplice to murder? It wasn't like he was helping a mass murderer, but he was aware of it. Not doing anything was technically doing something, wasn't it?

"I need to know your commitment to discretion," Skyler said. "There's a lot at stake here, and no one can suspect a thing."

"I've been doing this for years, lady. I'm a professional."

Where was Gloria? She hadn't come back yet. Had they dragged her into their scheme somehow? Holding her hostage under the table?

Kit shook his head again. He needed to get more sleep. The restaurant was full of people, and surely someone would have noticed a twenty-four-year-old being held against her will. Unless somehow the whole restaurant was filled with government agents, all of them here as backup for whatever Skyler was doing…

That was even more ridiculous. He needed more information.

"Your website has quite the list of names," Skyler said. "I haven't seen anyone with your level of variety before."

"I like to keep things interesting."

Did hitmen have websites now? Had Kit been living in the dark, so sheltered by his life surrounded by eight-year-olds that he hadn't realized contract killing was a common business nowadays?

"Ever shot a gun before?"

"No, ma'am. Why would I need—"

"Ever dealt with kids before?"

"Hang on." Pete sounded nervous now. "No one said anything about kids."

Kit felt sick. Was Skyler planning on having some kids *shot*? He grabbed his phone, his hands shaking as he considered his best plan of action here. He would probably need proof of something shady for anyone to believe him. Could he sneak his phone over the wall and record the rest of the conversation without being noticed? Probably not.

Wait, what kind of hitman had never used a gun before? Kit put a hand over his heart, willing it to stop racing so he could think more clearly. He was being completely ridiculous and letting his imagination run wild. He was smarter than this, and he was glad no one was here to witness this little dip into insanity.

Get a hold of yourself, man.

Skyler let out a sigh. "I don't think this is going to work. The kid thing is non-negotiable. And here I thought I was dealing with a *professional*. Thanks for your time."

"Wait! I need this job!"

"And I need someone willing to do whatever it takes."

As something banged on the table—Pete's knees, maybe—Kit jumped back to his original bench so it wouldn't look like he'd been eavesdropping. He meant to keep his eyes down, but when Pete came around the corner, Kit accidentally met his gaze.

And found the man crying. *What the...*

Wiping his nose, Pete hurried for the door and nearly slammed it into another man who was on his way in. "Sorry," he grunted before disappearing into the rain outside.

The newcomer frowned, glancing back at the door for a second before pausing when he saw Kit. This guy looked nothing like a hitman, so he probably wasn't there for Skyler, but Kit still didn't like the look of him. With a combover and pants hiked up high to cover a beer gut, he stood there with shifty eyes and fidgety hands.

"You here for the Montague chick too?" he asked.

Kit immediately went on high alert. This felt like an *actual* threat. "Yeah," he said, even if it was a lie.

The guy settled on the edge of the bench next to him. "It's crazy, right? What she's offering?"

Kit narrowed his eyes, gripping the vinyl on either side of his seat. Skyler had given a dollar amount to Pete at the meeting, but it seemed like this one knew that information already. "She hasn't told me," he said.

The guy chuckled. "Me neither. But the ad said it would be worth our while, right? I mean, how could it not? All I had to do was take one look at her to know she'd be a good time. Fine piece of a—"

Kit moved so quickly that he surprised even himself, grabbing the guy by the collar and shoving him against the wall. "I'm going to give you five seconds to leave," he growled, making sure he was too quiet to be heard in the dining area.

Thank goodness the man didn't question his ability to follow through with his silent threat. He pulled himself free of Kit's grasp and stumbled back out into the rain without a backward glance.

"What have you gotten yourself into, Sky?" Kit muttered, grabbing his phone again as Gloria returned to her station without a clue of someone else having been in the lobby.

"Sorry about all this craziness," she said. "Did you want a table?"

Kit shook his head, typing Skyler's name into his phone to see if he could find this so-called ad. Whatever she was doing, it was going to get her into a lot of trouble. That much was clear.

THREE

SKYLER HAD HOPED MORE people would show up, but as her hour ticked down, her disappointment grew. Pete had been a bust the minute she saw him, but despite him being physically all wrong, she'd wanted to give him the benefit of the doubt. His resume had been the best out of everyone who contacted her, with a whole bunch of acting gigs over the years. But if just the mention of kids made him nervous, he would never last the whole week.

Sebastian wouldn't have been her first choice either, but he'd been the most eager of all of the applicants when he messaged her. The fact that he hadn't shown up had, quite honestly, been a relief. She didn't like to judge, but she really needed someone young and at least decently handsome. Sebastian was…not that. The comb-over in his profile picture had nearly made her laugh out loud. At that point, he should have just embraced the baldness instead of fighting the losing battle.

At least Freddie showed up, but from the minute he'd sat down, he'd been so nervous. If he couldn't even pass an interview, he definitely couldn't make it with the real thing.

Two others had agreed to meet her tonight, but Skyler had been sitting at her table for twenty minutes now with nothing but chips and salsa to keep her company.

She should have known this tactic wouldn't work, but she had still let herself hope. Clearly she had been watching too much of the Hallmark Channel lately. She didn't even like Hallmark movies! They were too full of unbelievable romance, like a wealthy and successful woman falling for the down-on-his-luck guy she hired to be her fake boyfriend. *So ridiculous.* That would never happen in real life.

This was a waste of her time, but she couldn't bring herself to leave.

Nibbling on a chip, Skyler resisted the urge to poke her head over the wall and see if Christopher was still there. She *knew* he was still there because she'd kept hearing muffled conversations on the other side, too soft for her to hear what he was saying, but she would recognize that voice anywhere. Even if it had gotten deep enough to send a shiver through her. Despite him growing up—and growing up *well*—she'd known it was him the minute she saw him, but he definitely hadn't recognized her. That shouldn't have been a blow to her ego, but it was. She'd thought about the guy pretty frequently over the last seventeen years.

He had clearly forgotten about her.

Middle school in Diamond Springs had been all of four months of Skyler's life, but those four months had been some of her favorites.

"Miss Montague?"

Skyler turned to the man who had approached her table and nearly squeaked in surprise. She recognized Max from his photo, but he was a million times more handsome in person. "Yes! You must be Max. Please, have a seat."

He sat and flashed a bright white smile that knocked the wind out of her lungs. "Sorry I'm late. Traffic was crazy, and you didn't give me your phone number to let you know I was running behind."

Skyler grabbed a menu to fan herself. "No problem."

"Have you ordered yet? I'd love to buy you dinner to make up for it."

Almost bursting into laughter at the ridiculousness that was suddenly her situation, Skyler shook her head. "Not yet. Apparently, there was a problem in the kitchens or something."

Seriously, Max looked like he had stepped out of a magazine photoshoot, touch-ups and all. He had the kind of smile that made women swoon and sparkled in the sunlight and probably sent old ladies to the hospital with heart attacks.

"Order whatever you want," he said. "I hear everything here is delicious."

Skyler couldn't remember the last time anyone had told her to order whatever she wanted; that was usually her line because she made a whole lot more money than any of the guys who agreed to go out with her. Or, she *had*. Before she moved back to Diamond Springs for a pipe dream.

"So," she said after a waitress had taken their orders, "what convinced you to respond to my ad? Most people have been in it for the money." And this guy looked like he didn't need a dime.

Max flashed another megawatt smile. "I'll admit, I was more intrigued than anything. You don't usually see stuff like this outside of movies and books."

"And you have some acting experience?" Though, at this point, Skyler wasn't sure that needed to be a requirement. All Max would have to do was smile, and he would win everyone over.

Taking a sip of water, Max nodded. "Not a lot, mind you. Just local theater things. I love working with the kids."

Skyler wished the waitress hadn't taken away her menu. She was ready to swoon. "That sounds perfect," she breathed as she slowly overheated from the inside out. But she should probably dig a little deeper before she hired the guy. "And you're free the week of the fifth?"

"I was supposed to be on a business trip, but it got canceled."

"How fortuitous."

Max laughed, and it was the most beautiful sound she'd ever heard. "Fortuitous. I like that word. Though, I thought this felt more like fate."

Though she tried to hold it back, Skyler let out a giggle followed closely by an unflattering snort. "Sorry."

"Don't be sorry for being adorable."

What in the world was happening? This couldn't be real. Skyler reached for her water glass to try to cool herself down, but she got caught up in Max's smile and, instead of grabbing her own glass, slammed her fingers into his and knocked it over, right into his lap.

"Oh!"

Max jumped up in a flash, running into a waiter with a tray full of food. Both of them went crashing to the ground in a sea of sizzling fajitas and way more beans than any one group of people should be allowed to eat.

Skyler clapped a hand to her mouth as she watched the scene descend into chaos. Though Max repeatedly told the terrified waiter he was fine while shaking beans from his sleeves, he still looked furious as he marched to the bathroom to clean himself up. That had definitely been Skyler's fault. But before she could drop down and help clean up the mess, someone slid into Max's abandoned seat.

"You're hiring a fake fiancé?"

Skyler blinked, too caught off guard by Christopher's sudden appearance to realize what he'd said at first. "Uh, yes?"

His thick eyebrows slid downward. "Are you completely crazy?"

Skyler rolled her eyes. "Hey Skyler, nice to see you again. I can't believe it's been seventeen years since I kissed you under the bleachers. You look great! How have you been?"

He had the decency to turn crimson as he continued to stare at her. "Hey Skyler," he growled out. "Nice to see you again."

She lifted her eyebrows when he didn't continue.

This time *he* rolled his eyes. "I can't believe it's been seventeen years."

"Since…"

He sighed, finally losing the scowl. "Since I kissed you under the bleachers." His scowl shifted into an almost-smile. "You look great. Really."

Though she'd told him the same in the lobby, that had been a lie. Christopher looked like he had had the worst week of his life. Even worse than Max getting showered by queso and sweet pork. He was a mess and looked like he hadn't slept in days.

That didn't make him any less attractive, though. Seriously, who would have thought Christopher Morgan could have such a glow up?

"How've you been?" she said.

He sighed again. "How have—"

"No, I'm asking you. How have you been, Christopher?"

"Kit."

"What?"

He shrugged as he slumped in the seat. "I go by Kit."

"Oh." That actually fit him better. When they met on the first day of sixth grade, Skyler had struggled to call him Christopher, but he had insisted on everyone using his full name. It wasn't like she'd known him for very long, but the nickname Kit felt more like him.

She wished she'd known that back when they were friends. *More* than friends.

He wasn't looking at her anymore, his focus currently on the empty chip bowl in front of him. But then he glanced down. "Is this seat wet?" Then he seemed to notice for the first time the absolute mess on the floor next to him, his eyes going wide.

Skyler snorted, which turned into a giggle, which turned into a full-on laugh complete with several more snorts as she finally processed the last five minutes. "Wanna get out of here?" she asked.

Kit's eyes went even wider as he glanced in the direction of the bathrooms. "But what about—"

"Oh, I highly doubt Max wants to come to my family reunion with me and pretend to be my fiancé. Not after that fiasco. Maybe if I'm not here when he gets back, he'll think the whole thing was just a strange dream."

Kit grinned, looking more alive than he had a minute ago. He may have looked different, but that smile was exactly how she remembered it. "That's a relief, because he's definitely married."

Skyler gasped. "He is not!" She'd done a ring check the moment she saw him.

"He totally is. I'll prove it to you."

Too intrigued to say no, Skyler nodded and stood when he did. He led the way to the front door, looking a bit like he'd peed himself thanks to the wet seat. Skyler didn't have the heart to point it out, as much as she wanted to. He had probably been through enough trauma, based on the exhaustion in his eyes.

"How are you going to prove it to me by leaving the restaurant?" she asked when he opened the door for her.

"We'll sit in my car. It's parked with a perfect view."

Too intrigued to question the sanity of agreeing to his plan, Skyler hurried through the rain and was grateful when he opened the door of a silver crossover for her so she could slip inside without getting soaked.

Once he was in his own seat, he pulled off his glasses and tried to dry them off on his shirt, though it was too wet to do too much good.

"I like your new ones," Skyler said as he put the thick frames back on his face.

He stiffened. "New? Oh, yeah. Right. Thanks. I've had these ones for, uh, a while." He shook his head as if to stop himself from rambling. "Back to your friend, Max."

"First of all, he's not my friend." Skyler felt like she was grinning like a madwoman, but she couldn't stop. It was like she was suddenly back in junior high, making up stories about the teachers and fellow students and getting in trouble for laughing during class. She and Kit had been terrors that semester when they were in school together, and she hadn't been giddy like this since moving away. "Second of all, there's no way he's married, and you've got nothing to prove."

Kit narrowed his eyes. "A single guy doesn't spend his free time with kids unless he's a teacher."

"How do you know he's not a teacher?"

"Because *I'm* a teacher. And there's no way he's one of us."

"You're a teacher? Really? I thought you wanted to do—"

"Changed my mind," he said quickly, turning his head to look out the window.

Skyler wondered why he would deflect something like that, but she was too fixated on his theory to change the subject. "You still haven't proven he's married. You're just throwing out theories."

Smiling a little, Kit nodded toward the restaurant. Max had finally returned to the table, a strange expression on his face as he gazed at Skyler's empty seat. He looked sad, but also…relieved?

"Wait for it," Kit muttered.

Max dropped a couple bills on the table, and then he reached into his pocket and pulled something out. Skyler couldn't see what it was until he slipped it onto his left ring finger.

Her jaw dropped. "No!"

"Yes."

"But how could you possibly know that?"

"I have incredible deduction skills."

"How?" Skyler demanded, punching him in the arm.

He laughed. "The tan line on his finger."

"What if he just got divorced?"

"His haircut wasn't nice enough for someone looking to date."

"Neither is yours."

"Hey!"

"How did you know, Chris?"

He winced, losing the lightness that had been in his expression for the last few seconds.

It took Skyler a second to realize her mistake, though she wasn't sure why he would care so much. "Sorry. Kit."

Dropping his chin to his chest, he groaned, then looked back at her. "*I'm* sorry. It's just been so long since anyone called me—duck!" He grabbed her arm and tugged until their heads were right next to each other by the radio.

Skyler assumed Max was leaving the restaurant, but she honestly didn't care about the reason for hiding. This was more fun than she'd had in years, and she was having a hard time holding in her laughter as they hid from view.

"So are you gonna tell me how you knew he was married?" she asked in a whisper, though it wasn't like Max would be able to hear them.

Kit snorted a little laugh. "He was wearing his ring when he came into the restaurant and was having a conversation with his wife about his kid's soccer game."

"What a creep! And he was going to spend an entire week with me and lie to his wife about being on a business trip?" She shuddered. "Thanks for saving me from being a home-wrecker."

Kit lifted his head, glancing out through the rain. He must have decided they were safe, because he sat up all the way and relaxed in his seat. "You're only a homewrecker if you're doing it knowingly," he said with a shrug. "For what it's worth, I think you might have convinced him not to cheat."

"I'm just mad he even had the thought," Skyler grumbled. "Why are men such pigs?"

"It's not just men."

Glancing at him, Skyler tried to figure out what his expression meant. He looked angry, but it seemed to be more than a defense of his gender.

"I'm mad I let him go back and talk to you," Kit said after a moment.

Skyler frowned. "Let… Hang on, were you screening my applicants?"

He smirked at her.

She punched him again. "Rude! What if Xander was the perfect candidate?"

Chuckling, he shook his head. "I'm still not sure exactly what your plan is, but Xander would have made an awful fiancé."

"Why?" He'd looked pretty good on paper.

"Because he immediately started flirting with me when he walked through the door."

"Oh. What about—"

"Don't even pretend you wanted Mr. Comb-over to be your man," Kit said, raising an eyebrow in challenge.

Yeah, she wasn't going to argue that one. "He was probably as much of a creep as Max, wasn't he?"

"Worse."

"Well, it's not like I had a ton of people responding to my ad." Skyler sighed, wishing she hadn't needed to place the ad in the first place. If she had been able to prove her own abilities six months ago, she wouldn't have been in this mess.

"Can…" Kit wrapped his fingers around the steering wheel. "Can I ask why you need a fake fiancé?"

"Why does anyone?" Skyler ran her finger down the window, following a raindrop as it slid downward and connected with several others. The rain had slowed, leaving them in a thick almost-silence. "My stepdad doesn't think I could possibly run a business on my own, so I had to invent a man to take my place."

Kit cleared his throat. "I'm going to need more context," he said after a moment.

At least he hadn't immediately agreed with Lloyd, though he didn't sound like an advocate for her side either. "Well," she said slowly, unsure if she could trust a guy she hadn't seen since she was twelve, "it turns out that when you want to convert a residential property into something commercial, you need to change zoning laws. That requires a public hearing, which requires local government involvement, which means dear Stepdad Lloyd had to step in to help because he has friends in the government here. Only, he's under the opinion that I couldn't possibly know what I'm doing, so I may or may not have told him that my boyfriend and I were working on the project together. But that didn't give him a lot of confidence in him sticking around, so Boyfriend became Fiancé a few months ago. It was a grand occasion for celebration. But…"

She took a deep breath and bounced her knees, knowing she was about to sound all sorts of crazy. "But Fiancé isn't actually real. Neither was Boyfriend. And now Stepdad wants him to come to our family reunion in a week because he thinks it's about time he meets his future step-son-in-law."

She finally chanced a look at Kit, who was definitely staring at her like she was crazy. He opened his mouth, closed it, opened it again, and then he fixed his gaze on his hands on the steering wheel.

"How…" He took a deep breath and tried again. "How long have you been, uh, dating your fiancé?"

Skyler had perfected her story so well that the answer came easily as she played with the very fake diamond on her finger. She'd bought the ring at a pawn shop when she concocted her engagement, and she'd gotten eerily used to wearing it, even when she didn't need to. It worked pretty well to keep unwanted attention from guys who thought a bare hand was an invitation to flirt. "Almost a year and a half."

"And how have you avoided your family meeting him?"

"He travels for work. It's very classified, so I can't talk about it."

He turned to her, his jaw hanging open. "You made your fake fiancé a secret agent?"

Skyler shrugged. "They don't ask questions, so I don't have to answer them. I never said he was a secret agent."

"How have you avoided pictures?"

"Because he doesn't want to risk being connected to me." When she said it out loud, it sounded pretty stupid. No wonder Kit looked ready to make a run from it. Never mind this was his car. "Okay, so my story is pretty terrible, but it's been working!"

"Until now."

"Until now," she agreed. "If I show up to the reunion alone, Lloyd is going to start to wonder."

"Has the property been rezoned already?"

Skyler slumped in her seat. If only it were that simple. "Yes, but Lloyd offered to pay the mortgage to help us out. I can afford the remodel on my own, but I don't have enough to cover the monthly payments until the business is up and running."

"What kind of business is it?"

"A bookstore."

"In the middle of a neighborhood?" Kit's voice had risen half an octave. "Are you sure that's going to—"

Skyler folded her arms. "If you start questioning my business plan," she warned, not that she had a threat to go with it.

Kit held his hands up. "Sorry. I don't actually know anything about business. It just sounds risky."

"It *is* risky. But it'll work. The neighborhood is one of those neighborhoods that's either newly wed or nearly dead. The old ones want something to keep them entertained that is nice and quiet and won't draw in a bad crowd, and the young ones love the idea of having something unique within walking distance. I'll have a whole kids' section too, and the nearest library is a twenty-minute drive, so I'll have a rentable section to fill the void. I've done my homework."

Kit seemed to process that as he watched her, and it was only then that Skyler realized how weird this was. She was practically baring her soul to a guy she didn't even know. Okay, so yes, technically they dated in middle school, but it was the kind of dating that twelve-year-olds did, where they held hands in the halls and passed notes in class but never interacted outside of school. And yes, Kit—Christopher at the time—had been her first kiss.

But seventeen years was a long time. A lot could change, and Skyler hadn't even been in the state for most of that time.

She wasn't sure what she hoped to gain by convincing the guy of her plan. It wasn't like he could help with—

"How much are you offering for a stand-in?" Kit asked.

Skyler's breath caught. "What?"

"The ad didn't say. How much are you willing to pay?"

"Ten thousand dollars."

His hands slipped, dropping his face into the steering wheel and honking the horn with his chin. "Excuse me?" he spluttered as he sat back up.

Skyler shrugged. "Small price to pay for my dreams."

"That's not a small… Why don't you use *that* for the mortgage?"

It was a valid question, but she had a ready answer. "Because that would barely cover four months, and I know it'll take longer than that to get my profit margin high enough."

"Ah." He cleared his throat, clearly thinking things through before he said something he couldn't take back. If he offered to help her, she would say yes without hesitation. She wasn't sure if that made her desperate or as crazy as he probably thought she was.

"What if…" He clenched his hands, only to open them and scratch his arm. Maybe he wouldn't be a good choice after all, if he couldn't even suggest it. Skyler didn't even know if he could act. He'd been pretty good when they were kids, but that meant nothing if he had lost the talent. "Maybe I could…" He clenched his jaw.

Skyler held her breath. It wasn't like she had any other options unless she decided to risk it with Pete. At least Pete could pull off the secret agent part…

Kit groaned, dropping his head onto the steering wheel again. Without honking this time. "What if I play your fiancé?" he said, his words muffled.

Skyler bit her lip to keep from laughing. "Yes, that's *really* convincing. I can tell this is something you really want to do."

"It's not that," he replied, sitting up again. "I want to help you. Really. It's just…"

"Just what?"

He scrunched up his face. "My friends are never going to let me live this down."

FOUR

"I'M SORRY. YOU'RE GOING TO *what*?" Oliver ran a hand down his face, clearly exhausted. "Someone please tell me I fell asleep and dreamed that Kit Morgan—*the* Kit Morgan—is going to be in a fake relationship."

"Nope," Cam replied. "That was real."

"Very real," Ben confirmed.

Kit wanted to bury himself beneath the couch cushions and disappear. For how stupid he already felt for even considering Skyler's plan, his friends' reactions were only making it worse. It wouldn't have been so bad if Kit hadn't gotten annoyed with every single one of them for doing this exact same thing with their own relationships.

He'd gone back and forth over the last several days, trying to decide if it was even worth doing. But he'd told Skyler he would help her, and it wasn't like he could back out when her family reunion was only a few days away. He always kept his promises. Still, the idea didn't sit well with him.

He'd done the whole engaged thing before—for real—and that hadn't ended well. He couldn't imagine a fake engagement going any better. Especially with the after-effects Angela had left behind.

"Anyone else feel like we're a glitch in the Matrix?" Oliver asked, though he definitely looked like he was falling asleep in his spot on the couch. Apparently, Orion wasn't a great sleeper at night, though the baby was fast asleep on his chest right now.

Kit clenched his fists on his thighs. "This isn't the same thing you guys went through," he argued, even though he knew he was wrong. "She just needs someone to play a part for a week. That's it."

Ben snorted a laugh where he sat on the floor, his eyes not leaving his tablet where he was busy drawing panels for his next graphic novel. He and his girlfriend, Allie, had been picked up by a big publisher a few months earlier and were on a deadline for their second book, which meant he was almost constantly drawing something. "Oliver was *just* helping Madi and her friend," he said. "And Allie *just* needed someone to keep her ex away."

"And Lani and I *just* needed to keep our businesses afloat," Cam added. "Look where that got us. I'm getting hitched in less than three months."

Kit's whole body started to itch as he thought about Cam's upcoming wedding. Cam Martinez hadn't been able to commit to anything in his life, but now he was only a few months away from marrying a girl he'd only been dating for four months. Kit had thought he could count on Cam to remain single. Just like him. He was happy for his friend, of course he was, but the fact that Oliver and Madi had a kid now and Ben had recently bought a ring meant Kit was months away from his whole life turning on its head.

More than it already had.

At least Kit had finally figured out the laundromat and had clean clothes again, though he wasn't fond of showering at the gym like he'd done the last couple of days. It seemed the water line problems were a bigger fix than anticipated, and his house was still without water.

"You said she's paying you?" Cam asked just as Oliver started to snore. Though a few months ago Cam would have thrown a pillow at Oliver or found some way to prank him, now he simply smiled.

Things were definitely changing.

"He didn't use to do that," Madi said, appearing in the doorway to the TV room where they'd gathered for their Wonder Boy meeting. She whacked Cam in the side of the head as she passed him on her way to pick up Ri. "Oliver didn't snore until you broke his nose, *Cameron*."

Cam bit the inside of his lips, clearly amused. He and Oliver had gotten into a fight back in February, something they probably should have done when they were teens instead of spending a decade and a half believing they didn't like each other.

"I didn't mean to break it," Cam said, turning a little green. That meant he was lying, though Kit guessed it was at least half true due to Cam not actually throwing up. The strange phenomenon in which he couldn't lie without tossing his cookies had always baffled Kit and the other Wonder Boys—the name Madi had given their group of friends when they were teens—though it definitely came in handy. Sometimes. Not so much when Cam *did* lie and ended up vomiting all over. There were few instances where that was actually useful.

Grinning at her snoring husband, Madi brushed some hair from Oliver's forehead before making her way to the stairs with her sleeping baby in tow. "You should probably let Ollie sleep," she told Kit. "I'm pretty sure he's been spending most of the night watching Orion breathe. What are you guys talking about, anyway?"

Kit threw a pillow at Cam out of reflex, distracting him before he could say anything about Skyler. "I'm helping a friend with something, so I'm going to be out of town next week."

Madi narrowed her eyes. "You don't have friends."

"Ouch," Cam said at the same time Ben said, "What do you call us?"

"You're his brothers," she said with a roll of her eyes. "Don't tell me if you don't want to, Kit, but I'm having lunch with Kailani tomorrow, so I'm going to find out anyway."

Kit sent a glare toward Cam, who lifted his hands in surrender and complained, "I haven't said anything!"

"Yet," Kit grumbled. For the most part, Cam couldn't keep a secret to save his life, though Kit had to admit the man could be surprising at times. By some miracle, he hadn't said anything about Kit's failed engagement, but it was too much to ask him to keep quiet about this too.

Since his sister would know about Skyler tomorrow anyway, Kit sighed. "There's a high chance I'm going to pretend to be someone's fiancé for a week," he said, then cringed.

But Madi only smiled. "Oh, this is going to be good. Can't wait to hear all about you falling hopelessly in love with your fake fiancée!"

As soon as she disappeared around the corner, Cam sat forward. "So? How much are we talking?"

Kit pulled off his glasses to pinch the bridge of his nose. This was a bad idea. "Ten thousand dollars."

Even Ben paused his drawing, glancing up. "Uh, is she loaded?"

"Or desperate," Cam countered.

"Maybe both," Kit admitted. If she could afford a complete remodel to turn a house into a bookstore, she had to have quite a bit of money saved up. Just not enough to pay for the building and land. He didn't even know what she'd been doing with her life for the last seventeen years; they hadn't kept in touch.

That was what happened when a girl disappeared at Christmas and never came back. Honestly, Kit had been sure he would never see her again, and he was still reeling from today's encounter.

Skyler Montague.

Kit's first kiss.

First love.

First a lot of things.

"So, how do you know this girl, anyway?" Cam asked, pulling Kit out of his thoughts. "Please tell me you didn't agree to be some stranger's fiancé."

How could Kit word things so he didn't have to tell them the exact truth? Ben was the only one who even knew Skyler existed—Cam hadn't become their friend yet and Oliver went to a different school that semester. If Kit was lucky, Ben had forgotten all about her since they hadn't shared any classes. Kit had done his best to keep her a secret from everyone, as if someone else knowing her would break the spell he'd been under that semester.

"I know her from school," he said vaguely.

Ben glanced up, curiosity in his narrowed eyes, but Cam asked the best possible question. "She's a teacher?"

As much as Kit hated lying to his friends, letting them believe he knew Skyler from work would save himself a whole lot of embarrassment. So he shrugged, picking at a seam on his shirt until he realized the whole thread was unraveling and leaving a hole in his sleeve.

Of course it was.

At least the shirt was clean.

"You know what'll happen if this turns into a romance, right?" Cam said.

Kit narrowed his eyes. "You watch too many chick flicks. We're not going to be sneaking around behind the principal's back and making out in supply closets." Especially because he no longer had a job at the school, though that knowledge would stay secret until he found himself a new job. No point in making his friends worry for no reason.

Hopefully that new job would be better than flipping burgers. He liked the people who flipped burgers, but he couldn't afford his house on minimum wage. Not that his house was doing him much good at the moment... At this point, he wasn't even sure if he wanted the house. He'd bought it when things with Angela were looking promising, and she had picked all the colors and styles of the things inside.

Four years since she cheated on him and ended their secret relationship, and the only thing Kit had really changed was the cabinets.

Exhaustion settled in thick and heavy as he considered his next move. He needed to think short term before he overwhelmed himself. He still had two days to kill before he had water in his house again, based on the new timeline the workers had given him, and then the next week was covered by Skyler's family reunion. After that...

"We should probably let Oliver get to bed," Kit said, sitting up as if about to leave.

The others took their cue, Cam and Ben both picking themselves up off the floor with mumbled agreements for needing to go home. Ben only had to walk across the backyard to the guest house he rented from Oliver, but Cam had to drive across town to his apartment next to Kailani's. Honestly, it was a miracle Cam had stayed this late in the first place; he didn't like to leave his fiancée's side for very long.

Kit had done his best to keep Cam from disappearing from his life, but at this point he was pretty sure it was a losing battle. Just like getting Ben to show up more than twice a month or Oliver wanting to leave his idyllic home life with Madi to hang out. All things Kit was losing.

"That's not a bad thing," he mumbled as soon as the guys were gone. They hadn't even noticed he didn't follow, which both helped his situation and made him feel like crap. He knew that was stupid, thinking his friends were moving on without him, but his heart almost always spoke louder than his head at first.

It was a matter of endurance most of the time, and logic always won in the end, bringing him back to solid and steady Kit.

It was exhausting.

"Hey," he said, kicking Oliver's foot.

Oliver snorted awake and immediately began a frantic search for his baby.

"Madi has him."

Oliver paused, blinking up at Kit before running a hand down his face. "Oh. Thanks. How long was I out?"

Holding out his hand, Kit smiled before tugging Oliver to his feet. "Just a few minutes. You know you don't have to watch your baby sleep, right? You need sleep too."

"I know. But I can't help it. He's too cute."

Cute wasn't exactly a word Kit ever expected Oliver to use. Not seriously, anyway. But he wasn't wrong; Orion was undeniably cute.

"Did the Boys leave?" Oliver asked, blearily looking around the empty room.

Kit grinned. "You called them the Boys," he said, though Oliver's horrified expression said he'd already come to that realization. "I thought you hated calling us the Wonder Boys."

Groaning, Oliver started making his way toward the stairs as he grumbled, "I hate it so much. But Madi is apparently rubbing off on me." He paused in the hallway on the main floor of the house, turning back to Kit with one eyebrow raised. "Why are *you* still here? It's past your bedtime, isn't it?"

As much as Kit knew he was going to hate this part, he was grateful for the intro. "Actually, I was hoping I could crash here for a couple of days?" He hadn't meant that to come out as a question. He cleared his throat. "My water got shut off. Because of a broken water main," he added quickly, before Oliver started offering to pay his bills for him.

That was the thing about Oliver Hamilton. He was obnoxiously wealthy from selling his software company a few years ago, but despite having every right to be a pain in the neck about it, he was generous to a fault. He'd paid for Cam and Kailani's apartments through the end of the year and had been funding Ben's legal battle with his first graphic novel, just because he could.

Oliver cocked his head. "I'm surprised you would ask me."

"Why? You have a giant house with extra bedrooms, so—"

"No, I'm surprised you're asking at all. This seems like the sort of thing you would power through so you don't have to change up your routine."

Kit resisted the urge to let out a deep sigh. It wasn't Oliver's fault that he expected Kit to never stray from the same thing day after day. Kit had been playing a part for so long that he sometimes forgot he liked variety. And okay, yes, he had never loved anticipating change, and the thought of doing something new always made him itchy and uncomfortable.

That didn't mean he hated it. There was something to be said for the thrill of defying expectation. Not that Kit had done that in years. Even Angela had been the safe and logical choice; Kit hadn't done anything out of the ordinary for so long that it was almost laughable to think he could do it now. He hadn't strayed from the norm since the middle of sixth grade...

"I'll be fine," he muttered, scratching his arm. "It's only for a couple of days, and then I'll be helping Skyler out."

Oliver shook his head, his smile growing by the second. "Still can't believe you got yourself into a mess even worse than mine. Worse than Cam, which is saying something. His relationship was televised."

Kit clenched his jaw, pushing past Oliver to head to the nearest guest bedroom. "This really isn't a big deal. I help people all the time."

"Not like this. This is..."

Kit glanced back, a prickling sensation spreading across his arms when he saw the look on Oliver's face. "What?"

Oliver's eyebrows pulled lower, his jaw working along with his tired brain. "Why do I get the feeling this is going to change everything? How are you okay with this?"

Because my life is already falling apart. Because I'm tired of pretending I'm something I'm not. Because you don't know me like you think you do.

"I've known Skyler for years," he said, not bothering to mention she had been out of the state for nearly two decades. "This is just business, and I needed something to fill my summer anyway."

"Why have I never heard about Skyler?"

Holding back a groan, Kit pushed his way into the guest room and sat on the edge of the bed, pulling his glasses off his face and pinching the bridge of his nose. He could easily tell Oliver the truth, and Oliver would probably keep it a secret if he asked. But the fact that Oliver was worried about the outcome, on top of his new dad exhaustion, meant Kit would need to keep the truth to himself.

"I'm sure I've mentioned her," he said, immediately feeling guilty about the lie. He most definitely hadn't told Oliver about Skyler. That semester of junior high with Skyler had been the one semester Oliver went to a different school.

The one semester Kit let himself be something different.

His hand strayed to the leather bracelet he always wore, pulling it tighter against his wrist. "There's really not much to say about her. We ran into each other at Maravilla, and she needed some help."

"How do you know her?" Oliver asked, though half of it got lost in a yawn. He'd slept through the explanation before, which gave Kit a chance to find a different explanation if he wanted to. But more than likely, the Boys would keep teasing him about this, and he needed his answer to be consistent.

"I know her from a different school," he said, fighting a grimace. How many times had he lied to Oliver over the last few years? Too many. And he hated it every time. This technically wasn't a lie, but it still felt like one.

"Teacher?" That word got lost in yet another yawn.

Time to end this conversation and hopefully never speak of it again. "You should really get some sleep," Kit said, giving him a pointed look. "You can't do anything for Orion if you're exhausted."

Brushing a hand through his hair, Oliver nodded. "Yeah. Yeah, you're right. Need anything?"

Kit shook his head. He'd brought a duffel bag in anticipation of staying a couple of days, though he couldn't do anything about sleeping in a strange place. He would probably sleep terribly, but anything was better than getting up in the middle of the night to use the bathroom and having no water.

"Thanks for letting me stay, Ollie."

"As if I would ever say no."

They stood there for a second, the awkwardness filling the room between them. They used to be so close, friends since kindergarten, but after everything went down with Angela, Kit had pulled away. He hated keeping secrets from his oldest friend, but he hadn't had the courage to tell him he was dating someone, let alone engaged. After years of always living one way, it had been too much of a change to share.

Angela hadn't wanted him to tell anyone anyway, and then things had gone south, leaving Kit broken and too wounded to want to be around someone who had seemed to have it all.

"Well." Oliver patted his leg with his fist, glancing around the room. "See you in the morning?"

"Yeah."

Once Kit had retrieved his things from his car and changed into pajamas, he lay in the bed for a long time, staring at the dark ceiling like it might tell him what he was supposed to do with his life. Maybe, after the reunion, he would have a better idea, but he wasn't holding out hope.

At this point, what he really needed was some of the undying optimism he'd had as a kid. Those few months that Skyler knew him, Kit had been happier and freer than ever, and nothing had gotten him down. What would twelve-year-old Kit—Christopher—do in this moment?

"He wouldn't have gotten this low in the first place," Kit muttered, rolling over and forcing himself to try to get some sleep.

Getting twelve-year-old Kit back would take a miracle, and he was pretty sure his luck had run dry years ago. But that wasn't going to stop him from trying. Kit Morgan was a lot of things, but he wasn't the type of guy who gave up.

FIVE

FOR A WOMAN WHO HAD spent most of her adult life in the high intensity lawsuit world, Skyler was terrified. Well, nervous. Maybe it was just excitement? She wasn't entirely sure; all she knew was her heart rate had been elevated all morning, waking her up at four and convincing her to bake a batch of mint brownies.

She hadn't stress-baked like that in years, and it was going to do nothing to help her figure. Though she didn't particularly care how she looked, years of pleasing the higher-ups at work had ingrained in her the need to dress to impress. Especially when it came to business deals.

Kit Morgan was supposed to arrive at her bookshop any minute now so they could make a plan for the reunion, and Skyler definitely wanted to impress.

"Just a business deal," she reminded herself as she pointlessly swept the front porch of the house she was converting. Construction of the interior was still underway, so there was going to be all sorts of mess for the next couple of weeks. "Just business."

That hadn't stopped her from going back to the few photos she had from middle school. Growing up with a mother who treated every failed relationship like a reason to wipe the slate clean and start over somewhere new had taught Skyler the impermanence of things. She rarely kept anything from the past, but her few months in Diamond Springs had felt important somehow. She hadn't wanted to fully let go of the happy times she'd spent here.

Almost all of those happy times included Kit. He'd been the closest thing to a best friend she ever had as a kid, and his chaotic energy had matched Skyler's so well that it made her feel less like the weird new kid and more like she belonged somewhere for once.

One of the pictures she'd found had been from their home economics class during the kitchen unit. Kit had bet Skyler she couldn't balance the bag of flour on her head, and of course she'd had to prove him wrong. The bag had fallen within seconds, covering Kit from head to toe in flour when he tried to catch it for her.

Skyler had taken a selfie of the two of them with someone's Polaroid camera before the teacher made them clean up, and that picture had been in a box since the day she moved from Diamond Springs. Now, however, it sat on her kitchen table, first and foremost in her thoughts all morning. The flour-covered kid in that picture had been the brightest spot in Skyler's life, though at this point she was pretty sure she had idealized him. Still, that hadn't stopped her from wondering what he was up to over the years or wishing she could joke with him about something stupid one of the paralegals said. No one had ever understood her the way he had.

"Did the broom get heavy or something?"

Skyler jumped, looking up to find Kit on the walkway leading up to the porch. She hadn't noticed him approaching, and he stood only a few feet away. How long had he been standing there? "What?"

He nodded toward the motionless broom in her hands as he stuffed his own hands into the pockets of his tan slacks. "That, or you forgot how to sweep. Deep in thought?"

"Oh." She leaned the broom against the side of the house and let out a little laugh. "Something like that. I'm glad you stopped by."

He shrugged. "I told you I would."

Why did Skyler suddenly feel so awkward? She'd never had an awkward moment with Kit before—not even at Maravilla—and she wasn't sure how to fix it. Skyler Montague didn't *do* awkward. She was calm and confident and never got her feathers ruffled. This was all Kit's fault. "Um, wanna come inside? It's a mess, but at least it's starting to look more like a bookstore."

With another shrug, Kit followed her into the house and immediately began looking around the half-gutted space, giving Skyler a chance to really study the man. It had been almost twenty years since she saw him, after all, and he was so different from the preteen she'd known. Christopher the gangly goofball had been traded for a tall and solid man with a striking jawline and a fair amount of muscle.

Not that she could really *see* his muscles. Though she'd felt it every time she punched him at the restaurant the other night, he kept his bulk hidden beneath a button-up shirt and slacks. He looked like he was ready for parent-teacher conferences. Wasn't school over at this point? It was *June*, and he had to be warm in his long sleeves.

Skyler had spent the last three years in Baltimore, Boston before that, and summers in Diamond Springs started way earlier. She'd been in skirts and loose blouses since early May.

"This will be a reading room and cafe," Skyler said, still scrutinizing Kit as much as he scrutinized the open space. "I'm getting real hardwood put in, and there will be a bunch of chairs and sofas around the fireplace."

"Won't you have people who come in and read without buying anything?" Kit asked. He took a few steps around the room, his eyes following the lines of the unpainted walls as if imagining what the space might look like when it was finished.

Skyler couldn't help but smile despite the question sounding mildly critical. "That will definitely happen, but that's where the café comes in. I can make a pretty decent amount of profit on coffee alone. Plus, a lot of readers are more willing to buy a physical book when they already know they like it, and more sales come from rereads than you would think."

"You'll have to pay someone to staff the café," Kit said next, moving closer to the little kitchen. A wall separated it from the front room with a six-foot window open between them. "And are you planning on running the store yourself, or will you have employees on the payroll?"

"You sound so businessy."

Kit glanced back at her, a shadow of a smile on his lips. It wasn't a full smile, though, and Skyler had to wonder if he was feeling as awkward about this reunion as she was. Kit hadn't been awkward in middle school, nor at the restaurant, but he stood too stiff to look comfortable about the situation. It was so unlike him. Or, the version of him that she had known.

"I'm not," he said with a shrug. "But a couple of my friends have started businesses, so I know some of the things they've struggled with."

"What kind of businesses?"

"Oliver had a—"

"You're still friends with Oliver?" Skyler cringed, annoyed with her own interruption. "Sorry, I just… That's really surprising." And it made her wonder if he would have remained *her* friend if she hadn't been dragged away. The thought made her shiver.

Kit lifted a dark eyebrow, his expression a mix between confusion and surprise. "You remember Oliver?"

"I mean, it's not like I ever met him—you know that—but you talked about him all the time. He'd be hard to forget." Skyler had been so jealous back then, even though Oliver went to a completely different school. She'd never had a friend the way Kit had Oliver, and she had always wanted a close relationship like that. "How's he doing?"

Shrugging again, Kit leaned against the countertop bordering the kitchen. He kept his head down as he spoke, like he didn't want to give anything away. "He's married. To Madi."

"Like, your sister, Madi?"

"Yup."

"You totally called that one." Skyler grinned. Kit had complained about it all the time, the way his sister and Oliver acted like they were the only two people in the world, but Skyler had always thought Kit secretly wanted them to get together. Who wouldn't want his best friend to become his brother?

Kit shrugged. "They just had a kid a few days ago."

"Oo, so now you're Uncle Kit?"

He flinched, though he turned away as if to hide the discomfort that flashed across his face. "Yeah," he muttered, unbuttoning his sleeves and rolling them up as he made his way into the next room. "He's adorable, but it's…a lot. So, how are you going to organize things?"

Choosing to accept his change of topic—she knew deflection when she saw it—Skyler followed him as she explained her vision. "Each room will be a different genre, with the more popular subjects toward the back to help sell the less interesting topics." She had already had someone come in and take out several walls, connecting all of the bedrooms with open doorways so a person could go through each section continuously. She just needed to paint the walls, and then she could start putting in shelves.

"And upstairs will be…" But she stopped her explanation, her eyes locking on Kit's wrist. "No way."

Following her gaze, Kit turned bright red. "What? Oh. Um. I can exp—"

Skyler grabbed his arm and lifted his wrist to eye level. "You kept my bracelet?"

He hadn't just kept it. It looked like he'd *worn* it. For seventeen years. Though it was falling apart in several places, the worn leather band had the same uneven pattern she'd stamped into it when they were kids, a faded mishmash of stars and zigzags and swirls. On one corner near the tie was the letter C. On the opposite was an S.

"I can't believe you still have this," Skyler whispered, more reverent now than shocked as she ran her finger over the familiar design. "I gave this to you right before Christmas." It was then that she looked up and realized she had pulled Kit so close that their faces were only a few inches apart. His eyes had locked onto hers, dark and stormy.

Kit swallowed. "Right before you disappeared," he muttered, and then he freed himself from her touch and took a step back, his hands clenched into fists. "I have some things to take care of today, so should we go over the plan?"

Skyler felt the change of subject like a slap to the face. Apparently, she was the only one interested in going down memory lane. That was fine, even if it meant things would remain awkward until she figured out how to interact with the man. If she could face down an unfeeling jury in a full courtroom, she could have a conversation with her fake fiancé.

"Yes, we should get down to business," she said, disappointed in herself for thinking they could be familiar with each other the way they'd been before. She couldn't keep that disappointment out of her voice, even though she tried. "I've got some chairs out back and lemonade in the fridge. Unless you'd like to keep things strictly—"

"Sorry, Sky." Kit ducked his head, tucking his hands back into his pockets before flashing her a smile she didn't fully believe. "I didn't mean to be abrupt. It's just been a…week."

This time Skyler took a step back, a rock settling in her stomach as she examined the man in front of her. It was like he'd put on a mask. Or taken one off? Either way, his whole demeanor seemed to have shifted, leaving him bright and cheery in a way she'd never seen before. The sudden change put her on edge, and she reminded herself that Kit Morgan was basically a stranger.

She'd known the preteen version of him, Christopher, for only a few months almost two decades ago, and she would do well to remember that.

"I'll meet you out back," she said and led the way, stopping in the kitchen as he continued on. The moment the back door closed behind him, she stomped her foot and let out what she called a *gream*, a mix between a growl and a scream. "What are you doing?" she asked the empty kitchen, wishing she had a mirror so she could properly scold herself. "You're being weird. Stop being weird, Skyler."

But it was so hard not to be! Christopher Morgan was the first guy she'd really had a crush on. The first guy whose hand she held. The first—and only—guy she thought she might be in love with.

"Twelve-year-olds don't fall in love," she told herself, then pointed to the door. "And that is *not* Christopher. That's Kit, a guy you don't even know. A guy who's just here to help you out for a week."

"A guy who can hear everything you're saying." He poked his head around the corner and grimaced, making her realize only the screen door had been closed.

Skyler clapped a hand over her mouth, barely stopping another *gream*.

At least Kit seemed to have relaxed, his smile more natural as he pulled the door open for her. "I'm glad to know this is as weird for you as it is for me," he said when she joined him on the back patio. "And twelve-year-olds can totally fall in love."

"Did you?" Skyler winced as soon as the words left her mouth. *You can't ask something like that, Sky!*

But Kit grinned as he settled in one of the several Adirondack chairs that sat around a gas fire pit. "I don't kiss and tell."

And before Skyler could react to that bombshell, he said, "This yard is amazing. Did you do all this?"

Skyler looked out over the sprawling garden that had drawn her to this house in the first place. Amidst lush trees and cobblestone pathways, a little brook gurgled across the property, adding a sense of wildness to an otherwise suburban neighborhood. Wrought iron benches sat at various intervals along the path, surrounded by wildflowers, and a bright yellow butterfly floated in the summer sunlight to the soundtrack of birdsong—thanks to the many bird feeders hanging in the trees.

"Believe it or not," she said in a hushed tone, "it was like this before I got here. The last owners were this darling senior couple who spent most of their time out here, dreaming of a life in the countryside. The creek runs through half the neighborhood, but this property is the only one that has much access to it."

"You are going to have this open to the public," Kit guessed, his eyebrows high. "Another place for people to sit and read. To escape."

That was exactly why Skyler had come back to Diamond Springs in the first place. It was small enough and had good memories attached to it. Plus, her mom was here again. And Lloyd. He probably wouldn't have offered to finance anything far away from him. Besides, she'd come back to get away from the suffocating life she'd gotten trapped in. To breathe again.

When Kit's eyes focused on her instead of the garden, she cleared her throat, also clearing away the numbness that had started seeping into her soul. "Should we talk about next week?"

Though he hesitated, as if he could see the shadow that had fallen over her, Kit nodded and sat up straight. "Or maybe we can talk about the elephant on the porch?"

Skyler glanced at the decorative ceramic elephant sitting in the corner, though she was pretty sure that wasn't what Kit was talking about. "This is weird, right?"

"Only if we make it weird. We dated when we were kids, then moved on with our lives and became different people. Water under the bridge."

When he put it that way, Skyler could easily see an argument for treating him just the same as she would have one of her other applicants. "Thank you, by the way."

Kit's eyebrows rose a fraction. "For what?"

"For saving me from the total creeps who answered my ad."

"Yeah, I definitely wasn't about to let that comb-over guy anywhere near you."

"I can take care of myself."

When Kit smiled, it changed his whole bearing, pulling him up a little straighter in his seat. It was like he kept changing his mind on how he wanted to present himself but didn't seem to realize he was doing it. And Skyler, who had spent the last several years of her life reading juries and opponents, didn't like it.

He was hiding something. She just didn't know what.

"I'm sure you can," he said with a little chuckle, and his hand drifted to the bracelet on his wrist. "Do you remember that time Kegan Blake said you would never be able to keep up with the track team, and you challenged him to a race after school?"

Laughing, Skyler settled a little more easily into her chair. Kit wasn't some criminal trying to get away with wrongdoing, and she needed to stop making every little thing a reason to distrust him. Maybe he was just uncomfortable, like she was. Besides, she couldn't expect him to be the same kid she used to know. "I'm pretty sure I threw up after I beat him."

"But you still beat him. You were like that with everything, and something tells me that hasn't changed." He glanced back through the door into the bookshop, his smile still holding strong. "I think you've got a good plan for this place, and I'm excited to see how it turns out."

Did that mean he intended to be around beyond the reunion? Skyler certainly wouldn't mind having a friend, especially one she already—sort of—knew. But as she sat there gazing at the man before her, uncharacteristic cowardice hit her hard, and she couldn't bring herself to ask him if that was what he'd meant.

Instead, she took a deep breath and put on her down-to-business smile that she'd used in the courtroom and during staff meetings. "Well, we only have a couple of days before the reunion. Should we get planning?"

Though he hesitated, Kit sat forward and nodded once, his expression determined. "Let's do this."

SIX

Given the week he'd had, Kit probably should have expected his morning with Skyler to be uncomfortable, but he hadn't realized he would turn into a complete jerk after getting virtually no sleep the night before. When he'd realized how awful he was being, he'd overcompensated and gone psychopathic cheery. He probably should have eaten something this morning instead of letting his nerves convince him to skip breakfast. Kit had never done well on an empty stomach, and he was clearly losing it with the way he couldn't stick to a single personality. He didn't even need to be anything but himself right now, but that seemed harder than anything.

It was Skyler's fault. Just when he thought he might get a chance to recalibrate and go back to normal, she made that…sound.

He wasn't sure what it was, but he decided to call it a *scrowl*, the love child of a scream and a growl. That, plus her comment about falling in love in junior high, made Kit pretty sure he wasn't going to make it through the next week. Maybe if he hadn't been running on fumes for days now, but with everything in his life throwing him off balance, it was taking everything in him not to start pacing as his skin prickled.

This felt so much like sixth grade but in the worst way, and he had a feeling he was heading straight for another personality overhaul whether he wanted it or not. If this morning was any indication of his inability to pick one thing and stick with it, that could get interesting. He hadn't been this volatile in years, and he really didn't like feeling so unstable.

"So, Lloyd has three cabins up the canyon," Skyler said, pointing at the map she'd pulled up on her phone. "They're all in a row, and the family is divided up—"

"Did you say *three* cabins?" Kit scratched the back of his neck, stopping himself a second later. Starting that would only make the itching worse. He was fine. This was only going to be a week, and then things could go back to normal. Mostly.

Skyler rolled her eyes. "Sometimes I think the only reason Mom has stuck with Lloyd this long is because he's loaded."

"How long have they been married?" Kit tried to remember back to sixth grade. He couldn't recall much, but he was pretty sure Skyler and her mom had been on their own back then.

"Eight years."

"Sounds pretty permanent."

"Not when it's my mom as half of the equation." Letting out a deep sigh, Skyler stretched out her long legs.

Not that Kit was paying attention to her legs. She was just taller than he'd expected, and his awareness had nothing to do with her short skirt leaving a good deal of her fair skin exposed. *Look away, Kit.*

"Commitment and my mom are like chocolate and strawberries," Skyler said. "They don't go together."

Kit snorted. The look on Skyler's face was so full of disgust that he couldn't help but laugh. "Excuse me? Chocolate and strawberries are a great combination."

"Only if you're crazy."

"You're calling eighty percent of the population crazy?"

"Yes, but only because you're making up that statistic."

"Pretty sure it's true."

"Moving on." Skyler cleared her throat and pulled back. She'd gotten a lot closer than Kit realized, though that could have been him bridging the gap as well. He was barely on his chair anymore. "Lloyd's family is, well, huge."

"Hence the three cabins," Kit said.

"Exactly. I have no idea exactly how many stepsiblings I have, and I haven't met most of them. Just seen pictures. I don't even know which cabin we'll be in, but Lloyd makes the cabin assignments based on who he thinks will get along the best and/or who he thinks needs to get better acquainted. Otherwise, I would prepare you for who we might encounter the most. Regardless, the whole family will be there, so it's going to be chaos."

Maybe it was because Skyler Montague was sitting in front of him, but each new piece of information made him feel even more like he'd been thrown back into junior high. With Oliver at a different school and Ben in completely different classes, that first day had been his worst nightmare for the whole summer leading up to sixth grade. Instead of the same hundred kids he had known for the last six years of school, he had been about to be surrounded by strangers. People who didn't know him.

People who had no expectations.

When that realization had struck him as he sat in that first class, waiting for his name to be called during roll call, something had changed in him. *No one knew him.* And that meant he couldn't disappoint anyone. It had brought out a strange sense of freedom for a kid who always strove to live up to expectations and be the best version of himself. Or rather the version he thought everyone wanted him to be.

He had been feeling uncomfortable ever since he pulled up outside Skyler's bookstore, but as he sat there remembering the moment he chose to be Christopher instead of Kit, he almost thought a weight lifted from his shoulders.

For the first time all week, he could breathe again.

"Tell me about this fiancé of yours," he said, a bit too much eagerness filtering into his voice and making him almost cringe. No need to get too excited about becoming someone new. It wouldn't last.

Skyler pulled her eyebrows low. "My *fake* fiancé?"

"Yeah. I need to know who you've made him so I can match as much as I can."

"Right." She tucked her phone in between her legs, and though for the most part she looked perfectly calm, one leg bounced ever so slightly. She seemed nervous about this part. What, was he some impossible-to-play character? "Well, I already told you that his job is really vague."

"Secret agent," Kit said, unable to resist rolling his eyes. He could be a lot of things, but a spy would never be one of them.

Skyler pursed her lips, fighting a smile. "I never said that."

"The implication is bad enough. But I can work with that." At least, he hoped he could. It would certainly take some crea-tivity on his part. "What's this guy's name?"

"Uh." Skyler swallowed as red climbed from her neck to her forehead. "About that…"

Was he about to regret agreeing to this? It was only a name; how bad could it be? "Sky."

"His name is Chris."

His stomach twisted, leaving him feeling off-kilter as he sat there and probably turned the same crimson shade as her. "Chris," he repeated, his voice a little strained. "That's…that's my name."

The squeak that came out of her was probably supposed to be a sound of agreement, but it came out strangled. Clearly she thought this was as weird as he did. "I needed something believable."

"So you picked *my* name."

"You were my first crush."

"Seventeen years ago."

"So? At least you won't have to try to remember it, right? It's not like I planned for *you* to be my fake fiancé. I thought I'd never see you again."

Kit rubbed his jaw, suddenly glad he hadn't eaten breakfast this morning as his stomach twisted tighter. Mostly glad… All of this would probably be easier to swallow if he had eaten something first. "Chris the super spy," he muttered. "Have you given me a personality?"

"You like being spontaneous."

"Ha!" He winced. He hadn't been spontaneous—not really—in years. Pretty much since the sixth grade. But he *did* enjoy it. "Sorry. I'm just processing. What else?"

Though she sat stiffly, as if reluctant to continue, Skyler pressed forward. "You like the outdoors when you can get out, but you also like staying in and reading." That was mostly accurate, though he wasn't sure how to feel about that. "It's why we came up with the idea for the store—we spend a lot of time reading together. I like mysteries and nonfiction, and you have been big into the classics lately. You're more of a meat and potatoes guy than a health nut"—also accurate—"though you stay in pretty good shape."

Her eyes fixated on his torso, making him want to sit up a little straighter in case he had a gut. He didn't—Cam would never let him—but if such a thing were to magically appear, it would happen this week.

"And you don't like kids," she finished with a full-on grimace.

A sharp pain stabbed somewhere near Kit's liver—he didn't actually know where his liver was, but thereabouts—and he almost jumped to his feet in protest. "You want me to hate kids?" Even just saying it out loud made him feel dirty. Everything else had fit with him pretty seamlessly until she blindsided him with this one. He could do a lot of things, but he wasn't sure he could even temporarily *pretend* to dislike kids.

Skyler shrugged. "Yeah, well, *I* don't like kids, so why would I want my fake fiancé to be all over them?"

He had to stand. As prickly itchiness spread across his body, he shook out his hands and started pacing before he fell apart. "You told Pete that kids were non-negotiable."

"You'll have to interact with all the nieces and nephews. But I wanted to make sure I would never get pressured into having kids. Not that my fiancé is real in the first place, but I didn't want to get anyone's hopes up."

Why hadn't he known this about her before? *Right.* Because the last time he saw her, they were twelve. They'd been a little more focused on the principal's unibrow and the way it did a strange wave-like motion when he got animated. "Okay," he said, then said it two more times for good measure. "I can try that. But you do know what my job is, right? I spend more time with kids than I do adults."

"Not in the summer though, right?" She hopped up to match him, surprising him yet again with her height. At six foot four, he was used to towering over people, especially women. She only stood four or five inches below him, taller than most women he interacted with. She was built gracefully though, long and lean, with legs that went on for—

Stop looking at her legs. What is wrong with you?

"Right," he agreed, blinking and forcing his eyes back up to her face. This felt like a step in the right direction though; he hadn't really looked at a woman since his engagement fell apart.

"What do you even do during the summer?" Skyler asked.

"What?"

She smirked, apparently amused by his confusion. "You know, when you're not teaching. What do you do with all your free time?"

He didn't want to tell her. For some reason, not even Skyler could be trusted, even though Kit had been dying to share his hobby with someone for a while. He was by no means an expert craftsman, but the more he got into woodworking, the more he loved it. Although, Skyler was the only one who knew how he'd gotten into it in the first place…

"I've been, uh, doing projects around the house," he muttered. "Little things here and there." *Also known as building custom cabinets and stools.* "And I spend a decent amount of time with Oliver and the other Wonder Boys."

Skyler lit up, grabbing his arm and apparently not noticing how tense he went at the contact. Flames seemed to shoot from her fingers into his skin, far from comfortable. *Relax, man. You're fine.* He forced a breath, willing away thoughts of Angela before he lost his careful calm. He'd been doing so well.

"Isn't that what Madi called you? Wonder Boy?"

Kit cleared his throat, feeling like he'd swallowed a bag of rocks, and then he subtly shifted out of her reach. It was hard enough pretending he wasn't completely thrown off balance by her very existence, let alone the reminders of their few months together. He'd forgotten how often they used to touch back when they were kids, like they'd known each other their whole lives.

Twelve-year-old Christopher Morgan had fallen head over heels in love with Skyler the moment she first grabbed his hand. Thirty-year-old Kit didn't need to fall into the same trap. Especially when there were too many reasons why it probably wouldn't last. He was too messed up at this point to be good for anyone.

"Wonder Boys turned into a name for the whole group after I met Cam," he said with a stiff shrug.

Skyler cocked her head. "I don't remember Cam."

"He transferred to our school after…" Maybe it would be a good idea for him to examine why it was nearly impossible to mention Skyler moving away without feeling dizzy. One day she'd kissed him under the bleachers and wished him a Merry Christmas, and then she never came back.

Logically, he knew her mom had probably had to relocate and took Skyler with her, but Kit had never gotten over the fact that she never said goodbye. Skyler had just disappeared without a trace. Not even a phone call, even though she and Kit had often spent late nights talking on the phone during the school year. She could have at least told him she was leaving.

Heart thumping in his chest, Kit slowly lowered himself back into his chair. "When Madi turned twelve, no one showed up for her birthday party, so Oliver, Ben, Cam, and I tried to cheer her up." He wasn't sure why he was telling Skyler this. Perhaps he just wanted her to understand a little more about him. He didn't know why that would be important, when he would be someone else the entire week, but that didn't stop him from talking. "Madi adopted the Boys as her honorary brothers, and now we're all family. They know I'm helping you, but…they don't know anything about you."

Skyler sat too, her sharp gaze making him feel exposed. She seemed to discern more than the average person, which was definitely going to put him on edge all week if he didn't get a hold over himself. "Was Ben that one friend you wouldn't let me meet?"

Pulling off his glasses, Kit cleaned the lenses with the hem of his shirt and pretended he couldn't see the curiosity in Skyler's eyes. At least that was better than the pained way she'd looked at him in school the day he shoved her around a corner so Ben wouldn't see her after class. There had been a lot of reasons for keeping her a secret, but none that made him sound like a good person.

He hadn't wanted to share. He was different when he was around her. He was terrified of meshing old and new for fear of losing anything good.

"I'm trying to keep this agreement separate from my life," he said without answering her question. "Anything else I need to know about Chris?" He resisted a shudder at the name. That was going to be both easy to deal with but also awful, depending on the moment.

She pursed her lips, likely disappointed, but she shrugged it off. "That's the beauty of not being able to talk about him much because of his job. No one knows much, so you can generally be yourself and no one would know the difference."

Except for the disliking kids part, which still had him ruffled. Besides, there was no way he was going into this as the Kit everyone knew. Not only was Kit trying to keep this whole thing from affecting his life, but he wasn't necessarily a fan of his general self.

He scratched his arm, skin prickling again. "Sounds good. Is the end goal to make them like me or hate me?"

"Liking is preferable. And hopefully this week will hold them over until the store is up and running, and then I can break up with Chris once the store is paying for itself."

What if it doesn't? Kit was too much a coward to ask. If the bookstore didn't work out, would she disappear again?

"I have a packing list for you," Skyler said, grabbing her phone again. "I'll email that over to you, as well as a loose itinerary. Apparently, these reunions are a whole production. And if you give me your bank account, I'll send you half now, and you'll get—"

"You should pay me after." Kit shifted in his chair, feeling like he was sitting on a bunch of needles. Apparently, the thought of getting paid to spend time with a woman didn't sit well, and his body was not being shy about telling him. "If I do a good job. I would hate to accidentally mess everything up for you and have you be out a lot of money you could have used for the store."

Though Kit wanted to start pacing again, Skyler smiled at him and seemed to relax more than she had since he arrived. She was definitely a lot stiffer than he remembered her, like she wasn't used to interacting with people. Whatever she'd been doing the last several years, it had muted the brightness he had loved about her back in school. It was still there, just harder to notice.

"Please," she said. "If you're anything like the kid I knew in sixth grade, this week is going to be a walk in the park for you. Remember that time you convinced Mr. Gonzalez that the fire alarm was going off and we all needed to go outside?"

Kit couldn't hold back the laughter that bubbled up from his chest. "I still don't know how I got him to believe he had temporarily lost his hearing. Or how the whole class went along with it. I have never seen that many people be so quiet."

"I kept almost busting up and you had to hold your hand over my mouth for ten minutes." Skyler grabbed his arm, right below the rolled-up cuff of his shirt.

Kit's good mood vanished like a gust of wind had blown it away, leaving him tense and uncomfortable again. Though he hoped she hadn't noticed, Skyler immediately pulled her hand back. He wanted to tell her it wasn't her fault. That he reacted that way to anyone touching him unexpectedly. That every point of contact was a ghostly reminder of his ex-fiancée.

But there was no way to explain that without getting into his whole life story.

Clearing his throat again, Kit pasted on a smile as he glanced at his watch.

He wasn't wearing a watch.

Great.

"I should probably go," he said anyway, rising to his feet. "Unless there's anything else I need to know before Sunday?"

Big green eyes blinked up at him. "No, I think that was the basics. And you're good for the whole week, right? Summer break and all that?"

Stuffing his hands into his pockets, Kit hoped his panic didn't show on his face. He had been ignoring his joblessness the last couple of days, putting his focus into Madi and Orion, but eventually he would have to face reality. If he couldn't find a job, he couldn't afford his house, and then he would have to sell and move back in with his parents.

He shuddered. It had taken a lot of willpower to move out in the first place, no matter how much he wanted it. If he moved back now, he might never be able to leave again.

"Yeah, I'm good," he said, gladder than ever that he didn't have Cam's problem of throwing up anytime he tried to lie. "Meet you here Sunday morning?"

"Eight o'clock," she confirmed. "I'll walk you out."

As they passed back through the converted house, Kit tried again to picture the place as a bookstore. It would be unconventional, but that might be the thing to make it work.

"Out of curiosity," he said, pausing in the front room and looking around, "what kind of shelves are you putting in?"

The question seemed to catch her off guard, making her take a step back as she lifted her reddish-gold eyebrows high. "Oh, uh, ones that fit books? I don't really know; I've got a guy coming in next week to start building custom shelves for all the rooms, so hopefully the contractor is done with the walls and flooring before he starts."

Kit hoped she had hired someone good. He could tell Skyler had a specific vision for the place, and the shelves would either add to the appeal or kill the vibe if they were done poorly. Though he was trying not to think too hard about it, he couldn't help but start imagining what *he* would do if given the chance to build something like that. He would put in some variety and flair, changing up the design for each distinct room to better fit the genre they held.

Shaking himself out of the creative hole he'd almost slipped into, Kit flashed Skyler a smile and pushed through the door, reminding himself that he was only going to see Skyler for the next week, and then it would be best to cut ties.

Before his heart got the idea to hope.

SEVEN

SKYLER HAD SEEN HER FAIR share of actors in the courtroom. Clients and opponents alike had learned to play the jury, presenting themselves to their best advantage even when in direct opposition to what they were saying on the stand. Skyler had learned to read body language just as well as she listened to the way a person said something, and she liked to think she had a pretty good grasp of what a person was thinking and feeling.

At least, she'd thought so until she met Kit Morgan.

The first couple hours of their drive had been quiet. Kit said he hadn't slept well the night before and promptly fell asleep in the passenger seat, his face pressed against the window and his mouth hanging open. Skyler had wished she wasn't driving so she could study him a little better without him being aware of her gaze.

Now, however, Kit was wide awake as Skyler filled her tank with gas because she'd forgotten to do that before they left. The moment they stopped, he pulled a hat over his head and hopped out of the car. Skyler watched him duck into the convenience store like he was afraid of being seen, and she wasn't sure what to make of his strange behavior.

He had been different every time she saw him. Back at the Mexican place, he'd been so much like his preteen self that it had felt like they were back in middle school again. When he stopped by the shop, he had been calm and collected for the most part, all business. Now he was acting like he would rather be anywhere than seen with her.

It was like he was on a pendulum, and she hoped he would center in the middle somewhere eventually instead of swinging so wildly. She needed the guy she knew back in school if this was going to work. Otherwise, she was never going to be comfortable around him.

"Who are you really, Kit Morgan?" she muttered just as the pump clicked to a stop.

Kit came out of the store a moment later, head down and hands in his pockets. He had a plastic bag looped around one wrist and a bottle of fancy, expensive water tucked under one arm. He honestly looked like some celebrity trying to avoid the paparazzi.

"You good?" she asked when he reached the car.

As his eyes rose to meet her gaze, a little smile played on his mouth that set Skyler's heart beating faster. Strange as he was acting, the man truly was attractive. From the rich brown of his eyes to the striking cut of his jaw, Kit Morgan would be able to work a crowd with that smile of his. Was he secretly a movie star and never told anyone? He certainly had the face for it.

"I'm good," he said before slipping back into the car and closing the door behind him.

Skyler quickly finished up with the gas, determined to get to the bottom of things. She was not about to spend an entire week on her guard because Kit decided to act all weird. There were few things she hated more than people lying about who they were.

And no, the irony was not lost on her.

As soon as they were back on the road, she gripped the steering wheel tight and pretended she was wearing heels instead of slip-ons. Heels always helped her feel more powerful. "Spill it, Morgan."

He paused halfway through twisting the cap on his water bottle. "Spill it?"

"Not the—I mean, tell me why you're acting so weird."

"I'm acting weird?"

"Are you going to answer every question I ask with a question?"

"Are you going to keep treating me like I'm on the stand?"

Her jaw dropping, Skyler pulled her eyes away from the road long enough to see his smirk. "I didn't tell you I was a lawyer."

He chuckled, opening his water the rest of the way and taking a sip. "You didn't have to. I feel like I've been under interrogation since Friday, and I can't picture you as a detective. So either you're the nosiest person I've ever met, or you were a lawyer before you decided to pull a one-eighty and start a bookstore."

Skyler relaxed a little when his smile grew, though she wasn't about to stop grilling him. "How did a third grade teacher get so good at reading people? You did it with Max at Maravilla too."

He shrugged. "Eight-year-olds aren't all that different from adults sometimes. I had to learn to read their emotions so I knew how best to interact with them. Besides, I've always noticed things."

"I remember." Skyler loosened her grip on the steering wheel. "You realized I was struggling in math before our teacher did. *And* you knew I was desperate for a friend even though I kept saying I was fine."

His ears turning pink, Kit kept his gaze out the window. "I never want anyone to feel like they aren't seen."

Well, if that wasn't adorable, Skyler didn't know what was.

"Okay, Mr. Sees-All. Are you going to tell me why you're acting like someone is after you? You're not using me to run from the law, are you? Because if you'll recall, I *am* the law."

"You *were* the law," he corrected with another little smirk. "And I'm not acting weird. I'm acting like Chris. You should be used to this by now."

"You do remember Chris isn't real, right?"

He clapped a hand over his heart. "Ouch. I'm pretty sure I'm real, Sky. You know, sometimes I wonder why I agreed to marry you."

"You're saying *I* proposed?"

"Of course you did. At first, I thought maybe it was just for your bookstore, but you've proven me wrong. I know you love me."

Excluding middle school, Skyler had known this man for less than a week, and yet her face burned at the thought of loving him. *Twelve-year-olds can totally fall in love.* Clearing her throat, she shook her head. "I'll allow this one. But I'm pretty sure a secret agent wouldn't look so shifty in a gas station. You're supposed to blend in."

"I'm not a secret agent."

He sounded so confident that Skyler would never be able to convince him of the contrary. Even though she tried. "But that's the only—"

"I've seen *Mission Impossible*," Kit said, rolling his eyes. "I know there's no way a relationship can last without the person I love being in danger."

Laughing, Skyler relaxed even more. He was starting to feel like Christopher again, and she had never been more comfortable around someone than she'd been around him. "You do know that movie is fake, right?"

"As fake as this relationship."

"So if you're not a secret agent, what is your job?"

He waited to respond until she looked at him again, and his eyes narrowed. "Wouldn't you like to know?"

She would, actually, but she didn't want to interrupt this playfulness that was so familiar. This was the kid who liked pranks and keeping people on their toes and living life to the fullest. She'd missed him, and her life had been pretty gloomy for the last couple of decades. She could use some of his sunshine.

"So, you're really going to go all out for this, aren't you?" she asked. "If you're already in character, I mean. We're still an hour away from Laketown."

"That is the least creative name I have ever heard."

Skyler laughed. "You think that until you realize there's no lake anywhere close to Laketown." She had been to the little mountain village only once, over Christmas a couple of years ago, and she had spent three days trying to figure out how far the lake was from the cabins. Eventually, her mom realized what she was doing and explained the paradox.

Kit seemed to study her for a moment, as if trying to decide if she was lying, and then he took another sip of water. "Well, that is…unique."

"That's the best word to describe this place."

Reaching into his bag, Kit pulled out a package of spicy corn chips and tore it open. Then he paused and glanced at her. "You don't mind food in your car, do you?"

The smell of the chips hit her nose hard, and Skyler grimaced before holding out her hand. She had never had food in her car, but she wasn't about to be a grump and tell him no. Vacuums existed for a reason. "As long as you share, no."

He obliged, placing a small handful on her outstretched palm. "I'm totally going off of assumptions here, but based on the fact that you're doing a whole house remodel and starting up a business full of inventory, and you drive a QX60, I'm going to guess you were a good lawyer."

Though she tried not to be conceited when she could help it, Skyler couldn't deny the way she'd risen high enough to be offered a position as a partner in the firm after only a few years. "I was a fantastic lawyer," she admitted. "It took a lot of hard work and dedication."

"What made you quit?"

She nibbled on a chip, trying to decide how she wanted to answer that question. She still didn't fully understand her own motivations, but she knew the basics. "I was tired of climbing. And I wanted my life to mean something. Running a bookstore was that thing that I wanted to do as a kid but never thought about seriously because it's not a 'real' job that makes lots of money, you know?"

Kit didn't respond, though he looked like maybe he understood with the way he pursed his lips. Instead, he pulled his phone out of his pocket to read a text—a long one, from the looks of it. And when he chuckled and started typing a response, Skyler felt inexplicably jealous of whoever was on the other side.

She and Kit hadn't had cell phones back when they knew each other, so outside of late-night phone calls on the landline, they had mostly just talked while at school. Skyler didn't even like texting, but she had a feeling she would like texting Kit Morgan.

"Talking to Oliver?" she guessed.

"Isla," he replied.

"Who's Isla?"

"Cam's fiancée's sister. She thinks she's in love with me."

Skyler choked on a bit of chip. "Excuse me?" It wasn't that she didn't think someone could be in love with Kit, but it was the way he said it so casually. Had he turned into some sort of playboy over the years? Who talked like that?

Chuckling, he finished his text and slipped his phone back into his pocket. "That was a terrible way to say that. We went out a couple of times a few months ago, and I told her she was great but that we weren't meant to be anything but friends. She knows we aren't ever going to be more than that."

"Are you sure she knows that?" Skyler mumbled under her breath. If she knew a guy was grinning at his phone and typing back long responses every time she texted him, she would totally think he liked her.

A moment later, his phone was back in his hand with another lengthy text from the poor, hopeless Isla.

Skyler gripped the steering wheel a little tighter. "Does she always send you such long texts?"

"Do you always read other people's messages?"

She huffed, hating that he was so good at throwing questions right back at her. She was used to people being too intimidated by her to talk back. "I wasn't reading your texts. I can barely see them from here, and I'm too busy driving."

Kit spoke while he typed an equally long response, which must have meant he was some sort of superhuman. "We've been on the road for almost three hours, and I'm pretty sure you've answered at least three emails and watched a dozen TikToks. We're lucky to be alive."

Skyler gasped. "I haven't…" She stopped herself as soon as Kit raised a thick eyebrow at her. "…watched more than five TikToks," she finished with a wince. "And there was only one email. Besides, my car has that driver assist thing, so it's pretty much driving itself. I thought you were asleep."

"I thought a fancy lawyer from Maryland was too smart to watch mindless videos."

"Not all of them are mindless! I've been watching a lot of book-related ones to get a good idea of what's popular right now. I'm doing business."

"While driving. On your way to your vacation."

She let out a humorless laugh, shaking her head. "Oh, if only this *could* be a vacation. Lloyd is probably going to spend the whole week talking about the bookstore, and I'm going to be so focused on making sure I don't blow my cover—and that you don't blow it either—that it's going to be a miracle if I make it out of this week alive. I think it's way too much to think even you could get me to relax, Morgan."

When Kit was silent for a long time, Skyler glanced over at him and found his expression fairly unreadable. Whatever it was, it was somewhere between pity and amusement, and she hated it.

"Don't look at me like that," she snapped.

Kit didn't flinch. "Do you know why I offered to do this?"

"Because you were afraid I was going to get myself murdered by a cheat or a perv."

"Well, that, and because I could tell you really want this. And you needed help from someone who would give it their all." He shifted in his seat, his voice softening as he gazed at her. "I know it's been a while since we were around each other, Sky, but have you ever seen me not commit to something?"

As much as she didn't like needing reassurance when she had always applauded herself for her confidence, she swallowed her pride and shook her head. "Not even when you went through that goth phase for a week."

He grinned, back again to looking like the guy she knew. It was like the familiar parts of him were right underneath the surface, every once in a while making an appearance. "I thought we agreed to never talk about that week."

"*We* agreed to nothing."

"Skyler." He sounded more serious now, and she glanced over to get a look at his face. He watched her carefully, eyes never leaving hers. "You're paying me good money to be here, and I've never been one to back down from a job that needs doing. I'm going to make sure you get a vacation, and I'm going to make sure no one ever suspects that you and I haven't been together for the last two years."

"Year and a half," she corrected.

"Eh, that's only because you're not counting that time between our first date and when you finally agreed to be my girlfriend."

"What?" He was talking nonsense.

"You might not have known it then, but for me it was love at first sight. That first moment I saw you in Maravilla. But the timing wasn't right, and it took seven months before you finally agreed to go out with me again."

"Is that so?"

Kit chuckled again, grabbing his phone once more and smiling at the novel Isla had written him. "That's how I remember it, anyway."

Skyler had no idea what to say to that, mostly because he was so convincing that she had to wonder if this week was going to be a disaster after all. But the biggest question in her mind?

Who in the world was this man?

EIGHT

THIS WAS A MISTAKE.

Kit bit his tongue as Skyler pulled up outside a massive cabin—really just a fancy house surrounded by trees—with half a dozen adults lounging on the large porch on the second floor. Was he really about to pretend to be someone's fiancé for an entire week and expect everything to go well? Yes. Yes he was.

And in true Kit fashion, he'd spent his morning going completely overboard.

Skyler wanted mysterious, so he'd been mysterious. But he'd gone too far in the opposite direction of his usual self, and he wasn't sure how long he could keep up the persona he'd shown her in the car. The calm, confident white knight would likely be his downfall unless he suddenly turned into a professional actor.

But he'd panicked! During the drive, he'd dived too deep into thoughts of what could go wrong if he failed her, and now he was supposed to not only play the part of fiancé but also make sure Skyler relaxed during the reunion. All while ignoring his own life falling apart back home.

No big deal.

For some reason, Kit was really good at biting off more than he could chew. At least he was also good at hiding the fact that he was overwhelmed. For the last twenty minutes, he had been silently repeating everything he'd learned in his improv class, hoping those two months of community center classes from two years ago would be enough to get him through this week.

Rule number one: Never break character. That wasn't actually the first rule, but it was the most important in this context. He'd been good at that rule his whole life. Up until last week when everything fell apart and left him teetering. He would have to find a solid footing again if he wanted to be convincing.

Rule number two: Always agree to your partner's reality. He thought about that one for a moment, throwing a glance toward Skyler. She seemed to expect him to act the same way he had in junior high, thrown every time he did something that didn't fit the mold. After a lifetime of living up to expectations, that part should be easy.

But could he really act the same way he had back then? Did the carefree and spontaneous Christopher Morgan still exist? He had been so confident, and Kit was…not. Not anymore. He could pretend all he wanted that he had his life together, but that hadn't felt true for a long time.

Four years, to be exact.

As Skyler gripped the steering wheel and stared up at the lounging people who hadn't noticed the car pull up, she looked like she was gearing herself up for battle. Was it really going to be that bad? That didn't help his anxiety over this whole thing.

Kit cleared his throat, swallowing his insecurities and forcing himself to focus on the girl next to him. If he kept in mind the knowledge that her entire business rested in his hands, he would hopefully be able to concentrate. At least until he had a chance to get a moment alone. He had perfected the art of keeping a straight face no matter what his students said to him, only letting it out when no one else was around.

"Hey," he said, keeping his voice steady. Better to not show any weakness. "It's just your family, Sky. They're not out to get you."

"Ha!" Skyler nodded toward the gathered group. "You haven't met Heidi yet. Do you see her? The literal goddess dressed in white with perfect hair?"

Kit squinted. He could see who she was talking about sitting in a large, cushy armchair, and though the woman was undeniably beautiful, he had no idea what that had to do with anything. "Okay?"

"She owns a lifestyle company," Skyler said, speaking as if the words tasted bitter in her mouth. "Whatever that means. She has a perfect trophy husband who runs a nonprofit in Africa, and two perfect kids—a boy and a girl—who have perfect grades in school and play all sorts of instruments and are always polite. I'm not even technically related to her except through marriage, but that hasn't stopped Lloyd from holding her life up as the gold standard."

Shifting in his seat, more than ready to get out of the car and stretch his legs out after being cramped for so long, Kit wished he knew more about Skyler's family so he could be better equipped to help her. He had seen what happened to a person when they were held to high standards—Oliver had lived his whole life that way—but that didn't mean he knew how to fix it.

"You know you don't have to prove anything to anyone, right? I'm sure you could find a way to get your bookstore without your stepdad's help."

Skyler growled a little. "Tell that to my bank account."

"You're tenacious. You'd find a way."

"You don't even know me, Kit."

"Chris." Though the name tasted bitter, he waited until she looked at him with one delicate eyebrow lifted high, and then he pried her fingers from the steering wheel to kiss her knuckles. "From now until next Sunday night, I'm Chris. Your loving fiancé and the man who is going to back you up no matter what. Okay?"

Her expression did that thing it had been doing since the moment he showed up on her front porch, like she was confused and curious and frustrated all at the same time. It was exactly the sort of look he would expect with the way he'd been acting since seeing her again, but he didn't know how to fix it. After years of living his life exactly the same way, this sudden course correction had him fishtailing and making up terrible metaphors.

Before he got too deep into this thing, he needed to find the balance between Kit and Chris—figure out exactly who Skyler needed him to be this week—so he stopped flip-flopping. He would have to remember all of the parts of himself that he had tucked away years ago, but if anyone could pull Christopher out of him again, Skyler could.

Skyler took a deep breath, holding it for a few seconds before letting it all out in a sigh. "You sure you're up for this?"

No, he wasn't, but he took a deep breath, gearing himself up for what was sure to be an absolutely chaotic week. As long as Skyler got what she needed, he could make it through.

"Let's do this."

As Kit stepped out of the car, he closed his eyes for a second and ran through everything he had decided about Chris Morgan. (Because yes, Skyler had used his last name too. Not weird at all.) He had lain awake all night, half from nerves and half from listening to Oliver and Madi look after a fussy baby Orion. It had given him plenty of time to craft a backstory and important details about the persona he was adopting, even if it left him dead on his feet. As long as he stuck to the plan, he'd be fine.

And as long as he ignored the itching sensation that had been driving him crazy all morning… Clearly, his body didn't like his plan.

Maybe he needed a new plan. He was definitely a bit rusty.

"Skyler! You're here!"

Kit followed Skyler's eyes up to the porch, where a young woman who looked to be in her early twenties waved to them. Unlike the apparent goddess, Heidi, who raised an eyebrow at them before returning to her conversation, this woman seemed genuinely excited to see Skyler.

Skyler, on the other hand, looked a little nauseated. "Hey, Micah."

Micah spun and disappeared, blasting through a door on the ground floor only a few seconds later. She tackled Skyler, who barely managed to keep her balance, and then jumped right into an excited stream of words that all smooshed together. The only things Kit caught were, "Excited, party, hot tub, and sexy man."

Out of context, all of those words were absolutely terrifying. He wasn't sure they would be any less so *in* context.

"I'm so glad you're finally here," Micah finished in a rush of air, and then she lowered her voice, glancing up at the porch with shifty eyes. "Heidi has been in a mood all morning. Apparently, Tanner got in a fight at school, and Isabelle wants to quit violin. I'm so ready for a conversation that doesn't involve the Wonder Twins."

Kit snorted a laugh at the familiar nickname, immediately regretting his lack of control when both women turned his way. "Sorry," he mumbled. "I wasn't trying to…" He didn't even know what to say to finish that sentence. Regardless, he liked the sound of these kids already, just from the name they'd been given.

Fortunately—or maybe unfortunately—Micah's full attention turned to him, her blue eyes wide with interest. "Is this your man?" she whisper-yelled.

Skyler looked ready to drag Kit back to the car and drive away, her whole body tense. "Uh, yeah. Chris, this is my stepsister, Micah. Micah, this is my fiancé, Chris."

For all the time he'd spent planning for this moment, Kit hadn't expected the overwhelming longing that hit him straight in the chest. Especially with all his friends pairing off and getting married, he'd desperately wanted to hear those words. To know someone loved him enough to devote her life to him while he did the same.

Even as a kid, he'd never wanted anything more than a family to call his own.

He stuck out his hand, forcing a smile. "I'm probably going to forget your name, but it's nice to meet you, Micah." He sounded completely miserable, and he needed to get a hold of himself if this was going to work.

He didn't need to dwell on the fact that Angela hadn't wanted to tell anyone they were engaged after she agreed to his proposal. No one except her best guy friend. Though, he should have seen that one coming…

Micah beamed at him, shaking his hand with enthusiasm. "You're the luckiest man in the world to have snared someone like Skyler. Have you guys set a date yet?"

How long had Kit wanted someone to ask him that question? Years. And he didn't even have an answer.

"Not yet," Skyler said. She grabbed his hand, pulling it away from Micah's grip and lacing her fingers with his.

Kit barely managed to keep from tugging his hand free, holding his breath. This just kept getting worse—he kept getting worse.

"We're pretty focused on the bookstore right now," Skyler added. Then she looked at him with mild desperation in her eyes, like she had no idea what to say next.

Kit cleared his throat. He needed to sit down. Take a deep breath. Figure out why he was struggling so much to act normal. But he couldn't do that until he greeted the family gazing down at them. "I'm pushing for sooner rather than later," he said, glad when his voice came out clear. "But you know Sky. She's the boss."

Micah giggled, clapping her hands as if he'd told her she could plan the wedding for them. "That's so true! Do you guys want help with your luggage?"

"That can wait," a rough voice said above them.

Skyler tensed as soon as she looked up and made eye contact with the graying man staring them down. "Hey, Lloyd."

So, this was the infamous stepdad? With how stiffly Skyler stood there, Kit had to wonder what sort of man this guy really was. All he knew was Lloyd held Skyler to a high standard but clearly cared about her endeavors. He was maybe a bit misogynistic, but beyond that? Kit had no idea what to expect.

And, for some reason, that pushed him right back into overdoing things. "Mr. Taylor! *So* good to finally meet you! I've been hearing *so much* about you from Sky"—he grabbed her by the waist and tugged her against his side—"that I feel like I already know you." *Calm down, Kit.*

Lloyd raised an eyebrow before glancing back at the rest of the gathered adults as if hoping he was hallucinating the strange man still waving at him.

Kit tucked his hand into his back pocket, only just now realizing he was still wearing the hat. So he grabbed that and stuffed it into his back pocket, leaving him with no idea where to put his hand now.

Had he always been this big of an idiot? He could hear Oliver's voice in his head telling him *yes*. That wasn't helping.

"Uh, you okay there, Chris?" Skyler asked under her breath.

Kit clenched his jaw and nodded. After his display this morning, she probably thought there was something wrong with him. And she was probably right. He'd been here for all of five minutes and was already making a fool of himself. *Just pick one thing and stick with it, you dummy. Preferably not what you're currently doing.*

Lloyd cleared his throat and gestured toward the house with a jerk of his head. "We've got lunch ready. Better come in before the horde arrives."

Micah grabbed Skyler's hand and tugged her toward the door with enthusiasm, and Skyler grabbed Kit's hand in a death grip as if she thought he would abandon her. The three of them formed a little train going into the house that probably wasn't doing any favors for the first impression Kit was making.

"The littles are in the pool," Micah explained. "Stella wanted to get all the food ready before they came inside. You should see how delicious it all looks! Stella's practically a professional chef now, and she was teaching me how to make soufflé before you got here."

Stella… That was Skyler's mom, if Kit remembered correctly. And with the way Micah said her name, she seemed to revere Stella. Skyler, on the other hand, still looked ready to run and was practically dragging her feet as they made their way up the stairs.

Kit barely got a look of the bottom level of the cabin—an open concept, modern-looking gathering space and a dark hallway—before he lost his view. At the top of the stairs, he found himself in a room made almost entirely of windows, with a large mahogany dining table, an enormous stone fireplace in an open living room around the corner, and the nicest kitchen he'd ever seen. It beat out even Cam's apartment, which was part of the most upscale building in Diamond Springs.

Just how rich were these people?

"You must be Chris."

Kit snapped to attention when a woman appeared from a walk-in pantry looking like a grown-up version of Skyler. Not that Skyler didn't look grown up. In fact, Skyler had definitely grown, aging into a beautiful woman with high cheekbones and a slender, graceful build, with her eyes just as green and mesmerizing as—

An elbow to his ribs brought Kit back to his senses.

"Hi," he choked out, extending his hand despite the five-foot granite island separating him from Stella Montague. Or was she Stella Taylor?

Stella's eyes crinkled in the corners as she smiled and brushed her hands on the flowery apron she wore. "I finally get to meet the man who stole my daughter's heart. I'm so glad you could come!"

And then the room went silent.

Micah bounced on her feet, her eyes darting between the other three, and Skyler was staring at her mom like she'd never seen her before, and Kit knew it was his turn to say something, but he was too busy looking at his outstretched and untouched hand like it had betrayed him somehow.

Had he always been this awkward? He didn't think so. He usually talked with strangers just fine.

Think, Kit. How would Chris act?

"Sorry," he said, pulling his hand back and running it through his hair. "I got lost in thought for a second. Thank you for letting me tag along this week."

Stella cocked her head. "We were surprised you were able to make it. Skyler said your schedule is all over the place."

"Yes, well, I don't have a lot of control over things." That much was obvious.

"Does your organization send you all over? Anywhere dangerous?"

Kit stifled a laugh before it escaped and made things even more awkward. They really did think he was a spy for some secret agency! Skyler must have had to spin that tale really well for anyone to believe her—must have come from her skills as a lawyer in convincing people to see her side.

"Lloyd said something about lunch," Skyler said, finally jumping into the conversation. "Do you need any help, Mom?"

"Oh, no, I've got everything handled. The littles are probably on their way already, and the only thing left is to bring the potato salad out—"

"I'll get it!" Skyler reached for the giant bowl of salad and hoisted it into her arms as if some tragedy might strike if she didn't do her part to help out. "You've done plenty already." The last word came out in a grunt as she struggled to hold onto the thing.

Kit had never seen a bowl that big before. "Do you need some help?" he asked, holding out a hand to steady the bowl for her.

Skyler flashed what he guessed was supposed to be a smile but looked more like a grimace. "Nah, I've got it. I'll just bring it to the—"

The room suddenly filled with shrieks and screams as a stampede of wet kids in swimsuits burst through the back door, heading straight for them on their way to the front deck. Kit reacted instinctively, grabbing the bowl at the same time three different kids barreled into the back of Skyler's knees. She collapsed, pushed forward at the same time, and slammed into Kit. His grip on the bowl slipped. He tried to catch it—so did Skyler—and next thing he knew, they were both on the floor.

Covered in potato salad.

The kids disappeared a moment later, the only sign of their existence a trail of water leading from the door to the front of the house.

"Oh dear," Stella whispered.

"Are you okay?" Micah added, her eyes wide. Somehow, she had avoided the catastrophe and remained potato free.

And Kit, seeing the tension in every part of Skyler's body as she lay motionless on the wood floor next to him, burst into laughter.

He knew that wasn't the response Skyler probably wanted, with the way she glared at him, but he couldn't help it. It had only taken fifteen seconds for complete disaster to strike, and that felt a whole lot better than the awkwardness he'd contributed to. Reaching over, he wiped some sauce from her cheek and grinned at her.

"Relax," he reminded her. "You're on vacation."

"That doesn't mean I want to be covered in pickle juice and mayonnaise," she grumbled back.

Kit grinned. "Do you know what this reminds me of?"

She flicked a handful of potato at him, shaking her head. "I thought we agreed to never bring that up."

They had, but Kit couldn't help but be reminded of the day before Thanksgiving break back in sixth grade. Skyler had signed them both up for a pie-eating contest in one of their classes. After about a million eating contests with Oliver over the years, Kit had won by a landslide, and Skyler had been so mad that she tried to throw her remaining pie in his face. But Kit had expected that—again, from experience—and dodged the pie, which ended up directly in their *teacher's* face.

Once he sat up and pulled Skyler with him, Kit brushed some potato out of her hair. "Best detention of my life," he whispered so only she would hear.

Skyler flushed bright red before turning to her mom. "Do you know what room we're in? We should probably shower before we smell like pickles the rest of the week."

Stella had pressed a hand to her mouth in horror, but she nodded and pointed behind her. "Lloyd put you in the west cabin, in the green room."

"Right next to me!" Micah said with obvious glee in her voice. "I'll go get your bags if you give me the car keys."

Though she winced, biting her lip like she might argue about their placement, Skyler reached into her potato-smeared bag and gingerly held out her keys. "Thanks, Micah."

"Sorry about the mess, Mrs. Taylor," Kit said, struggling to get to his feet without slipping. As soon as he was up, he offered his hand to Skyler. "It tastes delicious," he added and then winked at Skyler.

She rolled her eyes before grasping his hand. "You're such a dork, Morgan."

"And yet you still love me." Those words came out so easily that at first Kit didn't realize what he'd said. Only when Skyler slipped and tumbled into his arms did the comprehension hit, and he tensed.

It wasn't like it was strange for a fiancé to say something like that, but Kit barely knew this woman. And as much as he liked holding her, she felt entirely awkward in his arms, like she was doing everything she could to avoid touching him too much. He figured he should do the same thing out of courtesy, which meant they stood there holding each other at arm's length as if they might get messier by getting close.

Skyler's eyes lifted to his, her expression unreadable.

Kit swallowed.

"What in the world happened in here?" Lloyd's deep voice filled the room.

Skyler squeaked and slipped again, grabbing Kit's stiff arms and nearly pulling him down with her. "A mishap with the kids," she said thinly. "We're going to go clean up."

"You're in—"

"Mom told me." Setting her jaw, Skyler grabbed Kit's slimy hand and pulled him out the back door without looking back.

Kit barely got a glimpse of the sprawling deck with a wide pool before Skyler dragged him around the corner of the house and along a cobblestone path leading toward two other equally large cabins. Several people of varying ages stared at them as they passed on their way to lunch, and a few asked Skyler if she was okay, but Skyler forged ahead without deviation until they reached the farthest cabin.

As far as Kit could tell, the cabin was empty, everyone having trekked to the first cabin for lunch. This one felt a little more rustic, more wood and brick than the first one, and he could imagine spending a good deal of time lounging in front of the fireplace on one of the several cozy-looking couches and armchairs.

"Not bad," he said, lifting his eyebrows.

Skyler kicked off her shoes with a huff. "Leave it to Lloyd to put me in the smallest and oldest cabin. I told you he doesn't like me."

"You didn't say that, actually."

She rolled her eyes. "Come on. Our room is at the end of the hall."

They were halfway down the hall when something clicked in Kit's mind, and he stumbled a bit. *Room.* As in single. And it wasn't like this was a hotel with sleeper sofas or extra rooms to book. Something told him he was about to get incredibly uncomfortable about the sleeping situation.

"Mind if I shower first?" Skyler asked as she opened a door on her left. "Micah should be here in a minute with our stuff, but I have a change of clothes in my purse."

"Why?" Kit eyed the bag draped over her shoulder.

Lifting an eyebrow, Skyler looked at him like his question didn't make sense. "In case of emergencies. You don't carry a change of clothes?"

He held his arms out. "Where would I put them? And what kind of emergencies are you running into on a daily basis that require a backup outfit? That's just weird."

She made that noise again—the *scrowl*—and stomped straight into the bathroom that sat between their room and the next one over.

Chuckling, Kit settled himself on the floor and grabbed his phone to distract himself from thoughts of the week ahead. Isla had sent him several more texts detailing the bachelorette party she was planning for her sister, details that Kailani was probably going to hate. Kit would have to rein Isla in before she accidentally convinced Kailani to elope.

Cam would probably go along with that if given the choice. He had proposed after only a few months of knowing Kailani and seemed more than ready to jump into the relationship headfirst. Getting married six months after meeting her? It would be some sort of record if Oliver hadn't proposed the literal day after he and Madi started dating. They'd gotten married three months later, despite Kit's protests, but it had worked out for them because they'd known each other their whole lives.

Cam, on the other hand… He'd been scared to let himself love for so long that his dedication to Kailani made him seem like a different person entirely. Kit hoped he knew what he was getting himself into. Except, Cam was too smart to dive into something if he didn't think it was a good idea. Maybe it would all turn out okay.

After typing out a text—or several—to Isla, cautioning her about going overboard, Kit moved on to the group chat he shared with the Wonder Boys, hoping they would be free for a distraction while he waited for the shower. If nothing else, he wanted to make sure they were all okay.

> Kit: How is wedding prep going?
>
> Cam: Oh, there is no way we're talking about my wedding when you're off playing fake fiancé.
>
> Oliver: Have you crumbled under the pressure of your lies yet?

Well, they were definitely available, though Kit didn't particularly love their lack of faith in him.

> Kit: You underestimate me.
>
> Cam: You're panicking, aren't you?

Leave it to his friends to know him too well. At least in this instance.

> Kit: I have no idea how I'm supposed to keep this up for
> a week.

He was getting there, though. A few more hours, and he would probably have the role figured out. He could feel it. So much for planning all night… He liked making plans, but something told him he was going to have to follow his gut on this one. So far, his plan had been a disaster, and Skyler's family probably thought he was a weirdo.

"They wouldn't be wrong," he muttered as another text came in.

> Ben: I lasted two months. What's your excuse?
> Kit: Not all of us are perfect. Have you proposed yet?
> Oliver: He's being awfully silent for someone staring at his
> phone right now.
> Ben: Do you have a camera in the guest house I don't
> know about?
> Oliver: I can see you from Ri's window. You should really
> close your curtains before you start living up to your
> laser name, Watchdog.
> Ben: You know spying on people is creepy, right?
> Cam: Until you've had your entire relationship televised,
> you're not allowed to complain.
> Oliver: When are you going to stop talking about that stu-
> pid TV show? We get it. You're rich and famous now.

Kit chuckled, feeling much calmer knowing his friends were perfectly fine without him. It wasn't like they hadn't been on their own before—all of them had gone their separate ways for college—but Kit liked feeling needed. He *craved* being a part of their lives. Oliver was stuck with him as his brother-in-law, but the others had no reason to stick around. What if they moved away or simply moved on, and they ran into trouble and needed help?

How was Kit supposed to be there for them if they were all gone?

"You okay, Kit?"

Kit looked up as Skyler came out of the steam-filled bathroom dressed in an outfit that looked like it belonged more in a courtroom than a mountain cabin. Her outfit on the drive had been just as formal and businesslike, and Kit was pretty sure that would only make her stand out among her family. Maybe he would help her with the whole relaxing vacation thing starting with this. "Is that a pantsuit?"

Skyler glanced down as she squeezed water from her reddish hair into a towel. "Uh, no?"

"Objection, Your Honor."

"It's more comfortable than it looks."

It was going to be even harder to make this woman relax than he'd thought, but as Kit stood to take her place, he realized he hadn't noticed any discomfort since the potato incident. He hadn't been acting; he'd just *been*. It seemed letting go of expectation was working in his favor.

It had worked in sixth grade, and maybe it would work again here. He wouldn't know until he really put it to the test, when other people were around.

Hopping up, he paused at Skyler's side instead of heading straight for the shower. "Please tell me you're going to change as soon as Micah gets here with our stuff."

"She isn't here yet?" Skyler glanced at the door as if expecting it to open on cue. "And like I said, this outfit is comfier than it—"

"Wear something normal for the mountains, or I'll be embarrassed to be seen with you." With that and a wink, Kit slipped into the bathroom and closed the door.

Even if he failed at everything else, Kit would make sure Skyler loosened up and relaxed. Just like he needed to do himself.

NINE

Micah showed up five minutes after Kit started up the shower, huffing and puffing with Kit's duffel on one shoulder and Skyler's two suitcases trailing behind her. Skyler had planted herself on the bed to brush her hair with the travel brush she always kept in her bag—for emergencies—and she was so frustrated by the events after their arrival that she didn't even care that Micah jumped onto the bed to join her.

"I'm so glad you're here!" Micah said with way more enthusiasm than she needed to. "Hopefully you got all of the potato salad out of your hair."

Skyler sighed. "Yeah, I'm all good. Thanks for getting our stuff."

"Of course! Anything for my favorite sister."

Resisting the urge to frown and hoping Micah didn't want her to return the sentiment of favorites, Skyler slid off the bed and opened up one of her suitcases. She didn't know what Kit expected her to wear, but she would change into something else per his request. It was the least she could do after that disaster in the kitchen.

"How long has my mom been cooking like that?" she asked.

It wasn't that Skyler didn't like Micah, but they'd only been around each other a few times. Skyler barely knew her, but she did know Micah had way more energy than any twenty-four-year-old should have. Micah was like the golden retriever of people, all innocent and friendly and incapable of thinking poorly of anyone.

Skyler was none of those things, and she honestly had no idea why Micah even liked her.

"Stella started watching cooking shows with Heidi a few years ago and wanted to get better," Micah said with a shrug. "She's so good!"

"Great." Grabbing a pair of khaki shorts and a blouse, Skyler bit back grumblings about her childhood of eating boxed macaroni and cheese most days. Her mom definitely hadn't been a cook back then, and Skyler had had to teach herself how to make dinner when she was ten. It was nice that her mom had found a hobby, but how long would it last?

As she quickly changed from her "pantsuit," as Kit had called it—it was definitely a jumpsuit—Skyler fought for a change in subject as well.

"Has Lloyd made any changes to the itinerary?"

Micah shook her head wildly, now hugging a pillow. "Not unless there's something you want to add. I'm sure Dad would be happy to make a change for you."

Fat chance of that. Skyler would so much rather have an open schedule anyway so she could have a chance to check in with the contractor every day. She hated being away from the shop for an entire week when things were so close to being done, but Lloyd had insisted she stay the whole week.

"Is that fair happening in town again?" she asked as she returned to her seat on the bed.

Micah grinned. "Yes! Oh, but you missed it last year."

"I heard all about it." Mostly from Micah, who had felt the need to text her every day with reunion updates even though Skyler had been deep in a court case and didn't actually care. "Who else is here?"

"Everyone."

Skyler dropped her brush, watching it bounce off the bed and clatter to the floor. "Like, *everyone*?" When she'd told Kit the whole family would be here, she had been hoping it was an exaggeration to better prepare him. She didn't want to actually be right.

Micah snickered. "Why do you think you ended up in the singles cabin? There are a million kids here this year."

"Yeah, I noticed." She would probably have the bruises from the collision all week. She'd been prepared for kids, but not the *entire* Taylor clan. If she remembered right, amongst his many marriages, Lloyd had acquired or sired ten kids, five of whom were married. Four of the five couples had several children apiece.

Kit had thought it strange to have three cabins, but it made perfect sense when one took into account the Taylor horde. At least this cabin would be kid-free so Skyler could get away from them when she needed to, but the thought of so many kids running around still had her sweating.

"I hope they don't overwhelm Chris," she muttered, thinking more of herself.

Grabbing Skyler's arm, Micah shook her head with enthusiasm. "No, see, I came up with a plan, and the Briggs Sibs are going to become Chris's best friends. I just wish we didn't have Sam in our cabin, but they don't have kids, so…"

Skyler fought to remember who was who. She could memorize a million facts about a court case, but she'd never had a firm grasp of her mom's new family. Then again, she'd never really tried. "Isn't Sam your half-brother just like the Briggs trio?"

"Technically, yes?" Micah shrugged one shoulder. "But Sam is annoying. I have enough half siblings that I'm allowed to say I like the Briggs half better. Sometimes I think Dad likes them better too even though they're only his step kids."

Hopefully Skyler would also like the Briggs side better, because she'd never been all that fond of the Taylor side on the rare occasions she actually attended family events. "Let's hope that your plan..."

The bathroom door opening cut her off, and Skyler turned to tell Kit his clothes were here. But instead of words, only a squeak came out of her mouth.

Kit Morgan was *ripped*.

She'd known he was decently strong after meeting him last week, but as he stepped from the bathroom in only a towel, Skyler had an up-close view of every inch of muscle. Where did a third grade teacher get abs like *that*? It was like the teacher thing was only a cover, and he spent the rest of his time saving babies from burning buildings and stopping armed robberies with his bulletproof chest. Was Kit actually Superman?

"Wow," Micah breathed behind her.

Skyler smacked her. "Feeling better?" she asked, cursing the strain in her voice.

Kit flashed a grin as he crossed the room to where his bag lay. "As much as I love potato salad, I'm not sure I need it in all my nooks and crannies."

"You have a lot of those," Micah said breathily.

Skyler smacked her again. "Shouldn't you be at lunch, Micah?"

"I guess." Micah took her time climbing off the bed and moving to the door, her eyes locked on Kit as he dug through his duffel. Either he hadn't noticed her drooling, or he was good at pretending he was oblivious.

"Can you close the door behind you?" Skyler growled.

Micah winked before doing as she asked.

Kit straightened up, clothes in hand, and seemed to be holding back laughter as he said, "She seems nice."

Skyler threw a pillow at him. "Don't go getting an ego, Sir Clearly-Goes-to-the-Gym-a-Lot."

"That's a mouthful. And one of my best friends is a personal trainer. What do you expect?" He slipped back into the bathroom, though he left the door open, standing just out of sight as he got dressed.

Skyler had *dated* a personal trainer on and off for a few months, but that didn't mean she was carved from stone. Kit had definitely made an effort, something she was not going to complain about.

And to think, she could have ended up here with Mr. Comb-over. Kit even beat out Cheating Scumbag when it came to attractiveness.

"Why don't you like Micah?" Kit asked.

"What?" Skyler's stomach did a little flip. "Who said I don't like her?"

Reappearing with his shirt in hand—thankfully, he wore a pair of jeans instead of the towel—Kit raised an eyebrow at her. "Are you sure you were a good lawyer? Because your poker face sucks."

She rolled her eyes. "Cut me some slack. I was caught off guard by all of…that." Her heart pounded a little faster as she unashamedly watched him slip his t-shirt over his head. Sad as she was to lose the view, at least she could think straight again. "You could have warned me you were hot."

"You think I'm hot?" His grin widened as he folded his arms and stood taller.

Oh goodness, this was not the kind of conversation Skyler wanted to have right before introducing her fake fiancé to her entire family. But how was she supposed to resist that easy smile of his? "Why do you think I kissed you in sixth grade?"

"Actually, I wanted to talk to you about that." He plopped himself down on the bed next to her, turning slightly pink. "Do you expect me to kiss you this week?"

If Kit was pink, Skyler was probably a deep red. "Oh. Uh. I hadn't thought about that. But clearly you have."

He shrugged. "It seems like something that people prob-ably do when they're engaged. Though I doubt anyone would notice if we didn't. It's just, uh, I guess it depends on how authentic you want this relationship to be."

He was making *her* decide? She supposed that made sense, with this being her stupid scheme, but he was being so casual about it. Just like he'd been when he said Isla was in love with him. He'd never answered her unasked question of whether he was a player.

"How many people have you kissed?"

Kit blinked. "Does that matter? I've never had mono or anything, so—"

"No, I'm just…curious." Skyler cringed. "You don't have to answer that. It doesn't matter."

"Four."

"Oh."

He raised an eyebrow. "Oh? What does that mean?"

Another wave of heat spread through her face, and she turned her focus to the fringe on the blanket spread over the bed beneath her. "I guess I expected more. Especially because you're so…"

"Hot?" he supplied.

Sudden laughter burst out of her, and her shoulders relaxed as she met Kit's grin. He'd always been good at that, making people more comfortable, and she was so glad he had kept the skill over the years. "Wow," she breathed. "I sincerely apologize for being so weird about all this."

"You're not being weird." He pursed his lips when he looked at her, then chuckled. "Maybe a little weird. But I don't blame you. I keep feeling like we're back in Mrs. Frasier's class, but we're different people now."

"I know that." Skyler put her hand on his arm, wanting some kind of contact before she slipped too deep into memo-ries of those days. But Kit tensed beneath her touch, just like he'd done on her porch, and she immediately pulled her hand away. "We don't have to kiss if you don't want to," she said quietly. "Like you said, no one will think—"

"No, we probably should. Just in case." Though he frowned down at his arm—he clearly didn't like being touched—he leaned in closer.

Skyler's eyes went wide. "What? Now?"

"We should probably practice."

What in the world was happening? "You want to practice kissing," Skyler repeated. "You don't even want me to touch you."

"That's not…" He huffed a frustrated sigh and ran a hand through his wet hair. "You can touch me. I'm just…out of practice."

"Of being touched? Or kissed?"

He scrunched up his face. "Both."

That made no sense. Twelve-year-old Kit had been the most physical person she'd ever known, constantly holding her hand or brushing eyelashes off of her cheek or putting his arm around her shoulders. Even before they started "dating." What had changed?

As if he could read her mind, Kit sighed. "It's been a long time, Sky. I'm not the kid you knew."

"Then who are you?" Skyler hadn't meant to ask that question, but if she was going to spend the next week with this man, she couldn't use up all of her energy trying to figure out how he might act at any given moment. "You're all over the place, Kit."

This time, she held out her hand, waiting for him to take it.

He gazed at her fingers for a long time in silence, his jaw tight. When he finally slipped his hand into hers, he seemed to settle further into his spot on the bed and relax a little. "I don't know who I am," he said, so softly that it was like he was terrified of those words.

Skyler had no idea what to say to that, though she wished she knew how to get him back to the teasing version he'd been a moment ago. People skills were not her strongest suit. Not unless she needed to catch someone in their lies.

This was something completely different.

"Why did you agree to help me, Kit?"

He met her gaze, his expression unreadable. "Because you needed help."

He seemed to mean that, but she had a feeling there was more. "And?"

He furrowed his brow. "And my water's out, so I needed a place to stay." When Skyler didn't say anything, he dropped his chin to his chest. "And I guess I thought it would be good for me, having a chance to play a different part for a change."

"*Different* part? Were you already playing a part?"

His expression tightened. "You have no idea."

TEN

AS HE WALKED HAND IN hand with Skyler back to the main cabin, Kit thought maybe Cam was onto something with his nonstop honesty. He felt lighter than he'd felt in years. He hadn't even said all that much, mentioning they should go to lunch before Skyler could dig any deeper after his comment about playing a part, but admitting out loud that he hadn't felt like himself in years had been more freeing than he'd expected.

Maybe he should have said that to someone years ago. The problem was his closest friends would have laughed at him and told him there was no one who hated change more than him. In their minds, that was true.

And okay, they were right—to a point. Kit liked things being orderly, and he wasn't especially fond of surprises. But sometimes he wished he could step back from the put-together adult and just be goofy for a little bit, the way he'd been as a kid. He wanted to try something new and not get weird looks about it.

For the first time in years, being at this reunion meant he didn't have to think about disappointing anyone by doing something they didn't expect. Skyler was the only person in the world who really knew the wilder side of Kit Morgan. Not even the Wonder Boys had experienced it to its full degree, though that thought did sober him a little. He didn't like hiding things from his friends, but he knew they needed their leader to be steady and unchanging.

This week was going to give Kit a chance to truly relax for the first time in years before he pulled himself together again.

Skyler nudged his side. "So you're really not going to talk about—"

"Nope." Kit grinned when Skyler scowled up at him.

"You can't just drop something like that and expect me to leave it alone," she complained. "I really think this is something you need to talk about."

He squeezed her hand "You're right. But now isn't really the time. We can talk tonight, after we practice our kiss." A shiver ran through him at the thought. The last time he had kissed Skyler, he hadn't known what he was doing. It had been strange and unfamiliar, but he'd enjoyed it. A lot. They'd gone off to Christmas break immediately after that, and then he didn't see her again until she appeared in Maravilla last week.

More than anything, he was curious to see if they'd gotten better at it over the years. He liked to think he had improved since then, but something told him Skyler had had plenty of practice. He'd seen the look of embarrassment in her eyes when he'd told her how few people he had kissed.

The longer he gazed at her, the redder she became. "You really think we need to practice?" she asked, biting her lip.

Did she have any idea what temptation that presented? Kit counted to five before he said anything, keeping his eyes fixed ahead of him instead of watching her worry that lip between her teeth. He had no idea if he would even be able to kiss her, but even thinking about it felt like a win. "Unless you think you can make it look natural in front of your family," he said, fighting a grin. He knew exactly how she would respond to that.

Her eyes went wide. "Practice it is."

They had reached the back deck with the pool, and Skyler paused before they got to the door. "This is the big test," she said, thrusting her shoulders back and standing tall. "If we can't make them believe we're a couple in the next ten minutes, it's game over."

Weirdly, Kit wasn't feeling the stress that he had been earlier. Maybe because of the truth he'd admitted, or maybe because he thought way too highly of himself. He had always liked loose and relaxed Kit. Either way, he hoped his newly returned confidence wouldn't backfire on him. "Don't worry, Sky. I'm going to make them love me."

Then he grabbed the door and forged the way inside.

The kitchen had been cleaned up, though Kit spotted a bit of potato salad beneath one of the stools. Voices carried into the house from the front porch, more than he would have expected, but as the two of them stepped outside, all of the adult conversation faded to nothing. (The kids, on the other hand, continued shouting and screaming from their short table in the corner.)

Kit took in the dozen pairs of eyes staring at him before he tugged Skyler toward her mom. "Mrs. Taylor," he said, "I am truly sorry for what happened to your salad. I was looking forward to eating it, not wearing it."

Stella, who had turned pink the moment Kit started talking, seemed to relax a bit as she smiled at him. "Oh, it's nothing. The littles aren't being the littles unless they destroy something. I'm glad to see you got cleaned up. Have you officially met my husband, Lloyd, yet?"

As much as he tried to remain calm, Kit tensed as soon as he made eye contact with Lloyd. This was the man who held Skyler's prosperity in his hands and the one who, more than anyone, needed to believe this relationship was real. Kit tightened his hold on Skyler's hand and pulled her closer.

"It's an honor to finally meet you, sir," he said, holding out his free hand.

Lloyd gripped it hard, his expression stoic. From his salt-and-pepper hair and goatee to his fit form and tall stature, he certainly used his intimidating demeanor to his advantage, blue eyes cold and piercing. "So, you're the man with the vision."

Kit winced both from the handshake and from that comment. Skyler wasn't kidding when she said her stepdad didn't think she was capable of running a business on her own. His blood starting to boil, Kit matched Lloyd's strength and stood a little straighter. He may not have been bigger than Lloyd, but he was taller. "Honestly, most of that has been Sky. I'm not great with business, but I'm good at following directions."

"Hmm." Finally releasing Kit's hand, Lloyd took a step back and folded his arms. "I suppose we will have to get to know you this week. After all, you're going to be family. Right?"

"Right," he agreed.

"It's a good thing you were able to get away from work to join us. What was it you do again? It must keep you exhaustingly busy to keep you away this long. We were starting to wonder if you really existed."

As Lloyd narrowed his eyes, he seemed to be ready to challenge the whole relationship. Skyler must have decided the same thing, because she pulled Kit over to a large table where some younger adults sat and watched the exchange. "Micah!"

Kit wrapped his arm around Skyler's waist before mouthing a silent apology for the interruption to Lloyd across the deck. "Thank you again for bringing in our luggage, Micah," he said, glad to avoid making a fool of himself by trying to act like some super spy in disguise. "Skyler, want to introduce me to your stepsiblings?"

Skyler let out a deep sigh, though she put on a believable smile right after. "You should recognize most of them from all the photos I showed you," she all but growled.

Kit kissed her cheek. "You know how bad I am with names, Sweetie Pie."

Oh, she definitely didn't like that pet name, her gaze on fire despite her smile. "Of course. Lloyd's three daughters, from separate marriages: Georgia and her husband, Vic; Heidi and her husband, Stephan. And Micah."

"No husband," Micah said brightly. "I have three other half siblings, though. Briggs instead of Taylor. This is Houston and Brooklyn—they're twins. And my oldest brother, Chad."

Kit already knew he would legitimately forget who was who, and there were still a few adults at the table. He'd probably have better luck with all the kids, but he kept his smile intact as Skyler continued with the introductions.

"That's Samuel," she said, pointing, "and his wife Stacy."

"Tracy," the woman mumbled with a scowl.

Skyler didn't seem to notice. "And Paul on the end there with his wife, and, uh, Mike? And his wife. And then…" She cringed as she turned to the horde of children. "The kids. Honestly, I don't know any of their names."

A few of the adults pointed out which ones were theirs, but they seemed to recognize it as a lost cause. Many of them looked worn out, and Kit fought against a smile. Not that he had his own kids, but he'd seen the bittersweet relief of parents dropping off their kids for the first day of school in the fall. Summer vacations were hard. Maybe he could do something to help…

Not if Skyler had anything to say about it.

"Nice to meet everyone," Kit said with a forced smile, feeling queasy at the thought of pretending to dislike the kids. He would definitely rather be hanging out at their table right now. "I'm Chris, and I've been looking forward to this trip for weeks."

"It's nice to see you're real," one of the men said before his wife smacked him. "What? Dad thought he wasn't real."

Kit laughed. "I can be a bit of a hermit when I'm working. Thankfully, I'm in between projects right now." Should he have been concerned about how easily the lies slipped off his tongue? It was almost true… "So, what's for lunch?"

He and Skyler loaded up plates of food, which all looked delicious, then took their seats at the end of the big table. Conversation had resumed among the Taylors, leaving Kit and Skyler to have a small moment to themselves.

Kit had been too nervous to eat breakfast, so he was desperate to dig in, but Skyler just sat there, staring at her lap and looking frustrated. All in all, he'd thought things had been going pretty well, but she seemed to think the scheme was doomed. Or maybe this was just her default reaction around her family.

Taking a bite of salad, Kit watched her for a moment, trying to figure out what would help her the most. Did she need reassurance? Praise? Did he need to jump the gun and kiss her now to add to the illusion?

He nearly choked on the piece of spinach he was chewing. He hadn't suggested they practice solely for her benefit. He was going to need to work up to that moment, all the while hoping it wouldn't throw him right back into memories of Angela. If he couldn't even be touched by a person without being reminded of his ex-fiancée, he didn't hold out a lot of hope for anything more. Even if he wanted it.

Skyler's expression shifted, her gaze still downward as she smiled a little. Then twisted her lips in the way she always did when she concentrated.

Kit narrowed his eyes. He'd seen that look too many times in his classroom to ignore what was happening. "Give it to me," he said, holding out his hand.

Skyler's eyes snapped up. "What?"

"Your phone."

She turned bright red, though she put on a falsely innocent expression. "I don't have—"

"You're a terrible liar, you know that?"

Gritting her teeth, she seemed torn between scowling and smiling. "I just need to answer this email from the contractor."

Kit shook his head. "At lunch? No way. *Vacation*, Sky. I'm sure it can wait." He was still holding his hand out to her, and he'd caught the attention of her siblings, who all watched with interest. "Hand it over."

Skyler's eyebrows rose. "No."

"I'm not going to spend the one week I get with you this summer sharing you with your phone." Kit tensed, though he hoped that simply sounded like they were both busy. Not that they would never see each other again after this.

Skyler swallowed hard, her gaze icy as she gripped her phone tight against her chest. He could imagine the things she was saying to him in her mind right now, chief among them being she wasn't paying him to tell her what to do. Skyler had never liked being bossed around, not even when it came to teachers telling her which chapters to read in a textbook.

Kit had figured that part out quickly. They'd sat next to each other in history, and he'd asked her if she understood the reading homework because she'd looked terrified when their teacher announced a pop quiz. She'd told him she hadn't read it but knew all about the next unit and would make up her grades then.

Skyler marched to the beat of her own drum, and Kit had always loved that about her. But this week would only work if there was some give and take.

"I'll give it back later," Kit said, softer this time. "Please don't put me on the backburner."

Someone—probably Micah—let out a little whine of sympathy, and it was at that moment that Skyler seemed to realize just how closely they were being watched.

Clenching her jaw even harder, Skyler stuffed her phone into his hand. But then she slipped off the bench and disappeared into the house without a word, leaving Kit with a pit in his stomach because he'd clearly made the wrong choice.

Not that that surprised him. So far, he hadn't done very well with adult Skyler, like she had broken the part of him that had always been pretty good with people. Somehow he had forgotten that he couldn't talk to a grown woman the same way he did his students.

He should have just asked her to put it away.

Groaning internally, he was about to jump up and follow her to apologize when the man sitting next to him clapped an arm around his shoulders.

"Well, you've sold me," he said.

Kit blinked. "What?"

"Sam, would you stop?" the man's wife groaned.

But Sam's grin only grew. "We were all convinced Skyler was lying about being engaged, but no man in his right mind would do what you just did if you hadn't been together for years. A hired fiancé would have been terrified of talking back to Skyler Montague."

His wife pressed a palm to her face.

As his guilt grew, Kit fought for something to say. "She's been working too hard lately," he muttered. "I'm trying to get her to take a vacation for once."

"Heaven knows she needs it," the female twin said. Brooklyn? Kit was pretty sure her name was Brooklyn. "Having her here is going to make Stella so happy."

"But only if she's actually here," another woman grumbled. "If I have to hear one more sob story about the prodigal daughter…" She met Kit's gaze and shut her mouth, wrapping her hand around her husband's arm. "Sorry."

Though tempted to hear more about what her stepsiblings thought about her, Kit figured he should go make sure Skyler was okay. Shrugging out of Sam's hold, he slipped from the table and ignored the way Lloyd and Stella watched him as he passed. Let them think what they wanted.

The dining room was empty as he entered, as was the kitchen, but thankfully Skyler hadn't gone far. She sat balled up in an oversized armchair in the living room around the corner, her arms curled around her legs and her chin on her knees. She didn't even look at Kit as he crouched in front of her, her eyes fixed on the large fireplace.

"I'm sorry," Kit said. "You asked me to help you relax, and staring at your phone all day isn't going to do anything for you. But I shouldn't have treated you like one of my kids."

That got her attention, her eyebrows pulling together. "There are third graders with cell phones?"

"I really wish I could say no to that."

She stared at him for a second and then said, "How are you so good at this?"

"What?" Frowning, Kit resisted the strange urge to take her hand. That wouldn't do him any good right now, especially when he had no idea what she was talking about.

Skyler huffed a sigh. "They already love you. It's been, like, fifteen minutes, and they already like you better than they like me."

"I thought you wanted them to like me."

"I've been part of this family for eight years, and I didn't even know Stacy's name."

"Tracy."

Skyler threw her hands in the air. "See?"

Though he wanted to smile, Kit kept his expression neutral. Clearly this wasn't about the phone, but he needed to gather more information before he knew how to help her. "I'm sorry for embarrassing you in front of your family," he said gently, holding her phone out to her. "I know the bookstore is important to you."

"Yeah," she agreed without taking the phone. "It is. But, honestly, that email was just an update telling me everything is on schedule. It doesn't really need a response. I just…"

Kit placed the phone on the end table and waited for her to continue, unsure if she needed a push or if he had to let her admit things on her own. Back when they were twelve, she'd always done better when things were on her own terms, but she'd changed enough since then that he had no way of knowing how she ticked without spending more time with her.

She sighed. "I feel so out of place here, you know? Like, all of these people have become a family over the years even when some of them aren't related, and I'm always the one on the outside looking in. My own mother treats them more like her children than she ever did with me."

This time Kit did take her hand, clasping it between both of his and giving her a little smile. "I'm not asking this to insult you…"

Skyler quirked an eyebrow. "That's a terrible way to start a sentence."

"I know. But how much have you *tried* to be a part of this family?"

Squirming, she locked her gaze on the fireplace again. "A little. Not a lot. I've always been…busy."

"Busy, or scared?"

When she met his gaze again, her eyebrows dipped down in confusion. "Are you a therapist in your spare time?"

That got a little laugh out of him. "This is nothing compared to therapy. Answer the question."

"Terrified." As soon as the word left her mouth, her shoulders relaxed a little, which seemed to confuse her. "I guess I never thought it would last."

"So you never tried."

"Yeah."

Kit smiled, glad that she was trusting him enough to have this conversation. "Well, I hate to break it to you, Sky, but your mom seems pretty happy. I think she's sticking with this one."

She scrunched up her nose. "I think you're right."

"So, what are you going to do about it?"

Moving her legs to the ground, Skyler took a long, deep breath. Her eyes were unfocused, like she was thinking up some grand plan, and Kit held back his smile as he waited.

Skyler had always been great at making plans, and he couldn't wait to see what she came up with. How would the girl who was always on her own finally become a part of her family?

"I have no idea," she breathed, meeting his gaze again and looking at him like he was her last hope.

Kit laughed, squeezing her hand between his. "Well, it's a good thing you've got me, isn't it?"

"Definitely. I'm glad you're here, Chris." Then she ran her fingers through his hair.

His entire body went on high alert, and not in a good way. It was like her fingers brought an electric current so strong that it coursed through him and left him frozen solid, while his skin erupted in an itchiness that was more painful than uncomfortable. His muscles tensed, his stomach clenched, and he fell backward onto his rear end, barely managing to catch himself with one hand as his legs crumpled.

Gasping, he shut his eyes tight and put all of his focus into not throwing up. "Wow, that sucked."

At least he hadn't eaten much yet.

"Uh." Skyler sounded distant and muffled. "Yeah, we're definitely talking about that."

Kit lowered himself onto his back, throwing an arm over his face as he stretched his body out and tried to breathe in deep. "I'd rather not," he moaned weakly. He'd thought he'd gotten over that, but clearly he was still broken. It was the hair thing. No one had done that since Angela, who used to do that whenever she wanted something from him. Maybe if Skyler hadn't called him Chris at the same time…

Angela had called him Chris. She thought the name Kit sounded childish, and Kit hadn't been able to convince her otherwise.

Skyler grabbed his arm, using only her fingertips to move it from his face, and then she stretched out next to him on the floor. Close, but not close enough to touch him. "I'm not going to share the one week I get with you with…whatever that was."

Grimacing, Kit turned his head to look at her. He'd been holding onto this secret for years, but what did he have to lose? He probably wasn't going to see Skyler after this week, and she would never tell his friends or family because she was never going to meet them.

Besides, he was way too tired to pretend that kind of reaction was normal.

"You can talk to me, Kit." She was right. He'd always been able to talk to her when they were kids. Sometimes for hours.

He decided to just go for it, regardless of how she might look at him differently. He was sick of keeping all of this to himself. "I was engaged four years ago."

Skyler's eyes widened, though she tried (and failed) to sound casual. "Oh? What happened?"

He took a deep breath, figuring he should probably get it all out at once. Rip off the Band-Aid, so to speak. He kept his eyes on the ceiling as he spoke. "She cheated on me. With her best friend. Apparently, she'd been in love with him for years but never told him. She was doing some laundry at my house while I was at work because her machine broke, and I guess he came over to talk. He must not have liked hearing that I'd proposed, and he decided to profess his lifelong love. I came home from school and found the two of them…"

He swallowed as fire licked his skin. He really didn't need to revisit that moment of leaving work early and seeing the two of them locked together. In *his* house.

Shutting his eyes, he shook his head and clenched his hands into fists. "We weren't meant to be. I know that now, but… That day broke me. She was always so affectionate, and every touch…" He shuddered as ghostly memories of her hands washed over him. He hadn't been the same since the day he silently sat in the living room and watched her walk out of his life forever. She'd given him one last kiss on the forehead, as if that was enough to make up for how easily she threw away the time she'd taken from him. If Cam hadn't come over that day and found him, who knows what might have happened to him. How long would he have sat there on the floor, staring at the wall?

He had never felt as small as that day, when he realized the last year of his life had all been a lie. He had just been a means to an end. The four years since had been an uphill battle to get back to the confident man he'd been before, one he hadn't won yet by any stretch of the imagination. He was getting there, but he could really use a push.

"Kit?"

He didn't want to open his eyes and see the pity in her expression, but he did it anyway.

Skyler pursed her lips together, and she seemed to study him for a long time. "I'm really sorry that happened. That sucks."

"Yeah," he croaked. Movement caught his eye, and he watched with trepidation as she lifted her arm and—so very slowly—moved her hand until it hovered over his heart. She started with the tip of her pinky, then the next finger, one by one until her whole palm pressed against his chest.

If she felt the wild beating of his heart, she didn't say anything. She simply kept her eyes locked on his, a little smile on her lips. "Will you let me help you? You were a friend to me when I badly needed one, and you taught me to be comfortable in my own skin. I want to do the same."

A new sensation bubbled up inside him, one that felt both foreign and familiar. With his skin still prickling and taking up most of his bandwidth, he couldn't really name the warmth in his chest, but he knew it was something he wanted to hold onto.

"Okay," he whispered, even if he wasn't sure that was a good idea. He was already stretched taut by everything that had happened last week, like a rubber band pulled to its limit. But if anyone could get him to relax and settle into something real, Skyler Montague could.

She had done it before. Maybe she could do it again.

ELEVEN

GROWING UP WITH A MOTHER who focused more on finding her next boyfriend and less on being a parent hadn't made it easy for Skyler to acknowledge her emotions. She knew this about herself, and she'd done a lot to try to fix it. Well, she'd done a little. Being aware of her issues was better than nothing.

The courtroom hadn't helped. In order to rise through the ranks, she had needed to tuck away any vulnerability and prove to the men around her that she had what it took to get the job done. She had to be flawless, and strong, and fearless, no matter how she actually felt. Convincing Lloyd to help her had taken the same skills, with some added manipulation in there. Throughout her life, Skyler hadn't let herself think too hard about what she might have been missing out on when it came to emotions because she had managed to get everything she wanted without them.

Lying on a decorative rug next to Kit while he laid himself bare had blown a hole through her world view, and—true to form—she didn't know how to feel about that.

"Ready to move yet?" she asked after they'd been lying there in silence for at least five minutes. The longest five minutes of her life, honestly. She felt exposed, even if it was only to him. Being vulnerable wasn't how she operated; it was dangerous.

Kit shook his head without opening his eyes. "Nope."

"We can't stay here forever."

"I know."

"Sooner or later someone is going to—"

Kit grabbed her hand where it lay on his chest, entwining their fingers. "I haven't told anyone about Angela," he said, his voice thin. "No one even knows I dated her. Except for my therapist. And Cam, but he doesn't know the full scope of the aftermath. He thinks I'm just sad."

"Are you sad?" Skyler asked, keeping her focus on the way Kit held her hand so firmly. Actively. He hadn't seemed all that miserable about his stupid ex-fiancée, but what did Skyler know? She'd barely been able to admit that her crazy family scared the crap out of her, and she didn't have Kit's incredible ability to read people's emotions outside of a courtroom.

Taking a deep breath, Kit held it in his lungs for a few seconds, then let it out slowly. "Not anymore. I'm just broken."

"You're not broken."

He let out a single laugh when he turned to look at her. "Did you see that just now? I fell apart when you touched me. That's not normal, Sky."

"You say that like I'm anywhere close to normal. Normal is a stupid concept." And yet she'd done everything she could to fit in wherever she went. The one time she hadn't worried about being like everyone else was in the sixth grade. With Christopher. "I think we both have some things we're working through," she said with a sigh. "I meant it when I said I want to help you. I want to break you out of whatever this thing is that won't let you get close to someone."

He gazed at her intently as he asked, "What exactly is your plan there?"

Oh, she was definitely in way over her head, but she still smiled and pulled their clasped hands up to her lips. "This isn't bothering you, is it?"

He shook his head. "When I'm in control of things, it doesn't bother me at all. It's when I'm caught off guard. When my brain thinks she's there again."

Skyler loved that he was being so open about all of this, even if she didn't have much of a plan to help him. Maybe he just needed practice? "I still can't believe someone would trade you for someone else," she muttered. "She really did a number on you, didn't she?"

He shrugged. "Like I said. Broken. It didn't help that I…" His eyebrows slid together, and he let go of her hand so he could sit up.

Thank goodness. Skyler was getting tired of being on the floor. "That you what?"

As he clenched his jaw, he clearly didn't want to keep talking. "We don't need to do this. This week is about making sure you get your bookstore, not fixing—"

"We're friends, right?"

He blinked. "Sure."

Though she didn't particularly like that vague response, Skyler kept going. "Friends help each other out. What's on your mind?" She grabbed his hand again, and even though he tensed, she held fast. He would have to get used to it at some point. She would too. She'd spent so much time on her own that showing affection wasn't exactly the easiest thing in the world. She hoped it would be easy with him, though. Kit was the only person in the world who had ever made her want to hold onto someone.

Staring at their hands, Kit seemed to think about her question for a long time. His expression was pretty blank, making him impossible to read.

Along with refusing to show emotion, Skyler also had a problem with patience. "Come on. We used to tell each other our problems all the time."

Kit laughed. "Twelve-year-old problems are nothing compared to the crap I deal with now. Can we just…" He took a deep breath. "I want to get away from my problems for a while. Not put them under a microscope."

Skyler understood that to her core. That had been her entire life. "We can't run away from them forever." Even if she'd tried.

"No, but I think we could both use this week to have some fun. I haven't had a real vacation in years because I've been busy with…things. And you clearly need a break."

She raised an eyebrow. "Things, huh?"

"Don't push your luck."

Grinning, Skyler rose to her feet and then pulled Kit up with her. "Fine. Let's have some fun. But don't think you'll be off the hook when this week is over."

"I'm smart enough to know you don't let important things go."

A strange spark ignited in Skyler's chest when he grinned at her. It wasn't like he hadn't smiled at her before, but Skyler hadn't been this close to him when he did it. She hadn't been holding his hand. He hadn't put that intonation into his words that almost sounded like flirting.

"So," she said, clearing her throat and shifting a couple of inches away from him. "What exactly is this week going to look like? I maybe forgot how to have fun, and I'm not so sure I was ever good at it in the first place. And we can't forget the real reason you're here."

Kit adjusted his glasses, likely stalling as he looked around the room. "Can't forget about that," he agreed. "If it helps, Sam believes we're a real couple. I can't speak for any of the others, but I don't think you need to worry."

"Yet." It had only been an hour.

"Maybe…" Kit cleared his throat and pulled his hand free so he could grab his phone. "Maybe we should outline our goals for this week so we can make sure we're not going in the wrong direction."

Skyler barely bit back a laugh. "Christopher Morgan being organized? I never thought I'd see the day. Didn't you once mix up all of your homework and turn everything in to the wrong teachers?"

"We don't need to talk about that," he replied, turning red as he typed. "It only happened the one time. I'm usually pretty organized, but there are a lot of things about that semester that were…different."

Interesting. Kit had mentioned playing a part, and Skyler couldn't help but wonder if he'd been playing a role back then. Everything about him had been so natural. "Good different or bad different?"

"Depends on who you ask."

"What if I ask you? Did you like who you were back when I knew you?"

He looked up from his phone, his expression once again unreadable. How did he do that? It was like he had spent his life learning how to hide, but he did it with the flip of a switch. Skyler had hidden most of her life, but the only time she *didn't* wear a mask was with him. The rest of the time, she had to *try* to show emotion.

"I loved who I was," he admitted after a long moment, and then he went back to typing. "But that doesn't mean I hate who I am now."

"I thought you don't know who you are."

He pursed his lips. "You and your memory are going to be trouble, aren't you?"

"That's my middle name."

"Skyler Trouble Montague. Sounds right."

"It's actually Lilith." Skyler grimaced. "I'd rather it was Trouble. What's your middle name?"

He gasped dramatically. "You don't know your own fiancé's middle name? What kind of girlfriend are you?"

"How's that list of yours coming?"

"Duke. My dad's name. And don't knock the list."

Skyler grinned. She'd missed this. Even as awkward preteens, they'd been able to talk and banter so easily. No one else really seemed to understand how their back-and-forth made sense, but everything about the two of them had always felt so natural.

"I meant it," she said, snaking her fingers around his wrist to pull his phone into view. He didn't seem to mind that touch, but he also seemed pretty focused on his phone and might not have even noticed. "I'm not even a little bit organized outside my head."

"I am well aware. Pretty sure you're the reason I mixed up my homework. You rubbed off on me. Besides, that was the day I asked you to be my girlfriend, so I was, uh, distracted."

Skyler rolled her eyes. "You say that like I hadn't put a note in your locker the day before telling you I liked you." She'd done it in a rare moment of emotional bravery, not knowing if Kit—Christopher—liked her back or even if her crush was real. She'd never been in a place long enough to like any boys, so liking Kit had been new and terrifying.

"Either way, my disorganization was your fault." Though he turned red again, Kit nodded toward his phone. "So, what do you think?"

He had written three things on his phone, straightforward and to the point.

1. Get to know the Taylor family
2. Have fun throughout the week
3. Be the best fiancé(e) ever

"Best fiancé ever, huh?" Skyler liked the sound of that one, though she couldn't ignore the fact that he had given her the same task. She hadn't really thought about how she was the other half of the engagement and needed to play the part as much as he did. She could hardly let her family fall in love with him while losing respect for her if she didn't give as much as she took. The problem was she had no idea how to do that. "You forgot to add me helping you get used to being touched."

Kit scrunched up his nose. "Does that sound as dirty to you as it does to me?" He laughed when she smacked his arm. "It's part of Number Three. If I were really your fiancé, I wouldn't be afraid to touch you."

"Are you really afraid?"

In response, he feathered his fingers along her arm and up to her throat, engulfing her entire body in goosebumps with his whispered touch. When he tucked some still-damp hair behind her ear and leaned in to brush a kiss against her temple, her breath caught in her throat.

"Nope," he whispered. "Like I said, when I'm in control…"

Skyler would have no problem surrendering control if he was going to be like that. Maybe now would be a good time to practice that whole kissing situation.

"Oh, sorry, am I interrupting?"

Skyler jumped away from Kit and turned to find her mom standing there with red in her cheeks. "Mom. Um."

"Not interrupting," Kit said, sounding entirely unaffected by that point of contact they'd just lost. "We were on our way back out."

Mom coughed a little. "Of course. Uh, everyone was going to take a walk up the road, if you were interested in joining. But I suppose you'll want to eat first."

Skyler's stomach rumbled in response, making Kit laugh. "Yeah," she said with a smile. "We should probably eat. I know too well what happens if I keep Chris away from food for too long."

"You know me," Kit said with a chuckle.

That part was actually true. Skyler had once convinced Kit to skip lunch so they could walk to a nearby pawn shop, and she had never seen a grumpier person than a hungry Christopher Morgan. He took hangry to the next level.

Hand in hand, they followed Stella back outside to the almost-empty table. Only Micah was left, though she seemed torn between staying put and joining the rest of the family.

"You okay?" she asked Skyler in a loud whisper.

Skyler swallowed her immediate response of snapping that she was fine. Micah had been nothing but kind over the last eight years, and yet for some reason she had always gotten on Skyler's nerves. Maybe it was her endless positivity and enthusiasm, or the fact that she had been a perky sixteen-year-old cheerleader when Skyler first met her. Getting to know her better would have to be a big part of Goal Number One.

Putting on a smile, she patted Micah's shoulder. "I'm fine," she said as gently as she could. "I've just been a little stressed over the bookstore getting done, but Chris is right." She turned her smile to Kit, noting how much easier it was to smile at him than it was with Micah. "I need a break."

Micah brightened. "Sounds like you picked the right man." She winked.

"No doubt."

"That man is hungry," Kit reminded her, glancing at their clasped hands that prevented him from heading to his full plate of food.

"Right. You should go on the walk, Micah. Maybe we can catch up when you get back."

Oh goodness, did people often cry when shown basic kindness? At the first sign of Micah's eyes filling with tears, Skyler leaned into Kit as if he might be able to keep the girl's emotion at bay.

"I'd like that," Micah choked, and then she scurried off to follow Mom.

The instant she was out of sight, Skyler plopped onto the bench where her plate still waited and dropped her head into her hands. "What is wrong with me?"

Kit spoke through a mouthful of food. "What do you mean?"

When she looked up, Kit had somehow already eaten half his burger. She made a mental note to make sure she didn't keep him away from food during the week. "I mean she just acted like that was the first time I've ever been nice to her."

"Was it?"

"Maybe?"

Grinning, Kit swallowed and reached across the table to take her hand. "Don't feel bad. You have a lot of *lawyer* to flush out of you. It'll take some time to be human again."

"I resent that." Skyler pointed her fork at the man, giving him a playful glare. "Lawyers aren't all bad, you know."

"What kind of lawyer were you, exactly?"

"Corporate. A good one."

Kit raised an eyebrow as he shoveled a forkful of macaroni into his mouth. Once he'd swallowed, he asked, "So you were basically a shark?"

"If you mean I went up against my opponents, who were usually in the right, and massacred them…" She wished she could make herself sound better, but there was a reason she'd left her job so easily. She hadn't exactly been making the world a better place. "Yeah."

"Remind me not to get on your bad side."

"Speaking of bad sides, you're going to have to tell me how to be a good fiancée."

Kit choked on the bite of pasta salad he'd just put in his mouth, coughing for several seconds and turning a deep crimson until he could breathe again. Skyler hadn't meant to spring that on him, but it wasn't like there was a good way to admit she'd never been good at relationships. Avoiding vulnerability had also meant avoiding attachment, which was great when moving from city to city but not so much when trying to put down roots or make connections.

"I don't know if I'm the best person to ask," Kit said after a long while. "Clearly, my attempt at being engaged wasn't very successful."

"But at least you *have* been engaged."

"It lasted less than a day, Sky. She cheated on me the next afternoon."

Though she hated Kit's stupid ex even more now, Skyler pressed forward. "I haven't even had a boyfriend. Technically." She cringed when Kit's face went slack with surprise. Nothing like admitting failure as an adult to put herself in her place. "Relationships aren't really my thing."

Swallowing hard, Kit seemed fixated on his almost empty plate for several seconds. What must he think of her? "There's no way," he said, answering her unspoken question. "You've been in a lot of relationships."

"Nope."

"But look at you!" He swept his arm over her as if that explained everything. "You're Skyler Montague. You had half of the sixth grade in love with you within the first month of school."

Though she felt the thrill of his praise down to her toes, she didn't appreciate the exaggeration. The only person who ever talked to her in sixth grade was Kit. "I've barely lived in one place for longer than a few months, Kit. Even when I did, I've always focused more on school and work than building relationships. Besides, why would anyone want to date—"

"Because there's no one in the world like you." Turning red again, Kit cleared his throat and shook his head. "I still don't think I'm going to be all that helpful, but I'll do what I can. Honestly, just treat me like you did in junior high, and you'll be fine."

She furrowed her brow as she watched him look everywhere but at her. Had she really treated him like they were truly a couple? They hadn't even held hands until Halloween, two months into knowing each other, and Skyler had known nothing about being a girlfriend. That hadn't changed.

"You'll tell me if I do something wrong, won't you?" she asked. "Like spending too much time on my phone answering emails?"

He rolled his eyes. "Yeah, you're not going to be spending *any* time answering emails. I'm going to hold onto your phone the rest of the week because you just said that."

Skyler had never considered herself addicted to her phone, but maybe that was because no one had ever asked her to put it away. Or maybe that was just because she didn't like someone telling her what to do. She swallowed the anger that rose in her chest and reminded herself that Kit really was trying to help her. She was paying him to do a job, and it would be a good idea to let him do it.

"Fine. Just know that means you have to be as equally entertaining as TikTok, or I'm going to get bored really fast."

He smirked, shaking his head. "That defeats the purpose of Goal Number Two, don't you think? And One and Three, if we're getting technical. If you want to get to know your family, Skyler, you're going to have to put in some effort. Same with having fun."

"I'm pretty sure making tie-dye shirts will never be fun," she grumbled back. Though she knew Lloyd and her mom wouldn't be surprised if she didn't participate in all of the activities they'd planned for the week, she also knew she needed to do everything she could to stay on her stepdad's good side. That meant making shirts and playing charades and doing her best to not make anyone cry.

Kit sat forward, linking his fingers together as he studied Skyler. The sunlight glinted off his glasses, making his eyes difficult to see. It was unnerving. "Here's the plan," he said, sounding official and—Skyler would never say it out loud— sexy, acting so in charge. "I don't care if you think it's the worst idea in the history of the world, but we are going to do every single activity on the list starting this afternoon. We're going to go all in, just like we used to in Mr. Gonzales's class."

Skyler pursed her lips. "You're right. That's the worst idea I've ever heard."

"No, listen." He hopped up, circling the table and straddling the bench next to her. He looked more excited than she'd expected after the day they'd had so far, and she couldn't help but want to do whatever he said. "So many of my kids over the years have held themselves back because they're so worried about what other people think of them. They're too afraid of what *might* happen, what might go wrong, that they can't even see what they're missing out on. I know you've got a lot going on in your life and you have a lot riding on this week, but if you want to accomplish all three of our goals, this is the best way to do it. I would make a pros and cons list for you if I thought there would be anything negative about it, but there isn't. Trust me."

She did trust him. It didn't matter how long it had been since she last saw this man; she knew he would never let her down. "Okay," she said, though she felt a little queasy thinking about the ridiculousness she was about to put herself through. "But only if you promise to never leave my side."

"I would never do that."

She believed him. But that didn't limit the fear she felt.

Kit held up his little finger and grinned at her. "Pinky swear."

Goodness, she hadn't done a pinky swear in years. As childish as it felt, linking her finger with Kit Morgan's meant something, so she latched on and nodded, trying to ignore the growing spark in her chest but epically failing.

If she made it through this week alive, she would not be coming out the other side as the same person.

Kit Morgan would never let that happen.

TWELVE

WHO WOULD HAVE THOUGHT ANONYMITY would be the greatest thing to ever happen to him? Just like sixth grade, knowing that no one in this cabin knew anything about him had liberated Kit from a lifetime of expectation. It was like having a fake username but in real life, though he had a feeling pretending to be Skyler's doomed fiancé would be even more fun than leaving ridiculous compliments in the comment section on the video of Oliver's fancy presentation that he'd done several years back.

Convincing Lloyd that Skyler could absolutely run a business on her own would be a lot more rewarding than telling the world he appreciated the way Oliver said the word "utilization."

It didn't hurt that Skyler had loosened up a lot while they cleaned up from lunch before everyone returned from their walk. They'd spent an hour reminiscing about the old days as Kit washed dishes and Skyler dried, laughing until they cried about some of their antics. Kit could pretend all he wanted that he had lived his entire life going in one direction, but Skyler made it impossible to ignore those few months when he'd been someone completely different.

The days of Christopher Morgan had been some of the best days of his life, and Kit was glad to have them back for a little while.

True to Skyler's frustration, the afternoon's scheduled activity was making matching tie-dye shirts to kick things off. Though she grumbled the whole time her mom laid out all the supplies, Kit kept his hand wrapped around hers so she couldn't run away. He had never actually done tie-dye before, and though he would probably never wear the shirt after this week, he was looking forward to seeing how things turned out.

"Number Two," he reminded her under his breath when she started bouncing her leg in her seat.

She shot a glare at him. "It's not like I could have forgotten in the last hour and a half. I just don't see the point of—"

"There doesn't have to be a *point*. Do you see how excited the kids are?" He pointed to the horde of children ranging from two to seventeen, most of them hovering around the supply table in anticipation. "That's the fun level you should be at."

"Ha! You say that like I'm actually capable of behaving that way."

Rolling his eyes, Kit tugged her a bit closer on the patio chair they were sharing. "Oh, don't even pretend I haven't seen you be the most enthusiastic reader in English class. You were terrifying as Lady Macbeth."

That got a real laugh out of her. "Who in their right mind lets sixth graders read Macbeth? We're lucky we didn't all turn out to be psychopaths after that. Wait, didn't you read Macbeth's part?"

"I had to do Jeff Fenton's homework for a week to convince him to trade parts with me so I could be your husband." Kit's heart stumbled in his chest as soon as he remembered that little tidbit of information. They'd read the play in October, before he and Skyler started dating, and he'd been desperate for any way to interact with her more. Reading lines with her hadn't exactly been romantic, but he'd lapped up every second of it, imagining a world where they were husband and wife for real.

Maybe without the murder.

Skyler snickered and bumped her shoulder into his. "You were such a dork. And terrible at reading lines. Remind me again why I agreed to let you come with me this week when you were so bad at acting?"

"Because you wanted me." Heat flared in his face. He hadn't meant to end the sentence there. "I mean, because you wanted me to protect you from cheaters and creeps."

Though she had to be aware of several of her stepsiblings watching the pair of them with interest, Skyler turned to face him and leaned in so close that his heart jumped into double time. "Oh, I wanted you."

Was it a terrible idea to throw away the plan to do a practice kiss tonight and just go for it right now? Kit wasn't so sure this moment wouldn't work to their benefit, and her pink lips looked mighty tempting. But a little voice in the back of his head reminded him that Skyler had admitted to being nervous about this relationship of theirs, and she'd never had a boyfriend. Had she even kissed anyone since junior high?

With the way she licked her lips just now with the very tip of her tongue, he assumed she *had*. That, or she was more of a natural at this dating thing than she realized. Everything about her on the surface level was fair and delicate, her soft green eyes big and alluring, but it was what lay underneath that had always intrigued Kit. She was so much stronger than she looked and never backed down from a challenge. He knew the intimacy of a fake engagement terrified her, but that hadn't stopped her from holding his hand for the last twenty minutes.

Maybe he could start by kissing the freckles on her bare shoulder and work his way up with the hope that her lips would be ready for him when he got there.

When the horde of kids started screaming, hopefully for joy, Kit let out a groan and pulled himself away. "You're not getting away that easily tonight," he warned her, pleased to see her turn a stunning shade of pink. Had she been anticipating the kiss as much as him?

"I wasn't expecting to," she replied before hopping to her feet and joining the line to gather supplies.

"Looks like she got over it," someone said behind Kit.

He turned, trying to remember the other twin's name. Austin? No, Houston. "I'm really good at groveling," he said as he stood. "You're Micah's brother, right?"

Houston nodded, eyes slightly narrowed as he seemed to examine Kit. "Same mom, different dad. Mom married Lloyd after the divorce and had Micah. Died a few years later. It's confusing; technically, we're not related to Lloyd, but..." He shrugged, stuffing his hands into his pockets. "He was nice enough to take us in after our dad took off."

Though he was having a hard time following the dynamics, Kit looked over at Lloyd, who had sat himself down in a corner with a beer and seemed to be overseeing everything without participating. He had the same stoicism he'd had at lunch. "I can't say I know him very well yet, but that surprises me."

Houston laughed a little, nodding. "He's loving in his own way. Hard on us, but he really likes seeing his family succeed. Sorry about Sam earlier. Sometimes the Taylors don't know when to keep their mouths shut."

"Sorry about your parents," Kit replied. "And don't worry. Skyler and I aren't exactly a typical couple, so I don't expect people to keep to their own business while I'm here. I know I've raised a lot of questions."

"A few, yeah." Houston squinted, standing a little taller. He looked to be about Kit's age, somewhere in his late twenties, and carried himself with the confidence of a man who knew exactly who he was. Blond hair, blue eyes, enough muscle to give Kit a run for his money—put him in a suit, and he would look right at home in a big-city boardroom or schmoozing clients on a golf course. At the moment, he wore a t-shirt and jeans with a worn baseball hat, and somehow he still looked impressive.

Houston cocked his head. "You're not really a secret agent, are you?"

"Is that what people think?" Chuckling, Kit knew he would have to drag that out as long as he could, if only to keep himself entertained. "I wish I knew what Sky's been telling you guys. Speaking of, I should probably go help her. She looks a little lost."

He hurried over to Skyler's side before Houston could ask any more questions, and then he wrapped an arm around her waist and pulled her back against his chest. He didn't miss the stiffness in her body for the first few seconds, but she relaxed fairly quickly. It was *definitely* a good thing he hadn't kissed her. They would have to work up to that. "I thought I was the one who needed to learn," he muttered in her ear.

She giggled, reaching up until her fingers found the side of his head and slid into his hair. "Yeah, well, this is going to take some getting used to."

He shuddered, either a remnant of his reaction to this move earlier or because he really liked the way her fingers brushed his scalp. Maybe both. "Tell me about it. So, what's the plan here?"

Skyler gestured to the table, which had already been mostly raided by the kids. "From what I understand, we need shirts, rubber bands, and way more creativity than I'm capable of."

Kit looked around the patio, searching through the various kids to see if any of them looked like they knew what they were doing. Most of the younger ones had recruited their parents or an aunt or uncle, but a few of them seemed determined to do the job on their own. Spotting two children who didn't look like they might start a fight with the bottles of dye, Kit decided they were probably their best bet.

"I have a plan," he said, searching through the piles of shirts until he found his size. "Do you trust me?"

"I thought we already established that."

"Good."

Loaded up with supplies, Kit led the way to the corner where the two kids were quietly working. He'd just about reached them before he realized Skyler had stopped halfway there, her eyes wide and horror in her expression.

"Uh, everything okay?" he asked when he returned to her side.

She twisted her mouth, glancing around before she leaned in and whispered, "Those are Heidi's kids."

Heidi was… Kit fought to remember. "She's the perfect one, right?"

Skyler scowled. He must have guessed right.

"What does it matter?" he asked, shrugging. "It's these two or that fifth grader who has already turned his hands purple."

Though she smiled a little at the sight of the boy making a massacre of his shirt with the dye, Skyler still seemed reluctant. "I don't know, Kit," she whispered. "They're probably her little spies, and they'll tell their mom all about how I can't even tie-dye a shirt properly."

"How do you know you can't do it? You haven't even started." Kit looked around, hoping to find an alternative, but he had a feeling these kids could use the attention. With the way they so swiftly went off on their own, they probably didn't get much of it. Particularly with so many rambunctious kids to fill the space around them and make them disappear.

"Okay," he said, taking a deep breath. "You don't have to come with me, but I'm going to go work with the Wonder Twins. It's up to you what you want to do, but don't forget your very important goals."

He made it two steps before Skyler latched onto his arm. "This is extortion. You know that, right?"

Laughing, he pressed a quick kiss to her cheek, paused for a second to register how much he liked doing that—probably a little too much—and then he led the way to the corner and knelt on the patio. "Hi, guys. We were hoping you could teach us how to do this."

Both children stiffened, their amber-colored eyes widening in unison. The boy looked around the patio, as if searching for his parents, while the girl seemed to be frozen in place with fear.

Skyler and the girl looked remarkably similar at the moment, and Kit couldn't help but grin. "I'm Chris, by the way," he said, ducking his head so he wasn't so tall. "And this is Sky. She's kind of your mom's sister."

Skyler hissed in a breath but said nothing.

"What's your name?" Kit asked.

Blinking a couple of times, the girl glanced at her brother, then said, "Isabelle."

"How old are you, Isabelle?"

"Eight."

No wonder these kids had stood out to him. "Does that mean you're going into third grade this year?"

Isabelle nodded, her lips puckering into a little smile. "Tanner is eight too."

"Whoa, are you guys twins?"

Another nod.

"Did you know Houston and Brooklyn are twins too?"

"Really?" That came from Tanner, whose eyes locked on Houston across the patio where he was talking to one of the other men. "I didn't know that. They don't look like each other."

"Twins don't always look like each other," Kit replied. "People used to think my sister and I were twins, but we're not. I'm two years older."

"I'm older too," Tanner said, puffing out his chest a little. "By three minutes."

Unable to stop his grin, Kit grabbed his white shirt and held it out to the two kids now that he had their full attention. "Do you guys know how to do this? I've never done it before."

"Me neither," Isabelle admitted. "We were reading the instructions online."

When she showed him the iPhone she'd been hiding in her lap, Kit resisted the urge to grimace. They were definitely too young to have access to the internet like that, but at least they were using it for a good purpose today. "Well, then you must be experts by now. I'll do what you do."

Isabelle, who was clearly more tenacious than her brother, walked their little group through the steps, starting with getting their shirts wet and then choosing what sort of style they wanted to do. Kit offered to help Tanner with spinning his shirt into a design and getting the rubber bands secured, while Skyler attempted to assist Isabelle, though the two of them got rather giggly pretty quickly.

"I don't remember laughing being part of the instructions," Kit said, poking Skyler in the ribs.

She yelped. "I thought the goal was to have fun."

Skyler Montague was ticklish. Tucking that information away for future use, Kit stuck his tongue out at her. "We're having fun too, but at least we're quiet about it."

"I like when Izzy laughs," a quiet voice said.

Kit's grin dropped, and he spun back to face Tanner. The kid was watching his sister so intently that he hadn't seemed to realize he was in the middle of stretching a rubber band around his shirt. Recognizing some sort of significance, Kit leaned in closer. "She has a great laugh, doesn't she? I like Skyler's laugh too. I'm just teasing them. But I meant what I said about having fun when you're quiet too. We're having fun, right?"

Tanner ducked his head, aligning his rubber band perfectly as he spoke. "Mom didn't want to come to the reunion.

She said she has too much work to do, and Dad hates being outside."

Kit glanced around the patio, eyebrows furrowed. He was surprised Tanner had decided to trust him so quickly, but he wasn't about to waste the opportunity. "Where are your parents now?"

Tanner shrugged.

Micah had said something that morning about Tanner getting into a fight and Heidi being upset with both kids. This absolutely wasn't any of his business, but instinct told him that these kids needed him this week as much as Skyler did.

"You know what?" Kit said, putting as much energy into his words as he could. "It's okay if your parents have to work. They have jobs so they can pay for things like your house and food. Luckily for you, kids don't have to have jobs yet, so you get to have all the fun you want."

Tanner perked up a little, as if he hadn't realized his life could be independent from his parents'. "Do you have a job?"

Ouch. He should have seen that backfire coming. Absently scratching his arm, he shook his head. "Not right now, but that means I get to find a new one."

"You don't want to teach anymore?"

Kit nearly jumped a mile high when Skyler grabbed his arm; somehow he'd forgotten she was right behind him. She'd probably been listening to everything he said, and he clenched his jaw in frustration with himself. "Maybe that's a conversation for later," he muttered. Then, louder, he said, "I think we're ready to dye these bad boys!"

"I don't know what colors to do," Isabelle moaned. "I want pink and yellow and red and blue *and* green, but the instructions say to choose three colors or less."

"You can do however many colors you want," Skyler said before Kit could tell her the same thing. "This shirt is all about you, Isabelle, so you gotta make sure you use every single color you want to. That way everyone will know that it's yours and just as unique as you." She tucked a blonde curl behind Isabelle's ear and gave her a huge grin. "This is the part where you get to be creative."

And maybe the part where Kit started to wonder if he'd ever gotten over his crush on Skyler Montague.

Why in the world did this woman think she didn't like kids?

"What colors are you going to do, Chris?" Tanner studied his options with his eyebrows low, like he was being quizzed on complementary colors.

Kit put on a thoughtful expression. "Hmm, that's a really good question! I like all the colors, but I want to make sure I pick something that makes me look good."

"Green."

Kit met Skyler's eyes.

As she blushed, she shrugged a little and then dumped a bunch of purple dye onto a section of her shirt. "You look good in green."

His smile stretched so wide that he thought it might fly off his face. "Thank you. You're great at giving compliments."

"Did you just turn your thank you into a return compliment?" she replied, raising an eyebrow. "You are so weird."

It was a habit from teaching. His kids always needed more validation in their lives, and he always tried to show them how to praise people for things within their control. "Only because you make it easy to say good things about you," he said with a smirk.

"Are you boyfriend and girlfriend?" Isabelle asked with wide eyes.

Though Skyler spluttered a little, as if she didn't think she would ever get asked that question, Kit reached over and picked up Skyler's left hand to show off the ring she wore. "I'm going to marry her someday."

It happened without warning. Without wondering. But the moment those words left his mouth, he knew they were absolutely true. But that was nonsense! He'd known grown-up Skyler for less than two days' time collectively, and yet… And yet Kit had never had anything hit him that hard, like it had just been waiting for him to realize it.

As Skyler continued to help Isabelle squirt dye onto her shirt, Kit watched her for a long time, trying to understand why he wasn't completely freaking out about this little revelation he'd just had. Maybe because he knew he couldn't know the future, so there was no way for him to know if the thought would ever come true.

But at the same time, he had to wonder why he so badly *wanted* it to come true when he barely knew this woman.

Nothing like a little insanity to spice up a summer afternoon.

THIRTEEN

"WHY DID TODAY FEEL LIKE it lasted a week?" Skyler collapsed onto the plush couch in the third cabin's living room, completely exhausted and strangely satisfied. She hadn't expected to enjoy tie-dyeing in the slightest, especially when she ended up with red dye all over her fingers and looked like she was escaping a murder scene—apparently Isabelle had missed the part that recommended gloves—but she hadn't laughed that much in a long time.

Unlike her snooty, stuck-up harpy of a mom, Isabelle was sweet and genuine and immensely prone to giggling so hard she cried, and that had made Skyler relax almost instantly.

It didn't hurt to have Kit right beside her, drawing in her family members as they took turns trying to get to know him.

It was just like sixth grade, when he somehow managed to befriend everyone with half a conversation and a generous helping of smiles. Even when Kit kept his responses suspiciously vague, no one seemed to bat an eye. They even talked to Skyler, something no one but Micah had ever made an effort to do before.

Speaking of, Micah had settled on the other end of the couch from Skyler, though she sat upright and alert. How did she not get exhausted being so bubbly all day long? "You didn't even go on the walk with us," she said brightly. "I thought you were used to being around people all day."

Skyler laughed. "Talking to a jury that can't talk back is not the same as trying to have a conversation with a four-year-old who can only talk about canned corn. Not just corn in general. *Canned* corn, specifically."

"Yeah, Callum is a weird kid. He's cute, though. So…" Micah glanced at Skyler's closed bedroom door as if Kit might come walking through it in a towel again. "Why didn't you tell me your fiancé was totally hot?"

"Why don't you talk a little louder so he can hear you?"

Kit had gotten in a dye-fight with the older kids on the lawn and had made the mistake of waiting until after dinner to hop in the shower; he'd been in there for a while, probably trying to scrub through a few layers of colorful skin.

And Micah wasn't the only one hoping to get another view of that man's abs of steel. Skyler had purposefully declined joining the others from the cabin—Micah's single siblings and the one couple who didn't have kids yet—for some time out in the big hot tub. Secretly, she hoped Kit would be up for doing the hot tub with her later, after everyone else had gone to bed.

Hugging a pillow, Micah snickered. "Seriously, I can't believe you've been together for eighteen months and I haven't heard a single thing about how he looks. You've got a Greek god for a fiancé and all you've been able to say about him is that he's busy? The man looks like a superhero!"

That wasn't entirely accurate, though Skyler couldn't argue too much. Kit was attractive without question, but he had a softness to him that she'd never seen in anyone before. He was like a boulder at the edge of a river, smoothed around the edges but still mighty and majestic.

"Didn't you say he didn't do well with kids, though?" Micah continued. "I thought for sure the Wonder Twins would run away."

"I guess he is better than he thought."

Yeah, Kit had completely ignored that aspect of his fake persona, and Skyler wasn't even mad. No wonder he had put up a fight when she told him that part; Kit was a natural. Once the kids realized Tanner and Isabelle were having a blast with him in their little corner, he'd gotten swarmed.

The swarm had spread to the adults, then led to the dye fight, and then Chad and Houston had discovered Kit played basketball in high school and spent all of dinner talking about the last NBA season. Kit's attention had been pulled in every direction until he finally begged for the chance to shower and go to bed.

It had only been a few hours since Skyler had really interacted with him, but it worried her how much she felt that absence. That wasn't going to end well.

"So, uh…" Micah tugged on one of her auburn curls, letting it spring back and bounce. "What happened today at lunch? You looked really upset."

Skyler had promised Micah they would catch up, but she wasn't sure if she wanted that to mean having a heart-to-heart. Micah had decided they were sisters the moment Mom married Lloyd, but Skyler had never felt that connection the way Micah seemed to. Still, she would get an earful from Kit if he found out she didn't at least try to have a decent conversation. Once the man made a plan, he stuck with it.

"I've always been a workaholic," she said with a shrug. "Chris thinks I should be using this week to relax, but I can't stop thinking about the bookstore and how much I need to get done."

Micah raised her eyebrows. "Smart man. Did he steal your phone for the whole day? I don't think I've ever seen you without it before."

Skyler held up her hands to show they were empty. "I wasn't very happy about it," she admitted, "but he talked me down." And was incredibly vulnerable on the floor when he told her about his ex. "Honestly, it's been nice not checking on things constantly, and it made it easier to talk to people because my head wasn't somewhere else."

Micah pursed her lips, like she was trying not to laugh. "It's driving you crazy not having it, isn't it?"

"Oh my gosh, yes!" Admitting that felt so good that Skyler laughed out loud. Maybe Micah wasn't nearly as bad as she'd thought. "It's like I'm missing an entire limb! I know it's good to disconnect, but I don't know if going cold turkey was the best way to go. Chris was supposed to tell me if I had any messages, but he hasn't—"

"Unless you count your local congressman asking for your vote," Kit said from the suddenly open doorway, "you haven't gotten any messages."

Skyler's response—whatever it might have been—came out as a squeak that sounded like a poor, dying hamster breathing its last breath. Was there something magical about that shower that made him get hotter every time he came out of it? Seriously, a pair of sweatpants and a hoodie shouldn't have been that attractive, and yet Kit Morgan in all his wet hair glory stood in the doorway of their bedroom like—

"Oh." Skyler felt like something had just fizzled out in her brain to make way for the ignition of something completely different. *Their* bedroom. As in both of them. How, in all her planning, had she not made the connection that they would be sharing not only a room but a *bed*? Though there was nothing wrong with couples sleeping separately until they got married, she couldn't very well sleep on the couch, or Lloyd would sniff out trouble in paradise and call everything off. And no way did she want to sleep on the bedroom floor, though she would do it if she had to.

Kit furrowed his brow. "You good?"

She nodded, knowing he probably wouldn't believe her. So much of her past life had been about lying and manipulation, but she would never be able to lie to Kit. Not when he had always been able to see right through her.

"Did you still want to practice tonight?" he continued, his eyebrows still pulled down low in swoon-worthy concern. Or maybe the swoon was coming from the notion of kissing the man in the immediate future.

Skyler practically saw Micah's ears perk up at the sound of Kit's question. "Practice? What are you guys practicing?"

"Daily affirmations," Kit said without missing a beat, though he cringed a little as if he'd forgotten Micah was sitting there.

"Oo, I love affirmations!"

Good for Micah. Skyler thought they were stupid unless they were a euphemism for making out behind a tree, in which case she was okay with them. Even if she was a little terrified. Kit said he'd only kissed three other people over the years, but something told her he'd learned a thing or two from those women. With the way he reacted to physical contact—and with him growing up to look like Clark Kent—his fiancée must have been all over him. Why else would physical contact be such a trigger?

Skyler's two attempts at kissing post-Kit hadn't exactly gone well, and she still felt bad about Matt's broken nose. The poor paralegal had gone for it after their third date, and Skyler had gotten so tickled by his mustache that she sneezed, her head smacking right into his nose.

She could talk all the talk she wanted. Wear the six-inch heels, slay in the courtroom, prove to every man who doubted her that she deserved a spot at the table. But she would never be able to claim she had any idea what she was doing when it came to the really important things. When it came to relationships, of any kind, Skyler couldn't walk the walk.

"Sky?"

Maybe she wasn't ready for this. Kit was so far out of her league that she would always be several steps behind him.

"Today was really tiring," she said, feeling the sting of disappointment in every inch of her body. "Maybe we can practice tomorrow?"

Unless she was mistaken, Kit was as disappointed as she was, his shoulders dropping and his smile shifting into something less real. "Of course. You had an exciting day. I guess we'll just go to...bed?" With the way that sounded like a question, he had clearly realized the same problem she had.

And he likely hadn't found a good solution to their one-bed situation.

"We'll talk more tomorrow?" Micah said warily as Skyler rose to her feet.

"Yeah, sure."

As soon as they were both in the bedroom with the door closed, Kit grabbed a pillow. "I'll sleep on the floor."

Skyler grabbed the other end of the pillow. "I can't let you do that."

"Sure you can."

"But I'm paying you."

He narrowed his eyes, giving the pillow a gentle tug, though she held fast. "Exactly. Why would you pay me so *you* can sleep on the floor?"

"I hate when you get all logical."

Have mercy, he shouldn't be allowed to use a smile like that when in the middle of an argument. It made her want to say yes to anything he said. "You'd think the lawyer in you would like me being logical," he said.

Skyler barely held back a *gream*, knowing Micah would probably hear and come running. Instead, she tried ripping the pillow from his hands but didn't even move it an inch. "Christopher Duke Morgan, you are not sleeping on the—"

"Why don't you want to practice?"

Skyler dropped the pillow. This was worse than arguing about the bed. "It's not that I don't want to practice. I do!"

Kit raised an eyebrow.

Skyler groaned. "I *really* want to practice, okay? I'm too curious not to. But I really am exhausted." And she needed a little time to figure out why she was freaking out this much. It was only a kiss, and not even a real one. Kissing Kit's face off didn't mean they were in a committed relationship. There was no need to panic.

"Okay?" Dropping the pillow at his feet, Kit folded his arms, his frown still firmly in place. "So what's the problem? It's not like we haven't done it before."

That was the problem. That little moment in time that had never left Skyler's heart or mind in the seventeen and a half years since it happened. If she let herself be pulled back to those blissful days, the separation would be ten times as brutal at the end of the week. No matter how much she had enjoyed watching Kit play with all the kids today, it had only reminded her how often he had talked about having a family someday.

He was going to make an incredible father. And Skyler…

Skyler didn't see marriage in her future, let alone kids and the white picket fence and the whole shebang. She had seen too many relationships fall apart—mostly her mother's—and picked up too many pieces to want to risk being broken herself. Even Kit, who was the best person Skyler had ever known, had been shattered on the rocks by his whirlwind engagement.

He may have still had faith in a future with someone, but she didn't.

"I am feeling way too dramatic to practice with you right now, Kit Morgan," she breathed, massaging her temples. "Sorry."

She could practically see him chomping at the bit, wanting to argue in the silence that followed, like he wanted to push her to admit the real reason she was being so weird.

But when he spoke, his words were calm. "You always had a hard time running on little sleep. You should get to bed before we have another sleep talking incident."

Skyler looked up, a measure of peace settling over her when she saw Kit's smile. "I almost answered the question correctly, even dead asleep on my desk."

Kit rolled his eyes. "If you think Georgie Porgie was the first president of the United States, you may want to look into going back to school."

"I said almost."

"You also said he sailed the ocean blue in 1492."

"I'm going to bed. On the floor."

He gently grabbed her elbow, holding her in place and giving her a look that might have made her melt if she didn't have a thick shell around her heart. It would take more than those puppy dog eyes of concern to get through that barrier. "You know you can tell me anything, right?"

That would have been true with anything but this. They'd been a pretend couple for less than twenty-four hours, and if she told him that she was panicking because she was falling for him all over again, she had no way to know how he might react. There were too many different versions of Kit in there, and she didn't want to set off the wrong one.

"I'm okay," she said, putting her hand on his arm and flinching when he flinched. Angela had really gotten to him, hadn't she? Skyler probably shouldn't keep arguing with him after everything that had happened today. "And I'll take the floor tomorrow night."

He smirked. "We'll see about that. Goodnight, Sky." Then he tugged her closer and brushed a tender kiss on her forehead, lingering there long enough that she shivered. "I can't wait to practice with you."

This man was dangerous.

Skyler almost didn't care.

FOURTEEN

AFTER A TERRIBLE NIGHT'S SLEEP, which he'd expected, Kit got up early, hoping to have some time to himself. He generally liked people, and as an extrovert he didn't do well with spending too much time on his own. But playing the carefree Chris Morgan all afternoon when he was internally freaking out had drained him.

Or maybe it was just the last week that had knocked him flat on his back.

Slipping into the dim kitchen, Kit thanked Lloyd and Stella for stocking the countertop with tea and coffee and quickly set about making himself a cup of green tea. He had looked at the itinerary for the day before falling asleep, and he would need more energy than what he'd gotten from a few hours of sleep. Not only had the floor been wildly uncomfortable, but his head had been swimming with thoughts of Skyler.

For all the time he'd spent getting after Oliver for thinking it was a good idea to propose to Madi after a day of dating her, this was a million times worse. At least Oliver and Madi had known each other their entire lives. Kit had known Skyler for four months, tops, and the seventeen years in between had turned them both into different people. No matter how many times they reminisced or how easily he slipped back into the rambunctious and devil-may-care Christopher he'd been back then, it didn't change the fact that he wasn't that person anymore.

And he didn't have a clue who Skyler was.

Logically, there was no way he could know he and Skyler would work long-term. But his heart didn't seem to want to listen to his head this time.

"You're up early."

Kit looked up just as Brooklyn, Houston's twin, padded into the kitchen in her pajamas and slipped onto a barstool. "So are you," he said, leaning against the sink.

She smiled, though it turned into a yawn a second later. "Habit. I teach high school, so I'm still on teacher schedule."

"You teach?" Kit flinched at his own volume. He hadn't meant to get that excited; Fake Chris Morgan wasn't a teacher. "What subject?"

She smiled. "Chemistry."

"I have a lot of respect for secondary ed teachers. Having been a teenager myself, I don't know how you deal with a school full of them."

Grin widening, she reached for a box of cereal on the counter and pulled out a handful. "We're a special breed." Despite what Tanner had said about the Briggs twins not looking similar, Brooklyn actually did look a lot like her brother, blonde hair and big blue eyes, with an overall softness about her. She didn't seem to have the exuberance of Micah or her brother, but Kit had only seen kindness from her as he observed the family throughout the day. Overall, the Briggs siblings seemed to be a good sort.

"Would you like some tea?" Kit asked, not sure how much he wanted to have a one-on-one conversation with anyone. Being in the group had made it easy to redirect topics to innocuous subjects that didn't involve the fake Chris, but he couldn't easily ignore a direct question if Brooklyn decided to pry.

She shook her head, though, slipping off the stool with her box of cereal in tow. "I'm good with my Captain Crunch, but thanks. I think I'll go enjoy some fresh air before the littles fill the mountainside with noise."

"Smart."

She paused at the door, glancing back. "I'm really glad you were able to come this year," she said softly. "Skyler always seems so lonely, and I've worried about her. So I'm glad you make her happy."

Face flaming, Kit grunted something incoherent and lifted his mug in a toast. He hoped Brooklyn was right and that he really did make Skyler happy. More so, he hoped they could keep this going after the end of the week even though Skyler had admitted yesterday that she wasn't fond of relationships. While that could have easily been because she'd never been in one, something told him she had purposefully avoided creating any tethers over the years. Her childhood had been spent bouncing from place to place, so it only made sense that her comfort zone would be away from deep attachments.

He hoped that could change, but if anyone knew how difficult it was to break out of a cycle, he did.

Sighing, he pulled his phone out of his pocket and grimaced at the dozens of texts he'd gotten throughout yesterday but ignored. How was it he could go days without hearing from some of his friends when they were in the same city, but as soon as he went somewhere else, they decided to blow up his phone?

Isla had texted several times as well. Kit gulped down some tea, thinking about what Skyler had said yesterday about Isla not knowing they were only friends. Was he leading her on? He'd told Kailani's sister multiple times that their relationship would never go beyond friendship, but beyond that he had always treated her the same as he had from the beginning because that was what Kit Morgan did. He didn't deviate. Once he made up his mind, that was it, and he became someone people could rely on.

Apparently, Isla was taking him paying her attention as a sign that there was a chance they could be more than they were.

He groaned. He was kind of a jerk. He could say his lingering trauma from Angela cheating on him gave him an excuse to have avoided a more direct conversation with her, but he didn't like pinning his actions on anything but himself. He would have to face her eventually and apologize for letting her think there was still a chance, however small. Isla deserved better than that.

Unwilling to face whatever she'd texted him today until he was more awake, Kit opened up the group chat with the whole Wonder Gang and frowned at the many texts inside it. They had started talking around ten last night, way later than usual.

Honestly, Kit was afraid of what he was about to read, mostly because chances were high he had missed out on something important and wasn't there. His friends were adults and could take care of themselves, but he had always been the one to help them through whatever they were dealing with.

Yes, Kit wanted things to change in his life. But his friends needing him wasn't one of those things.

Thankfully, as soon as he started reading through the texts, he breathed easier because the conversation contained only good things, starting with Oliver being Oliver.

> Oliver: Ben? Wanna tell me why there's a brand new car in our driveway in place of the death machine?
>
> Ben: New car?
>
> Oliver: I ran the VIN. I know it's yours.
>
> Ben: I don't know what you're talking about.
>
> Allie: YOU GOT IT???
>
> Ben: I was going to surprise you when I picked you up tonight, Als. Thanks a lot, Oliver.
>
> Allie: I'm going to miss the Death Machine.
>
> Ben: It was time.
>
> Oliver: Wait, does that mean...
>
> Madi: What does that mean???

> Cam: It means he got a hefty settlement check from the
> lawsuit.
> Ben: I don't know if I would call it hefty.

Excitement and happiness burst through Kit. Ben had spent his entire life being overlooked and accepting the bare minimum, and he deserved the world and more. Unfortunately, the graphic novel he'd created with Allie had been uploaded onto a website without their permission and exploded in popularity overnight, robbing them of a whole lot of potential royalties. Getting this settlement and the proper recognition for all the hard work he and Allie had put into their book was exactly what he needed.

The conversation hadn't ended there, though.

> Ben: By the way, Oliver, I'm moving out.
> Madi: You won! That's amazing!
> Oliver: It's about time. I've been wanting to turn the guest
> house into a home office.
> Cam: For what? It's not like you actually do any work.
> Oliver: That's what you think.
> Kailani: Does anyone else find it creepy that Oliver ran
> someone's VIN so easily?
> Allie: It was TOTALLY a hefty settlement. And we also got
> an advance on book 2. ;)
> Oliver: Perfect. Ben, you're paying for dinner next time we
> get takeout and you pretend you're too tired to get
> your own food so you mooch off of ours and say you
> can't afford to pitch in but eat the last fortune cookie
> anyway.

Kit groaned, wishing he'd been around to knock Oliver upside the head. Ben didn't need someone pointing out that this good news was in such stark contrast to the life he'd been stuck in before. Kit had tried so hard to convince Ben to believe he deserved more than the dead-end job he'd been working for years, but it hadn't sunk in until Allie came along.

Was that what Kit needed too? Someone who hadn't known him his whole life to give him a push toward better? He jumped back to reading, ignoring the slight itch in his palms.

> Madi: Yay!
> Ben: That was the longest sentence I've ever seen, Oliver.
> Madi: I meant yay for the advance, not for my dumb husband and whatever that was.
> Oliver: Thanks, Ben.
> Ben: It wasn't a compliment.
> Oliver: Don't care. And don't act like you wouldn't do the same thing, Lani.
> Cam: She so would. She's terrifying.
> Cam: Love you, babe.
> Cam: Come back! I didn't mean it.
> Cam: Okay, I did mean it. But I still love you! Don't leave me to watch the movie alone.
> Oliver: Nice one.
> Cam: Does that mean all of us are rich and famous now?

The conversation ended there, and Kit knew in his gut it wasn't because it had gotten late. Nope, his friends had realized that their successes didn't translate over to him. Pursing his lips, he fought for a response that wouldn't make him sound pathetic compared to his incredible tribe. He hadn't picked a career path that would get him fame and fortune, and he was okay with that. He'd never wanted a big life. Not in that way, at least.

> Kit: Congratulations, you guys. You absolutely deserve all of it. I'd better get a signed copy of both books before you're too famous for the rest of us.
> Kit: When are you moving? I'd be happy to help.

He sighed, knowing he probably came across as pathetic anyway. He should have put an exclamation point in there somewhere to spice it up a bit, but any attempts at adding some pep now would make him look even worse. He really needed to stop caring what other people thought about him, but that was easier said than done.

Groaning, he considered opening up Isla's texts but thought against it when Skyler's face popped into his head. She would get after him again if he was too eager to respond, and odds were high Isla had said something flirty. She always did. He would have to think of the best way to lay it all out for her without hurting her even more than he already had.

Kit stuffed his phone back into his pocket and vowed to leave it in the bedroom the rest of the day. Just to avoid temptation.

"Don't you look happy this morning?"

The smile that broke onto Kit's face at the sound of Skyler's voice felt like it belonged to someone else—like there was another part of him that was so excited to see her appear in the kitchen that it took over his motor function. Smiling at her hadn't felt strange yesterday… But yesterday Kit hadn't been stuck in his head like he was now. Despite being a guy who had always made sure his logical side won out, he hated that he was back to overthinking because he loved the way his heart thumped in his chest when she was around.

Who needed logic, anyway?

Apparently, all it took to change Kit Morgan was a little bit of renewed puppy love. He knew the chances of that teenage crush turning into something deeper were slim, and more than likely he would get his heart broken at the end of the week. But he couldn't find it in himself to care. Skyler brought out a freer side to him, one he'd been missing.

"Morning," he said, trying to stand as casually as he could while still looking manly. It was a fine line of folding his arms and leaning against the countertop without slouching too much and coming off as a lazy slob. "How'd you sleep?"

Coming to a stop only a few inches away from him, she glanced down into his mug and then stole it right out of his hand to take a sip. "Better than you, I'm guessing."

"I'm not letting you sleep on the floor, Sky."

"And I'd rather not get dirty looks when everyone sees these circles under your eyes. They'll think I'm treating you terribly." She reached up and stroked the tender skin above his cheekbones, right below the frame of his glasses. He was especially proud of himself for not reacting poorly to that touch, her soft fingers sending a warm thrill through him rather than a shock of discomfort. Definitely a nice change. "You were already tired before we got here."

He took hold of her hand and kissed the fingertips of her first two fingers, immensely glad there wasn't any awkwardness between them when it came to physicality—when he was paying attention. At least this way he could enjoy some parts of the moment while trying to get away from the thoughts of what he was going to do when all of this was over. For once, he needed to try *not* to be logical, or he was going to be miserable all week.

He wanted to stay in this bubble as long as he could and pretend he didn't know how it would all end.

"How about we continue this argument you're losing when we get to tonight?" he suggested, shifting his hold so he could start massaging her palm with his thumbs. "I have other ideas for this morning."

"Oh really?" She lifted a delicate eyebrow, moving in closer and lifting her chin. "Does it involve what I think it does?"

Kit's heart stumbled for half a beat, tripping over the way her voice in the morning was even smoother than normal. He would have expected some grittiness, but her velvety timbre sent a shiver through him. If he'd found her attractive back in junior high—no question of that—that was nothing compared to the temptation she was now.

But… As much as he wanted to kiss her, he didn't want to be interrupted by any of their cabin mates. If Brooklyn was up, the others probably would be soon.

"If you're talking about changing your outfit," he said, "then yes."

Skyler jerked backward a few inches, blinking in surprise before she glanced down at the light blue sundress she'd put on. She hadn't put on any makeup yet, but her unwrinkled dress and strawberry hair were immaculate. "What's wrong with my outfit?"

Still holding onto her hand, Kit guided her a step back and directed her to twirl. "It looks great," he said.

"But?"

"But you clearly forgot to check the itinerary today. Besides, who wears a dress in the mountains?"

"I would have checked the itinerary if I had my phone, but *someone* won't tell me where he put it." She punctuated her frustration with a weak slap to his chest.

Kit grinned, weirdly gratified to have gotten under her skin so easily. She deserved that much after his frightening revelation yesterday. She hadn't just gotten under his skin—she'd cut a door into his heart and moved in, putting up pictures on the walls and settling in to stay. "I told you there's nothing important on there."

"You can't expect me to believe I haven't gotten a single email in the last twenty-four hours."

"That isn't what I said."

"I just want to check on the—"

"The bookstore is fine." Kit tucked some hair behind her ear, hoping she believed him. Truth be told, he hadn't thoroughly read the emails that came in, but he'd skimmed them after Skyler fell asleep, just to make sure there weren't any issues she needed to solve. Everything seemed to be moving along nicely, and Skyler had been so relaxed yesterday while making her tie-dye. Keeping her from her phone a little longer would be good for her.

Once she realized Kit wasn't going to budge, she sighed and took a step back. "Fine. So, what's on the itinerary today? Why can't I wear a dress?"

"You mean you didn't memorize the schedule?"

She rolled her eyes so hard it was a miracle they didn't disappear into the back of her head. "It's like you don't know me at all. Why waste brain power on useless information when someone else can keep track of it for me? I've gotten too used to my paralegals and assistants telling me where to be and when."

"I'll bet you terrified them."

"You have no idea. What should I make for breakfast? I'm starving."

She swept past him to open the fridge and peer inside.

"Isn't there breakfast in the main—"

"Apparently, Mom loves making the meals for everyone," Skyler said, still with her head in the fridge. "But I have had to cook for myself my entire life, and it's hard to break the habit. Besides, I like cooking."

Kit frowned. "So, why don't you go help your mom?"

"Because cooking and cooking with my mom are two very different things. Pancakes and eggs?"

Kit grabbed the carton of buttermilk she handed to him, as well as a carton of eggs, trying to understand how she was being so casual about things. "I thought you and your mom got along really well." In fact, he'd spent hours on the phone with Skyler most nights in school, during which she often talked about how much she loved doing things with Stella.

"If acting like girlfriends instead of mother and daughter is getting along really well, then yes. But she's never been a mom. As soon as I graduated high school, things got weird between us, and…" Straightening up, Skyler scrunched up her face and squinted at him. "What is it with us and getting into deep, personal topics? We don't need to hash out my mommy issues."

"Even if it falls under Goal One? You're supposed to be getting to know your family, Sky. That includes your mom."

She cursed under her breath before opening up several cabinets in search of something. "You, my friend, have a bad habit of getting me to open up like I haven't spent my life with everything under lock and key. You can't control minds, can you?"

"Nope. But Ben can."

After opening up a cupboard filled with flour, sugar, and other baking supplies, Skyler glanced back. "You're not serious, right? I can't tell."

He chuckled as he set the eggs and buttermilk on the counter. "He can in the graphic novel he illustrated. He and his girlfriend wrote a book about the Wonder Boys, in a manner of speaking."

Skyler dropped the open bag of flour, which exploded upon impact in a cloud of white dust. Coughing, she tried to wave the cloud away but gave up a second later, leaping over the mess to grab Kit's arm. "Your Ben is Ben Nakamura? He wrote *Menace Unknown*?"

A little distracted by the sight of her covered head to toe in flour, Kit nodded. "How do you know about—"

"Literally everyone knows about that book, Kit." As her voice rose in volume, she picked up the half-empty bag of flour and stuffed it into Kit's hands, and then she grabbed a broom that was hanging on the wall. "I told you I was researching what's popular right now, right? And with the whole copyright lawsuit thing, that graphic novel is all anyone is talking about. Oh! Do you think he would do a signing at my grand opening?"

Kit raised his eyebrows. He'd known the book was popular, but he wouldn't have thought it was *that* popular. He'd been meaning to read it for months but hadn't gotten around to it. Did that make him a terrible friend? "I don't know. I could ask. Wait, don't…" Setting the flour bag on the counter, he grabbed his phone and opened up the camera.

Skyler immediately grinned and pressed herself up against his side for the picture. "I still have that picture we took in Home Ec," she said.

Kit's heart pounded a little stronger as he wrapped his fingers around her waist and pulled her closer. She'd kept it? Though he hadn't loved finding flour in every crevice and crease the rest of that day, he hadn't laughed so hard in his life than he had the day he ended up covered in flour thanks to Skyler's terrible balance. That day was the day he first thought about kissing her, though he hadn't been brave enough until just before Christmas break a couple of months later. He'd always wondered what happened to that Polaroid.

Knowing she'd kept the photo had his heart twisting in several knots, and he turned to press his nose against her cheek, forcing himself not to do more as he hit the capture button. He needed to stay focused on the conversation instead of getting lost in the past. Specifically in their kiss.

Once Kit had his picture—or several—Skyler brushed herself clean and then began sweeping as she kept talking like he hadn't interrupted. "That would be so cool if Ben was willing to do a signing. Really start the store off with a bang, you know? Hold that dustpan, will you?"

Kit did as directed, crouching down and holding it in place while she swept the flour into it. "Ben's pretty shy," he replied, thinking out loud. "He might not like being in the spotlight, so don't get your hopes up." Had it been Oliver, he would have jumped at the opportunity without hesitation, and Cam had been enough in the spotlight with his celebrity-owned gym that he would probably do it too in this situation. But Ben? Ben had grown up a lot over the years, but he tended to lift others up instead of himself.

"Allie would probably do it, if nothing else," he finished with a shrug.

"You know Allie too?"

"Well, yeah. She's dating Ben."

"Seriously? They're not only the most talked-about duo in the comic world right now, but they're also a *couple*? That's adorable!"

"For a girl who always said she hates icky love stories, you're awfully excited right now."

Laughing, Skyler did an exaggerated shrug. "What can I say? I like to be unpredictable. It keeps people on their toes."

"You sure you're a lawyer?" Kit asked, raising an eyebrow. "You're being especially cheerleader right now." He wasn't complaining. He'd crushed on several of the cheerleaders during his high school basketball days—not that he'd ever intentionally done anything about it. They just always seemed to have a peppiness he was lacking. Besides, this excited side of Skyler was a lot more fun than the stuffy businesswoman she'd been playing so far.

Skyler did a spin, making her dress flare out. "I'm not a lawyer anymore," she reminded him. "And I am definitely not a cheerleader."

"You're just trying to avoid talking about your mom," he guessed.

Skyler met his gaze, narrowing her eyes, and then she stalked toward him until she could wrap her arms around his neck and pull him close. He barely resisted flinching, though her minty breath on his mouth worked as a great distraction.

"We could talk about my mom," she whispered. "Or we could practice."

That sounded like a great idea. Kit slid his hands around her waist, feeling her tense beneath his touch. What would happen when he kissed her? It would have to happen eventually, but he wasn't sure he would come out the same on the other side. He had already fallen further than he was comfortable with, and kissing her would only make things worse. He had enough memories of their first and only kiss to know a second would be unforgettable. Was he willing to put his heart on the chopping block again on the off chance it might stay intact this time?

"We could practice," he agreed slowly, leaning in until his nose brushed hers. "Or we could talk about your mom."

Clearly he wasn't willing to risk it. Not yet.

Skyler sighed heavily and pulled away, leaving him cold from her absence. "I don't know if I'm ready to get into the nitty gritty just yet. What if I make pancakes and you tell me about those Wonder Boys of yours? How did Ben get into illustrating?"

At least she hadn't shut him down completely, but as Kit grabbed a mixing bowl to help Skyler make breakfast, he knew one way or another he would have to get this girl to trust him enough to open up. If he didn't, this week would just be another bittersweet memory, and he would be back to being on his own. That was the last thing he wanted.

He hadn't thought it possible after Angela ripped it to shreds, but his heart was telling him he was almost ready to move forward. Ready to fall in love. He just had to be brave enough to take the first step into vulnerability. He couldn't expect Skyler to trust him if he didn't trust her back, and he had no reason to think history would repeat itself.

Skyler wasn't Angela. And he wasn't the same man he'd been four years ago.

This could work. He *wanted* it to work. For both their sakes. But in order for this relationship to change from a sham to something real, Kit would have to do more than hold her hand. He would have to turn up the heat, so to speak, and stop finding excuses not to give in to the desire pounding in his chest. Kissing her would be the best way to show her that their compatibility hadn't changed during their years apart. Both emotionally and physically. The emotional part would take more than just a kiss, but the physical…

Assuming he was ever brave enough, he wasn't going to mind that part in the slightest.

FIFTEEN

"I'M NOT DOING IT." SKYLER crossed her arms over her chest, trying to look like she wasn't intimidated by the masks and armor in front of her. She was pretty sure it wasn't working. "You can't make me."

"No one is making you do anything," Mom said gently. "You can always come tie the quilt with us."

Of all the alternatives, it had to be that? Skyler scrunched up her nose. She might have considered subjecting herself to such a boring task if Heidi hadn't made an appearance this morning. She, apparently, was an expert at tying quilts, and she wanted to film the whole thing for her website.

Honestly, what even was a lifestyle coach?

"What if I just go spend a couple hours in the cabin?" Skyler suggested, knowing before Kit cleared his throat that he wasn't going to let her back out.

"One and Two," he said simply. *Stupid goals.*

Okay, so she had to admit that seeing Kit Morgan in paintball gear was downright mouthwatering. She liked the teacher look he generally supported, but boy did the man look good in camouflage with a rifle slung over his shoulder.

But paintball? Skyler was in no way athletic, and even after changing into jeans and a peasant top, she was poorly dressed for romping around the forest with a gun in her hands.

"We need you so we can have even teams," Micah said, her voice pleading.

Skyler did a mini *gream*, which sort of hyped her up. "Fine! Which team am I on?"

"I vote Chris is a team captain!" someone said. One of the teens. Honestly, Skyler would have been better off if they all wore name tags the rest of the week.

Kit grinned and saluted the boy. "With honor."

"Houston can be the other one," a teenage girl said, blushing bright red. *Gross.* At least Houston wasn't actually related to anyone in the family except Micah, but he had to be twice her age. He was a good-looking guy, but nothing compared to Kit.

Kit and Houston moved to the front of the group and did a quick round of Rock, Paper, Scissors. Kit won, apparently, because he picked the boy who had nominated him.

"Let me help you get your stuff on," Micah offered as Houston picked his twin for his team. "Trust me; you don't want to get hit with a paintball without some kind of protective layer, so you'll want to make sure your gear fits right."

Skyler breathed a thank you and started strapping herself in. "I'll be lucky if I make it out of this alive," she said at the same time Houston chose Vic and Kit called Micah's name.

Micah waved without looking away from fitting Skyler's helmet. "From the looks of things, Chris knows what he's doing. Just stick with him, and you'll be fine."

"Oh, I'm not leaving his side."

"As long as you two don't sneak off and have a little powwow behind a rock or something. I'm in this to win." Micah sent a glare toward Houston, who narrowed his eyes right back. "My idiot half-brother has beaten me six years in a row, and I am *taking him down.*"

Skyler didn't realize her jaw had dropped until Micah looked at her and giggled. "Paintball is bringing out a whole side of you I knew nothing about," Skyler said. "I'm a little scared of you right now."

Micah's continuing giggle broke through that fear in an instant. "Mostly it's just fun to shoot each other. Still, I do want to win. You ready?"

Most definitely not. "Wait, did I get picked for a team?"

"Like I would let you go anywhere without me," Kit said, appearing out of nowhere. With his helmet tucked under his arm and his eyes bright with excitement, Skyler momentarily forgot to breathe. "Alright, Blue Team, huddle up!"

As several people shuffled around Kit while the rest of the group hurried into the woods, Skyler noticed with concern their team wasn't exactly made up of heavy hitters. Aside from Micah's brother Chad, they mostly had the women and a bunch of kids. Why hadn't Kit picked a stronger team?

"So," Kit said, using his official teacher voice, "from my understanding, this is a combination of paintball and capture the flag, right? What are the rules?"

"You can get hit three times before you're dead," the teen said. He seemed to be matching Kit's intonation and even stood the same way. It was adorable. "But you have to go back to the starting spot after you get shot, and you hold your hands up in the air so everyone knows they can't shoot you until you're back at the start. Our flag has to be in sight and away from the cabins."

"Can we move our flag throughout the game?" Kit asked.

"I guess so." The kid—what was his name?—didn't sound very confident, but maybe that was because he was looking around at their team just like Skyler and realizing he had made a grave error in nominating Kit as captain.

Kit, on the other hand, smiled wide. "Okay, so as long as our flag is in the open, we're good. That's perfect. Now, I'm sure you guys have noticed that our team looks a little unconventional."

"That's one way of putting it," Micah said. She'd lost all cheerfulness from her expression. "Houston is going to kick our trash. Again."

"No, he isn't," Kit argued. "Not when we have a secret weapon."

"Which is what, exactly?" Georgia asked. She barely stood tall enough to reach Kit's shoulders and was eyeing the quilt with new interest.

Kit's grin inexplicably grew. "You, Georgia. And Micah. And you, Blake. All of you guys. Blake, what did your brother say when you showed up this morning?"

The teenage boy frowned. "He said I wasn't any good so I should play with the little kids."

"And Georgia, your husband laughed when you said you wanted to play."

Georgia narrowed her eyes. "He's definitely sleeping on the couch tonight."

"I have a better idea. What if you kick his butt in paintball?"

"I wouldn't mind kicking Hou off his high horse for once," Chad said with a chuckle.

"Oh, he's going down," Micah agreed. "I bet we could get Brook to turn traitor."

Skyler cringed when the two of them gave each other matching evil grins. They may have only shared half their DNA, but those two were definitely siblings. "Anyone else terrified?" she muttered under her breath.

"*You* probably should be," Kit replied. "You're going to be our flag."

"I'm going to what?"

Taking the length of blue cloth that waited for him on a nearby table, Kit stepped up to Skyler and swung it behind her so it rested on her shoulders like a cape.

Her stomach dropped. "Oh, no I'm not."

"Oh, yes you are. We need someone who won't go charging into enemy lines to get revenge, and you're likely to run away from the red team to avoid getting shot."

Skyler grabbed his hands before he could start tying it around her neck. "You got that right, buddy."

Kit laughed, enjoying this way too much. "Buddy?"

"Yep. *Buddy.* And that's what you'll be until you hide this flag somewhere else. Maybe up your—"

Kit moved in and pressed a kiss against her jaw, his lips warm and lingering as if he really wanted to take his time exploring that one spot. Did he always smell this good? His fresh scent made her slightly dizzy, as did the way his fingers brushed against her throat. The kiss distracted her so thoroughly with the heat that sparked from the point of contact that she didn't understand his smirk when he stepped back.

Or, she didn't until she realized he'd tied the flag around her neck while he'd kissed her.

"No fair," she squeaked. And if that was how she reacted to a relatively innocent kiss, she was doomed when they finally got around to the real thing. Had Kit been this intoxicating in middle school? No, because he'd been *twelve.* But that hadn't made Skyler crush on Christopher any less back in the day.

But Kit? Oh, Kit had a new light in his eyes, which she could see so much clearer right now because he'd put in contacts for the game, and every time those golden-brown eyes met hers, he seemed to be telling her a million different things. She wasn't as versed in romance as she would have liked in this moment, but she had a feeling she was supposed to like what his eyes were saying.

Honestly, *anyone* would be swooning with a look like that regardless of their fluency in romance.

"This is a good plan, and you know it," he said softly, sliding his hand down her arm until his fingers found hers. "You love my plans."

She would go along with any plan he came up with if he kept looking at her like she was the most important thing in his life. That couldn't be what was going through his head, could it? That would just be ridiculous. They'd only been pretending to be a couple for a day, and Kit Morgan was too smart to fall for someone like her. "Your plans are always overcomplicated and ridiculous," she mumbled, even though he was right. She *had* always loved the way he dove into everything without hesitation. Once he made up his mind, he was impossible to convince otherwise.

Skyler had always admired confidence, and Kit had that in spades.

"Trust me," he murmured, placing one more tantalizing kiss on her cheek. Then he stepped back and captured the attention of the team with merely a look. "I know this feels daunting, but I picked all of you for a reason. If we work together as a team—and show no mercy—this is going to be easy."

"Yeah!" a few people shouted, throwing their fists into the air.

Skyler felt weak in the knees watching him take command.

Kit grinned as if they'd already won. "Alright, blue team! Fan out! Everyone stays within a few hundred feet of Skyler, and we all move into red territory together. Watch your neighbor's back, and don't get killed. Let's go!"

Everyone scattered, far more eager than they'd been a few minutes ago, and Kit gestured in the direction the two of them would go. Straight into the trees toward where the red team had gone. "Don't even worry, Sky. You're carrying precious cargo, and I know our team has what it takes to keep you safe. And if they don't, then I've got it covered."

"What has you so confident?"

"This is mountain man laser tag. We got this!"

Skyler laughed, sounding a little crazed. "We don't got this. *You* got this. I got a ball of anxiety the size of Texas. I don't even know how to shoot this thing!"

"I'm not expecting you to shoot. That's why I'm here. My one and only goal is to look after you, and I don't intend to fail."

This paintball gear was way too warm. If Kit kept being adorable and looking at her so intently, she was going to overheat and pass out, and he would be left to defend her lifeless corpse. "You just made me carry the flag so you could show off and impress me, didn't you?"

"When have I ever tried to impress you?"

"Let's see." She ticked each item off on her fingers as she listed them. "That time you bragged about your math test. Mrs. Geller's class presentation. The pie eating con—"

"Okay, fine. I crave your approval like I need it to live and am desperate to make myself matter in your life. Are you happy?"

Skyler choked on her response when she saw the way he was looking at her. He meant it? "You do matter," she said, slowing to a stop. "You've always mattered."

His eyebrows pulled low, genuine fear tugging at the corners of his downturned mouth. "But will I matter next week?"

An air horn blared through the trees, followed by immediate air-powered gun blasts and several shouts. Kit waited a few seconds, as if hoping Skyler wasn't completely shocked into silence by that question, and then he stuffed his helmet over his head and pulled the mask over his face.

"Stay close," he said, his voice muffled.

As soon as Skyler had her own mask in place, she grabbed hold of Kit's jacket and let him pull her forward, all the while scanning the trees frantically for any sign of someone coming to attack her. The sounds of muted gunfire and excited screaming sounded eerie, like they were in the middle of a children's video game meant to mimic an adult game without the extreme violence.

"How is this considered fun?" she asked breathlessly. They weren't even running, and she was already winded from nerves. They'd barely been playing for five minutes.

Kit's chuckle vibrated through him. "I don't know. It's like you can be a different person when you're playing games like this. No one expects you to be calm and collected, and you can just—" He lifted his gun and shot so quickly that Skyler was sure he was shooting at nothing, but then Vic emerged from the trees several yards ahead with a scowl and started the trek back to his starting point, a bright blue spot on his shoulder.

"How in the world did you—"

Kit shot again, this time shooting off two paint pellets in rapid succession. A moan followed the second shot, and a kid jogged off to follow Vic.

Skyler rolled her eyes. "You know this is only going to make people even more convinced you're a spy, right? Look out!" She grabbed his arm to make him turn, and he fired a few times, nailing Houston in the chest with two bullets.

Houston looked furious, growling and pointing at Kit. "You and your flag are going down, Morgan." Then he took off running with his hands in the air.

"We should probably change course now that Houston knows where our flag is," Kit said and grabbed her hand, bursting into a run into a thicker part of the forest.

Skyler was tall, but she barely managed to keep up with his long legs and was more than glad when he stopped in a thicket of bushes. This part of the forest was quieter, though Skyler could still hear the muted sounds of battle to their left. No one seemed to be nearby, and yet Kit was still on full alert. "What now?" she asked in a whisper.

"Now—" He aimed his gun when a twig snapped, but he didn't shoot this time. "Micah."

Micah scurried down a small slope and joined them in their bushes. She'd already been shot in the arm, her elbow plastered with red. She lifted her mask at the same time Kit did so they could more easily talk. "Houston is in a *mood*," she said gleefully. "He thought they'd win this in five minutes, and he's furious that you have the flag on the move."

"Has anyone found the red flag?" Kit asked. He stood straight, gun at the ready, and could have easily passed for a hardened soldier with the way he focused so intently on every-thing around him.

"Georgia thinks she saw it right on the south border just a few feet from their starting point."

"Smart," Kit said, brushing his arm over his nose. He'd gotten fairly sweaty already, his hair sticking to his forehead in a strangely attractive way.

Skyler had gone on plenty of first dates over the years, mostly with fellow lawyers or businessmen from the city. With the way she wanted to leap into Kit's arms and taste the salty sweat on his lips, she'd clearly been going after the wrong type. Honestly, what was wrong with her? It was like she'd reverted back to the hormonal teenage years and was trying to under-stand her changing body.

Silently telling herself to grow up and admire the man like a sensible adult, Skyler crept a little closer to Kit's side. For safety reasons, obviously.

Kit looked down at her the moment her arm brushed his. "We should keep moving," he said. "Micah, tell anyone you see to start moving toward the back line. It's going to get tricky with everyone respawning right by the flag, and we'll get out-numbered fast if we're not careful." He grabbed Skyler's hand. "Ready?"

"I love a man in charge," she breathed, not even a little ashamed about acting like a lovesick fool. After all, that was the point, wasn't it? Goal Three was all about being a good fiancée, and a good fiancée would beyond a doubt be turned on by her man's manliness.

Kit seemed to forget for a moment that they'd been about to run as he stared at her, slack jawed. He gripped her hand tighter, leaned in, and their helmets clunked together before he grumbled, "This is no time for practice," and nearly pulled her off her feet when he started running.

If Skyler thought it wouldn't make Kit mad, she would have surrendered herself to Houston so she could end the game and get to that whole practicing thing.

Why in the world had she thought it was a good idea to postpone instead of jumping in last night?

SIXTEEN

THIS GAME WAS A TEST of patience in so many ways. Kit's instinct had always been to be on the front lines, taking down opponents as quickly as possible. There was a reason no one had beaten his high score in laser tag yet, and it wasn't because he was cautious.

But he'd seen the terror in Skyler's eyes right alongside the excitement he wasn't sure she recognized in herself, and he'd known that he would have to play defense this time around if only to keep her in the game as long as possible.

Besides, having her carry the flag had given him a great excuse to keep her close, and he counted that as one of his more brilliant ideas.

"There," Skyler said, tugging his arm like she'd done the last time.

Kit spotted Brooklyn quickly and fired off a few rounds, aiming for her legs in the hopes that it would hurt less. She still yelped, though she smiled at him to tell him she was fine.

"You could come to our side, you know," he called, remembering what Chad and Micah had said.

She laughed. "You want me to turn on my own twin?"

"Call it poetic irony."

Looking down at her gun, Brooklyn thought for a moment, then shrugged, her smile growing. "What'll you give me if I do?"

"A sense of satisfaction that you can only get from being an underdog."

"Is that so? I happen to like winning, and Houston always wins."

"Who is more excited about a good test score? The valedictorian or the kid who studied his butt off?"

She bit her lip, shaking her head like she couldn't believe she was thinking about doing what he said. "You're trouble, Chris Morgan."

"Chris." Skyler's fingers dug into his arm. "We should keep moving."

He winced, doing a quick visual sweep of the area to make sure they were still alone. "Right. Brooklyn, if you decide to change your loyalties, go ahead and give your flag to Blake. He'll take good care of it."

As she laughed and started the trek back to her base, hands in the air, Kit grabbed Skyler's hand and searched for their best path of travel. "Let's go this way," he decided with a nod to his left.

Skyler's grip was hard as they half walked, half ran through the trees, and Kit gave her a little squeeze of reassurance.

"Hopefully the game will end soon, but it's hard to say what Brooklyn will do." He spotted movement up ahead and shot quickly, missing his first shot but hitting Blake's older brother with the second. "You're being a good sport about all of this."

Skyler didn't respond for a long moment, probably overwhelmed by the game. "Is Brooklyn a teacher?"

He paused, trying to figure out why that would be the question she asked right now. "Yeah. Chemistry. I found out this morning."

"You found out she's an expert in chemistry this morning," she repeated.

"Uh, yeah? Is something—"

"We should keep moving." She pulled her hand out of his and tromped ahead, wobbling a bit in her Toms as she tried to avoid a slightly muddy spot. It wouldn't matter at this point, with her shoes already caked in dirt, but that didn't stop her from trying.

Kit frowned as he watched her. Had he done something wrong, or was it the game that was bothering her? Whatever it was, she looked both angry and hurt, and Kit thought back over the last several minutes. She hadn't been acting weird after his conversation with Micah, so it had to be…

He swore under his breath, heard someone behind him and shot several rounds until he made contact, and then he rushed forward to catch up to Skyler.

"Sky, wait!" He reached her just as he caught sight of Houston and Sam in the bushes just up ahead. "Duck!"

Thankfully, she did as she was told, giving Kit a clear line of sight. He shot quickly, though his aim was off as he scrambled to find a way to say he wasn't making a play at Brooklyn, so he only hit Sam. Houston got off a shot, which miraculously missed Sky by an inch, landing near Kit's foot.

Kit shot again, hitting Houston in the stomach.

Houston looked ready to throw his gun to the ground as he did a pretty good impression of Skyler's *scrowl.* "How?" he moaned, shaking his head. "You're inhuman, Morgan. But this isn't over yet."

Kit grinned and shooed him away, feeling pretty good about himself until he caught Skyler's glare. "I can explain," he said quickly, holding up his hands in surrender.

Rolling her eyes, Skyler plopped herself down in the dirt with a huff. "Explain what, exactly?"

He made sure the area was clear, then sat himself next to her, keeping his eyes on the trees and hoping she didn't take that as a sign that he was lying. "I don't know why you think I'm some sort of player, but I'm not."

"Isla, Brooklyn, pretty sure even Micah is crushing on you now because you're so good at flirting."

Kit sighed. "I'm not flirting. I'm friendly." And suddenly he realized how many times he had accused Oliver of doing the same thing. Oliver had always been the "flirt" among his friends, but in reality, Kit hadn't ever seen him genuinely flirt with anyone since high school. The only person he'd ever really done more with was Madi.

He groaned, lifting his mask so she could better see his face. "Maybe I'm a little too friendly," he admitted. "But I hope you know that the only person I'd flirt with is you."

She didn't look convinced. "I guess it makes sense that you would want to get to know Brooklyn better. She's gorgeous, and sweet, and a teacher like you. Maybe after this week you could—"

"Sky." He looped his arm through hers, tugging her up against his side. It was dangerous, staying in one place for too long and not being in a position to run, but he cared more about this woman than a friendly game of paintball. Without question. "I don't want to date Brooklyn. Yeah, I got a little excited about a fellow teacher, but I am literally surrounded by women every day when I'm at school. That doesn't mean I want to practice with any of them."

Her lips pursed together, gaze still wary but a little bit of hope brightening her eyes. "That shouldn't make me feel better, but it does," she admitted with a little smile. Then she gasped and pointed. "I see an enemy over there!"

Though instinct told him to grab his gun, Kit wanted to make sure things really were okay between them. He needed to fix the dynamic and bring them back to easy banter levels where they were both comfortable. Preteen Skyler hadn't been good with emotions, and he suspected she hadn't fully grown out of that over the years. So Kit pulled his eyebrows together and said, "Why are you talking about ocean life?"

Skyler turned to him. "What?"

"Anemone."

"Yeah, over by the—"

"No, *sea* anemone."

"That's what I said!"

"No, like…an anemone."

She cocked her head to the side. "Are you having a stroke?" And then she screamed when Houston took aim at them.

Laughing, Kit grabbed his gun and shot, the paint pellet hitting Houston right in the facemask. "Game over for you," he said.

Or it would have been, if half a dozen people didn't suddenly appear from the trees and surround the two of them. Kit leapt to his feet, unsure who to aim for because they all looked ready to murder him. Probably because he'd shot all of them at least once.

Skyler whimpered a little, likely anticipating the sting of being hit.

"They won't shoot you," Kit assured her quietly.

"How can you be sure?"

"Because then you'll have to go back to the starting point before anyone can touch you."

"So what do we do?"

"You get ready to run."

There was no way he was going to make it out of this alive, but he could see in the red team's eyes that every single one of them was out for blood. They would be too focused on making sure Kit finally got shot to worry about Skyler until they remembered she had the flag.

Catching movement in the trees behind Vic and Sam, Kit recognized Georgia and Blake creeping toward the red flag with determination. If he bought them enough time, they could grab the flag and win the game while Kit kept most of the red team distracted.

As much as he wanted to remain untouchable, letting the scorned Taylors win the game would be a whole lot sweeter.

"You ready?" he whispered to Skyler. "If I survive this, I'll meet you back at the cabin. I think it's about time we practiced."

Skyler squeezed his arm, shifting her stance.

He held up his hands, keeping his finger on the trigger of his gun to hopefully take out a few people before they got him. "Guys, let's talk about this."

Houston, now without his helmet so he could see, folded his arms and might have looked properly peeved if he wasn't fighting a smile. He seemed to appreciate Kit's competitiveness and hopefully wouldn't be a sore loser. Kit could see him becoming a friend, and with the way Houston dove headfirst into their animated basketball discussion last night, Kit had a feeling this man needed more good ones. He clearly didn't have enough people to talk to about his passions.

"Oh, I don't think you want to try talking your way out of this one, Morgan," Houston said, shaking his head. "You're good, but there's no way you can beat all of us."

Blake had the flag tucked in his arms as he and Georgia crept back toward the blue side, their grins huge.

Brooklyn cleared her throat behind Kit, pulling his attention away from the blue players before someone else noticed. It seemed she had switched sides after all, considering she probably had as clear a view of the two of them as Kit did.

Kit grinned, loving how quickly that tore the smile right off of Houston's face. "Pretty sure you already lost, Briggs. But if watching my execution will make you feel better..." He shifted his hands behind his head in a sort of surrender, even though he still held his gun.

Houston narrowed his eyes. "It will."

Kit got ready, feeling Skyler tense up beside him. *Now or never.* "Run!"

As Skyler darted into the trees, Kit got off two shots—only one of them hitting its target—before a barrage of paint knocked him to the ground.

SEVENTEEN

SKYLER HADN'T SPENT MUCH TIME with her mom's family over the years, and she had only just started to get to know any of them. So the fact that the entire blue team swarmed around her at lunch to celebrate their victory made her feel like she was in an episode of the Twilight Zone. People who had barely said a word to her over the years—like Georgia—even wrapped her up in a hug and told her how glad they were that she had come for the reunion this year.

Skyler tried to keep smiling, but all of it was a little overwhelming.

"You're their hero," Micah told her as the pair of them sat in the middle of the giant picnic bench the blue team shared. They finally had a moment of peace. "You and Chris."

"I didn't even do anything," Skyler complained. "I literally ran away from the fight and let Chris take multiple bullets for me."

She winced when Kit once again lifted his shirt to show someone his many bruises and welts. Who would have thought a third grade teacher would be so eager to show off his battle wounds?

"That man was born to lead," Micah said with a little sigh, her eyes glazing over.

"Will you stop drooling over my fiancé?" Skyler complained. It was bad enough that she'd basically accused Kit of flirting with Brooklyn; she didn't want to deal with these feelings of jealousy Micah's interest was stirring up.

Micah giggled. "Sorry, but he's just too…"

"Yeah." Skyler sighed. She'd dreamed about meeting Kit again after she left Diamond Springs the first time, but she'd never imagined he would grow up to have Henry Cavill's jawline. How was she supposed to keep this relationship fake when it felt so real?

"Did Chris get really hurt playing paintball?"

Skyler turned at the quiet voice, surprised to see Heidi's kid Tanner standing nearby, his worried eyes locked on Kit. He never talked to anyone, from what Skyler knew, so she had no idea why he had decided to talk to her now. She'd barely said a word to him yesterday when they were making their shirts.

The poor guy looked ready to cry as he stared at Kit's bruises.

"No, he's fine. Do you see him smiling?" And oh, what a smile.

Tanner shuffled his feet. "Why did so many people shoot him? Do they not like him?"

Skyler wasn't sure how to answer that, though she could tell Tanner needed some reassurance. "Um. I think they were just jealous that he was so good at paintball."

"Jealous?" He finally looked at her, cocking his head. "They were mean to him because they were jealous?"

"Uh, maybe?" Skyler wasn't equipped to handle little kid emotions. Not by a long shot. But Kit would probably know what was bothering Tanner. "You could go ask Chris. I'm sure he'd love to tell you about the game."

Tanner ducked his head. "I don't want to bother him."

"He totally wants to be bothered," Micah said. She was watching Tanner with wide eyes. "Go talk to him."

Skyler furrowed her brow as Tanner wandered off toward Kit. "Uh, what was that about?"

Though Kit had been laughing with Houston, he immediately turned his attention to Tanner when he noticed him standing there, like he was so attuned to kids that everything else disappeared as soon as one of them tried to get his attention. He kept his smile in place and even crouched down to get closer to Tanner's level as he listened.

Micah sighed as if she'd never seen anything dreamier. "I don't know what's bugging Tanner, but you were seriously wrong about Chris and kids. That man is naturally paternal."

Skyler had to agree as Kit stood, put his hand on Tanner's shoulder, and followed the boy into the house. "Yeah, I guess he's pretty good."

"Pretty good? I don't think I've ever heard the Wonder Kid speak before. Believe me, I've tried. Not even Brooklyn has been able to get through to him, and she's, like, the sweetest person on the planet."

"But she's not Chris," Skyler said, adding her own sigh to match Micah's. There was definitely something special about Kit, something she was pretty sure not many people got to see. Yeah, everyone had liked him in middle school, but he didn't open up to all of them. With most people back then, he'd been the class clown and ringleader. With Skyler, he'd been her rock. Someone to lean on and rely on.

Tanner had clearly realized that with the way he'd grown so attached so quickly.

"Excuse me."

Skyler jumped, recognizing Heidi's voice. She leapt to her feet, as if standing would make her feel any less inferior to the graceful and gorgeous woman. "Heidi."

Heidi narrowed her eyes. "Where did your fiancé just take my son?"

"I don't know. I think they went somewhere to talk."

"Talk." Heidi made air quotes with her fingers. "You had better tell me where they went, or—"

"What else would they be doing?" Her anger flaring, Skyler stood a little taller. It helped that she was the same height as Heidi, who wore three-inch heels. "What are you accusing my fiancé of, Heidi?"

Heidi's voice rose, a little frantic now. "Where is my *son*? Tell me, or I'll—"

"What's going on here?" Mom to the rescue.

"I'm trying to find Tanner," Heidi said brusquely.

Skyler didn't bother disguising her frustration and annoyance. "And I told her he's with Chris."

"Exactly the problem!" Heidi said, throwing up her hands.

Mom glanced between the two of them, no stranger to the unspoken rivalry they'd had from the moment they'd met. "Chris and Tanner are in the kitchen," she said, after a moment, putting her hand on Heidi's arm. "They're just talking."

"I told you!"

"Skyler, I don't think you should—"

As Heidi hurried into the cabin, Skyler was right on her heels, ready to defend Kit's honor with her last breath. Thankfully, Kit and Tanner were on either side of the massive countertop, Tanner sitting on a stool and Kit leaning on the granite surface. They both looked up as Heidi and Skyler approached, Kit looking moderately concerned and Tanner wiping some snot from his nose, though he didn't seem to be fully crying.

"Tanner, baby, what's wrong?" Heidi swept him into her arms, though he sat there stiffly, arms at his sides as she fussed over him.

Kit studied the pair of them for a moment before he stood up straight and said, "He was just worried about me. I got hit pretty hard right at the end of the game."

Heidi didn't even look at him, instead tugging Tanner off the stool and leading him back out onto the patio without another word.

"I hate her," Skyler said before the door had even closed. "She's such a snobby—how could she think—if she knew you were a teacher she would never think you would…"

Kit sighed, his eyes on the floor. "It wouldn't have helped. Being a male teacher has never been easy," he admitted. "Parents are always worried for their kids."

"But she had no right to think you're a—"

"Sky, it's fine." Kit wrapped his arms around her and pulled her in tight, for some reason comforting her instead of the other way around. She hadn't even realized how tense she was until she relaxed against him. "I'm fine. Heidi doesn't know me, and she is allowed to be cautious."

Gripping the back of his t-shirt, Skyler took in several deep breaths and settled more firmly against him, enjoying this spot more than she thought she would. They hadn't had a moment to themselves since the end of paintball, and she clearly craved his presence. Or maybe she had just never been held like this before.

"By the way, I'm sorry my family tried to murder you with paint," she said into his chest, loving that he had a good six inches on her. She could tuck her head in and feel protected in his hold.

He chuckled as he ran his fingers through her hair. "I don't blame them. I have a bad habit of getting really competitive. I credit growing up with Oliver, though Cam doesn't help at all."

Skyler wanted to see that winning smile of his. Shifting back so she could meet his gaze, she reached up and touched a bit of paint that had lodged in his hair. "Will you tell me more about the Wonder Boys? I wanna know all about these girls they've fallen in love with."

"Maybe later," he murmured, a fire igniting in his eyes that instantly sparked a matching flame in her belly. Oh, she could get used to a look like that. "I think it's about time we got to practicing."

Yes please. Skyler leaned up on her toes as Kit swooped down.

"Hey, will you guys help clean up the—oops." Micah let out a giggle in the doorway as the two of them broke apart. "Sorry. Stella wants to get started on the next activity, so we're cleaning up lunch."

Breathless, Skyler smoothed her shirt and was tempted to stick her head into the freezer for a second. They hadn't even made contact, and she was reeling. "Sure thing," she breathed just as Kit growled a little, his hands in fists.

At least she knew he wanted to kiss her as much as she wanted to kiss him.

As Skyler slipped out the door, Micah walked beside her and nudged her with her elbow. "I think you need to thank Heidi."

Skyler stumbled. "For what?"

"For creating a high-tension situation for you to use to your advantage."

"I wasn't…" Skyler shook her head, not even bothering to argue. The almost-kiss probably wouldn't have happened if Heidi hadn't thrown an unnecessary fit like that. "It's not like I haven't kissed him before," she said, picking up an almost empty bowl of watermelon. "It isn't a big deal."

Micah giggled. "Chris just tried to laser fry me with his eyes. Pretty sure he thinks it was a big deal."

They both glanced behind them to watch Kit heft a full garbage bag out of the can, his bicep bulging under his t-shirt. He had a few welts on his arms, angry red spots on his skin, but he didn't seem to mind, even when Stacy accidentally bumped into him. He simply gave her a smile and handed off the trash to Vic before jumping over to help Houston move one of the picnic tables.

"How have you not picked a date yet?" Micah asked, shaking her head. "I would have locked that sucker down the moment I laid eyes on him."

"Mm hmm."

When Kit laughed at something Houston said, Skyler melted a little. He was *so good* with her family, and she couldn't help but wonder how things would change if he stuck around after this week. Would she be able to convince him to keep being her fake fiancé until the store was up and running? She could tell him Lloyd wanted to spend more time with them.

"Hey, Sweet Pea." Lloyd's deep voice came out of nowhere, making both ladies jump. "Skyler. Hope you're having fun."

Skyler had managed to avoid Lloyd up to this point, and seeing his little scowl now made her feel like she was in trouble even though he pulled Micah into a quick side hug. "Yes, of course!" she choked out. "Paintball's not really my thing, but it was…interesting."

Lloyd's eyes shifted over the chaotic patio to where Kit was now deep in an enthusiastic discussion with Houston, who thankfully didn't seem to be holding a grudge over his loss. "It's nice to see Chris interacting with the family," he said, his eyes narrowing a little when Kit gestured wildly about something and then let out a boisterous laugh. "You didn't say he was so, uh, energetic."

"He usually isn't," Skyler said with a shrug. That sounded like a normal response, right? "I'm pretty sure he's having more fun than I am. Guess we both needed a break from the store."

Lloyd returned his attention to her with a grunt. "How's the store looking?"

Why did she feel like this was some sort of test? "Uh, the contractor should be finishing up with everything this week, and then I've got a guy putting in the shelves once the floors are done. I have a lot of the books on order already, and Chris is going to try to set up a book signing with a popular local author for our grand opening."

"That is very impressive," Lloyd muttered, and Skyler felt a rush of pride until he added, "Bringing in local talent will convince the community to support you."

She barely resisted the urge to roll her eyes. "That's what I thought," she said instead of telling him that it had been her idea. "I'll take some pictures of the store when we get back next week so you can see how things are coming along."

"I'm sure Chris has everything handled."

He had *nothing* handled because Skyler had done everything herself, though she would never be able to convince Lloyd of that. It was painfully clear that bringing Kit had been a good idea, even if it reinforced Lloyd's backward thinking. At least he wasn't telling her that the store would fail and he was wasting his time and money by helping her.

"Oo, are we making friendship bracelets now?" Micah clapped her hands, bouncing a little where she stood. "Daddy, do you want me to make you one?"

Lloyd immediately softened, his whole face shifting into a warm expression Skyler had never seen before. "Sure, Sweet Pea."

"I love making these! Come on, Skyler," Micah grabbed Skyler's elbow, not realizing Skyler was still holding the watermelon bowl until it slipped out from her arms and all over her shoes.

"Great," Skyler croaked, kicking a soggy piece from her toe.

Micah winced. "Sorry!"

"It's fine. They're covered in mud anyway."

"Stella can send them out to get washed," Lloyd grunted, back to his grumpy self.

They were her least favorite pair of shoes, and she'd only brought them on the off chance she might have to run or trek through the woods. At least they'd come in handy. Shaking her head, Skyler slipped out of them and gingerly picked them up by the heels. "I'll just throw them away. Thanks, though." She definitely wasn't about to ask her mom to pay someone to wash them. That was just ridiculous after eighteen years of using every home fix in the book because they couldn't afford stain remover.

Tossing her shoes in the now-empty trash can, Skyler followed Micah across the patio to where Houston and Kit were still deep in conversation.

"Basketball again?" Micah whined. "Don't you talk about anything else?"

Houston scowled. "I never talk about basketball because none of you dorks like it. You have no idea how glad I am to be getting Chris as a brother-in-law."

Kit met Skyler's gaze, a touch of worry creasing the corners of his eyes. Most likely, Houston would never see Kit again after this week ended, and Kit knew it. Clearly he was feeling some guilt over that fact, and Skyler didn't have a way to fix it.

She would do better to try to distract him. "Yeah, well, you're not allowed to use up all his attention," she told Houston and planted herself on Kit's lap.

Kit immediately froze, not even breathing for several seconds until he forced in a breath that sounded painful. "You'll always have my full attention whenever you want it," he said, his voice strained.

"Sorry," Skyler whispered, realizing she'd caught him off guard. He'd been so at ease all day that she'd forgotten how easy it was to trigger the whole Angela thing. She really needed more information about her if she was going to help Kit get over this touch aversion.

He shook his head minutely, his eyes tracing her face as he relaxed and slipped an arm around her back. "No apology necessary. Maybe one of these days I'll stop thinking you're her."

"Thinking she's who?" Micah asked. She'd taken a seat on Kit's other side and watched the two of them with interest.

Kit flashed her a smile. "My ex," he said, surprising Skyler with how easily he spoke that truth. "I don't know why she's still stuck in my head when she pales in comparison to my Sky." He pressed a kiss to Skyler's cheek, lingering there long enough that she shivered.

"You know," Skyler said, "we don't have to stick around and make bracelets."

Kit laughed, though his eyes smoldered a bit. "And what if I want to make bracelets? I need something to go with the one I've got." He held up his wrist, as if she needed a reminder about the leather bracelet she still couldn't believe he still had. What did it mean that he wore it so regularly? Or had he dug it out of a box somewhere after they ran into each other at Maravilla?

As if reading her mind, Kit tugged on the strap and pulled the bracelet higher up his arm to show her the stark tan line on his wrist. Skyler gasped and turned back to meet his gaze, her face heating when he quirked up a single eyebrow.

"I think I like you," she said on a breath.

"Good," Kit replied. "Because I like you too. So, are you going to stick around and make me a bracelet? Or are you going to walk back to the cabin on your own in your socks? Because I'm going to sit here and make *you* a bracelet."

As if Skyler could say no to that face. Still, she would have to keep some emotional distance between them unless she wanted her family to get a front row seat to their inevitable makeout if they spent too long gazing into each other's eyes. Kit's magnetism had always existed, and he had always been attractive. But this man with his muscles and jawline and warm brown eyes could change her life if she let him.

For good or bad, she didn't know.

Sliding off his lap and onto the bench next to him, Skyler reached for a bundle of green string. "Did we end up at a summer camp and I'm just now realizing it?"

Kit chuckled. "I'm guessing this activity was more for the kids, but Number Two requires us to participate."

Skyler rolled her eyes. Those goals were going to be the death of her. "You are the one who thinks this is fun. I'm only here because of One and Three. Otherwise I would be using this time to nap."

"You mean look for your phone."

She pointed the string at him and did her best to look annoyed, though his grin made her want to smile right back. Or maybe melt into a puddle. "Don't think I don't know the way your mind works, Morgan. I'll find that phone, and then we'll practice like no tomorrow."

"Careful what you wish for."

"I don't understand half of what you guys say to each other," Micah said, watching the two of them with utter confusion on her face.

"If I start dating someone," Houston said on Skyler's right, "and I act this ridiculous, someone put me out of my misery."

Across the table, Brooklyn threw a bundle of string at her twin. "You'd be lucky to have what they have, but you're never going to come close if all you date are supermodels who don't speak English."

"Hey, Mischa spoke English. *Some* English." He narrowed his eyes. "Her strength was in math, not linguistics. And I'm not about to take love advice from the girl who can't string two words together when she's around Mr. What's-His-Face Math Teacher down the hall."

Brooklyn gasped. "I told you that in confidence!"

"Yeah, well, you switched sides in paintball. Confidence broken."

"Oh, you are so getting toilet water in your coffee one of these days!"

Chad groaned from one of the cushy armchairs around the gas fire pit nearby, pinching the bridge of his nose as if he'd dealt with his younger siblings bickering one too many times. "You are twenty-seven years old," he complained. "Every year… It's like this place turns you back into middle schoolers."

Kit and Skyler busted up in unison. Apparently, Skyler wasn't the only one who felt like she'd been thrown back a couple of decades.

"What's wrong with that?" Kit asked. "Some people peaked in middle school."

"So not true," Skyler argued, giving herself a second to admire the adult version of Kit with all his muscles and confidence. He really had grown up so well, and while he wasn't exactly the same kid she'd known back then, he was still so familiar. He may have thought he didn't know who he was, but if this was how he acted normally, Skyler thought he was pretty great.

Kit grabbed her hand under the table and laced their fingers together, his thumb brushing the length of hers with a feather-light touch.

Even if her face was probably bright red as her heart pounded in her chest, Skyler didn't want him to let go for a second. "I thought we were supposed to be making bracelets."

His eyes burned with an intensity she felt down to her toes. "I like this better," he murmured, leaning closer.

"Chris, could you help me with my bracelet?"

They both turned to find Isabelle standing behind them with a handful of string. While Kit smiled and shifted to make room for the girl, Skyler let out a sigh. If her family could stop interrupting every potential moment with this man, she would be most grateful.

EIGHTEEN

THIS WAS FINE.

Dark room, comfy couch, cozy blanket, two dozen Taylors… The perfect circumstances to finally get his moment with Skyler. Ha! Kit couldn't imagine a worse place to be when all he wanted to do was be alone with this woman for more than five minutes.

Kit had spent three hours helping more kids than he could count with their friendship bracelets, all the while watching Skyler take over with Isabelle yet again, the two of them whispering secrets to each other with every knot they tied. Kit had loved interacting with all the kids, especially knowing he wouldn't get to do it next year in school, but his heart hadn't fully been in it.

It was stuck with Skyler. Which meant he was in serious trouble.

As the family gathered in the underground home theater in the second cabin, Kit tried to snag a couch at the back of the tiered room but was beat out by several of the married couples who had probably had the same idea he had. The littles all scurried to the bean bags up front, and Micah and her siblings spread out across the room, leaving one couch in the direct center of the room.

Right in front of Lloyd and Stella.

Groaning inwardly, Kit pulled Skyler forward and settled himself in his seat with the knowledge that this was going to be the longest two hours of his life.

They would have to look like an engaged couple without *acting* like an engaged couple. This was neither the time nor the place for a second first kiss, no matter how much Kit wanted it. Skyler would just have to wait.

And Kit would have to put his self-control to the test.

"What movie are we watching?" he asked, praying it wasn't *Frozen*. He had gone through way too many years of students getting that stupid song stuck in his head. The movie had come out years ago, and yet every Halloween he had at least three Elsas show up for the costume parade.

"We're watching the best movie ever," Skyler replied. "*Frozen II.*"

Kit stared at her for a second, searching for any indication that she actually meant what she said because the odds were high she was messing with him. But all he found was a blank slate. "You have no idea what we're watching, do you?" He held his breath.

She grinned. "Not a clue. But I enjoyed seeing you squirm for a second there."

Chuckling, he settled deeper into the couch, getting comfortable. He could do this. He'd be fine. But then Skyler reached over and tucked his arm around her shoulders, curling herself up against him even though he went completely tense.

Not fine.

"Relax," she whispered as the DreamWorks logo popped up on the screen. "It's just me."

That was exactly the problem. There was no way Kit could possibly be thinking about Angela right now with Skyler stretched out against him, her knee bent over his legs and her arm resting on his stomach, hand splayed against his chest. Did she have any idea how much it was killing him not to kiss her right now in front of everyone? No, because like an idiot he had been avoiding it at all costs. At what point did being strategic turn into losing his chance because he'd delayed things for too long?

He didn't really want to find out.

When the intro started up to *How to Train Your Dragon*, Kit counted his blessings. He liked this movie, and hopefully it would be enough of a distraction that he wouldn't focus on—he shivered when Skyler's thumb rubbed along his t-shirt, followed by the rest of her fingers in a smooth motion.

"You need to stop," he begged in a whisper. "I am *not* practicing with you in front of your mother."

Skyler snickered, scooching even closer. "Who said anything about practicing?"

"I swear, Sky, if you don't—" He jumped a mile high when his phone buzzed in his pocket. "Oh, thank goodness."

Skyler pressed her face into his chest to stifle her laugh, but a text from Oliver was more than enough to keep him distracted for now.

> Oliver: What do you think about a trip to Vegas for Cam's
> bachelor party?

Before Kit could even hit the reply button and start typing out what a terrible idea that was, Cam sent a text.

> Cam: Don't you dare say yes to anything he says.

Well, that was interesting. Did that mean Cam and Oliver were in the same place? *Without* Kit? Outside of anything that was a competition between the two, that had only ever happened once in the last decade, a few months ago. Kit's attempt at getting those two idiots to get along had backfired and sent Cam into a panic attack.

> Oliver: Seriously, he would love it, right? I can only imagine
> what that man would do with a slot machine.

Skyler reached over and tugged Kit's arm into view, unashamedly reading his texts. "I take it Cam is a gambler?"

"First of all, not even a little bit. Second of all, don't you know it's rude to read someone else's texts?"

"I want to see who is more interesting than me."

"Low blow, Sky."

Another text came in from Cam, even though Kit had yet to respond to either of them.

> Cam: Does it make me a bad friend if I break a guy's nose
> twice in six months?

Skyler snorted loudly, earning herself some dirty looks from the kids up front. "Okay, that's a story I'm going to have to hear."

"It was actually a touching moment," Kit said as he started typing out a text telling Oliver to stand down before he got himself a black eye. Before he got halfway through his reply, another text came in. This time from Ben in the group chat.

> Ben: Could you tell Oliver and Cam to stop duking it out
> on the lawn when they said they would help me
> pack?

"You've got to be kidding me," Kit grumbled. "I leave for two days and they're falling apart."

> Ben: Will you tell Ben it's rude to tell lies?

What in the...

> Oliver: Fun fact: Benjamin Nakamura can throw a punch.
> Who knew? Don't be shocked when you come back
> and Cam has a black eye.
> Cam: For the love of
> Cam: Just because I stole Cam's phone after he stole
> mine, it doesn't mean I punched him!
> Cam: I didn't punch him, Kit. But I want to.

Kit had never seen Ben get violent in his life. Not even when they played laser tag. He had to be really bothered if he was willing to get physical with Cam.

> Ben: When are you coming back? I think Ben is ready to kill us.
> Ben: Also, did you realize he still has the same phone he had in college? This thing is ancient. I don't even know how it still works.
> Oliver: Have you fallen in love with your teacher friend yet?

Kit swore and tried to hide his phone, but Skyler had already read the text. "It's not what it looks like," he said a little too loudly.

Lloyd cleared his throat.

Kit slouched lower on the couch, all too aware of the way Skyler had shifted away from him to her own half of the loveseat. He couldn't blame Oliver, who thought Skyler was a fellow teacher and who enjoyed teasing people a little too much. They'd all joked about Kit falling for his fake fiancé, but Oliver had terrible timing.

Now Skyler probably thought Kit really *was* flirting with Brooklyn when that couldn't be further from the truth.

Forget about watching the movie; Kit needed to figure out a way to fix this.

The problem was none of the Wonder Boys would have a clue how to deal with a problem like this. Oliver and Madi had literally pretended to get married once as kids—they didn't seem to remember this, and Kit would never remind them, not after he gave them a hard time for getting married so quickly. Ben was about as perfect as a person could get and would never give off flirty vibes unless he meant to. Cam had a built-in lie detector and couldn't lie without throwing up, which meant there was no one more honest and open than him.

Kit's circle of friends had never felt smaller than now.

Groaning, he opened up his phone—ignoring the Wonder Boys entirely—and finally looked at the texts Isla had sent him.

> Isla: I'm thinking a beach theme. Tiki torches, flower necklaces, the whole package. What do you think?
>
> Isla: Do you know where I can buy bags of sand?
>
> Isla: I tried this great Thai place you would love. We should go sometime.
>
> Isla: Lani just told me you're up in the mountains. Guess you don't have service.

Grimacing, Kit knew it would be a bad idea to jump right into telling her his dating problems after a day and a half of radio silence. But he wasn't equipped to help himself right now, and maybe this conversation would be what Isla needed to realize he wasn't interested in her. This wasn't going to be his finest moment, but he needed help. And Isla was way smarter than him when it came to dealing with people.

Once he made sure Skyler had her eyes fixed on the projector screen, Kit typed out a quick message, knowing Isla would respond immediately. That girl was never without her phone.

> Kit: I have service. I've just been busy.
>
> Isla: Doing what?

Was there any point to beating around the bush? With Isla, probably not. She was tough as nails, the sort of person who liked things direct. Whether she listened to those things was up for debate.

> Kit: I'm at a family reunion with a girl I dated in junior high.
>
> Isla: You dated someone in your family???
>
> Isla: Kidding. Bad joke.
>
> Isla: I'm going to be jealous of this girl huh?
>
> Kit: I'm afraid so.

> Isla: Darn. I really thought I had a shot. You did warn me
>   but I was hoping you were just playing hard to get.

Kit shook his head, marveling at her maturity levels for being only twenty. He supposed losing her leg to cancer when she was a kid had forced her to grow up quickly.

> Kit: I didn't mean to lead you on. Sorry.
> Isla: Don't be. Maybe now I'll start paying attention to the
>   hot barista who works the cafe in Lani's gym. He
>   might not be cuter than you but he's way funnier.
> Kit: Thanks?
> Isla: Whoever this girl is she's lucky.
> Kit: I'm not so sure about that.

He typed out the basics of the issue as quickly as he could, though it still ended up being a huge text. At least Isla was used to mini novels in her inbox, and she was never afraid to write them in return.

> Kit: I don't blame her for thinking the worst. You're proof
>   I'm not good at setting boundaries.
> Isla: The only thing that's proven here is you're an ex-
>   tremely good guy. Just be glad Brooklyn is the only
>   one she's worried about.
> Kit: Brooklyn and you.
> Isla: NICE. I love being considered competition.
> Kit: You're so weird.
> Kit: How do I fix this? I really thought I was making head-
>   way and then Oliver had to go and ruin things.

Skyler shifted next to him, and he froze, waiting to see what she did. But she only bent one leg underneath the other without even turning her head in his direction.

He waited a moment longer before reading Isla's response.

> Isla: I don't know anything about Skyler, but I know the
>   way we women think. This might have to be a grand
>   gesture moment.

Kit: ???

Isla: You know, the grand gesture.

Kit: Saying it again isn't giving me more information.

Isla: UGH. You need to watch more romantic movies. I can't believe I ever liked you. I'm definitely saying yes the next time the cute barista asks me out. As for Skyler...

Kit couldn't help but chuckle. They would never be a couple, but he could see the two of them easily staying friends. They'd first bonded during the competition that brought Cam and Kailani together a few months ago, but Kit had realized one date in that they were in two very different stages of life. Talking to her had always come easily, though, and as he waited for what he anticipated to be a long and winded set of instructions, he was glad to have her in his life.

But the text that came through several minutes later had him feeling like he'd been handed one of those trick ice cream cones that the street vendors used to mess with tourists. He'd been hoping for a huge scoop of rocky road, and all he got was an empty cone.

Isla: Show her she matters.

How was he supposed to do that?

NINETEEN

"I'M GOING TO PRETEND I fell asleep reading on the couch."

Those were the first words out of Kit's mouth after Textgate, as Skyler had started calling it in her head. Since the moment Oliver outed him and told Skyler all her fears were true. Since she realized she didn't know if she could trust anything Kit said to her.

He'd spent the whole movie on his phone, sending a million texts to who knows who, followed by a suspicious amount of Googling romantic comedies. When the movie ended, he grabbed her hand (to keep up appearances, she assumed) and walked back to their cabin in silence. The moment he was in his pajamas, he tucked a book under his arm and made his announcement.

"Smart," Skyler replied, and she meant it. For all the negative feelings she had about the man right now, she still didn't want to make him sleep on the floor. And no way was he sharing the bed with her when he clearly wanted to share it with Brooklyn.

Ew. Skyler shook her head. She was making assumptions, she knew, but she had yet to come up with some other meaning for that text Oliver had sent.

"Well." Kit looked around and patted the pockets of his sweatpants as if looking for something. "Goodnight, I guess?"

"Guess so," Skyler replied. How had they gone from mega flirting to being so awkward that she was sure the entire cabin could feel it? She hated this. She hated feeling jealous of someone as sweet as Brooklyn when she wasn't technically dating Kit, and she hated thinking the worst of him just because she had seen him play a part and switch personalities in an instant.

He'd said that text wasn't what it looked like. Why didn't she believe him?

She was a *lawyer* for crying out loud! She had perfected the art of reading people so she could know when to push on the stand and which questions to ask to get what she wanted. And while Kit stood there in the doorway looking miserable, Skyler knew he wouldn't do anything to hurt her, especially something like this. She *knew* it.

But that didn't make the feelings go away, and she didn't think she was strong enough to listen to him breathe all night until she could convince herself that he was telling the truth.

So she slipped onto the bed and muttered, "Hopefully the couch is better than the floor," wishing she didn't have to send him away.

Nodding once, he opened his mouth as if to say something but changed his mind, turning around and closing the door behind him. Skyler fell asleep with her thoughts locked on that closed door keeping them apart.

She woke to Kit frantically saying her name, his face hovering over hers in the darkness. "What?" she gasped.

He let out his breath all at once. She couldn't see much in the darkness, but he looked like he was barely holding it together. "You were crying," he said, his voice wavering. "You shouted my name. Were you…were you having a nightmare?"

She couldn't remember. One minute she'd been wishing he would come back, and the next… Her heart pounded an erratic rhythm in her chest, leaving her trembling, and she curled herself up in a ball. "I don't have nightmares," she said right as her tears started up again. Why in the world was she crying?

Kit sat on the edge of the bed and watched her for two seconds before he scooped her up into his arms. "I'm here," he whispered. "I know you may not want me here, but I'm—"

"Don't you dare leave," she whimpered and wrapped her arms around him, holding him tight. She hadn't had a nightmare since she was a kid, and even if she didn't have a clue what she had been dreaming about, the lingering fear felt all too real. She clung to him like she might fall apart if he let go, and he held her like he wouldn't move a muscle even if the world crumbled around him.

Hiding her face in his chest, she tried to match her breathing to his to calm down but realized he was barely breathing at all. "Kit?"

"You scared the crap out of me, Sky." His arms tightened around her, his whole body shaking until he dropped his head onto hers and finally relaxed with an exhale. "When I heard you screaming, I thought…"

"I'm fine," she whispered, sniffling through her tears.

"You're clearly not fine."

No, she wasn't fine. "Did you know my mom was with ten different guys before I turned six?"

Kit stiffened again, his breath hitching.

And Skyler kept talking. "She doesn't even know who my father was. Every time she found a new man, she introduced him as my new dad and pretended we were one big happy family. Most of them only lasted a few months before they disappeared in the middle of the night, usually taking our stuff with them.

"So then we'd move to a new city and start fresh. 'This is it, Skyler,' she'd say. 'I'm making changes, starting right now.' Six months later we'd be back in the car, on to the next town. The next apartment. The next school."

She pulled out of his hold only long enough to direct him to change positions and sit against the headboard. As soon as he was situated, she tucked herself under his arm, not caring if he didn't want her there. She needed him to hold her.

"I cried for three days when she made me leave Diamond Springs," she said quietly. "For the first time in my life I had a friend. A *home.* And when her latest fling broke her heart, she packed up the apartment while I was at school and picked me up with the trunk already full."

She couldn't hold back the sob that escaped her. "She'd only known the guy for two weeks, and I didn't even get a chance to say goodbye to the boy I was in love with."

She cried in Kit's arms for a long time, letting out years of pent-up sorrow and frustration. Kit didn't say anything, but he rubbed her back and held her hand, and each kiss he touched to the top of her head said a lot more than any words might have.

And when she'd finally cried herself into exhaustion, Kit tucked the blanket around her and whispered, "I loved you too."

TWENTY

HAVING BEEN A MORNING PERSON for most of her life, Skyler had always liked waking up. A new day felt like a fresh start, and the rising sun always seemed to fill her with a bright hope for something great. Dawn held promise and possibility and potential, and early mornings are always when she got her best work done. When she didn't have to answer to anyone.

As it turned out, the sight of Kit Morgan sound asleep just a few inches away was a million times better than waking up to work.

Breathing in deep, Skyler ran through what she remembered from last night, making sure she hadn't completely made a fool of herself by sobbing uncontrollably. Honestly, it had probably been a long time coming, and she felt so much lighter than she had in years, even more than she had the day she quit the law firm and moved back to Diamond Springs.

And Kit had stayed with her. That on its own buoyed her soul. It might have been just because she begged him not to leave, but he could have slept on the floor again. Instead, he held her hand like he'd wanted her to know that he would always be right there when she needed him. Even when she treated him unfairly.

Was this what a relationship was supposed to be? She'd seen too many failures and not enough success, and she never could have guessed that a guy she wasn't even technically dating would hold her through her tears and be a comfort she hadn't known she needed. Kit Morgan was the best sort of man, and she knew a life with him would always feel safe and stable.

But he deserved so much more than someone scared to risk her heart. What if they made this thing real, and then she got scared and left him? She never wanted him to be in her mom's position and feel like he wasn't good enough for anyone. Angela had already broken his heart, and it was a miracle he was still standing after that betrayal.

Would he survive that happening again?

"Do you make it a habit of watching people sleep?" Kit asked suddenly, opening one bleary eye and giving her a small smile.

Skyler squeezed his hand a little tighter. "This is my first time, but I'm enjoying it."

"You're beautiful in the morning."

She squinted. "Can you even see?"

He chuckled. "I'm not *that* blind. I can see you just fine, especially up close like this." He inched a little closer, though he kept himself on his half of the bed. He'd slept on top of the covers, creating a barrier between them, and Skyler had never disliked a blanket more. She wanted to be back in his arms now that she knew how good it felt to be held by him.

"I'm sorry about last night," she said.

"You don't have to—"

"I mean I'm sorry that I scared you. Not that I told you all of that." She brushed some hair off his forehead, loving the mess of it. It was somewhere in between straight and wavy, a dusty brown color that had always reminded her of an oak tree. Everything about Kit was like that; solid and strong. "Thank you for listening. And making me feel better."

He pulled her hand close and kissed her knuckles. "I'm sorry you didn't have any stability as a kid. I know I'm lucky. But..."

"But what?"

Pursing his lips, he shook his head as he massaged her palm and kept his focus on their hands. "I've spent my entire life in stability. And yeah, I can't complain about any of it, but everyone who knows me thinks I am perfectly happy to keep doing the same thing day after day. To be the same person I've always been. Being here with you has made it easy to be something different. Like I was back then. I don't feel trapped anymore."

How long had he been feeling that way? "You said you've been playing a role."

He nodded. "I mean, it's not like I've been something I'm not. I'm still…me. But there's a part of me that I lost after that first semester of sixth grade. Back then, for the first time in my life, I was surrounded by people who didn't already know me. I could be anything I wanted, and I didn't feel like I was going to disappoint anyone by changing."

Skyler frowned. That was what had him all twisted up inside? He was worried about disappointing people? She was pretty sure that was literally impossible. "What happened?"

"Oliver came back and didn't know I'd changed. My parents got mad at me for getting sent to detention. You left." He shrugged one shoulder as he lifted his gaze to hers. "I think part of me at the time thought that that version of me is what drove you away. So I went back to the way I'd been and hid away all of the wild parts of me. I went back to Kit, the perfect son, brother, friend, who never surprised and never disappointed."

If only Skyler had gotten the chance to say goodbye to him. By the time she ended up somewhere with a phone she could use, she'd somehow forgotten Kit's number, no matter how hard she tried to remember. He had always been the one to call her first, not the other way around, and it killed her when she couldn't find the right combination of numbers. And oh, how she'd tried. If she could have just explained what was happening, if they had kept in touch, maybe their lives would have turned out differently.

"I like this version of you," Skyler said, smiling. "It seems like it's somewhere in the middle, like you're finally embracing your two sides." When he met her smile, she ran her whole hand through his hair. Though the first time she'd done that he had freaked out, this time he didn't even flinch. He just watched her with so much warmth in his expression that something deep in her gut told her that that big, cracked heart of his wasn't going to belong to him much longer.

Skyler wanted his heart. She shouldn't, but she desperately wanted it to be hers so she had a reason to give him her own. But could she really be selfish and risk hurting him? His heart was still so fragile, and if she didn't hold it gently and treat it with all the care it deserved…

She shuddered, a little grossed out by her own metaphor. "What if we don't go to the fair today?" she suggested to distract herself from imagining a meaty heart beating in her hands. "What if we just stay here and…"

"Practice?" Kit raised an eyebrow.

Well, if he was going to suggest it. "Yes. Please. No more stalling, no more interruptions."

But Kit sat up, laughing to himself as he slid off the bed and took several steps away. "That's a bad idea, Sky."

"Why? Because I'm not Brooklyn?" She didn't mean that, and she immediately wished she could take it back. After the way he'd held her last night and stayed with her even when he didn't have to, it was a lot easier to believe him when he'd said there was nothing happening with Brooklyn. That didn't mean the jealousy had magically disappeared overnight.

Stuffing his hands into his hair, he bit his lip and shook his head. "I can only deny that so many times, Sky. You have to believe me when I tell you it's all a misunderstanding. I mean it's a bad idea because this week is about you and your family."

What did that have to do with anything? There had to be a real reason he didn't want to kiss her. "What about Number Three? I'm pretty sure a good fiancé would kiss his girlfriend."

Kit groaned. "Why'd you have to go and put a word to it? It was so much easier to resist you when we were calling it practice."

"I think we're past that point, Kit."

"Let me have my semantics, okay? It's the only thing keeping me sane."

"Why don't you want to kiss me, Kit?"

"Because I don't know if I'll be able to stop once I do." He grimaced as those words hung between them. "And I don't… I'm worried."

There was something so genuine in the way he was looking at her with all of his fear written on his face. His mask was entirely gone, leaving just raw and real Kit in its wake. Sitting up, Skyler tried to consider all of this from his perspective, but she needed more pieces to the puzzle. "Worried about what?" Did he know she was afraid she was going to leave him?

He swallowed. "I'm not really a 'casual' guy."

"And I'm a casual girl? I'm the definition of awkward and complicated, Kit, and since coming back to Diamond Springs I date even less than you do. But this doesn't have to mean anything. It's not like it's real." Did she really mean that? It would certainly be easier if she pretended all of this was fake. But she wouldn't be so jealous if there weren't some real feelings involved.

The change was subtle, but his expression shifted, his frown growing harder. "What if I want it to be?"

Oh.

Terrified by the idea of this becoming a real relationship and blowing up in her face, Skyler fought for something to change the subject before they both got wildly uncomfortable. They *so* weren't ready to have a conversation like that. At least, *she* wasn't. "This is off topic," she said with some hesitation, "but did you get a chance to talk to Tanner at all yesterday before Mrs. Perfect interrupted?"

Kit relaxed a little, apparently grateful for the new topic, and he shoved his hands into his pockets. "No. It usually takes some coaxing with kids, and Tanner seems even more closed off than most. There's something bothering him, but I don't know what it is."

"He said something about people being mean," Skyler offered with a shrug. "He was referring to how you got ganged up on in paintball, but I got the feeling there was more to it than concern for your misadventures."

That got his attention, his eyebrows pulling lower as he considered the new information. "You're probably right, especially if he's been getting into fights." He groaned a little. "If I could have just had a few more minutes with him, I think he would have talked to me."

"Maybe we can somehow get the Wonder Twins away from their parents at the fair today. I can't imagine Heidi and her husband wanting to go to something like that when they can stay at the cabin and work."

"Maybe. I'll have to be cautious, though. I don't want to put a strain on the family dynamic or scare Tanner into thinking he's in trouble."

"You must be a really good teacher." Skyler could imagine him teaching young minds and being an inspiration to all of them. Maybe one day she could see him in action, assuming they made it that far.

Kit grew tense, a shadow passing over his expression like the sun had just gone behind a cloud. "I was, yeah," he said, and then he snatched his glasses from the bedside table and headed for the door.

Her stomach did a flip, and her entire body almost did a flip as well as she tumbled out of bed to chase after him. "Kit!" she shouted after him. "What's that supposed to mean? *Was?* Kit!"

Only when she reached the living room did she realize the cabin's occupants weren't as asleep as she'd anticipated. Sam and his wife sat on the couch on their phones, though their screens had gone forgotten as the pair of them looked between Kit and Skyler with interest. Kit had paused near the kitchen, probably when she shouted his name, and he'd closed his eyes as if bracing for the inevitable.

Sam spoke first. "You just called your fiancé Kit."

As if Skyler wasn't fully aware of that. "No I didn't," she tried.

"You definitely did," Tracy—Stacy?—said.

Kit was clenching his jaw so hard that it looked like he might crack a few teeth, and Skyler felt a bit like throwing up. Of anyone, Sam was the most likely to go running to Lloyd if he figured out the truth.

Praise the heavens Skyler had been dumb enough to use a real person's name, and Kit had been dumb enough to agree to her stupid plan.

"Kit is short for Christopher," she said, folding her arms. "Excuse me for giving my fiancé a nickname."

Sam pulled his eyebrows low. "No it's not. That doesn't even make any sense." He turned to Kit, narrowing his eyes as if expecting to see someone different than before. "So if your name isn't really Chris, who are you, super spy? *Wait.*" He turned back to Skyler. "Was Dad right? Did you bring some-one to pretend to be your fiancé so he would keep paying for your stupid store?" His confused expression shifted into a glare. "That's sick, Skyler. I know my dad has money, but that doesn't mean you can—"

"Okay." Kit let out a little growl and turned back, stalking straight for Skyler. She had no idea what he was doing and wasn't sure how he wanted her to react, but he went past her and into the bedroom. He emerged a moment later with his wallet in his hands and practically threw it at Sam.

"Want to say any other stupid things," Kit snapped, "or are you done?"

Eyes wide, Sam just sat there for a second as if the wallet landing on his chest had stunned him, but then his wife grabbed the wallet and opened it, turning bright red as soon as she looked at what Skyler guessed was Kit's driver's license.

Sam's face turned an even darker crimson when he looked over and realized his mistake. "Oh," he squeaked, flipping through a few other things in the wallet as if hoping to find a different name than Christopher Morgan. "I thought…"

Kit reached over and snatched the wallet out of Tracy's hands, stuffing it into his pocket and heading straight for the back door without a word.

Skyler fought back a sigh of relief, knowing that would look wildly suspicious, but she wasn't sure what to say now. Stacy looked adequately repentant, and Sam just sat there gaping like a fish. It didn't help that he was technically right, but she needed him to think he was wrong.

"Thanks," she spat out. "You'll be lucky if he ever comes to a family thing again."

It was sort of fun stomping away after that, even though she knew the drama was far from over. At least Sam's idiocy had helped solidify Kit's existence, and no one else would be stupid enough to accuse Skyler of lying about everything. But now Skyler had to figure out why Kit had said what he did about no longer being a teacher. He'd said something when they were doing tie dye too, but she knew how much he loved his job.

She found Kit on the back porch, leaning his elbows on the railing and staring into the trees. He turned his head slightly when she stepped onto the deck but didn't look at her.

"Budget cuts," he said before she could ask. "Across the whole district. And with so many teachers out of work, any open jobs were already gone before I could even…" His head dropped, and he sounded so completely lost. "I don't even know what to do now."

Skyler wrapped an arm around him and held him tight, wishing she was as good at comforting as he had been last night. "Why didn't you tell me?"

"Because I wanted to get away from it all this week." He reached over and placed his hand over hers on the railing at such a glacial pace that it made her shiver. "I wanted to get to know your family." His fingers skated across her knuckles and up her wrist, leaving a trail of fire in their wake. "And have some fun, and…" He turned his head, leaning in until their noses brushed. "I wanted to be the best fiancé ever."

Skyler leaned back just before he kissed her, realizing he was right about the danger of doing something they weren't ready to dive headfirst into. Knowing what she knew now about his desire to make their relationship more than a fake one, she knew that if she kissed him, it would mean everything was changing. She ached to know how it would feel to have his lips on hers, but taking that step would leave her exposed. Vulnerable. Besides, she hadn't brushed her teeth yet, and she wasn't willing to subject him to that. "I can't believe I'm saying this," she said as Kit grimaced, "but I don't think we're ready to practice."

He dropped his head again. "It's stupid. But yes. When this was fake, it made sense, but now…" Grumbling to himself, Kit stood up straight and ran his hands through his hair again. He hadn't shaved at all since arriving at the cabins, and she couldn't help but imagine what he would look like with a full beard instead of the dark scruff he sported now. Based on what he'd told her back in the room about living the same way most of his life, he'd probably been clean-shaven throughout adulthood, but he would absolutely be able to pull off the lumberjack look. Put him in a flannel shirt and some boots, and Skyler would be done for. Tall, dark, and stupidly handsome mountain man.

Yummy.

"If you don't stop looking at me like that," Kit warned, taking a step back. "When are we leaving for the fair?"

She grinned, her heart picking up into double time. She was either excited or terrified, and she honestly had no idea which. "You tell me. I haven't seen my phone since Sunday."

"Oh. Right. I should probably—"

Grabbing his arm, she felt a thrill of satisfaction when that sudden movement didn't seem to affect him in the slightest. He even seemed to lean into her touch. Maybe curing him of Angela's lingering presence would be easier than she'd hoped. "I don't care about my phone," she said, shocked that she meant it. "Let's just have some fun today."

For the space of three breaths, they stood there and stared at each other with so much tension filling the space between them that Skyler was afraid to move for fear of it spilling over and breaking any sense of resolve either of them had.

Then Kit turned abruptly and tromped down the stairs into the trees despite being completely barefoot and in his pajamas.

TWENTY-ONE

LAKETOWN LOOKED LIKE ANY QUINTESSENTIAL mountain town, complete with a classy little main street full of family-owned shops and happy people waving to each other as they walked down the street. Kit was pretty sure the Taylor clan would be doubling the population as they piled out of the several cars they'd brought into town, and he hoped the horde of kids wouldn't leave the place a pile of rubble by day's end.

"Got any secret insider information on this fair?" he asked Skyler as he helped her climb out of the back of Paul's minivan.

She shook her head, tugging on her tie-dyed shirt. Apparently, she hadn't looked at the size when she grabbed it. It was too small, rising up every time she moved and showing off some of the fair skin on her waist. The denim shorts she wore were small as well because she'd borrowed them from much shorter Brooklyn when she decided she didn't have "fair appropriate" pants, and they barely covered a third of Skyler's long thighs.

Kit hadn't noticed that. It hadn't been his sole focus during the drive. Not. At. All.

"Micah told me all about it last year," Skyler said, "but I honestly wasn't really listening to her. I didn't have any goals back then."

Lacing his fingers through hers, Kit turned his focus to the Wonder Twins, who had miraculously been allowed to come without their parents. Stella had offered to help with the older kids who were still too young to be on their own, while the youngest children were to stay with their parents. The teens had already disappeared, hopefully in the direction of the fair.

"Let's give it a little bit," Skyler suggested, nodding toward Tanner and Isabelle. "Mom probably got specific instructions to not let them out of her sight."

"Good idea," Kit agreed, though he hated the way both kids hardly looked excited about the day's events. They kept themselves apart from the other tie-dyed kids surrounding Stella and Lloyd, their hands clasped together. At least they had each other? "We could wait a few hours. I'm sure your mom will be glad to let us take a few off her hands after they've been pumped full of fair food."

"How, exactly, is fair food different from regular food?"

Somehow, even after her confession last night, he had forgotten how different Skyler's childhood had been from his. He couldn't imagine never having a safe place to go when life got overwhelming, or not having someone to truly rely on. She was clearly reluctant when it came to relationships, but maybe, if she knew he would always be there for her, that fear would dissipate.

For now, he would make sure she had the best county fair experience of her life. "Oh, you have so much to learn," he said with a wink.

"That's not an answer, you know."

"I know."

"Hey!" Micah leapt out of Chad's SUV before he'd even shifted the car into park. "You guys want to hang out with us?"

"Only if Morgan is up for a little rematch," Houston said as he and the other two Briggs siblings stepped out of the car.

Kit let out a deep laugh, and he wondered when the last time had been that he'd laughed quite so easily. He hoped he could keep up a friendship with Skyler's stepsiblings no matter what happened with the fake engagement. He fully planned on keeping Skyler in his life however he could have her, and a man could always use more friends.

Especially when the Wonder Boys were all moving on.

"Oh, I don't think you want to go there, Briggs," he said, though his voice faltered a little. He wasn't prematurely trying to replace his best friends, was he?

Houston pointed down the street in the direction Stella and the horde were moving. "Ball toss. Right now."

By the time they reached the fairgrounds, Kit and Houston had fallen deep into trash-talking each other like they'd been friends their whole lives. Houston had a lot of similarities to Oliver in his bearing and demeanor, with a healthy dose of Cam's competitiveness. He even had some Madi in him when he offered a wager on the outcome of the ball toss. Joking around with him as they walked felt like home.

The difference was Kit, who miraculously didn't care one fig what Houston thought of him. It was nice. He stepped into the fair with all its shouting, laughing, bright spinning rides, and overwhelming smell of fried food and livestock, feeling like nothing could dampen his day.

"Time for your reckoning," Houston said when they reached the booth with stacked pyramids of milk jugs. "I'll even pay your way to make you feel better."

Kit had played basketball in high school, not baseball. But when a man is the only athletic friend of state champion short-stop Cam Martinez, he learns to throw a ball. Kit didn't even know how many hours he and Cam had spent in his backyard, tossing a ball back and forth and talking about girls, their futures, and life in general. Those days were some of the few days Cam had been willing to open up and be vulnerable about deep topics.

"Spend your money all you want," Kit said, rubbing his hands together. "But it's Skyler who will be walking away with that giant stuffed..." He blinked. "Llama?" He'd never seen that particular prize before.

Skyler latched onto his arm, bouncing in her sandals. "You're going to win me a giant llama?"

"Apparently."

Houston glanced at his sisters—Chad had wandered off as soon as they'd entered the fairgrounds. "Either of you want a llama?"

"Yes, please!" Micah said, while Brooklyn rolled her eyes. Kit honestly couldn't tell if the twins liked each other or not.

When the kid running the booth handed Kit his first ball, he tested its weight and watched the way Houston handled his own ball. Houston held it casually in his left hand, but his expression filled with concentration as he focused on his pyramid. Feeling confident, Kit turned to Skyler. "Kiss for good luck?"

Skyler smacked him. "How about you throw the ball and get me that llama?"

Kit threw the ball as hard as he could, but it slipped a little in his fingers and curved to the side, only knocking a few jugs from the stack. Could have been worse, but not his best performance.

Houston threw his ball a second later, only hitting the top jug.

Kit's second throw knocked over the rest of his jugs, which earned him an inflatable baseball bat.

The next two jugs toppled from Houston's pyramid.

Kit gripped his next ball a little tighter. He didn't like the way Houston didn't even flinch at his poor throw, despite how adamant he'd been that they make this a competition to see who could knock over the most jugs. He was pretty sure Houston didn't want to get hit with a paintball without a shirt on—the loser's fate—and yet he didn't seem to be trying very hard.

Kit managed to knock four of the six jugs off the table this time, but his stomach twisted when Houston cleanly hit the top three together this time.

Even Skyler noticed the precision, gripping Kit's arm again as they both watched the man warily.

"I think I've just been played," Kit stage whispered, cringing when Houston smirked in their direction.

"I don't think I ever told you what I do for work," Houston said casually, tossing his ball in the air.

Micah broke into a fit of giggles, while Brooklyn had pulled out her phone and seemed entirely disinterested in her brother's scheme, like she'd seen it a million times before.

Kit groaned, for the first time noticing the team logo on Houston's hat. "Don't say it."

Houston grinned and threw his ball across the booth, knocking the rest of Kit's jugs off the table with ease. "I'm the pitcher for the Sun City Red-tails."

Kit couldn't even be mad at him after the way he'd beaten Houston in paintball so thoroughly yesterday. He broke into a defeated laugh, holding out his hand for a handshake. "I'm not even going to keep trying," he said with a shake of his head. "I might ask for your autograph, though. I've never met a pro player."

"You still haven't," Brooklyn muttered as Houston grasped Kit's hand. "Professional isn't in Hou's vocabulary."

Houston spun to face her. "Are you still mad about me saying something about your teacher crush? I didn't even say his name!"

As the two of them started bickering again, Kit reached for Skyler's hand and nodded toward the inflatable bat she held. "Sorry it's not a stuffed llama."

She bonked him on the head with the bat. "This is probably more fun."

"Brooklyn might want to use it on her brother, though it won't do much damage."

"If I had known he was a pitcher, I would have warned you."

Kit let out an exaggerated sigh. "If only you had some reason to get to know these people better…"

This time the bat hit him with a lot more force, and though Kit tried to steal it out of her hands, Skyler jumped free and darted out of reach. "What do you think I've been doing? Goal One is coming along nicely, in my opinion. Now, what were you saying about fair food?"

That got the Briggs siblings' attention, their argument falling forgotten at the thought of delicious, deep-fried junk food.

Chuckling, Kit approached Skyler warily, in case she was still inclined to attack, and then he tucked her under his arm. "Nope. No food."

"But—"

"Not until after we ride the Tilt-a-Whirl."

The five of them looked at the spinning contraption a few hundred yards away, and even Kit's stomach wobbled just thinking about how that ride would destroy them. The ride hadn't been kind to younger Kit's constitution, and it would be even worse now that he was nearing his fourth decade.

But this was the fair. It was basically designed to make people sick, and they were going to do it right. Skyler deserved to experience everything she'd missed out on as a kid.

No matter how much it made her puke.

TWENTY-TWO

"WHO WOULD HAVE THOUGHT THE thing that would make me feel better was a deep-fried turkey leg?" Skyler had had her misgivings about the giant hunk of meat the vendor handed her, but Kit had promised her a churro if she at least gave it a try.

Not willing to throw away the opportunity for cinnamon sugar goodness, Skyler had taken a bite. Ten minutes later, she'd been picking the bone clean and wishing for more.

After riding every terrifying and definitely not up-to-code ride they could, most of them throwing up only a couple of times—Houston had the stomach of a four-year-old and seemed to vomit half his body weight throughout the day—the five of them had wandered through the vendor and artist tents before returning to the games and attempting to collect as many prizes for the littles as they could.

Then Kit had finally introduced her to fairground food, and Skyler mourned the thirty years of her life that had been missing such delicacies as deep-fried Oreos and a burger with donuts in place of a bun.

After they finished eating, Brooklyn said she wanted to check out the livestock, dragging Micah with her. Houston spotted a group of young women and made a beeline for them, immediately charming them with his smile and biceps, and disappeared with them.

Skyler didn't mind the chance to spend some alone time with Kit. Not even a little bit. Still, she'd enjoyed watching him in his element. Even with Houston's big personality, Kit had taken charge of their little group and led the way all morning, making sure no one did anything they didn't want to do but also pushing everyone to take a chance and be brave. He cracked jokes and held Brooklyn's hair when she threw up, and he bought everyone sodas after the Tilt-a-Whirl nearly spun their brains out of their skulls. He clearly loved seeing others enjoying themselves even more than having fun himself.

Skyler would give anything to see him like that all the time. To see him happy.

As they sat at the base of a tree in a grassy area close to the food carts, Skyler wondered if the bright, warm feeling in her chest meant she was falling in love with this man. It felt similar to the crush she'd had on him when she was twelve, and yet it was so unlike anything she'd ever felt before that she had to wonder.

Could a person fall in love in three days?

If the way Kit smiled every time he looked at her was any indication, she was pretty sure they could.

"Can I ask you something?" Kit stretched out his long legs, leaning back on his hands as he watched the goings on around them. The crease that formed between his eyebrows gave him a serious expression she hadn't expected to see in a place like this.

For all the years she pretended she was calm and collected under pressure, Skyler's heart pounded in her chest with that vague question, a mixture of nerves and excitement. "Sure."

He turned to look at her, the crease deepening on his forehead. "Why a bookstore? You said you always wanted to do that as a kid, but why?"

Shrugging, Skyler tore a blade of grass and spun it between her fingers. Even though this was the one person who would probably understand, she still hesitated to share. Kit would get that look in his eyes that he always got when he felt sympathy toward someone and wanted to help, but all of Skyler's hurts were in the past. He couldn't change her childhood any more than he could change the way Skyler craved being around him.

He said he wanted this relationship to be real, but that would never happen if she didn't let him in.

Dropping her gaze, she tore off a handful of grass and put it in a little pile in front of her. She could be brave, as long as she didn't stop talking. "I loved reading as a kid. It gave me a chance to escape and live the kinds of lives I wish I had. When every few months I got packed up and brought to a new town, most of my friends were fictional characters because they didn't have to get left behind every time we moved."

She added to her grass pile. "The library was always the first place I would find when I got to a new city, and I spent hours there after school while my mom worked whatever dead-end job she found. Books give lonely people a chance to experience love and friendship and adventure when life doesn't make it easy, and I wanted to build a place where people could feel safe because I never had that."

As she grabbed another handful of grass to keep building her pile, Kit wrapped his warm fingers around hers, stopping the movement. "I'm sorry," was all he said, but his eyes were saying so much more.

Tears pricked at her eyes. No one had ever seen her the way Kit saw her, and she could feel everything so much more strongly than she did before. The warmth of the sun. The tickle of the grass on her bare legs. The feel of Kit's strong and calloused hand encasing hers. She could feel each beat of her heart telling her that he was the best man she had ever known and she would be stupid to let him go.

"Sky," he said, leaning in. Skyler was so ready to finally experience his kiss, but then he frowned and pulled his phone out of his pocket. His brow furrowed as he read the text he'd gotten. "I don't like the looks of this," he muttered as his phone buzzed again.

Hopefully it wasn't bad news, though Skyler was almost grateful for the distraction. She was feeling a lot of big things right now, and she didn't know what to do with them. "What's going on?"

He rolled his eyes. "I thought getting Cam and Oliver to admit they actually like each other would have been a good thing, but apparently I unleashed a monster with two heads and half a brain cell. No, Watch, don't—" He typed a quick text, shaking his head like his friend might see it.

"Watch?"

"Ben. It's the nickname I gave him when I realized he needed something to call his own." He groaned again when another text came in.

Skyler shifted closer, snickering when Kit immediately shifted his phone so she could see the screen.

> Ben: I never thought I'd say this, but I'm considering murder. Oliver and Cam thought it was a good idea to wrap themselves in bubble wrap and start sumo wrestling in my living room.

He'd followed the text with a picture of a smashed and mangled coffee table.

> Ben: Going to kill them.
> Kit: Murder isn't the answer.
> Ben: Sure it is. Will you be my alibi?

"I built him that coffee table when he moved into Oliver's guest house," Kit grumbled right as a text came from Oliver in what looked like a group chat between the four of them.

Skyler's eyebrows shot up. "You built it? You're still woodworking?"

Kit didn't answer, keeping his focus on the phone.

> Oliver: I'll buy him a new one. It's fine.
> Cam: For the record, I won.
> Oliver: Keep dreaming, big guy.
> Cam: Dreaming of my victory? Easy.
> Ben: You guys were supposed to be boxing up the kitchen. And the only reason I'm texting this instead of telling you is because you're laughing too hard to hear me.

"See?" Kit said, pulling off his glasses and pinching the bridge of his nose. "Monster. Cam and Oliver have never gotten along so well that they turn into idiots, and I regret everything."

He didn't even look at the next text that came in on a different text thread entirely, so Skyler grabbed the phone.

> Allie: Kit, I know you're on vacation, but I think Ben is getting seriously stressed out. Can you talk to them?
> Kailani: Oh no.
> Madi: What did my dumb husband do now? I thought they were helping Ben move his stuff.

Skyler snorted a laugh. "You're in a group chat with all the ladies?"

He half-heartedly shrugged, his eyes shut tight. "Are you surprised?"

"Not really. Women do seem to like talking to you."

"The only one I care about talking to right now is you."

Since he was still closing his eyes, Skyler read through the last few messages that came in, then typed out a reply.

> Allie: They were helping him. For about ten minutes. Then they discovered how much fun it was to body slam each other while wearing bubble wrap armor.

> Kailani: Does anyone know how hard it is to return an engagement ring?
>
> Madi: Easier than returning a husband, I'd guess.
>
> Kit: Hi ladies! This is Skyler, the woman who borrowed Kit Morgan for a con. I don't know much about his friends beyond what he's told me, but I'm pretty sure you'll just have to ride this one out. Wonder Boys will be Wonder Boys, and all that.

She held her breath, waiting to see how they would react.

"Tell me the damage," Kit said, finally opening his eyes and returning his glasses to his nose. "Actually, I don't want to know. I want to go watch that hypnotist show that just started over here." He hopped up and tugged Skyler to her feet without even waiting for her response.

"You want to watch a hypnotist?"

"It'll be a lot more entertaining than whatever nonsense is happening in Diamond Springs."

The phone kept buzzing in Skyler's hand, her curiosity driving her crazy. Was it the girls answering her? Or was this more of the Boys complaining about each other?

As Kit found them a couple of seats as the hypnotist began his spiel, he squinted at his phone in Skyler's lap and then studied her face for a second. "You want to keep reading, don't you?"

Skyler bit her lip. "So badly."

He sighed. "Have at it. I'm going to distract myself with the show and pretend I'm anywhere but here. Sound good?"

Skyler didn't bother answering, diving right back into the phone.

> Madi: Oh.
>
> Madi: Kit gave you his phone?
>
> Allie: If they break any more furniture…
>
> Kailani: MORE furniture? That's it. I'm coming over.

> Allie: Aren't you at the gym today?
> Kailani: Yep. And Cam knows how much I hate giving my
>   clients to the other trainers.
> Madi: That will do the trick. It's amazing how well fear
>   works on them sometimes.

Skyler bit her lip to keep from laughing since that would probably pull Kit's attention back to his phone. She desperately wanted to meet these women who had managed to snag themselves the Wonder Boys.

> Kit: Tempting them with a kiss works pretty well too. ;)
> Madi: OH.
> Kailani: Oliver was RIGHT?
> Allie: Right about what?
> Madi: That joke that Kit was going to fall for his teacher
>   friend the minute he agreed to be her fake fiancé. I
>   didn't think it would actually happen.

"Oh!" Skyler cringed as soon as she spoke out loud, but Kit was still fixated on the stage. Oliver had been talking about *her* last night? No wonder Kit had said it wasn't what it looked like. Now she felt extra bad that she hadn't believed him.

Several texts came in a few minutes later from the Boys chat, and Skyler struggled to keep up with it all. How did Kit do this all the time? Or maybe the chaos was just because he wasn't nearby to keep everyone in check.

> Cam: KIT MORGAN WHAT DID YOU DO?
> Oliver: You sent Madi out to whisper yell at us?
> Cam: Why is Lani leaving the gym when she has training
>   sessions all day?
> Oliver: Who takes a baby with them to get mad at her
>   husband?
> Ben: Someone smart enough to know you won't shout
>   back and wake him up.

Skyler decided to step in so Kailani could have full credit for the obvious fear she was striking in her fiancé.

Kit: It wasn't me.
Oliver: BEN
Kit: It wasn't Ben either.

The phone went silent for a full minute, like she'd suddenly lost service, and she even checked the network connection—which was fine—before a text finally came through.

Oliver: Who is this?

Skyler wasn't sure what she'd said wrong—she'd barely said anything at all—but she loved that the Wonder Boys knew Kit well enough to know when they were talking to someone else. Maybe she should have defended Ben a little more; Kit had always had a soft spot for the soft-spoken artist, even when they were kids.

Oliver texted again before she could think of a clever response.

Oliver: Alright, Miss Temptress. How'd you convince Kit
    Morgan to give up his phone?

Skyler snorted. Madi must have told him.

Oliver: It would take a lot more than a kiss for him to hand
    that thing over.
Oliver: Wait, are we sure you're even with Kit?
Oliver: How do we know you didn't murder him and steal
    his phone?
Oliver: How do we know you're not some fifty year old
    serial killer with hair transplants?
Oliver: Are you holding him for ransom?
Oliver: I need proof of life.

Then the phone lit up with a video call.

Her heart kicking up a notch, Skyler glanced at Kit only to find him with his eyes closed, arms held out in front of him like several others in the crowd. She hadn't been paying attention to the hypnotist in the slightest—she didn't really believe in hypnotism—but it looked like he was testing the crowd to see who could be put under his spell. It seemed Kit had been willing to give it a try. Probably to get away from the chaos back home.

Slipping off her chair and sneaking far enough away from Kit that he wouldn't hear her, Skyler answered the call.

Three male faces filled the screen, with a brown-haired woman who had to be Kit's sister, Madi, cradling a baby in the background.

"Hi, Boys," Skyler said, sounding a lot more chipper and confident than she felt. These were Kit's closest friends, and he considered them his brothers.

"Oh, she's hot," the one on the right said, cringing the moment the words left his mouth. He was most likely Cam with his darker skin and ridiculous muscles. "Sorry. I meant to say you're very…I shouldn't finish that sentence."

"No, keep going," the man on the left said with a laugh. Oliver?

In the middle, the man who must have been Ben looked like he would rather be packing up the boxes strewn behind him. "Nice to meet you…"

"Skyler," she finished for him. "I've heard a lot about the infamous Wonder Boys."

"Idiotic, you mean," Madi said and then smiled and waved. "Nice to meet you, Skyler. Sorry about these dorks. How is the reun—"

"Wait!" Oliver held up the hand that wasn't holding up his phone. "We still haven't seen proof of life. Where's Kit?"

She located his tie-dyed shirt in the small sea of chairs. He was still sitting there peacefully while the hypnotist had already pulled a few people onto the stage. "Um…" Skyler watched

Kit for another few seconds; he didn't move an inch. "Do you guys know if Kit is susceptible to hypnosis?"

All three men burst into laughter.

"I take that as a yes."

"Please tell me he's already under," Cam said with a little too much glee.

Skyler flipped the camera so it was pointed toward Kit, who sat there with his arms high in the air and an expression of tranquility on his face. "This isn't normal, right?"

"You'd better be careful," Oliver warned. "The last time he got hypnotized, he tried to propose to the head cheerleader."

"Thankfully she didn't take him seriously," Ben said, rolling his eyes. "He's lucky he didn't get slapped."

Skyler didn't like the sound of that for so many reasons, one of them being that he'd called her a cheerleader yesterday morning; apparently he was a fan. She flipped the camera back. "Should I try to snap him out of it, or…?"

"That depends," Cam said.

"On what?"

"On if you want to see unfiltered Kit or not," Oliver replied. "Not many people get that privilege. If you get him up on that stage, he could give you all sorts of secrets."

Skyler was pretty sure she was already getting unfiltered Kit, but the temptation to see what he might do was a little too strong. If the situations had been reversed, Kit would probably keep her from embarrassing herself. But Skyler wasn't Kit.

"Yeah, I think I'm going to let this play out," she said, biting her lip to stop her grin from growing too big.

The Wonder Boys laughed again. "I like you," Oliver said.

Skyler hoped her blush wasn't very visible through the phone. She hadn't expected to react so strongly to a pronounce-ment like that, but she felt that praise all the way down to her toes. Kit's oldest friend liking her was like a strange stamp of approval she didn't know she needed.

"Okay, well, I'm going to hang up now so I can—"

"No!" Oliver said. "Let us watch!"

Skyler pursed her lips as she watched Kit get pulled up onto the stage by the hypnotist's assistant. She suddenly held a lot of power, and she was going to use it. "Tell you what. You guys help Ben pack up his things without damaging any more of his stuff, and I'll send you the video."

"Oh, I really like you," Oliver said with a laugh just before Skyler hung up and hurried back to her chair with no intention of recording anything.

The hypnotist had pulled five people up to the stage, all of them listening to him intently as he walked them through some sort of scenario involving a table full of their favorite foods.

"As you're getting ready to take some of your most favorite dish, someone you might not like very much, from your past life or now, comes up and takes all of it."

"Hey!" the older woman on stage shouted, while the teen next to her kicked the air and started crying. Kit immediately jumped to his feet, his expression murderous, and the other two simply looked defeated.

The audience burst into laughter, as the hypnotist moved into his next scenario, running from one thing to the next. Sometimes he focused on individuals, like when he convinced the teen that the others were her heroes and she should ask for their autographs, but most of the time he kept everything vague and innocent. Just enough to keep the audience entertained without embarrassing the "volunteers" too thoroughly. Skyler had to wonder if all of them were really that unaware of what they were doing, but she was pretty sure Kit wouldn't willingly act like a dog in front of a bunch of strangers. He must have really wanted to avoid his friends if he had let himself be hypnotized.

"Now," the hypnotist said, "imagine you've been away for a long time, and you're finally back where you want to be.

You see the person you've most wanted to see in the audience, and you're so excited to be reunited or meeting for the first time."

Most of the volunteers waved furiously, the middle-aged man even jumping up and down as he beamed at a woman in the audience who was laughing so hard she was crying. Kit didn't wave. He locked eyes with Skyler but didn't move.

"If you could tell that person anything, what would it be?"

Though the hypnotist held his microphone toward the teen so she could answer, Kit was suddenly on the move, leaping from the stage and walking with a purpose.

"Oh!" Skyler jumped to her feet but had nowhere to go, so she just stood there and waited to see what was about to happen.

Kit ignored the hypnotist's attempt to bring him back, brushing past a few people standing on the edges of the audience until he reached her row and started climbing over people. As he neared, his eyes locking on her mouth with an intensity that twisted her stomach, he asked, "Can I?"

Skyler nodded.

Kit grabbed her by the waist and pulled her close, capturing her mouth with his as the crowd cheered. But his kiss was…underwhelming. Skyler hated that she thought that, but after three days of buildup, she'd expected more from the man. Instead, he kept it gentle and quick, barely doing anything more than pressing his lips against hers.

Maybe they *should* have been practicing…

When he pulled away, he seemed unsteady, blinking several times and shaking his head a little as if snapping out of it on his own. Then he looked down at where his hands rested on her hips and jerked them back as if burned.

"What did I just do?"

Skyler tried not to sound completely glum. "You just kissed me."

Of all the faces Kit could have made, why did it have to be one of disgust? "I did what?" Then he cocked his head, licking his lips as if he knew exactly how mediocre it had been. "Are you sure?"

Skyler sighed. "Yep."

Kit glared at the hypnotist and seemed to debate doing something about the situation, but then he turned without a word and started walking away.

Skyler stood there for a second, dumbfounded, until she realized Kit wasn't coming back. "Wait. Kit!" Thankfully, the crowds were thick enough that she caught up to him quickly with some maneuvering, but even when she grabbed his arm, he kept on walking. "Kit, it's okay." Well, it wasn't really, but a terrible kiss was hardly enough reason to never speak to each other again.

"Nope," Kit growled. "And we don't have to talk about this. Ever."

"What is that supposed to mean?"

He was too strong for Skyler to pull him to a stop, but at least he didn't try to get away from her hold. "It means…nothing. Don't worry about it."

Oh, Skyler was worried, alright. She may not have been an expert in relationships, not by a longshot, but even she knew physical chemistry was an important aspect. They clearly got along as friends and could flirt until the cows came home, but what would happen if that physicality just wasn't there? That hadn't been a problem before now, but what if that lackluster kiss had ruined everything?

Skyler didn't want to think about that, but she knew they couldn't leave things unresolved.

"Kit, we should talk about this."

"I'd rather not."

As they approached the Ferris wheel, Skyler had an idea. Kit was still stomping forward, apparently with no destination in mind, and they *needed* to talk. So Skyler gripped his arm a little tighter, waited a few steps, and then shoved him as hard as she could toward the line for the wheel.

"What are you—"

"We need to get on," Skyler told the girl at the front of the line about to get on, pushing past her and forcing Kit into the seat.

Though the people in line complained, the operator didn't bat an eye, buckling them in before Kit could escape.

At least Kit didn't *try* to escape. That would have made this a lot more difficult. As the ride screeched to life and pulled them up just enough to let the next person on, he sulked in his seat, jaw clenched as he stared out over the bustling fairgrounds.

Skyler folded her arms. "Are you going to be a baby the rest of the day?"

He let out a single, humorless laugh, shaking his head. "Can we just drop it? Please?"

"No. Kit, you *kissed* me. And it was—"

He growled. "I don't need you to finish that sentence."

Skyler groaned. Why was he being so difficult? They could discuss this like adults and figure out what it meant for the future. As much as she hated the likely outcome, it would make the rest of the week so much easier if they were on the same page.

"Kit, it happened. We can't change that."

"I didn't want…" He shook his head.

"You didn't want to kiss me?"

"No."

Ouch. Maybe trapping them up here was a bad idea. So what, had the last three days of flirting and tension all been for show? Was everything about this man fake? He'd said just this morning that he was afraid he wouldn't want to stop kissing her if he started, but that clearly wasn't the case.

"No," Kit said again. "I mean… I didn't want it to happen like that."

"Like what?"

Kit squirmed, still looking everywhere but at her, like looking at her would only remind him of how terrible that kiss had been. Could he even remember it? Maybe he was just so disgusted by the idea in general that he didn't even want to think about it.

"Kit," she tried again. "We need to—"

He swore under his breath and pulled her in until their mouths collided.

OH.

As Kit's kiss engulfed her, everything became suddenly clear. This kiss was nothing like the last one. *Nothing.* This kiss was hungry. *Greedy.* Enough to make her melt through her seat and fall to her blissful death because nothing in the world could top this moment. Skyler fell into the embrace, holding onto Kit's arms for dear life as he tilted her head and dove deeper, drinking her in like he couldn't breathe without her. His hands wove into her hair, shocking her body with electricity starting at her scalp, and then they slid down her back with agonizing deliberation, like he was mapping out every inch of her. The man had *definitely* improved his technique over the years, and Skyler was two seconds away from getting lost in his kiss forever.

Not a bad way to go.

When his hands found her waist, his thumb brushing her bare stomach beneath her too-small shirt and sending a shiver through her that wasn't at all unpleasant, she pushed him back in an attempt to come back to reality.

She could barely get the words out as she said, "Maybe we should…"

"Yep," he agreed immediately, lifting his hands in the air and shifting back an inch. The distance did nothing to temper the desire in his eyes—he clearly hadn't had enough. His voice came out low and rough to match the burning in his gaze. "I did warn you. I've wanted to do that since seeing you in Mara-villa."

Skyler wasn't sure she would ever catch her breath after a kiss like that. So much for not having physical chemistry. Kissing Kit felt like drinking in sunshine and letting it fill her to the brim with light and happiness. She'd never felt so weightless. "Okay," she said.

"Okay?"

She laughed, grabbing his hand and loving the way he immediately curled his fingers around hers in a firm hold. "Don't look so worried, you dork. I mean okay, I totally get what you meant now. I want to slap that hypnotist for ruining our first kiss."

His smile returning, Kit leaned back in, but he only pressed his forehead to hers and closed his eyes. "Technically the hypnosis kiss was our second."

"I only care about the third. And maybe the fourth." Hooking her finger on the collar of his tie-dye shirt, she pulled him in again, loving how incredible he tasted. But there was more to it than that. She loved the way he took the lead, how he held her so gently, how without words he made her feel so wanted and valuable. Kit kissed the way he did everything else—without hesitation or reserve.

"How are the Boys?" he asked when he broke away again, probably to keep himself from going too deep into the kiss again. Though, his question didn't stop him from pressing gentle kisses along her jaw toward her ear.

Skyler laughed as another shiver ran through her at his touch. Oh, he was *so* good at this, and she wouldn't complain if he didn't stop. "They're fine. The girls have things handled."

"Good." His mouth found hers again, and though neither of them said it out loud, they both seemed in agreement that they would stay on the Ferris wheel as long as they could.

When they got back to the cabins that night, Houston cashed in on the ball toss bet, grabbing a paintball gun and lining himself up a few yards from Kit, who had stripped off his shirt as required.

"I don't understand men," Skyler sighed, though she couldn't complain about the view. Kit's skin was already mottled with bruises from yesterday's game, but he had willingly admitted his loss and didn't try to get out of his fate.

Micah giggled, throwing her arm around Skyler's waist. "Me neither, but I could watch them do this all day long."

Skyler scowled at her. "You're lucky I like you, or I'd make you go join him out there for your own punishment."

"Twist my arm. I'll happily get close to those abs any day."

Houston fired his one allotted pellet, which landed square on Kit's chest, right over his heart. And though Kit grunted and winced from the pain, he put his hand in the splattered paint and then pointed to Skyler with a purple finger, his smile as wide as ever.

TWENTY-THREE

Despite sleeping on a couch that wasn't quite long enough for him to fit, Kit slept better than he had in years. After Houston's paintball of triumph, he'd taken a shower, kissed Skyler goodnight for much too long but not nearly long enough, and then popped in a movie to give himself an excuse for falling asleep on the couch.

He couldn't be trusted to be in the same room as her after their Ferris wheel adventure.

He wasn't sure if he'd dreamed at all last night, but as he lay stretched out on the couch in the pre-morning light, he felt like the night had been full of Skyler. Not a bad way to spend a few hours. Yesterday had had a lot of bad and good, but even the bad had pulled him closer to Skyler and made him fall more and more in love with her. She'd filled him in on all the Wonder Boys' shenanigans, and when she told him what she'd said to them before hanging up, he'd nearly dropped down to one knee.

The only reason he'd held himself back was because Micah and Chad had been walking right behind them. Kit neither wanted them to find out the truth nor be witness to a moment he wanted to have all to himself.

Besides, it wasn't like he could *actually* propose to Skyler. They had only been a fake couple for three days and hadn't spoken a word about the future. Until he knew where they stood in her mind, he couldn't throw something like that out there. Not like Oliver and Cam had both done. Ben, at least, had had plenty of conversations with Allie about them getting married soon, so all he had to do was pop the question. Any day now…

Kit thought about texting Ben to make sure packing had gone well after Skyler's conversation, but he'd left his phone in the bedroom to charge. If he went in there and saw Skyler asleep in the mass of downy blankets, he would probably end up sliding in next to her and wishing he could wake up next to her for the rest of his life. He still wished that out here on the couch, but when he couldn't see her bedhead, he was less likely to try to do something about it and make a mess of things.

He had a feeling he was going to have to take things slow with Skyler, and that was not going to be easy.

Luckily, he only had to lie there and debate with himself for a few minutes before the door opened and the beautiful woman herself stepped out of the room.

She swept directly to the couch, leaning over the back of it and grabbing Kit's already waiting hand. "Good morning," she breathed.

"It most certainly is," Kit replied and pulled on her arm so forcefully that she tumbled over the back of the couch and landed sprawled on top of him, her hands splayed against his chest. "Better."

Skyler rewarded his clever manhandling by stuffing her hands into his hair and locking her mouth onto his in a kiss that left him dizzy.

After the hypnotizing debacle, which he still couldn't fully remember, Kit had been convinced that he'd blown his chances by giving Skyler the most pathetic kiss in the history of kisses. But trapped on that Ferris wheel, he'd pictured his life without Skyler in it—the same old boring Kit Morgan doing the same old boring stuff day after day. That future had terrified him, so he'd thrown caution to the wind and did his best to show her how he really wanted to kiss her.

Skyler had responded so easily and willingly that the Ferris wheel kiss had felt like they'd been doing that for years.

It felt the exact same way now. Like they were meant to be together.

"Gross."

Skyler pulled away and looked behind her, where Houston was standing with his eyebrows pulled low in disgust. "Not going to apologize," she said with a smirk. "We've been good all week."

"Somehow," Kit said, dropping his voice low and tucking some of her strawberry blonde hair behind her ear. He couldn't really put a word to the feeling in his chest right now as he wrapped one arm around Skyler and held her tight against him. He'd never been this affectionate with Angela—he'd never wanted to be—and she never would have lain on top of him like this, especially with someone else around. Only when her friend could see…

Kit should have known from the very beginning, when she told him that no one could know they were dating, that things were doomed to fail. He should have recognized that she was most physically affectionate when they spent time with her best friend, a man she swore up and down was just her friend even when Kit didn't ask.

He should have realized he had fallen in love with Skyler Montague when he was twelve years old and never fell back out.

"I thought I got lucky when Lloyd put me in the cabin with all the singles," Houston said, heading for the kitchen. "Last year I was next door to Vic and Georgia and—trust me— no one should share a wall with those two."

"That is not something I ever wanted to know," Skyler complained.

"If I had known I would be spending my precious vacation time watching you two make googly eyes at each other, I probably would have played this week's games instead of coming here. The Red-tails lost yesterday, by the way. That's on you."

Skyler scowled. "You're the one who left them without their *star pitcher.*"

Houston chuckled. "I am a star, yes. Thanks for noticing."

Now that someone else was definitely awake and in the shared space, Kit figured he should probably distance himself from Skyler before he really gave Houston something to complain about. Taking her by the shoulders, he pushed her upward and laughed when she grumbled something incoherent.

Once he'd sat up as well and put on his glasses, he threaded their fingers together to keep at least a little contact between them. "We should probably focus on Goal One today," he murmured. "We may have put a little too much emphasis on Three yesterday."

"But being a good fiancée does a really good job at helping with Goal Two. You want me to have fun, right? Besides, we were with my family for most of the day yesterday. I think One is covered." She spoke with a silkiness in her words that wasn't usually there so strongly, and Kit cursed her ability to completely unravel him with that voice of hers. He had always loved her voice, the way it slid over words in a lower timbre than most. Even when they were younger. Back then, it had given her a sense of maturity that fit the life she'd lived. Now, it basically turned his insides into a sticky mess of useless goo.

Kit was absolutely a goner. If things went south, he wouldn't be shattered like with Angela but completely obliterated.

Even if loving Skyler came with that risk, being here with her now made all of it worth it. He'd taken her for granted the last time, and he wasn't about to make that mistake again. However long he got to keep her, he would treasure that time.

"Did you guys hear what happened with the Wonder Twins yesterday?" Houston asked.

Kit's stomach dropped, and he spun to look at him. "What?"

Houston picked at a protein bar, pulling off a little piece and putting it in his mouth as he leaned on the kitchen counter. "Apparently, they disappeared for a while. Lloyd found them sharing a cotton candy by the petting zoo after a few hours of searching for them. Heidi was furious, obviously, and poor Stella was an absolute me…" He broke off when he met Skyler's eyes. "She felt bad."

Well, that was certainly a good way to ruin what had been a great start to the morning. "I should have talked to him," Kit moaned, sinking low into the couch. Instead, he'd been selfish and put his whole focus into Skyler. He *knew* something was off with Tanner, and they'd even made a plan to talk to the twins yesterday afternoon. Could they have avoided this if Kit had trusted his instinct like he usually did?

Maybe Skyler was right when she said being in the middle of Christopher and Kit was the way to go. He had gone full Christopher yesterday, and that had clearly been the wrong choice.

"We should talk to your mom," he said, rising to his feet. "Maybe the kids told her something."

Skyler nodded. "She's probably making breakfast."

They dressed quickly and hurried to the main cabin, Kit's anxiety for the twins rising. Tanner and Isabelle had already proven they weren't afraid to go at things alone, and eight-year-olds rarely saw the error of their ways when they were trying so hard to be big kids. Hopefully Lloyd hadn't been too hard on them.

"I'm sure they're fine." Skyler gripped his hand tightly as they walked down the dirt path. "This definitely isn't your fault, especially after the way Heidi treated you. You don't owe her—"

"I don't care about her. I care about those kids." He had never wanted anyone to feel like they were alone or had to do things on their own, and images of the young Wonder Boys flashed through his mind as they walked.

Five-year-old Oliver showing up for his first day of kindergarten in a suit and tie, not knowing how strange that was until everyone in the class started laughing at him. Kit hadn't had a suit back then, but he'd begged his mom to buy him one after school that day so Oliver wouldn't be alone.

Eleven-year-old Ben sitting in the corner of the yard every day at recess and eating lunch by himself because no one else seemed to notice he existed. It had only taken Kit a couple of days to see how lost and alone he felt, and Kit had asked him to come over to his house after school to help him with homework. Ben had quietly agreed, and Kit never once brought up schoolwork after that. Instead of doing homework, they talked for hours and played games with Oliver.

Thirteen-year-old Cam frustrated and hurt after his dad died in combat, leaving him with only his great-aunt for family. Kit hadn't known that at the time and stupidly thought the best way to help the angry kid was to try to convince him to go to class and focus on school. Cam had understandably lost his cool and punched Kit in the face. Their little fight in the school hallway had led to three weeks of detention, and Kit talked at Cam for days until Cam finally talked back and told him about his dad.

Twelve-year-old Madi, whose sweetness somehow convinced her classmates that she wasn't worth their time, sobbing in her closet because no one had come to her birthday party. Kit's heart had broken for her, and though he couldn't knock some sense into her classmates as much as he wanted to, he could share his three incredible friends who already acted like Madi was their little sister as much as his. He'd told the Boys to pretend they loved doing all the girly birthday things she had planned. They hadn't needed to pretend.

Every day in his classroom, Kit had seen kids go through highs and lows, and no matter what their life looked like outside of school, he had always done his best to make sure each of his students knew they had someone on their side.

Pausing at the back door of the first cabin, Skyler faced Kit and pressed her palm to his cheek. "I can see you overthinking this, Kit. That bleeding heart of yours is one of the things I love most about you, but you have to accept that there might not be anything you can do. Hopefully there is, but if there isn't, you have to be okay. I need you to be okay."

She needed him? Though his brain kept spinning, he leaned in and kissed her gently, thanking her for recognizing what he was feeling and being smart enough to know the reality of the situation. Tanner and Isabelle weren't his kids. They weren't his responsibility. But if there was a chance he could do some good in their lives, he was going to take it. He wished he had a way to tell her how grateful he was that she knew that about him. That she didn't see his desire to help as a flaw.

"I love you," he breathed.

And then he froze.

It wasn't that he didn't mean it, but it had just slipped out. Standing outside her mom and stepdad's cabin with an impending deep conversation looming over them. Of all the stupid times… He'd already ruined their second first kiss, and now this? Couldn't he have been smooth at least once?

Skyler hadn't moved, her green eyes wide as she blinked at him in the morning light. Her expression could have meant so many things: elation, pity, disgust, abject horror. Honestly, it could have been a mixture of all of those for how difficult she was to read right now.

And before either of them could say anything to break the building tension, the glass door slid open, Stella standing just inside. "Uh, good morning, sweetie. What are you doing up so early?"

Skyler spun around, setting her shoulders and standing tall in what Kit assumed was the pose she adopted while examining witnesses on the stand. "We came to help with breakfast."

Stella's graying eyebrows rose high as she led the way inside. "Really?"

"I cook all the time, Mom," Skyler grumbled.

"That isn't what I meant. You and Chris have steered clear of the kitchen since the potato salad incident."

Kit had practically forgotten about when they first arrived three days ago, and he couldn't help but snort a laugh at the memory of ending up covered head to toe in sticky sauce and soft potato. "I figured it would help my case to make a better impression," he said, glad that he'd gotten over his panic after that first day. Especially after this relationship with Skyler shifted into something more real yesterday, playing this role was less about acting and more about being himself. His *real* self. He hadn't had to hold anything back the last couple of days, and that had given him a chance to breathe.

"I don't want anyone thinking Sky made a bad choice," he told Stella with a grin.

Stella smiled at him warmly and then handed him a mixing bowl and a giant bag of pancake mix. "From what I've seen, you've been making all sorts of impressions this week. You seem to be a favorite around here, especially among the kids."

Perfect. He dumped a large portion of mix into the bowl, trying to appear casual. "I heard Tanner and Isabelle gave you a scare yesterday."

Stella sighed as she handed Skyler a bunch of eggs to crack open. "I don't know what they were thinking, but I can't say that I'm surprised. Tanner has been acting out more and more these days. Heidi isn't sure what to do with him, and she and Stephan are getting so busy with their careers. She's gone through three nannies in the last two months alone."

Well, that was likely part of the problem. Tanner didn't have anyone stable in his life. There was nothing wrong with working parents, but if the kids constantly felt like they were being handed from one person to the next, of course they would act out.

"Maybe I could talk to him?" Kit suggested. "We bonded the other day over tie dye."

"I already know half his problem," Skyler mumbled. She'd stopped cracking eggs as she listened, her eyes now hard and cold. "He feels like an inconvenience because his mom only cares about her own life."

Kit tensed.

Stella frowned. "How would you know—"

Skyler slammed her hands on the counter. "How do you think, Mom?" Then she turned and disappeared onto the front patio.

Kit was pretty sure he shouldn't get involved in this, but he could feel Stella's pleading stare. When he looked up and met her eyes, seeing nothing but confusion, he had to wonder if Stella even had a clue about the life she'd given her daughter.

"I'll go calm her down," he said, "but the two of you should talk about what things were like for her growing up." Then he hurried out after Skyler.

He found her pacing, her back so straight and shoulders so tight that she would be stiff and sore if she didn't relax soon. Though Kit planned to tell her the same thing he'd just told her mother, for now, he simply caught her as she walked and pulled her against him.

She melted into his arms like she'd been there a million times and knew exactly how well she fit. "I'm sorry," she said into his shoulder as her hands bunched up the fabric of his t-shirt.

"For what?"

"I doubt you expected this week to turn into an emotional mess. I should pay you extra for being my therapist."

Kit held her tighter, trying to tell her with his hold how much he would love to help her work through things for the rest of their lives. "Don't forget," he said instead of freaking her out, "you've been *my* therapist too. I don't think I could have told anyone about how much Angela affected me. Or how trapped I feel by my own life. Not even my actual therapist."

"What are you going to do when you get back?" Her voice was muffled against him, and she tilted her head up until her face pressed into his neck and made him shudder.

He made a non-committal sound in his throat. "I'm trying not to think about it, honestly. I still have a few days before I have to face my demons. But you…" He shifted and pressed a gentle kiss against her mouth, craving the taste of her. "You should talk to your mom."

Her lips hardened as she pulled away and glared at him. "What did you tell her?"

No matter how icy she tried to look, Kit could hardly see the jaded lawyer in her anymore. She had softened over the last few days, settling in with her family better than she probably knew.

"I didn't tell her anything," Kit assured her. "But you kind of did. And I think she would like to talk it out."

Groaning, Skyler pulled herself back into Kit's arms and held him tight, like she might not let go if he tried to get her to go back inside. "You know that thing I said about paying you extra? I take it back."

Kit had no intention of letting her pay him *at all*.

The patio door opened before either of them could say anything else, and Lloyd stepped out onto the deck. He studied the pair of them for a moment, his expression unreadable. They hadn't seen him much for the last day or two, and definitely not since Sam's accusation.

Kit held his breath. Just in case.

Lloyd grunted. "I was hoping you could help me with something this morning, Chris. A little project I have in the workshop."

Though he had no idea where this was going, Kit's stomach twisted in his gut. "Workshop?" Was that code for a place to go out and beat him up for lying to him?

"I hear you're into woodworking."

Kit's heart skipped a beat—or several—and he was pretty sure this man would never not be intimidating. "Where did you hear that?" he asked. Even if it was true, Skyler had only just discovered the fact yesterday. There was no way Lloyd or anyone else had overheard their two-second conversation about it.

Lloyd lifted an eyebrow, a hint of amusement in his mostly blank expression. "I think you know."

The blood drained from Kit's face, leaving him dizzy. *Oh no. Oh no no no.*

"What are you talking about?" Skyler asked, clearly sensing the panic rising in Kit's chest and threatening to trigger an Angela-worthy freakout. "Chris, what's—"

"He hasn't shown you his videos?" Lloyd asked with a smirk. "His talent is clear with the woodworking, if not with filmmaking, but I understand why he would want to keep it secret."

"I had a few months to kill," Kit tried to explain, though his voice wobbled to an embarrassing degree. He thought he'd drowned those videos. That they'd ended up buried so deep into the endless wasteland of the internet. All thirty views had been enough to convince him it was a terrible idea to keep going, and he hadn't looked back.

No one wanted to watch him struggle through basic woodworking skills while talking through each step and demonstrating what could—and usually did—go wrong.

Lloyd folded his arms, looking at Kit in a way that made him feel like he'd done something wrong and had just been sent to the principal. "Making a fool of yourself and calling it education is a risky endeavor. Though, you are surprisingly popular for having so little content..."

He was surprisingly *what*?

Fumbling for his phone, Kit pulled up the app where he'd uploaded the videos three years ago, though it took him six tries to remember his password. When he made it into his account, his most recent video stared up at him, fifty thousand views hitting him straight between the eyes.

TWENTY-FOUR

THERE WAS SOMETHING ENDEARING about the way Kit looked back at her as he followed Lloyd through the house and to the large building south of the cabin that Skyler had always thought was a shed. Apparently, it was some sort of workshop, and Lloyd had decided it was time to have some one-on-one bonding time with his future step-son-in-law. If the expression on Kit's face was any indication, he thought he was a lamb being led to slaughter.

"What project is Lloyd working on?" Skyler asked her mom once the men had gone through the back door.

Mom seemed reluctant to answer, but maybe that was because Kit was pushing them together. No matter what he'd said, Skyler was sure Kit had told his mom *something*. This teary, guilty expression wasn't a normal one for Mom.

"Uh, he won't tell me," she said eventually, brushing a bit of flour from the granite countertop. "He says it's a surprise."

"But he's actually working on something?"

"Why wouldn't—Skyler, just what do you think Lloyd would do to your fiancé?"

Skyler shrugged. "You tell me. I hardly know the man."

"Whose fault is that?"

Oh, so they were going there already? Skyler figured there was no point in beating around the bush, especially when she knew Kit wouldn't let her get out of having this conversation at some point this week. "Oh, I don't know," she said setting her frustration loose. "Why should I bother getting to know any of them when you're just going to get a new one soon?"

Mom gasped. "Skyler Lilith Montague! How dare—"

"What do you expect from me, Mom? It's not like I'm lying about how many men you've cycled through!"

"That's not fair."

"You know what's not fair?" Skyler folded her arms, trying to protect herself from the decades of pain and insecurity that seemed to be trying to swallow her whole. It wasn't working, and she was feeling everything. "What isn't fair is never having any friends. Never knowing if I was going to have a place to live when I got home from school. Watching my mother get her heart broken over and over and believing for my entire life that love was nothing but a fairy tale."

She was full-on crying now, something she'd rarely allowed before this week. What had Kit done to her? "What isn't fair is knowing that out that door is the most amazing guy I've ever known, but I don't know if I'm capable of loving him like he deserves because I don't know if I'm capable of love at all."

Next thing she knew, Mom's arms were around her in the sort of hug they'd never shared before. Skyler fell apart, wrapping her arms around Mom's back and crushing her but not caring. The two of them didn't fit well, and the hug wasn't nearly as comfortable as being in Kit's arms, but Skyler couldn't move. She didn't *want* to move.

"I'm so sorry," Mom whispered as she stroked Skyler's hair. She was crying too, her voice weak and full of emotion. "I was a mess. But I thought you were doing okay. I thought you were stronger than me. You always seemed so strong."

"A kid shouldn't have to be strong, Mom."

"I know. And I'm sorry. I'm so, so sorry. It took me a long time to realize how dangerous my life was, and I never should have dragged you with me."

They stood there in the kitchen for a few seconds longer before Skyler pulled away, feeling awkward but stronger somehow. Before Kit, she hadn't exactly been an affectionate person, and never with her mom. But though Mom was still crying, she seemed to stand a little lighter. Less worry in her shoulders.

Even Skyler felt better, and she silently cursed Kit for being right. They'd needed to talk, even if the conversation had been short and mostly one-sided. Maybe Skyler just needed to admit her hurts to feel better. Kit had probably known that.

Neither of them said a word as they made a batch of blueberry muffins and a tray full of pancakes and scrambled eggs. It was enough to be in the same space and learn to be around each other for more than five minutes, which hadn't happened in years. Mom seemed too overwhelmed with joy and relief to find any words, and Skyler couldn't stop thinking about what Kit and Lloyd were doing. But being with her mom was good for her.

When the muffins were done, Skyler grabbed a couple and wrapped them in a towel. "I'm going to take these out to Chris," she said, her voice coming out crackly after not using it for close to an hour. "He's probably starving, and he doesn't do well on an empty stomach."

"Skyler?" When Skyler paused at the door, Mom seemed to debate saying what she wanted to say, her eyebrows pulled low. "If the way you look at that boy means anything, you are more than capable of loving someone. You just need to trust your heart. I know I'm not the best example, but when I met Lloyd, I realized what true love was supposed to feel like. I know you feel that too."

As more tears welled up in Skyler's eyes, she hurried outside and gulped several breaths of fresh air before she fell apart again. She could really use a Kit hug right now, but not because she was sad and needed comfort. She needed to *thank* him, and kiss him, and maybe tell him she was in love with him because Mom was right and he deserved to know how she felt.

Especially because he had already told her how *he* felt, so there wasn't even the risk of finding out things were one-sided. She really should have responded to him earlier instead of gaping at him like a fish.

As she approached the open doors of the workshop, a shiver running through her, she found Micah, Brooklyn, and Georgia all standing at the edge of the opening and peering in. "What's going—"

"Shh!" Micah grabbed her arm and pulled her close, nearly making her drop the muffins. "Don't scare the wildlife."

What did she mean by "wildlife"? All Skyler could see was Kit, who…

She froze as soon as she caught sight of her fake fiancé dragging a fancy tool across a plank of wood with so much concentration that the tip of his tongue stuck out between his lips. Sexy as that was, his arms pulled her attention downward, muscles flexing every time he shaved a length of wood from the plank. He glistened with a sheen of sweat that had started to soak into his t-shirt collar, but it was the look on his face that had Skyler fully captivated.

She had never seen him this relaxed or content, and that was saying something. This moment topped even the couch this morning, like he had let go of everything else in his life and focused only on the task at hand.

A task he apparently still loved.

In sixth grade, they'd had to take a class that taught basic home skills. The first quarter had focused on cooking and sewing, and the second had been in the shop, learning how to use all sorts of different tools. Skyler had thought it was crazy to trust twelve-year-olds with power tools, and she had tried to get out of doing any of the projects. But Kit had fallen in love with woodworking on day one. She'd thought he'd given it up until yesterday when he mentioned making Ben a coffee table.

She still wasn't sure what videos Lloyd was talking about, but as she watched Kit bend down and run his hand along the wood like he was seeing if he needed to keep shaving, she knew she would have to find them and watch them.

If Kit Morgan belonged anywhere, it was a place like this.

When Kit hefted the piece of wood over his head, t-shirt lifting up with his toned arms and revealing a couple inches of straining abs, Skyler dropped the muffins. One of them rolled into the shop like this was a movie and bounced against Kit's foot, and he glanced down. Then looked over.

All four ladies waved, Skyler's a little weaker than the others.

Though Kit turned a healthy shade of red, he set the plank on the table where Lloyd was running a sander (and apparently oblivious to everything happening around him). As he brushed off his hands on his sawdust-covered jeans, he stalked toward Skyler with a ridiculously attractive determination.

Feeling self-conscious, Skyler picked up the other muffin, which had landed safe inside the towel, and held it out to him. "I brought you some breakf—"

Kit claimed her mouth before she could finish her sentence, kissing her like it hadn't been only an hour since they'd stood on the front patio. Like he hadn't been able to breathe without her. The ladies cheered, and Skyler pulled away as heat filled her body in a mixture of embarrassment and her reaction to Kit. She could barely stand straight and had to grip his arm to keep herself upright.

"What was that for?" she whispered breathlessly.

His grin stole any air she had left in her lungs. "Because I love…breakfast." That hesitation was slight, but definitely there. Was it because she hadn't responded to him earlier? She'd wanted to—she'd wanted to since the Ferris wheel—but she'd meant what she said to her mom.

What if she wasn't actually capable of loving him like he deserved?

Skyler swallowed, feeling like she might choke as she whispered, "I love…breakfast too."

Kit's eyes practically glowed as he tucked some hair behind her ear, like he'd been waiting to hear those words for years. Did he hear what she really wanted to say, or was he just so happy that she loved anything at all?

Glancing back at Lloyd, who now seemed to be a little *too* focused on his sanding, Kit grabbed Skyler's hands and tugged her around the side of the workshop to the hoots and hollers of the ladies who had been enjoying the show a little too long.

The moment they were out of sight, he pressed her up against the side of the building and dove right back into the kiss with so much enthusiasm that Skyler lost all ability to think straight. All she could do was grab hold of anything she could—his hair, his shirt, his hand—and hold on for dear life. Kit Morgan never did anything by half, and as his mouth guided, directed, explored with unrestrained urgency, he seemed to be showing her every little corner of his heart without hesitation.

Telling her it belonged to her now.

He pulled away too soon but not soon enough, leaving Skyler a puddle where she stood, and he retreated several steps as he fought to catch his breath.

Skyler wasn't sure she would ever breathe again. "Wow," she gasped, touching her swollen lips. "Where… What… Why…?"

Kit grinned, shaking his head. "You are intoxicating, Skyler Montague."

"Tell that to all the men who said I was too intense for them." She wasn't sure why that was her response. Maybe she just needed something to ground herself before her head got lost in the clouds.

Though he didn't move any closer, Kit's gaze smoldered. "Their loss. And they didn't know you like I do."

If he kept looking at her like that, Skyler was going to jump him and kiss him senseless. She needed a distraction. "I talked to my mom."

He softened. "And?"

"And I think we'll be okay. Eventually."

"What about you? Are *you* okay?"

She shook her head but smiled to let him know what she meant. "After a kiss like that? Of course not."

He growled a little, stuffing his hands into his pockets. "You are the worst sort of distraction. Lloyd and I were bonding."

"Do I want to know what that means?"

He laughed, one foot stepping toward her though he didn't seem to realize it. "Lloyd is building Stella a rocking chair, but he was having a hard time with the legs." Another step. "I showed him a few techniques, and we got to talking."

Skyler felt each step from her head to her toe, craving his nearness. But she also knew that if they burned too hot too fast, they could fizzle out before they'd even figured out what this relationship of theirs was going to look like. As much as she wanted to make out with him all day long, they needed to pace themselves.

"What are these videos Lloyd mentioned?"

That got him to stop approaching, his face twisting in a grimace. "I was secretly hoping you would get so distracted by my kisses that you would forget."

Was it truly that embarrassing? "Absolutely not. You can show me yourself, or I'll go grab my phone from the bathroom drawer and look them up myself."

He lifted one eyebrow, looking way too attractive as always. Was it strange to be attracted to an eyebrow? Skyler couldn't lift just one, but Kit did it with finesse. "You know where your phone is?" he asked.

She shrugged. It still felt strange to not care about whatever messages and emails she might have gotten, but Kit was an easy replacement. "Are you going to show me or not? I need something to watch while I eat breakfast."

He winced. "You're going to watch with everyone else around?"

She had been joking, but now she would absolutely have to show as many people as she could. Lloyd already knew about the videos somehow, and it would be a good idea to add some flaws before Kit became perfect in too many minds. Her family liked him a little too much. With how embarrassed he already was without anyone even seeing them, these videos would be perfect.

If nothing else, they would get Skyler one step closer to unlocking the full Kit Morgan. If she could unmask him entirely, maybe he would still be happy when he went back to his regular life.

TWENTY-FIVE

Skyler watching Kit's embarrassing instructional videos had been bad enough, but by the time breakfast was over, she had an entire crowd of people watching with her. Someone unearthed a mini projector they could hook a phone up to, and breakfast turned into a watch party against the side of the cabin with an unhealthy amount of laughter.

Kit sat himself in the corner and refused to move, and thankfully everyone was too busy watching him attempt a dovetail joint for the first time to bother him in the present. He could just sit there and hopefully die from embarrassment.

Somehow, this was way worse than kissing Skyler like he'd never survive if he didn't. Right. In front. Of Lloyd.

Apparently, he was so head over heels at this point that he completely forgot anyone else was around as soon as he saw her. It was almost Lloyd's fault. He'd pulled the classic dad move and asked Kit if he was taking care of Skyler properly, all while holding a nail gun like a shotgun. He may not have been an affectionate man, but he clearly cared about Skyler. So they'd had the whole talk—the one he'd never had with Angela's dad because he'd never *met* Angela's dad—and Kit had basically asked permission to marry Skyler.

Not that she needed anyone to give permission. But on the off-chance Kit wasn't the only one who felt their connection so strongly, he wanted to be prepared.

After Lloyd said he fully approved of their engagement and was glad to see Skyler so happy, Kit had been on cloud nine. So when he'd seen her in the doorway, he couldn't help but want to bring her up there with him.

Typical that he would panic and tell her he loved *breakfast*, when really he wanted to tell her he would spend the rest of his life with her if she let him. But Skyler said she loved breakfast too, and maybe he was reading way too into things because he was a hopeless fool, but she seemed to know he hadn't meant to say breakfast.

He'd meant what he said on the back porch before her mom found them, and he was eager to say it again. Just not with other people around.

The family burst into laughter, jarring Kit out of fantasies of a future with Skyler Montague. They'd started his first video over from the beginning, which was the worst out of all of them. He'd begun the video trying to be all serious, talking about the rules of safety when it came to woodworking, and then he'd nearly shot himself in the foot with a nail gun because he was so nervous about talking to a camera. He'd only kept that part in because he didn't know how to edit it out at the time.

"Why are they laughing at you?"

Kit turned so quickly that Tanner jumped back in fear. "Oh! Sorry! I didn't know you were there." Just how long had the kid been standing next to his chair watching him?

Tanner ducked his head. "I'm sorry."

"No, it's okay. I must have been thinking really hard and not paying attention." The family laughed again, but Kit didn't take his eyes off of Tanner. This might be his only chance to have an actual conversation with him; his parents were nowhere in sight. "They're laughing because I did something silly in the video."

Tanner's head dropped even farther, his shoulders sinking with it. He looked completely defeated. "I'm sorry they're being mean to you too."

Too? "Has someone in your family been laughing at you?"

Tanner shrugged. "No. Not really."

"Someone at school?" When Tanner didn't answer, Kit slid from his chair and knelt in front of him. "You can tell me anything you want to, Tanner," he said gently. "It's okay. But if you don't want to tell me anything, that's okay too. Is someone being mean to you at school?"

Tanner's little body started shaking just before the tears came. Then he threw his arms around Kit's neck and pulled himself in. "Mitchell and his friends make fun of Isabelle," he whimpered, though his tears made him difficult to understand. "They call her a baby because she sometimes cries when she's excited. I asked them to stop but they didn't stop so I punched Mitchell and then I got in trouble and he didn't and now Isabelle doesn't smile or laugh because she's worried that someone will..." The rest of his words disappeared into his sobs.

Kit held the boy gently, using only enough pressure to let him know he was there. Clearly Tanner had been bottling up his frustration for a long time for him to break down like this; Kit suspected Tanner generally kept his emotions close to the vest. But this was the sort of thing his parents should be handling. They should have seen how hard school had been for both their children. They should have noticed their daughter smiling less.

Yes, Kit had wanted to find out what was bothering Tanner, but he didn't want to be the one to fix it. He couldn't be the one Tanner turned to for help and comfort when after this week there was no guarantee they would ever see each other again. He needed someone he could rely on, and that couldn't be Kit.

Swallowing, Kit rubbed his hand up and down Tanner's back. "You're a good brother," he said, hoping he could word things right. "Isabelle is lucky to have you looking after her. But you know fighting isn't a good way to solve problems, right?"

Tanner sniffled. "I didn't want to. But I got so angry."

"Everyone gets angry sometimes. I would be angry with those boys too if they were mean to my sister."

"What do I do? We go back to school in two weeks and they're going to laugh at her again. She doesn't want to play violin anymore because they said she sounded like a dying penguin when she plays."

That was an oddly specific insult, though Kit tamped down the laugh that threatened to break free. "Does Isabelle like playing the violin?"

"Yeah. It's her favorite thing. But she's not very good."

"That's because it takes a lot of practice to get good at something. She shouldn't let anything stop her from doing what she loves just because she's still learning." Pulling away, Kit nudged Tanner to look at the projector screen. "I'm not very good at making videos, but you know what?"

Tanner sniffed. "What?"

"I had so much fun making them. Being silly is one of my favorite things to do, even though it means people laugh at me."

"But it doesn't feel good when people laugh at you," Tanner said with a deep frown. "Isabelle cries at night all the time because of it."

Kit's heart broke for these two kids who dealt with so much on their own. "No, it doesn't. But you know what? Other people's opinions don't matter. I know it's hard not to care what people think of you, and I still get embarrassed sometimes." He also lived his entire life based on other people's expectations, but that was not something he wanted to unpack right now. One problem at a time. "But at the end of the day, the only person who can tell me who to be is me." Or maybe he was going to dive right into self-therapy…

Why had he let the people in his life unknowingly decide who he was for so long? He couldn't control whether they were disappointed, and trying so hard had left him pretty miserable.

Tanner considered Kit's advice, his little face scrunching up as he thought about it. "Is that why you act so much like a kid all the time?"

Kit snorted a laugh as he sat back on his heels. "Exactly. I'm a lot happier when I'm not acting like a boring adult."

"And that's why Aunt Skyler wants to marry you." That part wasn't a question; Tanner said it with a nod and no trace of hesitation.

Kit grinned. "I hope so."

"So…" Tanner looked at the video right as recorded Kit accidentally sawed his bench in half and the family roared with laughter at the way video Kit just stood there, staring at the two pieces of wood in utter bewilderment. "So it's okay if people laugh at Isabelle when she's happy, because she's happy and that's the part that matters."

"Exactly."

"And I can play drums instead of piano because that makes *me* happy."

Kit winced. "Well, that one you might need to ask your parents about. Drums can be really loud. But if that's what makes you happy, then you should do that. Even if it's not until you're a grownup and can buy your own drums."

Tanner accepted that with an easy nod. "And I shouldn't fight people when they make me mad."

"You can just ignore them, and they'll probably stop being mean," Kit offered. "But if not, you can talk to your teacher. And you should tell your mom and dad what you told me."

His face twisted into a mixture of disgust and fear. "They won't listen. They don't care."

That was what Kit had been afraid of. Still… "I promise they do care. And I hope they listen. But if they don't, you have a whole bunch of family who would love to help you. You're never alone, Tanner."

Next thing he knew, Tanner was back to hugging him with a fierceness that made Kit's heart swell to bursting. "Thanks, Uncle Chris. I'm glad you're going to be part of my family."

And Kit's heart did burst because he had no idea if he would get to stay. If Skyler would love him long enough for him to prove they were meant to be together. If this week was going to turn out to be a bubble and their real lives would ruin everything when the bubble popped.

Across the patio, he made eye contact with Skyler as she glanced over at him while Tanner still held him tightly. Though she smiled, she must have caught his worry because it mirrored in her own face.

Maybe it was time they really sat down and talked about what was going to happen in a few days, when all of this was nothing more than a memory.

TWENTY-SIX

Despite being fully engrossed in Kit's videos, which were both hilarious and genuinely informational, Skyler knew the moment Kit looked at her from his seat of shame, like they were connected by an invisible string or a Wi-Fi connection.

But when she turned to meet his eyes, she found him on the floor with his arms wrapped around Tanner and an intense look in his eyes that sent her heart thumping in her chest. Not only was the sight of him holding the kid the most adorable thing she'd ever seen, but he seemed to be telling her so much with that look. Like he wanted her to know how important she was. It filled her to the brim, to the point where she couldn't keep it to herself anymore.

"Micah." She grabbed Micah's hand and pulled her off her chair, dragging her to an empty corner of the patio. "I'm in trouble."

Micah's eyes went wide. "What kind of trouble?"

"I'm in love with my fiancé."

As her tension dissipated quickly, Micah snickered. "I should hope so."

"No, you don't understand." Skyler grabbed her by the shoulders, hoping she wasn't about to make a huge mistake. "He's not really my fiancé. There never was a fiancé."

"Are you trying to tell me Chris isn't real? Because he's sitting right there, looking mega hot with that child in his arms."

Skyler groaned, forcing herself to keep her eyes away from Kit. He did look mega hot holding Tanner, and that was more terrifying than admitting the truth to someone who could easily turn around and tell her dad. "No, Chris is very real. But I didn't even know he lived in Diamond Springs until last week. He's…" Better to let it all out quickly. "I hired him to be my fake fiancé for the week because Lloyd doesn't think I can run my own business so I made up a fiancé and have been pretending to be engaged so he'll keep paying the mortgage."

Micah blinked. "What?"

"He's not real, Mic. I…hired him. To be my fiancé for the reunion."

It still hadn't sunk in, apparently, and Micah glanced between the two of them with the look of someone who couldn't make the math add up. The longer she thought, the more her eyebrows pulled downward. "But this morning… you guys kissed like…"

Heat flamed in Skyler's cheeks at the same time fear filtered into her chest and left her feeling shaky. Micah wasn't taking this well. "That was new. Like, *yesterday* new. Like I said, I think I've fallen for him, and it's not hard to see why. And I know how bad this looks and that I've been manipulating your dad, but—"

"Whoa, calm down," Micah said with a little laugh. She grabbed Skyler's hand and gave it a squeeze. "I know how my dad can be a pain in the butt sometimes, so I get it. What I *don't* get is how it took you this long to admit how you feel about that piece of man candy. Fake fiancé or not, pretty sure you've been making goo goo eyes at him from the minute you guys got here. I mean, look at him!"

She waved her arm in Kit's direction only to yelp because he was only a few feet away.

Skyler's stomach did a flip at the sight of him so close. "Hi," she breathed.

Kit's delicious pink lips twisted into a smirk. "Hi yourself. Want to go for a walk?"

"Yes."

"We'll miss the—"

"I don't care." Tugging herself free of Micah's hold, Skyler looped her arm through Kit's and pulled in close. She would take a walk with him over a water balloon fight any day. "Maybe we can practice some more while we're out."

Micah made a little squeaking noise, like she'd just discovered something. "Wait, with this whole thing being fake, when you say practice, have you guys been talking about—"

"Don't worry about it," Skyler growled and guided Kit to the stairs, her face on fire.

He waited until they were a good distance from the cabin before he said, "You told her the truth?"

Skyler appreciated his way of keeping his voice calm and casual. Maybe he was worried, angry, or relieved, but he didn't let any of that show. The fact couldn't be changed, anyway, which he probably realized. "I couldn't keep it in anymore," she said with a shrug.

"Are you prepared to deal if she tells Lloyd?"

No, she definitely wasn't, but she'd gotten good at acting on the fly. Sometimes while examining a witness she had to completely change her line of questioning halfway through. "Are you?"

"I'm not the one who spilled the beans!" he complained.

"But I thought you and Lloyd were besties now."

For some reason, that comment made his ears turn red, though he tried to hide it by picking up a stick and examining it as they walked along the dirt road. "I wouldn't call us besties. I wouldn't call *anyone* my bestie. I really need to stop saying the word *bestie* if I don't want to lose my man card."

Skyler snickered, grabbing his hand to make sure he didn't try to run away from the conversation. "How did Lloyd find out about your videos, anyway?"

"I have no idea. I thought they were buried so deep they'd never see the light of day again."

"Clearly not." While everyone watched, Skyler had read through the comments on Kit's phone, growing more and more impressed with every one. Sure, there were the trolls calling Kit an idiot or telling him that he was doing certain techniques wrong, but most of the feedback was positive. (Including the dozens of remarks about how ridiculously attractive Kit was, but Skyler had mostly ignored those.) "Kit, have you looked at any of the comments?"

He shook his head, his eyes fixed straight ahead. "The last time I looked at those videos, I only had a few views. I think the one comment I got was a spam bot giving me a link to find hot girls."

"Did you click it?"

"Of course. Had a great time."

Skyler gave him a little shove, glad when he laughed and loosened up a bit. "You really should go back and read the comments. People started watching a few months ago, and everyone keeps talking about how helpful you are and how nice it is to learn alongside someone who isn't afraid to fail."

Kit seemed to lose his voice, his eyebrows furrowed as they walked. It was like he had no idea he could ever influence another person, even though that was all he had ever done in his life. Even back in middle school, Kit Morgan had been the guy everyone was drawn to. The one who noticed things about people that no one else did. Who made sure no one felt forgotten or stupid when they didn't know something.

He was probably a great third grade teacher, but he would be so great at so many other things too.

"People are asking when you're going to release another video," she said, raising her eyebrows.

Kit's eyes widened, like he was panicking at the idea. "Another? It's been three years! I started making them a few months after Angela to keep myself from wallowing. But no one watched them."

"I told you. You got rediscovered just a few months ago."

"Yeah, but I'm lucky if I get into a woodshop once a month. I barely did anything last summer because I was too busy keeping Oliver sane while he waited for his wedding day to come. I don't even remember how to—"

"That's the whole point of your channel, isn't it? To learn as you go?"

Sighing, Kit shook his head. "Maybe. But I have too many other things on my mind to focus on something like that right now."

"Like what? You don't have a job."

"Thanks for the reminder. There's that, which I need to figure out, and Madi's baby. And Ben's moving, so he'll need help, and Cam's wedding is coming up, and then there's you."

Skyler's stomach did a little flip. Were they about to have a future talk? She didn't know if she was ready for that, even if she desperately wanted a future with Kit. She'd lost him once before, and she wasn't sure she could do that again. "What about me?"

His grip on her hand grew stronger, like now he was the one keeping *her* from running away. "There's a lot for us to figure out too."

"I like the sound of that. *Us.*"

"I was hoping you would say that." He smiled, leaning in closer. "What would you say to meeting the Wonder Boys when we get back?"

Skyler snickered, partly because he said it like he was asking her to meet his parents—the Wonder Boys were probably just as important—and partly because she felt like she already knew the Boys. "I met them yesterday, Kit. They love me."

He groaned, coming to a stop and searching the forest as if hoping to find something important within the trees. "They love you *now*. But that could easily change when they find out what you've done to me."

"What exactly have I done to you?"

He closed his eyes, wrapping his arm around her waist and pulling her in. "Everything. You've made me feel whole. But I'm not sure the Boys will see it that way. They've always seen me a certain way. You've changed me so much…"

Shivering, Skyler leaned deeper into his hold. Yes, the air had cooled around them with a stiff breeze, but the way he talked about her effect on him had her thinking their future would be easier to find than she'd thought. "You haven't changed, Kit. You're just not hiding anymore. You really think they won't like this version of you over the old Kit?"

He squirmed. "You've never disappointed someone like Ben. Or Madi. All of my friends rely on the old Kit and his pre-dictability."

"Do they?" Skyler knew this was a big thing for him, but maybe he was looking at things all wrong. "Because I've had your phone all morning, and you haven't gotten a single text since yesterday afternoon. Do they know about your videos?"

"They don't even know I do woodworking," Kit replied with a grimace.

There was no way. "How do they not know?"

"Because I haven't told them."

"Why?"

"Why do you think?"

"Kit." Skyler grabbed his face, forcing him to look at her. "You said in one of your videos you've been doing this for eight years. If I had any friends, and one of them told me he'd been doing something like this for more than a quarter of his life and never told me, I would be furious."

"Exact—"

"You're not listening to me. I wouldn't be mad because he deviated from what I knew about him. I would be mad because he didn't trust me to celebrate his accomplishments and accept that it is a part of him. I may not know the Wonder Boys very well yet, but I know you. And I know you have probably done so much for those men. You have given them a place to belong and be themselves. Do you really think they wouldn't do the exact same thing for you?"

"I love you."

Skyler's heart stopped beating for a moment.

He cocked his head to the side, his expression pretty calm for someone who had just said three important little words again after she hadn't responded before. "Is that weird? You didn't say anything last time, so I'm worried it's weird."

Skyler knew Kit too well to think he asked that question because he was hesitant about his feelings. He said it because he meant it, and his follow-up question had been a way for her to tell him if it was too much. Not to downplay what he'd said.

She loved him all the more for it. "Only if it's weird that I'm in love with you right back," she said with a little shrug, though internally a volcano had exploded, leaving her insides screaming and running for their lives.

Skyler Montague didn't love. She didn't dream. She didn't let herself hope for a future with anyone, because the only person she had ever been able to rely on was herself. Admitting that she actually felt something of any kind was like admitting she wasn't the same person she'd been a week ago.

In all honesty, she wasn't sure she was. Kit had a way of bringing out the best in people and changing them for the better.

Kit's smile stretched so wide that it shone brighter than the sun, which had disappeared behind a layer of clouds at some point. No wonder it had gotten cooler. "You love me," he repeated.

"Probably more than you love me," Skyler said. Why were they just standing there? She threw her arms around his neck, closing her eyes when he pulled her in tight and imagining herself staying there forever.

"That's not possible," he said before pressing a kiss to her forehead. "I've loved you for the last seventeen years." He kissed the tip of her nose.

"Oh really?"

He kissed her jaw, trailing kisses along her skin as he spoke. "Yep. I told you. Twelve-year-olds can totally fall in love. I love your fearlessness. Your ambition. The way you refuse to let me hide because you're the only one who knows every part of me."

"Will you just kiss me already?"

He obliged, starting off slow and gentle, like he wanted to savor the moment. As much as she knew they should take their time, Skyler had never told anyone she loved them before. This felt like a big deal, and that required a big deal kiss.

"Kiss me, you dummy," she demanded.

"Are you always this bossy?" But he directed her toward a nearby tree and lifted her up, tucking her legs around his waist and using the tree to help hold her weight. Once he had her situated, he bent his head and stole her lips for his own. And oh, did he kiss her. He turned the dial to eleven, a man on a mission as he explored and tasted and took charge in true Kit fashion.

Skyler turned to putty in his arms, thoroughly enjoying his expertise. If she had known kissing him would be like this, she would have thrown all caution to the wind and kissed him that first night they were here. Though tempted to let him do his searching unhindered, she turned the tables, sliding her fingers into his soft hair as she took over and led the way, feeling all too pleased when Kit dutifully followed directions and let her take command.

When the first raindrop hit her head, she moaned and glared up at the sky.

"It's just rain," Kit said before diving back in, but he paused when thunder rumbled in the distance.

Skyler dropped her head back against the tree. "You had to go and open your big mouth."

Kit smirked. "I was under the impression you liked my mouth."

"Okay, no need to get a big head too." She smacked him lightly on the arm and then slid back to her feet, her legs a bit shaky after that whirlwind of a kiss. Was it always going to get better every time? Because Skyler wasn't sure how they could top that, but the evidence pointed to her never recovering the next time this beautiful man kissed her.

Kit took his glasses back—at some point they had ended up in Skyler's hand—and led the way back down the road as the rain started to fall a little harder. "I was never like that with Angela," he said quietly, the air around them shifting with his mood. "I never felt like I *could* be. She was always the one to initiate anything physical, and I couldn't…" He lifted their laced fingers and kissed her knuckles. "Thank you. For setting me free. For letting me breathe again. I haven't felt like I…"

Skyler wrapped her other hand around his arm and leaned into him. She ached for the years he had lost because he didn't feel like he could be his full self. For the happiness he'd denied himself for the sake of others. How had anyone made him feel like he had to keep anything about himself locked up and hidden?

"Will you tell me more about her?"

Glancing over, Kit pulled his eyebrows low. "Are you sure?"

No, but it would help to know how deeply she had hurt him. "I want to understand what she did to you so I never do the same thing." Skyler hated that she sounded so small.

He pressed a kiss to her forehead. "You could never." Then he sighed. "She worked for the school district. She came around one day to discuss state testing, and we got to talking."

Skyler faked a gasp. "Kit Morgan hit it off with a woman? No way!"

He chuckled, and then he pulled her beneath a thick pine tree to get out of the rain. "Maybe it'll let up in a minute," he explained, glancing up at the gray sky. The thunder hadn't returned, but the rain came down thicker than ever.

Skyler didn't care about the reasoning. She just wanted him to keep talking. "When did you start dating?"

Shrugging, he leaned against the trunk and kept his eyes on his feet while he spoke. "She mentioned something about being new to the neighborhood and not knowing anyone, and on paper she seemed perfect for me. I thought… No one would find it out of the ordinary for me to date someone like her, so I thought it would be easier to ease my friends into the idea of me dating someone after I'd gone so long on my own."

"Why didn't you date anyone before that?" Skyler asked, even if she hated the idea of anyone else kissing this man. She had no right to be jealous when she hadn't been in his life the last seventeen years.

Kit glanced up, clenching his jaw. "I dated. But rarely more than one or two dates with anyone. If I'd gone beyond that, Oliver would have turned it into a big deal and probably accidentally scared her off with his enthusiasm. Or Cam might have thought I was leaving him behind like everyone else had."

"But what about *you*?"

He shook his head. "I've been stuck in the same life for so long that sometimes *I* even thought I was okay being on my own."

Squeezing his hand, Skyler yet again wished she'd been able to stay in this man's life longer than she had. What might have been different—for both of them—if they had had each other? She would have helped him realize he could never disappoint anyone by being his full, authentic self, and he probably would have convinced her to start the bookstore so much sooner because she would have had someone to cheer her on.

"So," she said, silently mourning the life they could have had together the last two decades, "what was different with Angela?"

Kit took a slow breath, holding it in his lungs for a moment. He looked like he absolutely didn't want to keep talking, but Skyler knew he would tell her anyway. "Things were comfortable with Angela because she fit right in with the Kit I became over the years. Maybe a little too well. She..." He shook his head. "She made it easy to pretend I was okay with completely letting go of the more lighthearted parts of me that didn't fit her ideology when it came to a partner. The parts of me left behind were exactly what she was looking for, something she told me all the time. The ego boost was hard to ignore, even if sometimes she made me feel like half a person."

Skyler frowned. "Kit, how could you think—"

"I know." He grabbed her hands, pulling her in closer. "There were so many things wrong with that relationship. I *know*. But that doesn't mean I didn't think it might be my only shot."

She knew too well how much Kit had dreamed of finding someone and creating a life with them, so Skyler couldn't fault him. Still, if she ever figured out Angela's last name, she was going to go give that woman a piece of her mind.

Kit sighed, as if he could see the revenge plot forming in her head. "Can I finish my story now?"

"Only if you want to."

He seemed to debate for a second, but then he nodded. "She said she wanted to keep our relationship a secret, and it was like she knew how hard it was going to be for me to have someone new in my life. A part of me thought it was fate giving me time to figure out how to make such a drastic change in my life work without upending the lives of my friends."

As much as she understood Kit's reasoning, Skyler couldn't for the life of her figure out why anyone would hide away the likes of Kit Morgan. And worse, why anyone would want him to hide the best parts of himself. She was still ruffled by that part. "Why did *she* want to keep your relationship a secret?"

He shrugged. "Only her best friend knew about us, and he… Looking back, I know she was just using me to make him jealous. And I always saw the way he looked at her. I think a part of me was convinced she was trying to move on because he was too much of a coward to do anything about the way he felt; I was glad to help her find that closure."

"You are too good at seeing the good in people," Skyler grumbled. "How could anyone choose someone else over you?"

That got a smile out of him. "He worked for a Fortune 500 company."

She rolled her eyes. "So does a Walmart greeter. You are a paintball king with a heart of gold who spends his summers planning friends' weddings and comforting little kids. You notice things no one else notices, and I don't think there's anyone in the world who doesn't feel worthwhile if you're around. You live big and love hard, and I've never met anyone so determined to stick to something once he makes up his mind." She pressed her hand to his solid chest, keeping her eyes locked on his because he was giving her the most intense look. The kind that made her melt. "And don't get me started on this bod—"

He cut her off with a kiss that would have knocked her off her feet if he hadn't wrapped his arms around her to keep her steady. This was a different kiss, no less potent than any of the others, but he took his time. Slow and languid, like he was telling her with each touch everything he felt because there were no words to express it for him.

A clap of thunder broke them apart.

"We should get back," Kit said, his reluctance written all over his face.

Skyler groaned, but he was right. The storm was clearly getting worse. "Thank you," she said. "For telling me about her."

He smiled. "I'll always tell you anything you want to know. I'm done keeping secrets from the ones I love."

As they locked hands and ducked back into the rain, Skyler considered that. How far was he willing to take that statement? "Does that mean you're going to tell the Wonder Boys about Angela? You're not going to go back to the way you were, are you?" She couldn't stop the fear from entering her voice.

Kit glanced over at her. The rain had started to leave droplets on his glasses, probably making it hard for him to see. "That depends," he said after a moment.

Skyler tightened her grip on his hand. "On what?"

"On if you'll be around to remind me to be my whole self." And the look on his face, serious and warm, said he really wanted her to respond to that.

Oh. Skyler had wanted this. She'd wanted to talk about what was going to happen after the reunion was over. Scared as she was to commit to something so out of her element, with a man so out of her league, she didn't want this to end when the week did. She wasn't sure she wanted it to end *ever*. But was she really brave enough to say so? Lifelong fears seemed to speak a lot louder than anything as she considered a future beyond a few months.

No one could argue they didn't have chemistry, but when it came to life goals… What if they were too different?

Lightning flashed above them, followed by thunder just a second later, and Skyler's foot slipped out of her sandal when they hit a patch of mud. The rain was falling thick and heavy now, putting them in a dangerous position if they didn't get back soon.

"Get on," Kit said, turning his back to her. "Your shoes are terrible."

"You can't even see," she argued, though he wasn't wrong.

Kit crouched down a little to make it easier for her to climb up. "We're going to have to work together to get back. Neither of us is any good on our own."

That sentence felt like it carried a lot more weight than the storm, but Skyler hopped onto his back anyway, locking her arms over his chest as his large hands latched beneath her thighs.

"I need you to guide me," he said, yet another sentence with a double meaning.

"Straight ahead," she told him, knowing their future would not be quite so easy to navigate.

TWENTY-SEVEN

KIT DIDN'T LIKE RAIN. HE had never liked rain. Wearing glasses most of his life had made it difficult for him to see the appeal, and he had grown to like being warm and dry. A torrential rainstorm keeping him from kissing Skyler didn't help his opinion, and when he finally stumbled into their cabin after what took way too long to get back from their walk, he had never been so glad to see a fire burning in a fireplace in his life.

"Are you guys okay?" Micah asked when the pair of them barreled in through the door. "This storm came out of nowhere!"

Most of their cabin had sequestered themselves in the living room with the crackling fire, a few of them playing a game of Monopoly while the rest watched a movie. Micah hurried over with a blanket and draped it around Skyler's shoulders before she shivered so hard she fell apart. Kit had felt bad for using Skyler as a shield from the rain, but she never would have made it back in bare feet, and her sandals had disappeared somewhere along the road.

"We just got started, Morgan," Houston said from where he sat on the floor next to the coffee table. "We could put a wager on the game if you want to join in."

Kit wanted a hot shower. He wanted to curl up in a ball in front of that fireplace with Skyler in his arms and never leave. "Yeah, no, I'm never betting against you again," he said, trying to smile. "Knowing you, you're probably some business mogul and know all the tricks."

"Suit yourself."

He didn't particularly like the way Houston looked like he was trying not to laugh, nor the way Brooklyn rolled her eyes from her place on the couch. If Houston really was a business mogul on top of being a professional pitcher, Kit was going to complain to whomever doled out circumstances and cry foul play. He and Houston were grossly uneven when it came to assets and luck.

Except when it came to relationships. Kit had won the jackpot there. Even after their conversation about Angela, which should have left him feeling sick and itchy, he was mostly just happy. It was like every glance at Skyler gave him a straight shot of dopamine, and he couldn't get enough of her.

"We should get you into dry clothes," Kit told Skyler, cringing when he heard how that sounded. He hoped she didn't think he was implying anything. "I mean—"

"You too," Skyler said with a wink.

Maybe a cold shower would be good for him. Or better yet, he should go back out into the storm until his imagination learned its lesson. What happened to his logic always winning out?

Skyler happened.

Both of them were quiet as they entered the bedroom and closed the door behind them, like they both knew everything had changed. Even yesterday hadn't felt quite so heavy, but neither of them had admitted to deeper feelings yesterday. Now that things were out in the open, how did they move forward?

Skyler still hadn't answered his question about if she would stick around, and as she shivered through her search for dry clothes, she seemed to be feeling the weight of that question with every passing second until she finally met his gaze.

"I know," she said, teeth chattering. "But I can't think straight right now. Let me warm up in the shower, and then we'll talk, okay? I promise."

Kit believed her. But just in case, he slowly moved toward her until he had her backed up against the doorframe of the bathroom, a bundle of clothes the only thing between them. "I'll hold you to that promise," he said in the gruffest voice he could manage, easy enough to do after carrying her piggyback through the storm. His throat felt like sandpaper. Then he grabbed a towel and stepped back like being that close to her hadn't short-circuited something in his brain.

Was it always going to be like that? Would he always lose every ounce of restraint he had when she looked at him with those big green eyes? Was kissing her always going to feel like she was the only thing that made life worth living? All of that aside, just being around her had made him happier than he'd been in years. Long before he met Angela. He had never felt like he needed to hide pieces of himself from Skyler, and she had never given him a reason to think she didn't love all of him. Not just the convenient parts.

A shiver ran through him, not entirely from his soaked shirt.

He peeled the shirt off on his way to his suitcase, only realizing he hadn't heard the bathroom door close when Skyler let out a little squeak. Flattering as her staring was, if she kept looking at him like he was a plate of chocolate cheesecake, there would be no stopping him from devouring her right on back.

"Shower," he growled, pointing at her. "Now."

Her lips pinched in a smile, but thankfully she closed the door and put a barrier between them.

Groaning, Kit changed into sweats as quickly as he could and then flopped onto the bed. He needed something to keep him from thinking about Skyler in the shower and turning into one of those creeps he hated, but a game of Monopoly with Houston Briggs was the last thing he needed.

Limited in his options, Kit grabbed his phone from the table where Skyler had left it and chose the person who would probably be the most helpful, even though Kit knew he wasn't going to like a lot of the conversation he was about to have. Of all his friends, Oliver had known him the longest. He would be least likely to sugarcoat things.

Oliver answered on the second ring, sounding a little too pleased with himself. "Finally at your wit's end?"

"I'm in love with her, Ollie." Kit exhaled, shoving his hand into his hair.

"Duh. I told you this would happen."

"No, you don't get it. I *love* her. How is that even possible? And how were you so certain it would happen? This is *me* we're talking about."

"Why do you say that like it's an argument against the fact?" Oliver asked. His amusement had quickly faded, and he sounded like he'd used to when they were younger. Before Ben and Cam, when it was just the two of them and they had all sorts of deep, serious conversations. As serious as ten-year-olds could get, anyway. "Kit, I don't think anyone in the world loves harder than you do. Besides, every time you said her name, it was written all over your face. She's the girl who gave you your bracelet, isn't she?"

Kit looked at his right wrist, where the worn leather sat next to the green and brown friendship bracelet Skyler had woven for him the other day. He'd had to fix the strap of the leather bracelet so many times that it was a miracle he could still wear it, but it had been on his wrist for the last seventeen and a half years. Even as a kid, he'd known Skyler was a forever kind of deal.

"How did you know?" he asked. None of his friends had ever questioned the bracelet's existence, which had never bothered Kit until now. Either they didn't care—unlikely—or they thought Kit didn't want them to ask. Maybe they'd never pushed him to be different because they thought he was actually happy as he was. He'd never given them a reason to think otherwise.

Had he been completely deluding himself in thinking his best friends would ever hate anything about him?

Oliver was quiet for a few seconds, like he wasn't sure he wanted to answer that question. "You're my best friend," he said eventually. "And as much as I like to think that me announcing that I was coming back to your school was the reason you were so happy at the end of that semester, I knew there had to be something more to it. You were different, but in a way that was like everything about you had been, I don't know, *emphasized*. You hadn't changed, you were just…more. Even Ben saw it.

"And then Christmas break was over, and we went back to school, and it was like the Kit we knew was gone. You went too far in the other direction until everything was muted. And you wore that bracelet like a shield."

Kit shuddered a breath. This wasn't why he had called Oliver, and he wasn't sure he wanted to hear what his oldest friend had to say. He hadn't thought he changed after he realized Skyler wasn't coming back. He'd thought he'd just gone back to the way things had been before he got his heart broken by Skyler disappearing. Had it really been that drastic of a shift?

"Ollie," he muttered as tears leaked from his eyes.

Oliver sniffed, clearly crying on his end as well. "I figured you were just growing up, you know?" he said, and Kit could imagine his shrug. He was probably sitting at his computer, a complicated coding project waiting forgotten on the dual screens. "But I always wondered if something—someone— was at the heart of it. Especially when you never really dated anyone."

Kit swallowed. "About that. I have to tell you—"

"I know about Angela."

"What? How?" And why had he never said anything?

Oliver sighed heavily. "I know I wasn't around much the last few years, but after Madi pulled me back into the group, I saw the signs. The way you tense whenever we talk about our soulmates. Every time you flinch when someone touches you. I know you too well to not see the—"

"Cam told you," Kit guessed, rolling his eyes.

"I didn't even have to *try* to get it out of him," Oliver confirmed without hesitation. "The man sang like a canary a month ago." He got softer, speaking more slowly. "But I still saw the signs of heartbreak, Kit. I figured you would tell me when you were ready. I'm… I'm sorry I wasn't really around when it happened."

It was Kit's turn to sigh, though he knew he would have to wrap this conversation up soon. Skyler would only be in the shower for so long. "I'm sorry I had no idea what your company was doing to you," he muttered.

Oliver had told him just a few months ago about his company stressing him out so much that he worked himself into the hospital. Kit had always thought Oliver just gave up when he sold his company because it hadn't come easily for him like everything else did, and he hated that he had thought so poorly of his closest friend. There were a lot of things he hated about the last few years.

"I should have been there for you," Kit said.

"You were busy getting your heart stomped on. And I wasn't there for *you*."

"Why are we so bad at being friends lately?"

Oliver chuckled. "Because life gets in the way sometimes. But we're never not going to be friends, Kit. No matter who you are or how much you change."

Kit felt like he was being repeatedly slapped in the face by things he'd been so sure were secrets. "How did you—"

"Give me some credit. I've known you almost my entire life, and I know how much you hate disappointing people. You wouldn't be asking if you weren't worried about how this kind of relationship will affect the rest of us. Logically, that means something would have to be changing."

"You are too smart for your own good sometimes," Kit said, even if he didn't mean it. "And you aren't as shocked as I thought you would be."

"Please. I went out to dinner with *Cam* last night and had a good time. I don't think anything could shock me at this point. Besides, there is no way the Kit Morgan I know would fall for a girl like Skyler, so it makes sense. If she makes you want to be that *more* version of you again, I love her already. So please don't tell me you called because you've already messed things up."

Kit couldn't stop the smile from growing on his face. "Is it crazy to love her as much as I do? I've only known her for a few days."

"You do remember I proposed to your sister the day after I told her I loved her, right?"

He did *not* need that reminder. Even though Kit had helped with the proposal, he'd been mostly convinced they were rushing into things way too fast and would crash and burn. He was glad to have been wrong.

"That's different. You've known Madi your whole life."

"If you think about it, this version of you has known Skyler *his* whole life. I may have only talked to her for a few minutes, but even I know she's perfect for you. Cam and Ben would probably say the same thing. But being in love with her now doesn't mean it's a forever thing. You don't have to overthink this."

But that was what Kit did. He measured every action against what everyone expected, forgoing emotion for the much safer logical side of things.

At least, he'd done that before Skyler.

Kit dropped his voice so she wouldn't hear what he was about to admit out loud. "I want to marry her, Oliver. I *want* this to be forever."

Oliver's smile was clear in his voice. "Then tell her. What do you have to lose?"

Everything. "What if it scares her away?"

"Then it probably isn't meant to be. I'm not saying you should *actually* marry her anytime soon. Not everyone can be as lucky as me. But telling her how you feel? Being honest with her? That's never a bad idea. Keeping her in the dark will only make her wonder."

The shower turned off, which meant Kit's time was up. "When did you get so good at giving advice?" he asked.

Oliver laughed. "I learned from the best. You're always there for us, Kit. Let us be there for you for once. No matter what happens, the Wonder Boys have your back."

Kit grinned, feeling like his heart might burst from beating so hard, like it had been limping along for years before now. This conversation had been better for him than he could have imagined, though he shouldn't have been surprised. Kit had always loved Oliver's carefree attitude, for the same reasons he loved Ben's quiet steadiness and the way Cam told it like it was. Kit may have befriended them to help them out, but at the same time he had needed them in his own life. He always had and always would.

"You called us the Wonder Boys again," Kit said with a grin.

"And if you tell anyone that I did, I'll tell Skyler about the time you peed yourself in the second grade because you were too scared to ask to go to the bathroom. Good luck!"

Kit sat up slowly, clutching his phone like it might keep the connection with Oliver going even though he'd hung up. The two of them had been friends since kindergarten, and even before Oliver married Madi, he had been like a brother to Kit. All the Wonder Boys were. Skyler was right, and Kit had no reason to think they would turn on him just because he admitted he wasn't being true to himself. If the others thought the same way Oliver did, that he'd lost who he was after Skyler left, maybe it was time he brought the full Kit—the real Kit—back for good.

Otherwise, he was going to be living scared for the rest of his life.

Skyler stepped out of the bathroom after a few minutes, and Kit opened his mouth to tell her about the revelation he'd just come to. But all words failed him when he saw her wearing one of his t-shirts over a pair of his basketball shorts that she'd rolled a few times to get them to stay on her hips. She was *wearing his clothes.*

Skyler bit her lip. "Nothing I brought looked comfy enough," she explained as she hopped up onto the bed next to him and snuggled in. "So I borrowed a couple of things. I'll give them back. Maybe."

He would give her everything he owned if that was what it took to keep her.

"Any Wonder Boy updates?" She pointed to his phone.

Yes, but Kit still couldn't find his voice.

Skyler must have taken his silence as a negative, because she had her own phone in hand a few seconds later and was pulling up her email. "I'm a little scared to look," she said as it loaded.

He forced himself to speak. "Just think of all the TikToks you've missed."

She elbowed him in the ribs. "Shut up. I think we need to celebrate the fact that I've stayed away this long. I just figured it might be a good idea to make sure the store hasn't burned down or something. Oh!" She sat up, elbowing Kit again by accident with a lot more force.

"What?" Kit asked through a groan, massaging his sternum.

"The guy building my shelves sent an email a couple of days ago. He said he had a family emergency and can't do the job anymore. He was supposed to be done next week!"

Moaning, Skyler flopped backward, and Kit barely caught her before her head smacked into his face. He'd forgotten how dangerous this woman could be when she was comfortable around a person and not paying attention, but he kind of loved this part of her. Except when emotions got big, she had never been afraid to be herself.

Skyler let out a little sigh. "This is going to delay the grand opening by a few weeks at least, depending on how quickly I find a new carpenter and how good he is at his job."

That was the email Kit had thought was innocuous, and though a thread of guilt weaved its way into his stomach, he knew a couple of days wouldn't have made much of a difference. Besides, Skyler had needed the break from reality as much as he had.

"You don't seem to be panicking as much as I thought you would," Kit said carefully, rubbing her arm in case she wasn't as calm as she appeared. But she really seemed more annoyed than anything, like the delay on the most important part of a bookstore was nothing more than a minor inconvenience.

Skyler curled into him, wrapping her arm over his torso as she cuddled in close. "Yeah, well, I researched a lot of different people in the beginning, so it's not like I'm fully starting from scratch. Besides, I'm pretty sure I know a guy who would do it in a heartbeat and probably do a better job."

"Oh? How much experience does he have?" Kit didn't consider himself an expert, but he wanted to make sure Skyler got the best she could. She deserved to have the store do well.

"A few years, though I don't think he does it all the time. It's more of a hobby."

"That sounds a little questionable. I'm sure there are more professional—"

"But I like this one. He's super attractive, and I would really enjoy watching him work."

Okay, Kit *really* didn't like the sound of this guy, and he had to fight to keep his tone even. "I'm not sure if that's the most important—"

"It's you, genius." Skyler sat up, shaking her head at him like he was the most unintelligent person she'd ever known. "Why would I go find myself a woodworker when I've got one right here?"

Kit swallowed, torn between embracing the flattery and succumbing to his anxiety over knowing he was absolutely not the best person for the job. "I appreciate your faith in me, Sky, but you saw my videos. I barely know what I'm doing."

"I also saw the cabinets you built for your house."

Frowning, Kit pictured her breaking into his house while he was staying with Oliver so she could make sure he wasn't some sort of psychopath before she brought him to the reunion. "When?"

Rolling her eyes, Skyler ran her hand through his damp hair. "I definitely snooped through your photos while I had your phone this morning. Kit, you are way more talented than you're giving yourself credit for. And that coffee table you made for Ben? It was gorgeous! I want to punch Cam in the face for breaking it."

"He deserves it," Kit grumbled. Maybe another punch to the mouth would even out that stupid crooked smile of his. Nothing like a little nerve damage from Cam's fighting days to make a man look more roguish than he had a right to look.

Tucking her legs underneath her, Skyler grabbed Kit's hands and smiled at him. "So what do you think? Want to work with me?"

It wasn't exactly forever, but at least she was making it clear she wanted to spend more time with him. Wishing he were brave enough to take Oliver's advice and tell her exactly what he wanted when it came to her, Kit smiled and squeezed her hands. "Of course I do. I just hope I don't disappoint you, and I can't guarantee a timely completion. I haven't built free-standing bookshelves before, so I might have to do a little learning."

"Oh, you could film the whole process! Turn it into another video!"

Kit really didn't like how excited she got about that, and yet his mind started making a plan anyway. He could talk about choosing the right wood, measuring for the space, making a detailed plan before ever making a cut…

Skyler pointed at him. "I can see you thinking about it. You totally want to make more videos."

"Make a fool of myself."

"They're compelling, Kit. People like knowing that even skilled craftsmen make mistakes. Besides, it would be great advertising for the store."

Groaning, Kit dropped his head against the headboard and shut his eyes. She *had* to bring the store into it, didn't she? Now how was he supposed to say no? "I guess…" He swallowed, his mouth feeling impossibly dry. "I guess, until I figure out a new job, I could…" He shook his head. Why was he fighting this so much? It wasn't like he had a better option. "Okay, I'll do it. Build your shelves, film my show, all of it. But only if you'll be with me every step of the way."

Skyler's soft smile brought an ache to his chest, and she moved to her knees to get close enough to push his hair from his forehead and press a kiss against his skin. She smelled of something flowery that overloaded his senses, and he closed his eyes as he breathed her in.

"Where else would I be?" she said.

Was it pathetic to start crying again? Kit didn't care. He let the tears fall as he pulled Skyler into his arms and held her tight, hoping he would never have to let go again.

TWENTY-EIGHT

THE RAIN CONTINUED THROUGH THE afternoon and into the night. Everyone kept to their individual cabins to avoid the downpour, so Kit and Skyler decided to join the others out in the living room where the fire kept everything warm and toasty. As Skyler squished onto the couch with Micah and Brooklyn for some girl talk, Kit reluctantly accepted Houston's challenge to a showdown on the latest video game.

Kit happened to be pretty good at video games, but he refused to underestimate Houston ever again. Thankfully, Houston was mediocre at best, so even though Kit kept getting distracted by Skyler's pink cheeks as she laughed with her stepsisters, he still demolished the pitcher and earned himself the opportunity to throw a paper plate full of whipped cream into the man's face.

Brooklyn gleefully filmed the whole thing and promised Houston she would be holding onto the video to use as leverage in the future.

All of them stayed up late, enjoying time without any of the married couples—Sam and Tracy had kept to their room—or any of the kids, finally trudging to bed around two in the morning.

Kit didn't even pretend he would rather sleep on the couch, and Skyler didn't stop him from going into the room with her. Exhausted from a full day of a wide range of emotions, they curled up together on the bed and fell asleep within seconds of lying down, Kit feeling more content than he'd ever remembered being. Holding her in his arms and listening to her breathing grow slower had him thinking he might actually get the chance to keep this a part of his life.

The next morning, Kit didn't want to move. Though they hadn't talked about it yesterday, he knew it would probably be a good idea for them to head back to Diamond Springs early. Skyler needed to check on the state of the store, and Kit needed to get started on the shelves as soon as possible if he wanted to get them done in time for opening day in July.

Besides, he missed the Boys, and they had a lot to talk about.

Skyler stirred a few minutes after Kit woke, immediately curling in closer to his chest. "How is it already morning?" she moaned.

Brushing her strawberry hair away from her face, Kit pressed a kiss to the top of her head. "I don't know."

"I think we need to go back today," she said next.

"That I do know."

"I'll still pay you for the whole—"

"Sky." He shifted back so she could meet his gaze. "If you think I'm really going to let you pay me for this week, you're not nearly as smart as I thought you were."

She frowned, bunching his shirt up in her fists. "I like to keep my promises, Kit."

"What if I trade in dollars for kisses?"

Her resulting smile radiated sunshine, her eyes bright and shimmering. "Ten thousand kisses? That could take a while."

Kit brushed his lips against hers. "I'm counting on that."

Something had changed last night while they played games with her stepsiblings. Yes, Kit absolutely wanted to kiss her—really kiss her—but a sort of contentment had settled over him during the night, leaving him feeling full. Alive. *Whole.* Being around her family had felt so natural and real, and every time Micah talked about going to Sunday brunch with Skyler, and when Houston said he could get Kit tickets for his next home game, it was like Kit could feel his life settling into something new.

Something good.

"I love you, Sky," he said, though that hardly covered the way he treasured every moment with her. It said nothing of how badly he wanted to know every detail of the seventeen and a half years he had missed of her life, no matter how long it took to learn it all.

Skyler smiled and returned his kiss with a gentle one of her own, speaking against his mouth. "Will you stop being the first one to say it? I love you. I don't want to add a *too* on the end because that makes it sound like I'm only saying it because you said it. But you can ask Micah. She knows I've said it without you saying it first."

Kit narrowed his eyes, glad that she was so close so he could see her without having to find his glasses. "Hang on, you told Micah before you told me?"

"Don't be such a baby."

"It's not being a baby when those words mean everything. Now I feel like she's watching us." He exaggerated a shudder, laughing when Skyler smacked his chest and loving when she kept her hand there, pressed over his heart. "You know I don't care about that, right, Sky? I only care about you. That you're happy."

"I'm happy," Skyler said, but something leaked into her expression, so subtle that Kit thought maybe he was seeing things. Imagining doubts that weren't there. The two of them had always been so honest with each other, even back in junior high, and he hardly thought that would change now.

Sighing, Skyler nuzzled back into him like she wasn't ready to face the world yet. "I'm less happy about telling my mom we're leaving early. Or Micah. I think even Houston will be sad to lose his new best friend. You guys were just starting to like each other."

Kit chuckled, but his laugh sounded forced. Maybe he hadn't imagined something after all if she was talking like Kit would never see her family again. "This doesn't have to be the end," he said. He hated that his voice wavered. He had been so confident all week, but now that they'd made the decision to go back, it was like the boring Kit had reared his ugly head and taken the reins of his logical side. The side that had been in control for years.

He had worried reality would force him back into that role, but he wasn't sure he was strong enough to fight the pull. Even after Oliver's confession about not caring who Kit was. There was something to be said for settling into routine and familiarity, and he'd been doing that for so long already.

Skyler mumbled something unintelligible into his shirt, which didn't help anything. It was like she didn't even have a way to say she agreed with him. Did she think this was going to end? But why?

Tension growing, Kit sat up and grabbed his glasses from the bedside table. "Guess we should pack," he muttered.

"Kit."

He pushed himself to his feet and started grabbing clothes at random, his skin prickling. "Do you think your mom will be up making breakfast? Maybe we can catch her before anyone else is awake and avoid—"

She had her arms around him from behind before he could finish a sentence he really didn't want to finish, and she pressed her face into his shoulder blades, hands locked against his chest. "Will you stop jumping to conclusions? Please?"

He tried to breathe, closing his eyes and wrapping his hands around her arms, but his chest felt too tight. He hadn't even really put himself out there, not in the way he wanted to, and already she was too freaked out to have an actual response. What would she do if she found out how he *really* felt?

"You're overthinking," she said. "I can feel it." One hand stretched over his heart, which beat in a feeble attempt at keeping him from thinking stupid thoughts like comparing Skyler's non-committal answer to Angela, who had been so good at skirting around the topic of their future together. He'd proposed because he thought it might show her that he meant it when he said he wanted a life with her.

What if he told Skyler he wanted her in his life for the rest of existence, and she responded out of obligation?

What if he'd moved too fast and ruined their chances?

"Christopher Duke Morgan." Skyler slipped around to his other side and faced him, grabbing his cheeks with her soft fingers and forcing his gaze down to hers.

The instant Kit realized she was crying, he softened a little in her hold.

"I'm not going to pretend I'm not terrified by how quickly I fell back in love with you," she said, her voice coming out stronger than he would have expected. "You and I have always felt inevitable."

He swallowed and brushed his thumb across her cheek, wiping her tears. "But?"

She clearly didn't want to finish her own declaration, her hands balling into fists against his chest and her tears falling thicker and faster. "But I never saw this in my future. I never saw you. I never saw…" She took a step back that felt like it split the air, creating a chasm that separated them. "I told you in the beginning. I don't like kids. I don't *want* kids."

Kit's heart cracked wide to match the space between them. He hadn't even thought about… He'd been so caught up in Skyler that he'd forgotten the one dream that had never changed throughout his life, no matter which role he played. He had always wanted a family, with lots of little kids running around. He wanted to take them camping and help them with their homework and watch them fail and fall and get back up and keep trying. He wanted to laugh and cry with someone he loved, raising their kids *together*.

"See?" Skyler pointed at him. "I know you, Kit. And I don't want to take that away from you."

"Not knowing what to do with kids is not the same as not liking kids," he tried, knowing that wouldn't be enough for someone who hadn't really gotten to be a child. She hadn't seen what a real parent should be like. "Sky…"

Skyler wrapped her arms around herself, still wearing Kit's clothes. He would never be able to look at that t-shirt the same, assuming he even wanted it back. If this was going to be the end, having that reminder would only make everything hurt more.

Was this really how things would end? One little fear, one little difference in goals? Okay, so it was a big difference—monumentally huge—but it didn't mean things had to end. They could talk about this. They could…

"Maybe we moved too fast," Skyler whispered, though she didn't seem to believe her own words. She loved him. Kit knew she did. But love wasn't enough if they wanted different things. If she was too scared to even try.

"Maybe we did," he agreed, not meaning a word.

He had seen the way she interacted with Isabelle, and she had been just as worried about Tanner as Kit had been. She would make such an amazing mother, but unless she decided that was something she wanted, none of that mattered.

Kit had ignored his logical side for days, since the moment they got to the reunion, but with his heart breaking, his head was the only thing he could hear. Even if he told her he loved her too much to give up on them because of this, even if he said they didn't have to have kids to build a life together, there would always be a part of him that would resent his choice. That desperately wanted that family he'd always imagined.

He hated that she might be right about all of this.

"I'm sorry," Skyler whispered.

Her expression was so mournful that Kit couldn't help but pull her into his arms and hold her, no matter how much it hurt him to be so close yet so far. Was this really it? He wasn't ready for it to be over, but he needed time to think. To process. To *plan*.

"We're still friends, right?"

That quiet question seemed to answer Kit's unspoken one and put a nail in the coffin of their short-lived love story, and he held her a little tighter. "Always." And he meant that, even if he knew he would never be the same.

This was *not* over. He wouldn't let it be over.

TWENTY-NINE

Skyler was the worst. The worst of the worst. One minute she was imagining waking up next to Kit for the rest of her life, and the next she was telling him she hated kids and they would never work. And she knew it broke him. She knew it was so much worse than what Angela did because Skyler wasn't ready to let Kit go. And he knew it. She could see it in his eyes as they packed up their things in silence.

But when he'd said things didn't have to end, everything in his tone and expression had told her how deep he was into this already. She'd suspected it, probably for a while if she was being honest with herself, but that confirmation had scared her. Admitting she was in love with the man? No problem. Picturing a life together where she could actually make him happy? Not so easy.

He deserved to be happy.

By the time they got everything gathered up and headed out into the living room, Skyler was pretty sure the deep sorrow in Kit's eyes would be enough to make her change her mind and beg him to forgive her for listening to her head instead of her heart. He probably *would* forgive her, but Skyler couldn't guarantee her guilt wasn't the only thing convincing her she'd made a mistake. Feeling bad wasn't the same as being on the same page. What if she went right back to being scared?

Thankfully, the only other person awake was Chad, who sat at the kitchen table with a cup of coffee and a book. He had joined them last night for games, though he wasn't nearly as exuberant as his younger siblings, and kindness eked out from the laugh lines at the corners of his eyes when he looked up at them.

"Heading out?" He seemed neither surprised nor expectant, which was nice.

Skyler nodded, wondering if Kit would say anything. He didn't. "I've got to get back to the store," she said. "Some things came up."

Chad sipped his coffee as he glanced between the two of them, like he was trying to read them like he'd been doing with his book. Skyler could have tried to hide her misery, but she was pretty sure she wouldn't do a good job. She still didn't know Chad well after this week, but he seemed to be skilled at reading people. He'd caught everyone's bluffs in poker last night and cleaned them all out. Even Kit, the master masker.

"It's been good getting to know you," Chad said after a moment. "Both of you. I'm sorry about the videos yesterday."

Kit tensed. "What?"

Chad's lips curled into the smallest of smiles before he took another sip of coffee. "Lloyd asked me to do some digging, and I thought he would be interested in those."

"But how did you find them?" Kit asked. "I don't even have my name attached to them."

"Private investigator," he said with a shrug. "It's what I do. For what it's worth, I didn't find anything else on you except… well, no dirt, anyway."

Squirming next to Skyler, Kit moved his hands from his sides to his sweatshirt pocket and back again. "Thanks?"

Chad nodded once, glancing between the two of them. "Hopefully we see you around again." He almost said it like a question, like he knew something he shouldn't. Maybe he just saw the tension between them and wondered if their relationship was going to last.

Or maybe he knew their engagement was completely fake and he was kind enough to keep it to himself.

Skyler grabbed Kit's hand, hating that he tensed as soon as their fingers touched. He hadn't done that in days. "We should probably get going. I'm meeting my contractor in a few hours." She let go of Kit's hand as soon as they were outside in the cool morning air, but then her heart twisted when he stole her suitcase from her grip so she wouldn't have to drag it through the muddy path. He was already carrying the other one as well as his duffel. "You don't have to—"

"Sky." He met her gaze for the first time since their terrible conversation, giving her a look that said he meant it when he told her they were still friends. Skyler had always thought men were weak when they complained about the friend zone, but now that she'd legitimately put someone in there, she was starting to understand the damage it could inflict. If she wasn't interested, that would be one thing, but she loved him more than ever.

But Kit deserved to have everything he wanted, and Skyler wasn't sure she could give him that.

By the time they reached the main cabin and stepped inside, Skyler felt like her emotions had risen higher and higher until they were right at the surface, ready to break free at the drop of a hat. Did people usually live like this? Or had she just been so good at holding her feelings so deep inside that anything other than stone cold felt extreme?

Either way, when Mom turned to greet them and caught sight of their suitcases, immediately bursting into tears, Skyler did the exact same thing.

"You're leaving?" Mom moaned. "But you only just got here. We only just…"

For the first time in as long as she could remember, Skyler stepped forward and pulled her mom into a hug. It was just as unfamiliar as the last time, but it felt more natural now, like if they did this often enough they would figure out how to do it properly. "I know," she said into Mom's shoulder. "But something came up with the store, and it can't really wait. I wish I could stay and help with breakfast."

Sniffling, Mom wiped her eyes on her apron, looking so much different from how she used to be. She held a matronly air about her, and Skyler noticed for the first time that she'd put on some healthy weight instead of being all bones and angles. Her hair and clothes were both nicer too, but mainly she just looked…happy.

"Oh, don't worry about that. I have some pastries you can take for the road. Heidi likes to help out, anyway." As soon as Mom said that, she winced. "I'm sorry. I know you don't like—"

"It's fine." Skyler shook her head "I'm glad you have people like Heidi and Micah to keep you company."

Right as she said that, Heidi herself appeared from the hallway that led to the bedrooms. She paused when she reached the kitchen and took in the scene, but for once she didn't seem to be looking down her nose at everything. In fact, she looked a lot less put together than she usually did, like she was actually human for once. She'd pulled her hair into a long braid and hadn't put on any makeup, and her clothes were a bit rumpled instead of pristine.

Heidi swallowed, glancing at Kit before approaching Skyler like she would a wild animal—cautiously optimistic for an interaction. "You're leaving," she said, not really asking the question. "Is it because I—"

"No." As angry as Skyler had been with Heidi and her assumptions, she didn't want to leave on a sour note. "No, I just have some business to take care of."

"I'm sorry."

"What?"

Heidi shrugged one thin shoulder. "I'm sorry for the way I treated you. I shouldn't have… I should have treated you like family." Then she turned her gaze to Kit, her eyes filling with tears. "Tanner told me what you said to him. He told me that you encouraged him to tell me what was bothering him. I had no idea Isabelle was being treated that way."

Despite never having the instinct for comforting before, Skyler took hold of Heidi's hand and gave it a squeeze.

Heidi sent her a grateful smile. "Thank you for seeing my children better than I could, Chris. I'm sorry I distrusted you."

Kit looked like he'd just swallowed a giant marshmallow and it was stuck in his throat. "Thank you," he said, his voice muted. "I'm glad he talked to you."

"He said you knew we cared about him," Heidi said, and suddenly she was crying too, all three women in the room in tears. "To think he wasn't sure… I clearly need to rethink my priorities, so…thank you again. Skyler, you picked a good one. He'll make a wonderful father someday."

Well, that did it. Refusing to look back at Kit's face, Skyler grabbed her suitcase from his hand and made a beeline for the door before she fell apart and had a breakdown from too many emotions swirling inside her.

To her horror, Lloyd appeared at the top of the stairway as soon as she reached it. "What's going on up here?" he asked, his eyebrows sinking low as he took in all the tears. Kit hadn't moved from near the back door, and Heidi looked like a mess, and Lloyd's expression hardened when no one spoke. "What did you do?" he asked Skyler.

Seriously? Skyler shook her head. "We have to go."

Lloyd didn't move, even when Skyler took a step. "Go? Where?"

"The store needs—"

"Let Chris handle the store. Your mother was looking forward to spending the whole week with you."

Blinking, Skyler stared at him and tried to comprehend how a man could be so completely stupid. How could he care so much about his precious daughters and still think a woman had no business running a…business? She was so angry that even her thoughts were getting all jumbled up, and that was maybe the worst part of actually letting herself feel things. She'd always been so good at keeping a straight face and not letting things get to her.

But after telling Kit so many times to be true to his real self, how could she sit by and let this infuriating man continue tearing her down? It was time to be honest for once.

"Chris?" she repeated, her voice rough from her tears. It made her sound fierce, which was nice. "You mean Kit, the guy I literally hired last week to pretend to be a man who doesn't exist?" Mom gasped, but Skyler refused to break eye contact with Lloyd, who hadn't even flinched. "You are so set in your backward, misogynistic ways that I had to invent an entire person just so you would take me seriously!"

She stood up on her toes, pretending she was in a courtroom and making her final statement in her favorite pair of heels. "Did you know I could have been the only female partner in my firm in Baltimore? Not only that, but the youngest too. I was top in my class in law school after getting a bachelor's in business summa cum laude. I had firms all over the country trying to poach me because I don't back down.

"And I threw all of that away to move to a city no one's heard of so I could build a bookstore because I wanted to do something I was actually passionate about and be happy for once. But *you*."

She poked his chest. "You have only ever seen a pathetic little girl who begged for money because she got in over her head. And you know what?" She poked him again, punctuating each word with her fingertip. "I. Don't. Need you. I can't completely hate you because you've made my mom happy, but don't expect me to show up for next year's reunion. You'll have to get updates about my life from Micah, but I doubt you'll care about anything I do or who I end up with. You have plenty of grandkids to spoil already."

Feeling her strength waning—anger was exhausting—Skyler pushed past Lloyd and down the stairs, wondering if she had just liberated herself or made the biggest mistake of her life. There was too much adrenaline coursing through her body to think straight, and she was sure she wouldn't be able to process the last couple of minutes until she started breathing again. Or maybe when they were halfway down the mountain.

But where was Kit?

Skyler shoved her suitcase into the trunk of her car and flopped into the driver's seat, gripping the steering wheel as she waited. She'd expected him to follow her out—who in their right mind would want to stick around after a display like that?—but at least five minutes passed before he appeared in the driveway.

"What took you so long?" she snapped through her open window.

Kit shrugged as he loaded up her other suitcase and his duffel and then slipped into the passenger seat. "I just had to clarify a few things with Lloyd. He's still willing to pay your mortgage."

"I'm not going to touch another penny from him."

"That's what I told him. You were terrifying, by the way."

At first, Skyler thought she should be offended until she looked over at him and saw the soft smile on his face. "Thanks," she squeaked, relaxing a little in her seat. How did he do that? She'd broken his heart half an hour ago, and he was trying to make her feel better.

Kit Morgan was worlds above any man she had ever met, and every passing moment tore her in half, like she was a per-forated piece of paper under pressure. Each tug of emotion broke through another cut and sent her running for the hills while she desperately tried to cling to the hope of creating something lasting and staying in one piece.

"Should we go?" he said, nodding toward the windshield. "You don't want to be late meeting your contractor."

"Yeah." Skyler's breath eased out of her lungs as she started the car, and rather than speeding off and spitting gravel, like she'd imagined when she was shouting at Lloyd, she eased the car around and onto the road.

Two minutes of silence was all she could handle. "What did I just do?"

Kit chuckled. Something in him had relaxed between their conversation this morning and now. Maybe it was because of Heidi's surprising apology, though Skyler hadn't thought he was all that bothered by Heidi's accusation the other day. "You just stood up for yourself," he said. "It was epic."

"Epically horrible. How am I supposed to pay for the store now?"

"You're Skyler Montague. You'll figure it out."

Though Kit pulled out his phone, Skyler wasn't ready to fall back into silence. Besides, she was still running a little high and had too many thoughts and questions to keep all of them to herself. "Why are you being so nice to me?"

His response came without hesitation. "Because I love you. And I promised to be your friend. I don't like to break my promises any more than you do."

"Oh. Really?"

He flashed her another smile. "Just drive, Sky. I'm going to text Ben and try to convince him to do a signing on opening day, and it could take a while. He doesn't like being the center of attention, but I think he'll do it."

"You really think so?"

Kit didn't answer, but his lingering smile was enough to keep her from slipping into a panic. If Kit thought everything would turn out okay, it probably would.

Skyler just hoped that related to their relationship as well, as friends or otherwise. She hoped they would be okay.

THIRTY

UNDER NORMAL CIRCUMSTANCES, KIT WOULDN'T spend an entire drive ignoring the person driving on a road trip, but these weren't normal circumstances. Not by a long shot. Though the morning had started out great, then took a mad turn for the worse, his heart had been beating a little bit stronger with every passing hour.

He was probably crazy for thinking things weren't as hopeless as he'd thought, but after the way Skyler had stood up for herself to Lloyd…

"She hired you?" Lloyd had asked as soon as Skyler had stormed off.

Kit had smiled despite everything. "Yeah."

"But your name is Chris Morgan."

Sam must have told him about seeing his license. Or maybe it was Chad, who had apparently looked into him.

"We knew each other in the sixth grade." It had been so freeing to admit the truth after the kindness Lloyd had shown him in the workshop. "She was my first love." He'd run his thumb along the smooth edge of his leather bracelet. "Not sure I ever got over her, to be honest."

It had been a complete understatement, something all three people in the kitchen seemed to realize at the same time. Heidi had looked a little confused, Lloyd pleased, but Stella had burst into tears again. "I remember you," she'd said. "She'd never been so happy, and Skyler left a part of her heart in Diamond Springs. I didn't want to make her leave, but…"

"You did the best you could. She made her way back eventually."

"Made her way back to you."

Kit had smiled. "I hope so."

"She always said she would never get married or have a family," Stella had said, clearly recognizing her part in that belief.

But Kit knew in his heart Skyler was on the cusp of something. He could see it in her eyes, and he just needed to be patient. He'd waited seventeen years for her; he could wait a little longer. So he'd apologized for lying, given Stella a bone-crushing hug that she returned with equal measure, and hurried out to the car after Lloyd admitted his mistake and offered to pay for the store.

Lloyd really wasn't a bad man overall. Just a little misguided. He'd said Skyler had never actually told him he'd been mistaken, so he'd continued to assume she wasn't doing everything on her own.

Half an hour into their drive, Skyler had finally relaxed enough to simply drive instead of constantly looking over at him like she wanted to ask him a million questions. Her focus on the road made it easier to put his plan into place, for which he was grateful, even if he wished he could just tell her what he suspected.

Ben, like he'd expected, agreed to the signing without needing any persuasion. As it so happened, he'd been looking for a good moment to propose to Allie, and doing it in the middle of their first book signing had instantly appealed to him, just like Kit thought it would. Ben may have been shy, but not when it came to Allie. He would go to the ends of the earth for that girl and declare his love for the whole world to hear. Nobody loved like Ben.

Cam was a little harder to convince when it came to his part in Kit's plan.

> Cam: First of all, I'm sorry I told Oliver about Angela.
>
> Cam: We were talking weddings not long after I proposed to Lani, and Oliver said something about how you probably wouldn't tell us you got engaged until after the wedding had already been planned, and it just slipped out.
>
> Cam: Second, you want me to lie to Skyler? Are you serious?
>
> Kit: I promise I'll make it worth your while. I just need a distraction.
>
> Cam: And me puking is the best you could come up with?
>
> Kit: Everyone else has other parts to play.
>
> Cam: Fine. But you owe me.
>
> Kit: Look up Woodshop Would.
>
> Cam: What is that?
>
> Kit: Me making it worth your while.

Kit sent texts to Kailani and Allie, who were confused but happy to help out, and when Skyler stopped for a bathroom break, he stole her phone and sent a message to her contractor to push back their meeting by an hour or so, asking him to confirm what time he would be at the bookstore. Then he deleted the text he'd sent so Skyler wouldn't see it.

When he texted Oliver and Madi once they were on the road again, he could hardly hold back his smile when they replied.

> Madi: Did Skyler steal your phone again? You want to do what?
>
> Kit: No, she didn't. And exactly what I said.
>
> Oliver: We should do what he says, Mads.
>
> Madi: I am literally sitting right next to you. Why are you texting me?

Oliver: So my best friend knows I'm fully on his side. Take
    whatever you need, Captain.

Madi: Hold on a minute.

Kit: I promise it's for a good reason.

He quickly explained the situation and his plan, keeping his phone screen pointed away from Skyler just in case. He hadn't forgotten her ability to answer emails while driving. It would have been so much easier to put this plan into action if he'd been able to talk instead of text, but the timing was important. He couldn't wait until they were back.

Madi: This sounds crazy. Especially for you.

Oliver: No, it sounds like the Kit I knew when we were
    younger. Remember that time he convinced my par-
    ents to let me spend the night?

Madi: When we slept on the trampoline. Yes, I remember.

Madi: I'm still not going to go to all the effort to name that
    star after you.

Oliver: Why not? I think it would be cool.

Madi: Because you picked one of the brightest stars in
    the sky for me, which already has a name, so I can't
    get a star named after me.

Oliver: I'll name a different one after you.

Madi: But that one's mine.

Oliver: You do remember that we have a kid named after
    your constellation, right? I think that should count.

Kit: GUYS. Focus.

Kit: I had to convince Ollie's parents that it was their idea.
    It's going to have to be the same thing this time too.
    She has to make the decision herself.

Madi: And you think this convoluted plan will work?

Kit: It's not that convoluted. And it has to work.

Oliver: It will work. We'll make sure it does.

Oliver: It's good to have you back, Kit.

Kit grinned, amazed that he could feel this optimistic when Skyler was sitting next to him looking completely miserable, like she would never be happy again. He really hoped he could harness enough of twelve-year-old Christopher's chaotic confidence to pull this off.

"I'm exhausted," he said, breaking the silence that had permeated the car all morning. They only had an hour or so before they reached Diamond Springs, and Kit didn't want Skyler to suspect anything. "Mind if I take a quick nap? You can wake me up if you need me to drive."

Skyler waved him away. "Yeah, of course. Anything you need."

Kit sent off one more text, which Isla responded to immediately, followed by a messy text from Cam in the big group chat.

Kit: This grand gesture thing had better work.

Isla: OMG I can't wait to hear all about it

Cam: !!!?!!? YOU GUYS ARE NEVERGOING TO BE-
LIEBE THIS VIDEO IM ABOUT TOO SEND YOU

THIRTY-ONE

THE LAST THING SKYLER WANTED to see was the edge of Diamond Springs coming into view. Yeah, okay, she was eager for her own bed in her flat, but coming back into town meant they were officially coming back to reality. She had been holding onto a shred of hope the entire drive, wondering if they could stay in the bubble just a little longer. Or maybe, if she kept driving, she would never have to say goodbye to the good times with Kit.

Instead, she nudged him awake and tried to sound happy. "Almost back home."

As he sat up, Kit grabbed his phone, which had buzzed in his lap several times while he slept, and chuckled as he read some texts. He must have been messaging the Wonder Boys all morning, trying to have them cheer him up, and it seemed to have worked.

"I told them about my videos," he explained, rubbing sleep from his eyes before letting out a huge, attractive yawn.

What was wrong with her? Yawns weren't supposed to be attractive! But a girl didn't wake up next to Kit Morgan without every little thing reminding her of what could have been if she were braver.

It suddenly dawned on her what he'd just said. "You told—how did they react?"

He flashed his phone screen at her, showing her the endless texts and GIFs he'd gotten. "They're maybe a little too entertained. Actually, could you drop me off at Oliver's house? I'm probably too tired to drive, and I know they're going to want an explanation for the existence of my channel. He can bring me to my car later."

Skyler was already running late, but the little detour was the least she could do after this morning's breakup. "Sure."

When she pulled up outside a literal mansion, her jaw dropped. "Uh, you never told me Oliver was filthy rich."

Kit grinned. "It's Madi too, honestly. She downplays her photography skills, but ever since getting married she's been specializing in higher end weddings and making top dollar. I doubt she'll slow down even with the baby."

"That's right! You just got a new nephew." Skyler's heart throbbed as Kit's smile shifted into one so sweet and loving that she could barely stand it. If he could get that kind of look in his eyes when he thought about a nephew, what would he be like with his own kids?

Honestly, she hadn't been able to stop thinking about that. While Kit slept, she had been trapped in the silence with nothing but her imagination, which had really started to run rampant and leave her heart aching for deeper connections with people. People like Micah, who had texted a dozen times during the drive to make sure Skyler was okay. Skyler hadn't responded, but she'd wanted to, which was new.

The weirdest part was how tempted she had been to call her mom and actually talk things out. The only reason she hadn't was because she didn't want Kit to be a part of that raw conversation. To see her fully vulnerable in a place she couldn't escape.

Yawning again, Kit grabbed his door handle to step out but paused when someone appeared from behind the house on her way to a car parked in the driveway. "Oh, looks like Allie is here."

Skyler gasped. "*The* Allie? The one who wrote *Menace Unknown*?"

"That's her."

Glancing at her phone, Skyler debated calling her contractor to see if he could meet her a little bit later. But right before she was about to grab it, he sent her a text telling her he would be at the bookstore at one. "Oh!" It was like he'd read her mind, but that meant she had more than an hour before she had to be at the store.

"Want to meet her?" Kit asked, raising an eyebrow.

"Stupid question," Skyler replied and slipped out of the car. "She only wrote the most captivating storyline I've ever read."

Kit waved, stopping Allie before she reached her car. "Hey Als! You have a minute?"

"Oh hey, Kit! You're back early." Allie looked so non-threatening and innocent that Skyler couldn't help but wonder how someone who looked as sweet as her could have written such a dynamic and sympathetic villain. The shape shifter in her graphic novel did the things she did out of fear and self-preservation, doing all the wrong things for the right reasons.

Skyler sort of knew how that felt, especially when Kit did a fancy handshake with Allie. She had no right to be jealous, and she'd taken a step back because it was best for Kit. But it sure felt like the wrong thing to have done.

"Allie, this is Skyler."

Allie's eyes went wide. "Oh, you're the one starting the bookstore! This is kind of perfect, actually. I was just going to go email my publisher about the signing, but it would actually be really helpful if I had some more details. Do you have a second to chat?"

Skyler glanced at the big house Allie gestured to. If she was here, that probably meant Ben was somewhere inside. While she badly wanted to meet the artist, Kit's best friend and sister were in that house as well. But how was she supposed to say no when Allie would be doing her a huge favor by doing the signing?

"Yeah, I've got a few minutes."

Allie grinned. "Great!" She grabbed Skyler by the hand and pulled her to the front door, letting herself into the house. "Ben is out in the guest house, but he and Cam are trying to pack up the last of his stuff so he can move into the house he bought us. We can grab him in a minute."

That made Skyler stumble a little. Cam was here too? Did the Wonder Boys often get together like this? Or were they just so close that they were at each other's houses all the time like friends were in sitcoms? Skyler had never actually met anyone who hung out as frequently as the *Friends* or the *How I Met Your Mother* crews, but maybe they existed in real life? Or maybe the Wonder Boys were just a rare breed.

With Kit Morgan as their leader, that was definitely true. He had a knack for helping people become exceptional.

"Madi!" Allie called when they reached a gorgeous, vaulted living room. "I'm stealing your studio for a minute!"

"Wait!" Madi appeared from around a corner, her eyes wide. "I'm in the middle of editing the bridesmaid photos we—oh! Skyler! I didn't think you guys were coming back until Sunday. Does that mean Kit is—Kit!" Madi passed Skyler, giving her arm a squeeze, and then took her brother in a death grip that made him wince. "Will you *please* tell Oliver he needs to stop watching Ri sleep? I don't think he's moved in over an hour, and I'm not sure if he's actually alive or if he finally passed out from keeping himself awake at night. He promised to help Ben with the website today."

"Oh, I thought they were done with that already," Allie said, frowning at Skyler as if she had something to do with the delay. "Oh well. Madi won't let us see the bridesmaid pictures until they're edited, so I guess we can just sit and chat here? I'll just write everything down on my phone instead of the computer." She practically dragged Skyler onto the couch.

"Did you ask Ollie to leave the room?" Kit asked, squinting toward the stairs.

Madi rolled her eyes. "What do you think?"

"I'll go talk to him."

"So," Allie said, pulling Skyler's attention away from Kit's retreating back where it wanted to stay, "you're opening on the eighth, right?"

To say Skyler was overwhelmed was an understatement, but she nodded as Madi joined them on the couch. "I don't know if I have many details to give you yet, though. I wasn't sure if you guys would want to do it."

Allie scoffed. "After months of wondering if anyone would even believe I was the author, you have no idea how excited I am for this. Kit said your bookstore is going to be amazing."

Skyler's heart thumped a little stronger. "He did?"

"It must be pretty great," Madi said with a kind smile. "My brother doesn't talk about anything unless he is really into it. Except woodworking, apparently."

Allie giggled. "I can't wait to go back and watch the rest of those. How did he keep that a secret?" She squeezed Skyler's hand, which she hadn't let go of since the driveway. "Turns out Kit made a bunch of videos where he—"

"I saw them," Skyler said, smiling despite herself. She would have thought being in the house, surrounded by the people Kit loved, would have been harder than this, but these ladies were so welcoming. She felt like she knew them so well already just from what Kit had told her about them.

Madi's eyes sparkled as she gazed at Skyler. "Are you the reason he decided to share them with us?"

There was no way to answer that question without things getting awkward because she would have to explain their complicated relationship, so Skyler was immensely glad when Kit reappeared on the stairs. Only, instead of a duffel on his shoulder, he had a baby in his arms.

If seeing him hugging a third grader had pierced her soul, Kit Morgan with a baby in his arms was a hundred times worse. There was no way a man could look more attractive than cradling a tiny baby in his big, strong arms.

Her stomach twisted at that thought. She'd never even imagined a man holding a baby before, but that thought had come so easily. Maybe it was just Kit. He was attractive no matter what he did. Like Heidi said, he would absolutely make a good father someday.

Skyler suddenly felt nauseous. That someday would have to be with someone else. Someone who could imagine herself having kids. She shouldn't have hated the idea of Kit loving someone else enough to have a family with her, but she did, and she worried that this jealousy for an unknown woman was the kind that would never go away.

And now that he had worked through a lot of the things holding him back, that someday would probably come sooner than later.

"You should have let him sleep," Madi said as Oliver appeared behind Kit, looking completely exhausted.

"He is asleep," Kit argued, eyes locked on his nephew.

"I meant Oliver."

"I wasn't asleep," Oliver said through a massive yawn. *His* yawn wasn't attractive… When he reached the bottom of the stairs, he blinked at Skyler before a grin crept up one side of his face. "You owe me a hypnotist video."

Skyler hated that her mind went immediately to the Ferris wheel that had followed the hypnotist's show. How long would it take before everything reminded her of her time with Kit? If she kept reliving their kisses over and over again, and if Kit kept looking completely adorable as he smiled down at baby Orion, she was going to be in trouble.

"That's too bad," she croaked. "I didn't take a video."

"No!"

"Hey Oliver," Allie said, "will you go get Ben for me? We're talking about doing a book signing at Skyler's store, so he should probably be a part of this."

"Is that a good idea, sending Oliver out with Cam out there?" Kit asked, finally looking up from the baby he held. He pierced Oliver with a glare. "Clearly the two of you can't be trusted on your own."

Oliver waved that comment away as he headed deeper into the house. "Lani stopped by to pick up Cam for a meeting with Brad," he said, his voice fading as he went. "No way she's letting the two of us get into trouble."

That meant the entire Wonder Gang was on the property, which sent Skyler's heart racing. This was Kit's family. The people he trusted more than anyone. Had he told any of them about how she'd broken his heart this morning? Did they even know he'd fallen in love? Honestly, Skyler wasn't sure if any of them even knew about Angela, and she had to wonder if Kit sharing his videos was the start of him being more open with his friends, or if it was simply a distraction from the pain.

"He's getting so big," Kit said, looking at his sister. "Isn't he?"

Madi smiled. "I think so. It's hard to tell this early on, but you haven't seen him in almost a week. You'd probably notice the difference more than I would."

"How are you feeling, Mads?"

"Good. Tired, but good."

"I'm going to be helping Sky get her store ready, but if you need a babysitter so you can have a break…" He glanced over at Skyler, giving her a soft smile before turning his eyes back to little Orion. "Just let me know."

Had Skyler cried enough today? Apparently not. Seeing how happy Kit was about the idea of watching his nephew had her heart trying to tie itself in a knot. He was always so happy around kids. Even kids he didn't know. Of course he wanted his own kids, but maybe…

Could he be happy without them? Could Skyler even ask that of him?

"Hey!" A deep voice boomed throughout the house, somehow not quite loud enough to wake the baby, and a giant man followed the shout, so much muscle on him that he made Kit look small and skinny. Cam was even more impressive in real life than he'd been on video. "What is this about you hanging out with *Houston Briggs* all week and I had to hear about it from Fancypants McGee here? Oliver doesn't even like baseball! Please tell me you got Houston's autograph."

Kit shook his head.

Cam slapped a palm to his face as Oliver, Ben, and a gorgeous Polynesian woman—Kailani, if Skyler remembered right from the texts—appeared behind him, crowding the living room. "What am I going to do with you, Morgan? You always do this!"

Skyler tensed, waiting for Kit to lose his smile or show any sign of pain or fear from his friend reminding him of his old ways, but Kit's grin only grew.

"Didn't think about it," he said with a shrug. "But I did beat him in paintball and *God of Battle 2*. And I got you tickets to the next game. Behind the dugout. He said he'd love to chat afterward."

Cam's jaw dropped. "Someone get this baby out of the way so I can hug the man. Lani?"

Kailani grabbed Orion, and Cam immediately leapt onto Kit in what looked more like a wrestle than a hug, the two of them stumbling deeper into the room as Kit struggled to hold Cam's weight.

"Nice to meet you in person, Skyler," Ben said, as if the guys hadn't turned their hug into an actual wrestling match on the floor and this was a completely normal moment. "I'm excited to see your bookstore when it's ready."

Skyler barely had the capacity to wave. She was too overwhelmed by all of this. By being welcomed with open arms, by seeing a new side of Kit when she thought she'd seen it all, by the notion of having this in her life forever if she could only be brave enough to consider something unfamiliar and terrifying. Kailani, with all her muscle and intensity, hardly looked like the sort of person who could have mothering instincts, and yet she happily made cooing noises to the little baby who finally seemed to be waking up.

"Allie," Ben said, "we just got an email from Zoe."

Jumping up, Allie rushed to his side. "What did she say?"

Kailani immediately took her spot on the couch, bringing Orion close enough for Skyler to finally get a look at the baby. He looked so tiny. Skyler had only seen babies from a distance or in movies, and they always looked so much bigger than this little bundle in Kailani's arms.

"I think it's time for your nap," Madi said.

Skyler felt a strange tug in her gut—she'd only just gotten a glimpse of Orion—but Madi stood and stepped over to her husband instead, who looked ready to fall asleep on his feet.

Oliver took Madi's hand, kissing her palm. "Only if you come with me," he murmured. "I know you're exhausted."

Madi turned and met her brother's eyes. Kit must have heard the exchange, even while tangled up with Cam on the floor, because he shoved himself free and hopped back to his feet. "I'll watch him," he said easily. "You need to get as much rest as you can."

Madi smiled. "Let me show you where the bottles are in case he gets hungry. I've got some extra milk in the freezer."

"You're losing your touch," Oliver told Cam, his sleepy grin making him look a little ridiculous.

Still on the floor, Cam narrowed his eyes into a glare. "I am not. I'm in peak shape."

"Yeah, you are," Kailani agreed, and her eyes roved over her fiancé with obvious appreciation. "I could look at that all day," she breathed to Skyler.

As Cam saluted and sent a crooked grin their way, Skyler could see the appeal. Cam was undoubtedly attractive—all the Boys were—but none of them held a candle to Kit. None of them got her heart pattering like he did.

"Are you going to completely fangirl when you meet Houston Briggs?" Kailani asked Cam. There was an edge of amusement to her voice.

Cam glared at her, and the two of them had a little showdown—Kailani was definitely winning—until Cam said, "No, of course not."

And then he threw up, right on the rug.

Skyler pulled her legs up onto the couch out of instinct at the same time Oliver shouted in protest. Allie ducked behind Ben as if he could protect her from the disgusting sight, and Kailani let out a deep sigh.

"Can you—" she said before setting Orion in Skyler's arms and helping Cam to his feet. "Come on, big guy. Let's get you cleaned up."

"We'll grab a mop," Ben muttered at the same time Oliver groaned, "I'm throwing that rug away. Ben, the mop is—let me show you."

And suddenly Skyler was alone.

She sat there, arms stiff and panic rising as she tried to figure out how she was supposed to hold the baby. Why in the world would they leave him with her? It probably hadn't been intentional, but if she wasn't so worried about doing something wrong or hurting him, she would be on her feet looking for Madi or Kit. Allie. *Anyone* who wasn't her.

"What am I supposed to do?" she whispered to the baby, unwilling to let anyone hear her admitting her faults. For some inexplicable reason, she wanted Kit's friends to like her and trust her, not be scared to let her within twenty feet of the littlest Wonder Boy. "I don't know what to do with a baby!"

Orion blinked sleepily, his eyes a strange grayish green, like they hadn't decided what color they were going to be yet. He wiggled inside his blanket wrap, looking like a little blond burrito.

Skyler shifted him so his head was in the crook of her elbow instead of in her hands, which felt safer than holding him out across her lap like she had been. She could hold him in one arm this way and make sure his blanket stayed tucked.

"You look like Kit," she said, frowning down at the baby. His features were all squishy, but she could see where the Morgan genes had come into play in his nose and chin. Maybe he would have brown eyes like his uncle, a rich color that reminded her of milk chocolate mixed with caramel. Skyler loved Kit's eyes. They matched his personality so well, warm and gentle with a bit of mischief sprinkled into the golden streaks.

Would Kit's kids take after him? She hoped so, both in physical appearance and personality. Anything was better than them taking after someone like Skyler. But no matter how they turned out, they would have the best father in the world, and he would teach them how to be good people. How to be kind and caring, and notice when someone was feeling lonely or overwhelmed. He'd show them through example more than anything, like when he offered to babysit so his sister could get some sleep, and when he helped a million and a half kids with their crafts.

"I'm not like that," Skyler murmured, brushing a finger over the wisps of blond hair on Orion's head. Everything about the baby was so soft and delicate, and she couldn't understand how anything could be so perfect. And he was going to have the most incredible family behind him. Skyler wouldn't fit in. "I'm not naturally caring, and I don't have all the right things to say to a kid. Not like he does."

Kit was so good at all of that that he basically had enough nurturing instinct for the both of them.

Skyler's chest grew tight, and she pulled the baby closer to her body, like hugging him might ease the tension that kept climbing. "I want to see Kit as a father," she whispered. "Is that crazy? Does that make me a masochist? Because I'm desperate to see that side of him, but I can't stand the idea of someone else being his other half. If he's going to have a kid, I want it to be mine."

Wait.

"Hey."

Skyler flinched.

Kit appeared from around the corner, his eyebrows pulling low when he found the room empty except for her. "Where did everyone…" His eyes locked on the little puddle of vomit that Skyler had somehow completely forgotten about because all she could smell was baby shampoo. "Cam?" he guessed and gave her a crooked smile.

"I have to go." Skyler got up as quickly as she could without jostling Orion, and then she stuffed the baby into Kit's arms as she mumbled nonsense. "Meeting. Baby. Bookstore. Looks like you."

"Sky."

Skyler had pulled open the front door by the time he spoke, and when she turned around, she found him watching her with confusion in his eyes.

"You okay?" he asked, looking so at ease with a baby in his arms that Skyler couldn't hold back her tears anymore. Fear flooded her body as she stood there. Fear that these new feelings of *maybe* were only temporary. Fear that she could never be good enough. Fear that she'd blown her chances at a future with this man by telling him she would never want what he did.

"I'll see you around, Kit," she whispered and slipped out the door.

THIRTY-TWO

IT TOOK EVERYTHING IN KIT not to chase after Skyler as she ran out to her car and drove off. For one, he didn't exactly want to run with a baby in his arms, but for another, he knew he needed to give her time. She needed space to process.

"Madi was right. That really was the most convoluted plan in the world," Oliver said, coming up behind him. The others filtered back into the living room as well now that Skyler was gone. "Are you sure it worked?"

"She wants kids," Kit replied. "I know she does." He'd seen it in her eyes before she ran away, and then there was what she'd said to Lloyd about grandkids back at the cabin. It could have been a slip of the tongue, but Kit was positive Skyler secretly wanted the whole family life she'd missed out on. "I had to help her see the truth."

"If you were anyone else, I'd call you crazy," Oliver muttered, and then he pointed to Cam. "You owe me a new rug, Martinez. You couldn't have at least done it on the hardwood?"

Cam scowled. "It was Captain Morgan's idea, so blame him! It's not like that reaction to lying is pleasant or controllable, you know. You're lucky it wasn't worse; I had a huge breakfast this morning."

"I think you're right, Kit," Madi said with a warm smile. "She's scared, but I don't think a family is as out of the question as she told you."

"What will you do if she doesn't change her mind?" Kailani asked. It was a valid question.

Kit looked at his friends gathered around him, trying to imagine a future where he was on his own. For the longest time, seeing his best friends fall in love had made him feel like there was something wrong with him. Why else would a cheating, secret fiancée be the closest thing he could get to a happily ever after? But this week with Skyler had helped him embrace the parts of himself he had kept hidden for years, and he hadn't truly felt the itch of discontent in days, when that used to be a constant feature of his life.

Maybe, all this time, his body had been trying to tell him that the only thing he was really afraid of was the walls he'd put up. If he had stopped living scared, he might have realized that no matter what happened in his love life, the Wonder Boys were family.

He would never be alone.

Taking a deep breath, Kit looked down at Orion, who stared right back up at him like he knew this was a big moment. "I've never wanted anything more than my own family," he said quietly, tears distorting his vision. "So it's a good thing I've already got a good one, because even if Skyler doesn't ever want her own kids, I'm still going to have a whole bunch of nieces and nephews to spoil rotten."

Skyler meant too much to him to let her go because of this. He hadn't said goodbye to her seventeen years ago, and he wasn't willing to let it happen now.

Oliver put his arm around Kit's shoulders, gazing down at his son with so much love in his eyes. "You did good, little buddy," he said, cupping Ri's head with his hand. "If this kid can't convince the love of your life to make a baby with you, nothing will."

Kit elbowed him in the ribs.

Laughing, Oliver slipped out of reach and grinned at him as he walked backward. "You're still willing to watch him, right? Because Madi and I are totally taking that nap." He grabbed Madi's hand and disappeared up the stairs before Kit could argue. Not that he planned to.

Cam took the mop Ben handed to him, but he narrowed his eyes as he examined Kit. "You're different. I'm not just talking about the beard, which I had no idea you could grow until now. You're…different."

Kit waited for the prickly sensation to finally make its appearance on his skin, but it didn't. He just felt happy. "Yeah," he agreed. "I am. I feel like myself for the first time in years."

"Oliver told me about junior high," Ben said, tucking his arm around Allie's waist. "You do seem more like the Kit who found me in fourth grade. But you don't have to change if you don't want to."

Kit grinned. "I want to."

"Cool. We're going to go watch the rest of those videos." He paused, his eyebrows pulling low as if he'd just realized something. "You built my coffee table instead of buying it, didn't you?"

"Your cabinets!" Cam added with surprise.

Chuckling, Kit shifted Orion so the baby's head rested on his shoulder, freeing up one arm to grab his phone. "Guess I've got some explaining to do. But first, Ben, I need the name of your realtor."

"Why?"

"Because my plan's not over yet."

THIRTY-THREE

"MICAH, I'M FREAKING OUT." SKYLER paced on her back porch, her phone pressed to her ear and her entire body sweating. Maybe that was because it was ridiculously hot despite being nine in the morning, or because she wasn't used to having girl talk when she'd never kept a girlfriend longer than a few weeks. Or maybe it was because Kit was supposed to show up at the bookstore any minute now and she had spent the last forty-four hours in a state of perpetual panic.

"Clearly you shouldn't have gone home yet," Micah said, laughter in her words. "I wish I was there so I could see you like this. You're always so perfect!"

"Ha!" Skyler tugged at the front of her blouse, trying to cool off her body by getting a little air circulation. "You say that like Heidi isn't your actual sister. I'm so not perfect."

"Did you know that Heidi spent all day in the pool with the Wonder Twins yesterday?"

That made Skyler pause. "Really?" So she hadn't just said those things to Kit to clear her conscience? "That's cool, I guess."

"Stephan hasn't even left their bedroom office except to eat, and I think Heidi is starting to realize that her marriage is just as bad as her parenting was. It's been a whole lot of drama since you left."

It was all so interesting, but Skyler didn't have time to dissect Heidi's transformation right now. "I thought we were talking about my drama."

Micah laughed. "You mean the drama of you realizing you threw away the perfect relationship for the stupidest reason?"

Skyler flopped onto one of the Adirondack chairs. "Being unsure if I want a family when the man was literally created to be a dad is not a stupid reason."

"An hour ago you said you *knew* you didn't want a family," Micah argued. "Now you're not sure? Which, by the way, is wrong. All that time you spent with Isabelle, you were basically unrecognizable because you were smiling so much. Besides, who would look at Kit Morgan and *not* want to have his babies?"

"Gross. Micah, you are just asking for me to hate you, you know that?"

"I stand by what I said. Kit is hot. H-A-W-T. And if you're not going to lock that down, I might just have to come visit you in Diamond Springs. And by *you* I mean *him*. We can't let a good man like that go to waste."

Skyler groaned, doing her best not to picture sweet and perky Micah putting the moves on Kit. Micah had been a cheerleader when she was younger, which meant she was exactly Kit's type. It made Skyler's stomach churn just thinking about it. "Will you stop?"

"This is what I'm talking about! You're in love with the man, and if the only thing holding you back is your *assumption* that he doesn't want to be with you because of the *possibility* of you not wanting kids, something is wrong with you. All sorts of married couples don't have kids."

"But this is Kit," Skyler argued. "You saw him this weekend! And when we were kids, he talked about it all the time. What twelve-year-old is cognizant enough to be thinking about having kids in the future?"

"Man, I wish we'd grown up together so I could have seen little Kit."

"I have a picture."

"WHAT? Show me right now!"

"Micah, can we focus? What am I supposed to do when he gets here?"

"Kiss his face off."

"*No.*"

"Tell him you want to have his babies."

"Micah!" Skyler rubbed her temple, unsure if this headache that was slowly building was because of Micah or the fact that she'd barely slept the last two nights. Every time she fell asleep, she dreamed about Kit and woke up on the verge of tears.

That probably meant something.

"Okay, do you want some real advice?" Micah asked.

"Do you *have* real advice?"

"I may be, like, nine years younger than you—"

"Five."

"—but I know what I'm talking about when it comes to love. I've read all the books."

Skyler glanced through the back door into the store, where dozens of boxes of books waited to be shelved. "You're going to tell me you're an expert on love because you've read a bunch of trashy romance novels?"

"*Please*. I read the *classy* ones. But I'm serious. Trashy or classy, these books resonate with people because they're real. All of those characters may be in less-than-believable situations, but the emotions—the reason people read them in the first place—those are all real things people feel every day."

Skyler switched her phone to her other hand and got up to pace again. "You're saying you've read a book about my situation?"

"Psh. You're nothing special."

"Do you have advice or not?"

Micah's smile came out in her voice, which had gotten softer. "Don't try to tell Kit how he feels. Just tell him how *you* feel, even if you think it's going to ruin everything. Even if you're not sure how you feel. Be straight with him. Unless both of you are totally honest with each other, you're never going to make things work. And I *know* you want to make things work."

Skyler was afraid Micah would say something like that, probably because she already knew that she couldn't project her fears onto Kit and expect them both to like the outcome. But knowing that and putting honesty into practice were two different things. "Micah," she sighed, "this is me we're talking about. I don't know how to be open and vulnerable and all that."

"Sure you do. You were doing it all week. You just didn't realize it because you trust Kit."

Pausing, Skyler considered that. "I trust him," she repeated. She'd always trusted him. From that first day of sixth grade, when he gave her a nervous smile as he sat down next to her in first period. All this week she had let loose and had more fun than she'd ever had in her life, even though she should have felt ridiculous making bracelets and playing paintball. But with Kit beside her, all of that fear had melted away.

What if the same could be true for her other fears?

"I don't think one conversation is going to be enough to fix you guys," Micah said. "But you have to start somewhere. Kit knows that you're scared of being a bad mom, and he won't pursue something with you if you and all of your baggage aren't something he wants. I have literally never met anyone as confident as Kit, and I'm related to Houston Briggs, so that's saying something. *Trust him.*"

Was that really what Skyler was afraid of? Being a mom like the Stella Montague she'd grown up with? She'd always thought she didn't like kids, and she certainly didn't like the idea of being bad at something. But the same thought that she'd had at Oliver's house popped into her head again as she stood there and stared out into the yard.

Kit Morgan had skills enough for both of them. And he was also an incredibly talented teacher who could help her learn to nurture. Heck, he might have even orchestrated that whole thing the other day to leave her alone with Orion and show her that babies weren't nearly as terrifying as she'd thought.

She cursed under her breath. He'd *totally* orchestrated that whole thing! It was classic mischievous Kit, the kid who convinced an entire class to be completely silent so their teacher thought he'd gone temporarily deaf. The guy who picked a paintball team built out of spite. The man who made her insides catch on fire every time he smiled because he was exactly what she needed.

She swore again, louder this time.

"Did you trip on something or have an epiphany?" Micah asked.

"I have to go."

"Wait, no!"

Skyler hung up and turned to head into the store, only she ran smack into a solid, familiar body. Hands gripped her arms to keep her upright, and then neither of them moved. Oh, he smelled so good. Or maybe it had just been a day and a half too long since she saw him last.

"Sorry," he said, his voice soft. "I knocked on the door, but you didn't answer, so I let myself in and saw you back here. I was going to announce myself, but then you body-slammed me."

Skyler didn't want to move. She had no right to be in his arms like this, but there was nowhere else she'd rather be.

"You okay?" he asked, shifting so his arms wrapped around her shoulders and held her closer. *Better now.* This man knew how to hug. "How did things go with the contractor? It looks great, by the way."

"It's not complete." She said that directly into his t-shirt as she wrapped her arms around his waist, and she desperately hoped he understood what she was really trying to say but was too scared to. "It needs you. I mean your shelves." *But mostly you.*

"That's why I'm here." When one of his hands snaked up her back and into her hair, Skyler curled deeper into his hold. He felt so safe that all of her fears sounded stupid, even if they were real. Kit would never let her fail. "I have something for you."

Reluctantly pulling away, Skyler looked up into his eyes but couldn't read anything in his expression. His mask was back in place, and she knew she'd put it there. Glancing down at the folded paper he pulled out of his back pocket, she forced herself to remember this was going to take time, just like Micah had said. But the fact that he was here meant she hadn't completely ruined everything.

"Shelf designs?" she guessed.

"Those are out in the car."

"Then, what is this?"

"Just read it."

Skyler took the paper, scanning over the photocopied contract though he'd only given her the last page, with the signatures. Something about a sale and… She froze. "You sold your house?"

He nodded, his face still missing any real sense of expression. "I'm taking Ben's place in Oliver's guest house in exchange for free babysitting."

"But I thought you had all sorts of plans for your house." What did it mean that he'd given up on that dream? Was he trying to tell her that he no longer had a place to make a home with her because they didn't have a future together anyway?

"I did," he agreed. "Until about a week ago."

He was definitely telling her they didn't have a future, and she'd killed his last dream, bringing him down to his lowest point. Jobless, homeless, childless. "Oh." Not wanting to see the emptiness in his face anymore, Skyler stepped past him and into the store. They could at least get the shelves figured out. Or maybe she would be better off finding a different person to do the job, someone who didn't hate her.

"Sky." Kit was right behind her. "I want to be your business partner."

She came to a dead stop in the middle of the front room. "What?"

"You heard me. I want to invest in your store, which you really need to name, by the way, so I don't keep calling it The Bookstore in my head. I'll pay the mortgage in exchange for a share of the profits when it's up and running."

Spinning around, she expected to find him ready to start laughing at his hilarious joke. But he looked perfectly serious, his hands in the pockets of his shorts. He looked so…normal… in his khaki shorts and a green t-shirt. Casual. Relaxed. He did *not* look like a guy who had just had his heart broken a couple of days ago, especially with her friendship bracelet sitting next to the leather one on his wrist. Why would he still wear those?

"You want to pay for the store," she repeated, trying to figure out what he was doing. Was this part of his convoluted plan?

As a little smile played at the corner of his mouth, Kit nodded. "Yep."

"And Oliver is okay with you moving in?"

He shrugged. "The guest house is separate from the main house."

He was being far too cool about all of this. Yes, he had loosened up and became more whole over the last several days, but Skyler knew there was still some of the unchangeable Kit in there. Leaving the comfort of his house and being at the mercy of his best friend could hardly be easy for him. What was his game?

Standing up a little straighter, Skyler narrowed her eyes at him. "How are you going to pay rent?"

"He's not charging me rent. Like I said, the only thing I owe him is watching Orion, and I would have done that anyway."

"And how are you going to pay for a mortgage when you don't have a job?"

"My house was worth more than I owe on it. And I was thinking of setting up a custom order shop on Etsy or something. Plus, it turns out you can make some decent money from sponsors and ads when you have a lot of views."

Skyler folded her arms. "And if that doesn't work?"

"I'll find another job."

"Do you have any idea what it takes to run a bookstore?"

"No, but you can teach me."

"Can you make coffee?"

"Barely."

"How did you get Cam to throw up on command like that?"

"Easy. You just have to…" He stiffened, eyes going wide as his mouth slowly fell open.

Skyler pointed at him. "I knew it!"

He held up his hands. "I can explain."

"How you totally set me up using your friends to trick me into falling in love with your nephew?"

A glorious smile broke out on his face. "Did it work?"

"Yes, but that's beside the point!" Skyler couldn't decide if she was angry or impressed, and her face felt like it was stretching in all sorts of weird angles as she fought the smile that kept coming. "Kit Morgan, you can't just go around ninja attacking people with big emotions!"

His smile hadn't faltered in the least. "You totally lawyered me just now."

"That's not a verb."

"You lawyered me the same way I teachered you."

"You know there's a word for that one, right?"

"Teachering is different from teaching. Obviously."

"Obviously." Skyler threw her hands in the air. "For goodness's sake! Why are we arguing about this?"

"Because I'm trying really hard not to kiss you right now, and I'm pretty sure I'm going to fail."

Letting out a *gream*, Skyler took a lap around the room while Kit watched her with hungry eyes. "You're supposed to hate me, Kit!"

"Why?" He folded his arms, accentuating his muscles and making himself look far too tempting.

"Because I can't give you what you want!" Had she just gotten closer to him? It was like she'd gotten caught in his orbit, circling slowly closer with every rotation around the room.

He shook his head. "You still believe that, huh?"

"Maybe I'm not as convinced as I thought I was, but the whole kid thing—"

Kit grabbed her, spinning with her until she was flush against him. "At what point did I tell you I want anything except you?" he asked, his face fully serious now.

Skyler fell limp against him, his strength the only thing holding her up at this point. "I want to give you what you want, but—"

"You're not listening." He lowered his head, brushing his nose against hers and teasing her with the softest of kisses. "If I have nothing else in my life, as long as I have you, I will be happy. I've had a Skyler-shaped hole in my life for the last seventeen years, and nothing else seems to fit quite right. Yes, I would love to have kids. Dozens of them. A handful of redheads because I've heard you're going extinct, and one who grows up to be a public defender because that's the only kind of lawyer I'll tolerate, and maybe a few teachers thrown in because teachers are the best. I would love to watch the way your eyes go all watery when you see your kid walk for the first time or shoot their first basket, and I would love to discover if you're the type of parent who takes a million pictures or forgets to document anything because you're too caught up in the moment."

He tugged her in closer, pressing his forehead to hers. "You know what else I would love? Building this store into something incredible and making so much money that we can travel the world—you and me. Taking all sorts of classes together and learning new skills. Being the go-to babysitters when Madi and Oliver need a break, and teaching bad words to Cam and Kailani's inevitable eight kids and watching them try to figure out where they learned it."

He pulled away and met her gaze, though Skyler was crying too hard to really see him. He brushed his finger across each cheek, wiping away her tears as if he hadn't just said the most beautiful words she had ever heard.

"I want a life with you, Skyler," he whispered. "And I don't care what it looks like as long as we're together. But I'm not asking for forever, no matter how much I want it. I'm asking for *right now*. One day at a time. Can you give me that?"

"I love you." She'd finally been the first one to say it, though it had nothing on Kit's speech. "I don't know if I'm ready to give you anything more than that."

He smiled, and there was nothing but love in his expression. "I know."

Still crying, Skyler lifted herself up onto her toes and met his lips in a kiss, and it felt like that kiss sealed their fate, locking them together in a promise that was so much more than three little words.

As long as they were together, nothing else mattered.

EPILOGUE

"I'M NOT TRYING TO KNOCK your wedding, Ollie, but this is so much better than yours." Kit yawned, brushing sand from his hair as he stretched out across his lounge chair. The ocean breeze was lulling him to sleep, and he didn't care in the slightest. It was nice to finally have a chance to relax.

Oliver let out a single laugh. "Excuse me, *who* did most of the planning for my wedding?"

"Kit Morgan did," Ben replied. "Pretty sure you had the schedule planned down to the minute, Kit."

"I did not." He totally had, but only because he'd wanted Madi's wedding to be perfect.

"Will you guys shut up?" Cam groaned. "I'm trying to meditate."

All three of them looked over to where Cam sat at the end of their row of chairs, his body so tense that he looked like he might snap his chair in two. They'd been under the shady beach cabana for twenty minutes, and though Kit was fully relaxed, Cam clearly hadn't gained anything from the massages they got an hour ago.

"Anyone have a coconut they need opened?" Oliver joked, poking Cam's bulging bicep.

Cam slapped his hand away without opening his eyes. "Best Man, you're failing at your job."

Kit snorted. "I don't remember 'keep Oliver from driving Cam crazy' being anywhere in the official duties."

"It was implied."

"I really don't see why you're so stressed," Oliver said with a grin. "You got your big celebrity billionaire friend to surprise you with a tropical destination wedding because you and Kailani have made him millions of dollars by making out in public every few hours."

Cam cracked one eye open. "Brad paid for the wedding because he could turn it into a bonus episode of Lovers' Quarrel and boost views for his next season."

"Isn't that what I just said?"

Sitting up enough to look at Kit over the heads of the other two, Cam shot him a pleading look. He really did look stressed, to the point where he couldn't see that Oliver was actually trying to help by distracting him from the impending ceremony. No matter how calm Cam had pretended to be over the last few months since proposing, he'd been throwing up at least once a day for the last week. Without even telling any lies.

Shaking away the drowsiness that had been sifting over him with every cool breeze, Kit rose to his feet and gestured for Cam to follow him. They walked down to the shore, where the turquoise Hawaiian water licked at their toes.

"What's really bothering you?"

Cam dug his toes into the wet sand, watching it smooth away with the next wave. "It doesn't feel real. Like, I'm waiting for the moment I wake up and find out all of this has been a dream."

Kit knew that feeling all too well. The last eight weeks with Skyler had been some of the best of his life, but it didn't matter how confident he was in his own feelings; he kept waiting for Skyler to realize she was so much better than him.

He'd watched her throw the biggest, craziest, most perfect grand opening, complete with an exclusive book signing with the author and illustrator of the world's most popular graphic novel. Their bookstore—which Skyler had named The Bookstore just to mess with him—had become a worldwide phenomenon overnight. It was the only place to buy signed copies of *Menace Unknown* thanks to a contract Skyler had written up with Ben's publisher, and people in the neighborhood had jumped at the chance to turn their spare bedrooms and empty basements into vacation rentals for the people who traveled to Diamond Springs just to get their hands on a rare physical copy.

She was born to run that store, and one of these days she was going to realize she had grown beyond Kit and the little life he could offer. All he had done for the store beyond paying the mortgage and building the shelves was a children's story time three times a week.

"I don't know if I have any good advice for you," Kit muttered.

Cam groaned. "Not even the great Kit Morgan can help me? I'm doomed."

Kit took a deep breath. He needed to do something to get Cam to calm down, but lately he hadn't felt as wise as he used to be. Spending his days with Skyler had involved random urges to put plastic wrap over her toilet and convince her there was a spider in her hair when she was deep in the middle of a mystery book. She may have brought out the best in him, but she brought out the worst too.

How had Oliver put it? She made him *more*.

Kailani did the same for Cam.

"Kailani loves you," he said. "Do you really think that's not real?"

Cam put his hand over his heart as if making sure it was still beating. "No. No, that's real."

"And do you think she's going to leave you?"

"Intentionally? No. But my dad didn't plan to die."

Kit frowned. He hadn't heard Cam talk about his dad in years. He'd died right before they met, his death the reason the two of them had even become friends.

"Here's a question," he said, putting his hand on Cam's shoulder. "If you could choose to go back and never meet Kailani, never fall in love and have that risk that you might lose her, would you do it?"

"Not in a million years."

Kit admired that conviction as he asked himself the same question about Skyler. If they only lasted this summer, would he still be glad to have done the things he'd done? The answer was an easy *yes*. His life had been fuller the last two months than the rest of it combined.

"There's your answer," he said, speaking as much to himself as he did to Cam. "We all get scared that we're going to end up hurt, but that doesn't mean the good stuff isn't worth it. Besides, do you remember how nervous Oliver was at his wedding?"

Cam chuckled, glancing back at the cabana where Oliver and Ben had managed to procure drinks with colorful little umbrellas in them. "I thought he was going to run away."

"Oliver doesn't get nervous. But he was terrified that day. And Ben? He literally gave Allie a black eye when he proposed because he was scrambling to keep it together. It's okay to be scared."

"You're not scared."

Kit turned back to Cam, his eyebrows high. "I'm terrified."

"Please." Cam scoffed, digging his toes into the sand again. "You didn't even flinch when Skyler dumped you. You knew exactly what to do to get her back."

Fighting a smile, Kit shook his head. "I cried like a baby that night. Madi thought it was Orion, but no. Just me and my miserable overthinking."

They were both quiet for a moment, watching the waves roll up the beach, and then Oliver and Ben appeared on either side of them.

"You two looked sad and pathetic down here on your own," Oliver explained, sipping his drink. "I hope now you know why I was so tempted to elope. This wedding stuff makes everything feel bigger. Scarier."

"Eloping was so much easier," Ben agreed with a nod.

Kit sighed, fixing his eyes on the horizon like he might find some sort of answer out in the ocean. He'd thought love would be so much less dramatic than this. He always imagined finding that perfect person and everything being nice and easy, like a reward for sticking it out until he met his soulmate. But he'd met his soulmate at twelve, and it had taken them more than seventeen years to become the people they needed to be before they found each other again.

After all of that, surely it had to last.

"Wait," Cam said.

The realization hit Kit like a truck, knocking him back a step, and he turned to glare at Ben. "You didn't."

His face turning a deep red, Ben lifted his left hand and let the sun glint off the silver ring on his finger. "I really thought you guys were more observant than this."

"When?" Oliver demanded.

"Two weeks ago."

"WHAT?"

Cam grabbed him and threw him into the water like he weighed nothing. "*Two weeks*?"

Ben came up laughing, scrambling through the waves to get back on his feet. "Seriously, I can't believe none of you noticed. Allie's wearing hers too, but the girls figured it out in about five minutes."

"I feel betrayed by my own wife," Oliver said, his hand over his heart as if wounded.

"I can't believe Lani kept a secret from me," Cam complained. "She knows how much I hate that."

Ben grinned. "We're going to do a ceremony in a couple of months for Allie's mom's sake, but we wanted to do it for ourselves first. With no pressure."

Then all three of them turned to Kit, who honestly wasn't sure how to feel about all of it. Ben was like a brother to him, and it hurt to know he'd missed such a big moment in his life. But at the same time, he knew Ben had never liked being in the spotlight. His very public proposal—at this point, very *viral* proposal because fans had filmed the whole thing—had probably scared him off from the idea of a wedding ceremony with others watching.

"I'm happy for you, Watch," he said, and he meant it. Ben relaxed into an easy smile, one Kit had never seen in the eighteen years they'd known each other. He looked so *happy*. "I'm glad you and Allie did things your way."

"I'm not," Oliver complained. "If I had known you would have reacted like this, Kit, I would have—"

"If you made me miss my baby sister's wedding, I would have murdered you," Kit said calmly. "And Cam, you're legally not allowed to elope because this wedding is now part of your contract, so don't even think about it."

"What about you?" Ben asked, the other two mirroring his worried expression.

Kit tried to smile, but he probably looked constipated. He hadn't brought up the idea of marriage to Skyler after his promise to take things one day at a time, too afraid that it would scare her off again. "Who knows if I'll ever get to that point."

The three of them glanced at each other, and Cam opened his mouth. Oliver wrapped an arm around Cam's shoulders before he could say anything. "Oo, look, I see some hotties coming our way!" He stuck his fingers in his mouth and tried to whistle, but he only blew air through his lips.

Though Kit's heart picked up its rhythm at the sight of Skyler and the others making their way across the beach toward them, he tried to keep his focus on the way Cam was suddenly fixated on the sand again. What were they up to?

"Hey, Wife," Ben said when the girls reached them.

Allie brightened as she took his hand. "They finally figured it out?"

"With a little help. Or maybe a lot of help."

"It's about time!" Madi complained as she slid into Oliver's arms. "Sometimes I wonder if you're really as smart as you look."

"Hey," Oliver said.

Kailani greeted Cam with a kiss, then pressed her palms to his cheeks. "I can see you panicking," she told him quietly. "Let's just pretend it's all fake and we're just here to have a good time."

"Yes, please."

Kit waited for his own greeting, but Skyler had stopped several feet behind everyone else and stood looking out over the ocean like she was trying to find the same answers as Kit. She looked amazing, her hair glowing golden red in the sunlight and her lightweight white dress blowing in the breeze. They'd been in Hawaii for nearly three days now, and her sunkissed skin was begging to be touched.

"Are you going to stay over there?" he asked her, stuffing his hands into the pockets of his shorts.

She grinned back at him. "I was hoping you would come over here. It's a little crowded."

Glancing at his friends, who had all become quite preoccupied, Kit gladly crossed the distance between him and Skyler.

She slid her hands through his open button-up shirt and around his waist, kissing his collarbone as he pulled her close. "This bare-chested look is a good look for you," she said with a smirk. "Why don't you dress like this at home?"

Home. He loved when she used that word. "Because I think it would scare away the customers."

She eyed his bare torso with the look of a museum curator examining a new acquisition. "Mm, I'm pretty sure these abs would double our romance sales if you were around to give them a preview of what they'll find in the books."

"Are you trying to convince me to sell my body?"

"Nah, the show would be free. Though…" She kissed his chest. "I do like the idea of keeping you for myself."

"I should hope so." Before she could keep trailing her kisses across his skin, he bent down and caught her mouth with his own, reminding her why she usually let him take the lead. She was good, but he was better.

Once she'd been thoroughly kissed, he took a step back and tucked her hair behind her ear, only for the wind to catch it again.

"I hate when you do that," she breathed, looking a little dazed and not in the least bit angry. "You always make me forget why I came over here."

He smirked. "You're welcome."

"Oh!" Bouncing on the balls of her feet, she grabbed his hand. "I remember! Did you know there are three weddings happening on the beach today? Apparently, Brad paid one of them to move up their wedding date to today so Cam and Kailani could have the beach to themselves tomorrow."

"Sounds like Brad." The fitness guru-turned-venture capitalist had been funding Cam and Kailani from the moment they got together, and nobody loved their love story as much as Breakout Brad. Not even the half a million fans who had watched the online show that brought them together.

"I was thinking," Skyler continued, and she was back to running her hands along Kit's stomach, "since we don't have any official plans tonight, we could go crash one of them."

Though distracted by her cool hands on his ribcage, Kit frowned at her. "You want to crash a wedding? Don't you have bachelorette things tonight?"

She shook her head. "You forget Kailani has a crazy early bedtime. Not even an all-inclusive resort wedding can convince her to stay up late. Though, I think she's really just nervous."

"Cam's a mess."

"You kind of look like you're a bit of a mess yourself."

How did she notice that? Sometimes Kit forgot that the only time they'd spent apart over the last eight weeks had been at night, when he forced himself to go back to Oliver's so they didn't burn too hot and fast. He'd spent more time with Skyler in two months than he had with Angela in the year they were together, and not even the Wonder Boys knew him as well as she did.

Smiling, Kit laced his fingers with hers and pressed a kiss to her forehead. "Wedding crashing sounds like a nice distraction."

"Distraction from what?"

"Nothing."

"Kit."

"You're not going to lawyer it out of me, so don't even try. I'm fine."

She raised an eyebrow. "Uh huh."

"Who's hungry? Are you hungry? I'm starving." He only made it one step before Skyler pulled him back.

"I will throw you in the ocean if you don't start talking, Christopher Morgan."

Her threat wasn't supposed to make Kit laugh, but it took every ounce of willpower he had to hold back his amusement. Glancing at the waves, he frowned. "Can you even lift me?"

She pointed at him, her glare making her look more attractive than she had a right to be. "You're asking for trouble."

"I'd love to see you try to—"

Skyler punched him in the stomach, knocking the air out of him, and then she pushed him off balance until he stumbled into the water.

He surfaced to the sound of Wonder Boy cheers, still fighting to breathe, and couldn't understand how that move had made him fall even more in love with the woman as she watched him with a smug look on her perfect face. She had never been afraid to stand up for herself, and he never had to wonder if she was getting what she wanted.

He had never minded looking out for people, but he appreciated that she made things easy for him.

"That's for the whole seaweed thing yesterday," she said, her smile growing as he stepped out of the water toward her. She seemed to like what she saw, her gaze filling with desire. "You know how scared I am of fish touching me. Hmm, I changed my mind about keeping you to myself. This wet Mr. Darcy look is really—"

Kit lunged forward and grabbed her around the waist, throwing her over his shoulder until he was far enough into the water to toss her in.

"I've always wanted to crash a wedding." Skyler tucked herself under Kit's arm as they walked down the beach toward the crowd and music ahead. After trying to dunk each other under the water, which quickly turned into some of the best kisses Kit had ever had, they'd hurried up to the hotel to change into dry clothes while the rest of the Wonder Gang joined Brad for a fancy dinner.

Kit had been torn about leaving, knowing Cam was still anxious, but Cam had told him that the best thing Kit could do was enjoy himself. "One of us should," he'd said as he fumbled to button his shirt.

So now Kit was wearing a pair of loose cotton pants Skyler had found him in the gift shop and a dry unbuttoned shirt over a t-shirt, which was apparently the Hawaiian beach equivalent of black tie. Or maybe Skyler just wanted to mess with him and get more revenge for him tickling her feet with seaweed and pretending it was a shark.

She really did bring out the teenage boy in him.

"So, how do we do this?" Kit asked as they neared the wedding. "Figure out the name of the bride and groom and pretend we're long-lost cousins?"

"You ask like I've done this before." She snickered. "But don't worry; I asked Isla for advice."

Kit groaned. "I never like when someone starts a sentence like that."

"Don't pretend she didn't give you the idea to sell your house for our store."

"And she is going to lord that over my head for the rest of my life like it's some badge of honor. We're lucky she offered to watch Orion tonight instead of making me stay behind while the Boys had their fancy dinner."

"Oh please, like your mom is ever going to leave that baby's side. Did I tell you she canceled our lunch date the other day because Ri smiled for the first time?"

Kit couldn't imagine anything better than Skyler and his mom getting along so well that they planned lunch dates without him. His parents had both welcomed Skyler in so easily, somehow without making a big deal out of Kit dating someone.

Their openness had made it easy for him to tell them about Angela and explain why he had been alone for so long. He was no longer hiding from the people he loved, and he would forever owe Skyler for giving him such a precious gift. If he could, he would give her the world in return.

He squeezed Skyler's shoulders. "Have you seen that baby? I'd cancel on you too."

"Uh, pretty sure you already have. More than once."

They'd reached the edge of the dance floor, and Skyler pulled Kit up without hesitation, twisting in time to the music like she'd been there from the first notes. "All we have to do," she said as she wrapped her arms around his neck and kept dancing, "is make sure anyone who talks to us thinks we're on the other side of the wedding. If they're a friend of the groom's, we're related to the bride. Easy!"

Kit frowned. "I doubt people will start conversations by announcing their relation to the wedding party. That sounds like what would happen in a romantic comedy. Why do I get the feeling you asked Micah for advice too?"

"Because I asked Micah for advice too." Grinning, Skyler pulled herself closer until Kit had to dance with her or look like an idiot. "There you go. This isn't so bad, is it?"

"I'm missing a hundred-dollar dinner for this," he grumbled back.

Skyler's eyes brightened as she held back laughter. "Did you Boys not have lunch today?"

He shook his head, suddenly fixated on the hollow spot in his gut that used to be his stomach. "Cam wanted to have a spa day for his bachelor party. It did not involve food."

"Cute! We went horseback riding and learned how to spear a fish."

Kit honestly couldn't tell if she was making that up or not, and he couldn't ask because Skyler tugged him toward an empty table and sat down in front of someone's half-eaten plate of food.

He grimaced. "Okay, I'm hungry, but I'm not that hungry."

"Excuse me?" Skyler waved down a waiter, then pointed to the plate in front of her. "I'm so sorry, but I think this chicken was undercooked. Is there any way we could get a couple new entrees? It tastes delicious, but I would hate to get salmonella."

The waiter nodded quickly and hurried off.

Kit shook his head. "You're diabolical."

"What can I say? I've still got a bit of lawyer in me."

"I know. It keeps me up at night."

Ten minutes later, they ate some of the best chicken Kit had ever tasted and then hurried off to the next wedding, grabbing plates of cake on their way.

The other two weddings were more of the same, though a few people actually came up to them to say hi. Skyler used her lawyer voice to convince people they remembered her, and Kit made himself so likable that no one cared they hadn't seen him before. By the time they'd eaten their weight in frosting and rice pilaf, the sun had started to sink below the water, leaving the sky painted in vivid pink and orange.

Skyler found a fairly secluded place beyond the weddings to sit in the sand and watch the sunset, nestling herself between Kit's legs and leaning against his chest. "I could stay here forever," she breathed.

Kit wrapped his arms around her. She probably meant staying on the Maui beach forever, but he let himself believe she meant staying in his arms. Maybe one of these days he would be brave enough to ask her if she was willing to give him more than a day at a time, but he doubted it.

He was happy as they were. It was too much to risk being greedy.

"Tonight was nice," he told her, kissing her jaw. "But you know I'm going to try to find a way to pay the brides and grooms for the food we ate, right?"

She leaned more heavily against him. "Oh, I already sent money to their honeymoon funds. I knew you would never steal from them. I just figured we've been so busy with The Bookstore that we could use a little fun."

"Life with you is always fun."

"Yeah?"

He kissed her temple. "Yeah."

As the sky got darker, they sat in comfortable silence, listening to the sounds of the surf against the backdrop of music and happy wedding guests. It was peaceful, a nice way to unwind before the chaos that would be the wedding tomorrow.

"Oh, I forgot," Skyler said. "A woman in the bookstore was asking about the shelves the other day, wondering where I got them because they would be perfect for her house."

Kit felt a twinge of pride for that. He'd had to redo one of the shelves entirely because he'd forgotten a technique until he was halfway through, but most of them had turned out better than he expected. And the videos that had come from that project had received triple the views of the old ones. He'd started to gain a good deal of traction teaching people woodworking, and he loved it. He had plans to start bringing on guests, particularly kids who wanted to learn. Maybe even starting a beginner woodworking class in Diamond Springs.

"What did you tell her?" he asked.

"I told her my scaredy cat boyfriend hadn't gotten around to making business cards or a website yet."

He groaned. "I'm not scared." He was totally scared. "I've been busy. *We've* been busy."

"You're allowed to work on your thing too, you know."

He wanted to, but a part of him was worried that if he took any focus off of his relationship with Skyler, something would go wrong. "Eventually," he said, hoping that would satisfy her.

It was fully dark now, and the only light around them came from the moon that had only just risen behind them. It was bright enough that they would easily make it back to the closest wedding and the lights around the event space, but not quite bright enough for Kit to see Skyler's expression. Was she happy? Was he doing enough for her? She would tell him if he wasn't—and she had—but he still worried.

"Do you see that?" she asked suddenly, pointing to something near the water.

Kit squinted. "Is that a light?"

"Let's go check it out." She was on her feet before he could argue that it was probably just someone out for a stroll. "Come on!"

Kit followed with a yawn. For having spent the whole day getting pampered, he was pretty exhausted, and he couldn't wait to get back up to his hotel bed and hopefully sleep like a rock. With the way his thoughts were spiraling, he wasn't sure he would manage it, but he hoped it for Cam's sake. Cam would need all the help he could get tomorrow.

As they got closer to the light, Kit realized it was a line of fire, and he hurried toward it a little faster. That wasn't normal, was it? He slipped past Skyler, heart pounding, until he reached the edge of the fire and realized it had been lit in trenches dug into the sand. Someone must have poured some kind of oil into the trenches, and the fire was shaped into letters that spelled out—

He cursed and turned to tell Skyler they were crashing someone's proposal. "I think we..."

Skyler was on her knees, a little velvet box in her hands. "I thought it would be a good idea to beat you to it this time," she said, giving him a wry smile. "I know you didn't ask for forever, but I'm going to."

He'd stopped breathing. He was starting to get dizzy, his vision swaying, but it was like he'd completely forgotten how to use his lungs as he stood there and stared at the woman who had completely flipped his life upside down in so many ways.

He finally managed a breath that sounded like a dying gasp, though he sank to his knees because he was afraid he would fall over otherwise. "Are you serious?" he whispered. He had hoped for this, yearned for this, but he hadn't been sure if it would ever happen. He'd also never in his wildest dreams expected to be on the receiving end of a proposal. That was supposed to be his job.

Skyler's smile grew bigger as she opened the box to reveal a titanium band inside. "Do you really think I would have enlisted the Wonder Boys to set all this up if I didn't mean it? I want forever with you, Kit. Don't you?"

He was supposed to say something. Some kind of response. But it was like his brain had sprung a leak and left him running on empty. "Yes," he finally choked out. That was the response he wanted, right? Of course it was. Anything else would be a lie. Yes, he wanted forever with this woman who made him feel more alive than anything else in the world. "Yes, of course I do."

Skyler grinned, holding out the ring. "Then marry me, Kit Morgan. I think it's time we start living that life you promised me."

SERIES EPILOGUE

seven years later
Madi

KIT WAS LATE. MADI COULDN'T help feeling nervous as she sat in the living room, waiting for her brother to show up. He'd loosened up over the years, but even when he was late, it was rarely more than ten or fifteen minutes. He should have shown up an hour ago. Her mind kept conjuring up worst case scenarios, and it was making her sick to her stomach.

She didn't know why she felt so nervous, but even though Oliver had tried to get her to hang out with him outside instead of staring anxiously at the door, she couldn't bring herself to move until Kit showed up.

"They probably had something come up at the store," she told herself, though that was stupid. They had no reason to be open on Christmas Eve. Maybe Skyler had gotten caught up with something and lost track of time. She tended to do that, particularly if she got a new batch of books in at the store. She liked to say she needed to sample them before putting them in front of the customers, but Madi was pretty sure she just liked reading the romances.

A car door shut outside, and Madi breathed a sigh of relief. Was she supposed to feel this much anxiety over her big brother? It should have been the other way around, and usually was, but every once in a while Madi got a strange sense of protectiveness when it came to her one true brother. And the others, honestly. She cared too much about her Wonder Boys to not worry about them.

"Kit got me pregnant again," Skyler announced as soon as she stepped through Madi's front door.

Kit groaned right behind her, somehow managing to make it through the door with a child in each arm. "Will you stop saying it like that? It's like you forget that it took both of us to make that happen."

Skyler giggled, leaning up and kissing him before relieving him of their one-year-old daughter. "But it's so much fun to make you sound like the villain."

"Yeah, well, this villain is going to take Oakley and find someone who won't make me sound awful."

"Ben is downstairs in the library," Madi suggested, falling into Kit's open arm for a side hug shared with his four-year-old. "Cam and Oliver are out back playing snow football with the boys."

Kit looked at the girl he held, the two of them making the same exact thinking face. "Football?" he guessed, and Oakley grinned, nodding. "I thought so. Let's go show them how it's done!"

"Don't forget her coat!" Skyler called as he headed for the back door.

"She's wearing it."

"And gloves."

"Got them."

"Scarf?"

Kit paused at the door, as if reluctant to turn around. "We forgot the scarf," he said dramatically to Oakley, who giggled and ran back to Skyler as soon as Kit put her on her feet.

"Thank you, Mommy." As soon as she was wrapped up tight, she hurried back to Kit and grabbed his hand to follow him outside.

Madi turned to Skyler with a wide grin. "When are you due?"

"July. We couldn't have planned a worse time."

"So this one was planned?"

Skyler laughed, shaking her head. "Of course not. Where would be the fun in that?" Hoisting Aspen higher on her hip, she seemed to study her daughter for a moment. "I think I want a boy this time," she said. "These girls have been way too easy."

Shouts rang out from the backyard, and Madi laughed. "Are you sure about that? The boys already outnumber us." She gestured toward the door, silently suggesting they go out to the heated porch to watch the game.

"That's because Cam and Lani keep adopting boys," Skyler complained. "Speaking of Lani."

They found her settled comfortably in an armchair on the porch, wrapped in a blanket that barely covered her giant belly.

"I thought you were napping," Madi said, grabbing another chair for Skyler before settling in her own chair underneath the propane heater. She pulled her legs up onto the cushion, glad to have the warmth overhead.

Kailani sighed, shifting in her seat. "These babies make that really difficult. It's like they won't stop fighting, and I feel every kick and shove. They definitely take after their dad. Cam!" She pointed to her two adopted boys, who had forgotten the game and were burying themselves in snow.

Cam looked over and snorted a laugh just before Oliver full-on tackled him into the snow.

Madi winced. Ollie was going to feel that hit tomorrow a whole lot more than Cam was. Why did they always turn into teenagers when they got together?

"Oh, you're going down, Hamilton," Cam growled, grabbing his sons by the arms and lifting them straight out of the snow. "Everyone attack Uncle Oliver on three! One. Two. Ri, you with us?"

Orion frowned, clearly torn between protecting his dad and making Cam happy. The kid aimed to please, a little too much like Oliver sometimes. When he glanced over and caught Madi's eye, she smiled at him.

"I'd tackle Dad if I were you," she said with a wink.

"Three!" Cam said.

All the kids rushed Oliver, Orion and Oakley included, until they had him flat on his back and each of them found a place to sit on top of him and hold him down.

"This seems a little unfair," Oliver said with a mock frown. "I'm getting too old for this."

"You're not even forty yet," Ben said. He must have heard the commotion and come upstairs, his boy right behind him with Madi's youngest taking up the rear with Allie. Danny *adored* Allie, probably because she read comic books with him every time she came over.

"Hey, Kit," Ben said. He pulled Kit into an embrace as Oliver struggled to free himself from the giggling kids. "Happy Breakfast Eve."

"I'm glad you're here," Kit replied. "I'm still mad you missed the last one."

"We were on tour and had a signing the day after Christmas. What did you want me to do? Charter a private jet to bring me back from London for a day?"

Kit scowled. "Yes."

"By the way," Skyler warned Madi, "Oakley had a meltdown this morning, so Kit didn't get breakfast."

Madi grinned. She'd seen Kit hangry far too many times to want to let him go too long without getting some food. Now that everyone had arrived, they might as well get brunch going.

"Ollie!" she called.

Oliver was on his feet in a flash, a kid in each arm. Cam grabbed his own armful, the two of them laughing about something and looking years younger than they were. Madi always loved when they got together like this, though it didn't happen often anymore. They still had monthly club meetings when they could, but most of the time it was the big things, like Breakfast Eve or her birthday.

"You're letting me cook this year, right, Martinez?" Oliver said.

"Not a chance. Last year you put cardamom in the waffles. Who does that?" Cam looked around at all the expectant kids surrounding him, his eyes glittering with excitement as he said, "Who's helping in the kitchen this year? Not you." He pointed to his boys, who looked up at him with far too much innocence for it to be real. "We talked about this. You two are on dish duty. Everyone else, follow me!"

Kailani laughed as Cam led the entourage of children inside. She struggled to her feet with Madi's help, and then they all followed the cacophony inside. "They poured syrup all over the cat this morning," she explained before settling at the kitchen table. "Don't ask me why. So they're grounded from the kitchen until they can catch the cat long enough to give him a bath. They really love cooking with their dad, so it's a pretty effective punishment. I just can't wait to stop finding tufts of sticky cat fur everywhere."

"We should get a cat," Kit said as he wrapped an arm around Skyler and kissed her cheek.

She snorted as she patted his chest and handed Aspen over to him. "Uh, no. Not unless you want me to take back the Christmas present I got you, though I've gotten a little too attached to his little waggy tail."

Kit laughed, and Madi nearly teared up at the sight of him so happy. It wasn't that he hadn't been happy before Skyler, but he had kept himself so restrained before, putting himself behind walls that left him muted and only halfway there. Sometimes she thought about when they were really young, when it was just the two of them and Oliver, and she missed the way they'd been back then. Before the world had gotten to them.

But things were good now. They were so different now that they were grown, but they were better.

"Hey." Arms empty now that all the kids were in the kitchen with Cam, Oliver touched her elbow and looked at her with worry in his eyes. "You okay? You were having a rough day yesterday too."

Honestly, Madi had never been happier, especially when she looked around at her growing family. Tomorrow, Mom and Dad would come over for Christmas morning, and Cam and Ben would be here all day today. The Wonder Boys always spent some time just the four of them, usually grabbing Madi to join in before they left. Those moments were her favorite.

"Did you ever think we would get here?" she asked, taking Oliver's hand as their chaotic family filled the kitchen.

"Sometimes I wondered," Oliver admitted. "But yes. I knew, one day, we would all have these incredible lives that felt so unreachable back when we were kids. Maybe we didn't talk about it all the time, but we all wanted this. For ourselves and for each other."

Madi tucked herself into his hold as her tears fell harder. She didn't usually cry this much, but maybe there was something about this year that had her especially emotional. Was it because Ben had been missing last year? Or what if…?

"You sure you're okay?"

She nodded, but not with a lot of confidence. Doing some quick mental math, she counted back the weeks, then felt her stomach drop. Or maybe that was just nausea. "Oh."

"Oh?" Oliver spun her around so she was facing him. "What do you mean, oh?"

She could be wrong, but… Smiling, Madi shrugged. "I think… I think I might be pregnant."

Blinking, Oliver stared at her for a second like those words didn't compute. He was usually pretty excited about this kind of thing, but maybe he'd thought two was enough? They hadn't talked about having another, and Danny was almost five.

But then a smile cracked through the shock on Oliver's face, quickly turning into a huge grin. "I knew it," he said, and then he turned to Kit and shouted, "You owe me twenty bucks, Morgan!"

Kit let out a groan, but it was quickly followed by a smile as he came and wrapped Madi in a hug. Kit hugs were the best hugs. After Oliver hugs, of course, which Oliver apparently felt the need to prove because he joined in, wrapping Madi up from the other side.

"Congratulations," Kit said, holding her tight.

"What are we celebrating?" Cam asked, already adding to the hug.

Ben completed the group only a second later, and Madi burst into laughter in the middle of them.

These Wonder Boys of hers were ridiculous, but they would always have a special place in the deepest recesses of her heart.

The End

Also by Dana LeCheminant

The Wonder Boys
Love on Camera
Love in Writing
Love on Display

Simple Love Stories (Sweet Love Stories)
Simplicity
Growing Young
Bittersweet Brews
In Front of Me
As Long as You Love Me
Dear Dalia
Let Go

Terms of Inheritance (Sweet Romance)
Forever You and Me
Holding On to Everything
A World without You
Love, Strictly Speaking

Historical Romances
The Thief and the Noble
A Twist of Christmas (part of The Holly and the Ivy Christmas anthology)
What Dreams May Come

About the Author

Dana LeCheminant has been telling stories since she was old enough to know what stories were. After spending most of her childhood reading everything she could get her hands on, she eventually realized she could write her own books too, and since then she always has plots brewing and characters clamoring to be next to have their stories told. A lover of all things outdoors, she finds inspiration while hiking the remote Utah backcountry and cruising down rivers. Until her endless imagination runs dry, she will always have another story to tell.

www.ingramcontent.com/pod-product-compliance
Lightning Source LLC
Chambersburg PA
CBHW070239200726
48293CB00005B/1707